ON THE STREETS OF MANHATTAN
Shirley Jackson's heroine learns the meaning
of total fear

IN A WEALTHY HOUSEHOLD IN INDIA
Ruth Prawer Jhabvala portrays a woman who
suddenly finds herself an isolated stranger

ON A TRAIN THROUGH AFRICA
Nadine Gordimer takes us on a journey of
shattering sexual revelation

IN AN ENGLISH NURSERY
Muriel Spark illumines the seeds of a woman's
destiny in an infant girl

ON A DANISH ESTATE
Isak Dinesen creates a masterpiece about the
price of motherhood

These are but a few of the places you will visit
in this dazzling collection of stories—

WOMEN AND FICTION 2

SUSAN CAHILL has taught literature and writing
at several universities in the New York area. She is
the editor of Women and Fiction, Volume I; the
co-editor of a number of anthologies; and the author
of *Earth Angels* and *A Literary Guide to Ireland*
(with Thomas Cahill).

WOMEN AND FICTION 2

Short Stories by and about Women

EDITED BY

Susan Cahill

A MENTOR BOOK
NEW AMERICAN LIBRARY

NEW YORK AND SCARBOROUGH, ONTARIO

NAL BOOKS ARE AVAILABLE AT QUANTITY DISCOUNTS WHEN USED TO PROMOTE PRODUCTS OR SERVICES. FOR INFORMATION PLEASE WRITE TO PREMIUM MARKETING DIVISION, THE NEW AMERICAN LIBRARY, INC., 1633 BROADWAY, NEW YORK, NEW YORK 10019.

Library of Congress Catalog Card Number: 75-21588

ACKNOWLEDGMENTS

"The Courting of Sister Wisby" by Sarah Orne Jewett. Reprinted courtesy of Houghton Mifflin Company.

Excerpt from *Pilgrimage* by Dorothy Richardson. Reprinted courtesy of Alfred A. Knopf, Inc., and by permission of Mark Paterson & Associates, Colchester, England.

Excerpt from *Kristin Lavransdatter* by Sigrid Undset. Copyright 1923, 1925, 1927, and renewed 1951, 1953, 1955 by Alfred A. Knopf, Inc. Reprinted by permission of Alfred A. Knopf, Inc.

"The Cooboo" by Katharine Susannah Prichard. Reprinted by permission of Angus & Robertson Publishers from *Happiness* by Katharine Susannah Prichard. Copyright © 1932.

"Sorrow-Acre" by Isak Dinesen. Copyright 1942 by Random House, Inc., and renewed 1970 by John Philip Thomas Ingerslev, c/o The Rungstedlund Foundation. Reprinted from *Winter's Tales*, by Isak Dinesen, by permission of Random House, Inc., and The University of Chicago Press.

"Outside the Machine" in *Tigers Are Better-Looking* by Jean Rhys. Copyright © 1960 by Jean Rhys. Reprinted by permission of Harper & Row, Publishers, Inc., and Andre Deutsch Ltd.

"The Petrified Woman" by Caroline Gordon. Reprinted by permission of the author.

"Sunday Afternoon" by Elizabeth Bowen. From *Ivy Gripped the Steps and Other Stories*, by Elizabeth Bowen. Copyright 1946 and renewed 1974 by Elizabeth Bowen. Reprinted by permission of Alfred A. Knopf, Inc., and Curtis Brown Ltd.

"The Gilded Six-Bits" by Zora Neale Hurston. *Story* Magazine, August, 1933. Reprinted by permission of the Estate of Zora Neale Hurston.

"The Wind-Chill Factor" by M. F. K. Fisher. Copyright © 1973 by *The New Yorker*. Reprinted by permission of Russell & Volkening, Inc., as agents for the author.

Excerpt from *Miss MacIntosh, My Darling* by Marguerite Young. Copyright © 1965 Marguerite Young. Reprinted by permission of Charles Scribner's Sons.

(*The following page constitutes an extension of this copyright page.*)

MENTOR TRADEMARK REG. U.S. PAT. OFF. AND FOREIGN COUNTRIES
REGISTERED TRADEMARK—MARCA REGISTRADA
HECHO EN CHICAGO, U.S.A.

SIGNET, SIGNET CLASSIC, MENTOR, PLUME, MERIDIAN AND NAL BOOKS
are published *in the United States* by
The New American Library, Inc.,
1633 Broadway, New York, New York 10019,
in Canada by The New American Library of Canada Limited,
81 Mack Avenue, Scarborough, Ontario M1L 1M8

FIRST MENTOR PRINTING, MARCH, 1978

5 6 7 8 9 10 11 12

PRINTED IN THE UNITED STATES OF AMERICA

For
Claire Hahn Becker

Contents

Introduction

This book is a sequel to *Women and Fiction*, the popularity of which has indicated a wide interest in the perspective of women on the human condition. The women in this case are supreme literary artists. For readers who seek understanding, and for lovers of literature as well, it is important that these artists be heard together, anthologized between the same two covers. For in such an assembly our sense of ambiguity is renewed. The experience of life brought to order by these women of vision is exhilarating.

Women and Fiction 2 contains twenty-six first-rate stories by outstanding writers who are women. There are no new names among them (though there are plenty of new writers to choose from, enough to fill at least another volume). Each is prominent in the place where she once wrote, or is now writing: Dinesen in Denmark, Lagerlöf in Sweden, Undset in Norway, Fussenegger in Germany, Ginzburg in Italy, Jhabvala in India, Gordimer in South Africa, Bombal in Chile, Prichard in Australia, Gallant and Laurence in Canada, Richardson, Manning, Rhys, Bowen, and Spark in England, and in the United States Dorothy Canfield Fisher, M. F. K. Fisher, Jewett, Gordon, Hurston, Young, Bowles, Jackson, Betts, and Cullinan. This geographical variety makes *Women and Fiction 2* unique among collections of writing by women. And it makes clear that literary expression by women is not confined to one culture or to a few recent decades. The tradition of the best women writers is international, transcontinental; it is older and wiser than the Women's Liberation Movement (Lady Murasaki, a Japanese woman, wrote *The Tale of Genji*—called by many critics the world's first real novel and one of its greatest classics—in the eleventh century). Accordingly, what I wrote in the Introduction of the first volume of *Women and Fiction* applies to the present volume as well: "no story has been included because it either illustrates or disputes a currently popular theory about Women. Vision and great craft have been the criteria of selection."

These stories are the work of women who have found their identity as writers, who know why they write. "Because I must," said Jane Bowles, and she spoke for everyone who has ever undertaken the toil of bringing back a life in words. "Because I can't do anything else," Jhabvala claims, which is only another form of Flannery O'Connor's explanation: "I write because I'm good at it." Because "I only feel half-alive when I'm not writing"—Elizabeth Bowen's art was her bread and wine. Readers of these stories will recognize at once— and savor—their seriousness. Everything that is banal is alien to them. They reflect the power of their creator's impulse: this tale must be told, and not for fame or money.

Each story is preceded by a brief introduction which offers some details about the writer's relationship to her work and the critics' response to her art. It is, of course, significant that in many cases the critical territory is quiet or unrevealing. How little of worth has been written about Sigrid Undset, Marguerite Young, Caroline Gordon, Jean Rhys, Muriel Spark, Elizabeth Bowen. One wonders: is it too farfetched to read the silence and the awkward attempts to understand these works as expressions in our day of those nineteenth-century sentiments typified by Poet Laureate Robert Southey's response to Charlotte Brontë, when she wrote to him and asked for his opinion of her poetry. He replied: "Literature cannot be the business of a woman's life and it ought not to be. The more she is engaged in her proper duties, the less leisure will she have for it, even as an accomplishment and a recreation."

One of the strongest Victorian prejudices against women as writers had to do with the conviction that motherhood and authorship were incompatible activities. To bolster this prejudice in the present century, the output of mothers who write or writers who mother is skimpy compared with that of male writers who are also fathers. But a surprising and growing number of women have made the marriage of the two vocations work (though at what personal cost one can only guess). At least twelve of the writers in this anthology, including Nobel Prize winner Sigrid Undset, have borne and raised children. Many of these writer-mothers do (or did) their writing at night, after the children have been fed, washed, read to, rocked, lullabyed.

*   *   *

For teachers who use this book as part of a course there are clusters of stories that can be considered together, their points of view compared and contrasted for the heightened perspective that such an approach can yield.

The nuances of heterosexual relationships—along with their political implications—are caught in their various lights and shadows by Nadine Gordimer in "The Train from Rhodesia," Gertrud Fussenegger in "Woman Driver," and Zora Neale Hurston in "The Gilded Six-Bits." One reads these three together, powerless to deny the truth that each re-creates, and immediately recognizes the dramatically different shapes that the relationship of man and woman may take.

The character of the mother in "Sorrow-Acre"—Isak Dinesen's masterpiece—and in "The Mother" by Natalia Ginzburg are indelible in the memory, exist in radically different worlds. Yet both share common ground.

It is interesting to compare the perceptions of the mature daughter and the adolescent one in the two brilliant stories of family relationships: "Idioms" by Elizabeth Cullinan and "A Bird in the House" by Margaret Laurence. One sees, the other suspects. A profound caring is the métier of both.

The experience of personal authenticity is recreated most convincingly in the relatively old-fashioned narratives of Dorothy Canfield Fisher ("The Bedquilt"), of Sarah Orne Jewett ("The Courting of Sister Wisby"), and of Selma Lagerlöf ("Eclipse"). These three worlds with their sense of timelessness and interior harmony seem antique when read amidst the urgent cacophony of our times. Yet there is a freedom of voice and action in each that gives them an amazing contemporary relevance.

A number of the stories reflect their writers' belief that our mad modern world is not the only one—there is an unseen world, call it the realm of moral values, or of diabolic forces, or of supernatural faith. A consciousness and acceptance of the mystery of things unites the otherwise dissimilar stories by Shirley Jackson, Muriel Spark, Margaret Laurence, Selma Lagerlöf, Isak Dinesen, and Nadine Gordimer.

Both Isak Dinesen in "Sorrow-Acre" and Eizabeth Bowen

in "Sunday Afternoon" are concerned with the clash between the values of the old order and the new. That clash is perceived in both stories by a young man who is all modern confusion and loneliness. In the manner of great storytellers, but in completely different tones, neither writer endorses one way of life in preference to another. Both belong.

Tillie Olsen has suggested that readers compare Fisher's "The Bedquilt" with Alice Walker's "Everyday Use" which appears in the first volume of *Women and Fiction*. Other correspondences between the stories in the two volumes come to mind: read Kay Boyle's "Winter Night" (Vol. 1) with Ginzburg's "The Mother" (Vol. 2); Gertrude Stein's "Miss Furr and Miss Skeene" (Vol. 1) with Manning's "Girls Together" (Vol. 2); Joyce Carol Oates's "In a Region of Ice" (Vol. 1) with Caroline Gordon's "A Petrified Woman" (Vol. 2); Eudora Welty's "A Worn Path" (Vol. 1) with Isak Dinesen's "Sorrow-Acre" (Vol. 2); Colette's "The Secret Woman" (Vol. 1) with Bombal's "The Tree" (Vol. 2); Doris Lessing's "To Room Nineteen" (Vol. 1) with Jhabvala's "The Englishwoman" (Vol. 2).

Teachers, students, and general readers may ask whether there is, after all, such a thing as women's fiction, female imagery, or feminine sensibility. What Professor Linda Nochlin says about painters in her book *Women Artists: 1550-1950* applies to writers as well. It is futile, in her opinion, to look for consistent feminine motifs where there is such vigor and variety of styles as exist today in painting by women. Yet "the fact that a given artist happens to be a woman rather than a man counts for something: It is a more or less significant variable in the creation of a work of art, like being an American, being poor or being born in 1900." In her book *The Female Imagination*, Patricia Meyer Spacks delivers a penetrating analysis of the ways this variable operates in fiction written by women, as does Mary Ellmann in *Thinking about Women* and Elaine Showalter in her essay "Women Writers and the Double Standard."

All this, however, is single-issue criticism. After a while, one grows impatient with theories about the nature of the female imagination and desires the fullness and freedom of the art itself.

SARAH ORNE JEWETT was born in South Berwick, Maine—"Deephaven" in her stories—in 1849. Her father was a distinguished physician who taught obstetrics at Bowdoin College. She got her education in his library (she favored the works of Carlyle, Lowell, and Matthew Arnold) and even more from the long trips she took with him as he made his rounds in the country districts around South Berwick. She came to know intimately the old people who were his patients. In her fiction she caught their accents perfectly. Lowell praised her use of dialect, "for flavor, but not so oppressively as to suggest garlic."

Her first book of stories, appearing at a time of great demand for regional studies of America, was an immediate success, winning her entree to the "Boston circle" of Howells, Whittier, Lowell, and Thomas Bailey Aldrich. Her stories, those close, accurate studies of plain people (from Flaubert, she said, she learned an "almost French clarity and precision"), have been described as easily the best work of their sort to come out of New England. They are idylls in prose, infused with what Edward Garnett called "a poetic realism." Lowell compared her to Theocritus, Kipling praised her grasp and vigor, Henry James admired her greatly. She has been criticized for being too genteel, for not writing about sex, for not feeling passion for a man in her private life. But her place in the main line of American literary expression is secure.

Willa Cather, who was her friend, and student of a sort, wrote the introduction to the collection of her best stories. Sarah Orne Jewett died in 1909.

Sarah Orne Jewett
(1849—1909)

THE COURTING OF SISTER WISBY

All the morning there had been an increasing temptation to take an outdoor holiday, and early in the afternoon the temptation outgrew my power of resistance. A far away pasture on the long southwestern slope of a high hill was persistently present to my mind, yet there seemed to be no particular reason why I should think of it. I was not sure that I wanted anything from the pasture, and there was no sign, except the temptation, that the pasture wanted anything of me. But I was on the farther side of as many as three fences before I stopped to think again where I was going, and why.

There is no use in trying to tell another person about that afternoon unless he distinctly remembers weather exactly like it. No number of details concerning an Arctic ice blockade will give a single shiver to a child of the tropics. This was one of those perfect New England days in late summer, when the spirit of autumn takes a first stealthy flight, like a spy, through the ripening countryside, and, with feigned sympathy for those who droop with August heat, puts her cool cloak of bracing air about leaf and flower and human shoulders. Every living thing grows suddenly cheerful and strong; it is only when you catch sight of a horror-stricken little maple in swampy soil—a little maple that has second-sight and foreknowledge of coming disaster to her race—only then does a distrust of autumn's friendliness dim your joyful satisfaction.

In the midwinter there is always a day when one has the first foretaste of spring; in late August there is a morning when the air is for the first time autumn-like. Perhaps it is a hint to the squirrels to get in their first supplies for the winter hoards, or a reminder that summer will soon end, and everybody had better make the most of it. We are always looking forward to the passing and ending of winter, but when summer is here it seems as if summer must always last. As I went

2

across the fields that day, I found myself half lamenting that the world must fade again, even that the best of her budding and bloom was only a preparation for another springtime, for an awakening beyond the coming winter's sleep.

The sun was slightly veiled; there was a chattering group of birds, which had gathered for a conference about their early migration. Yet, oddly enough, I heard the voice of a belated bobolink, and presently saw him rise from the grass and hover leisurely, while he sang a brief tune. He was much behind time if he were still a housekeeper; but as for the other birds who listened, they cared only for their own notes. An old crow went sagging by, and gave a croak at his despised neighbor, just as a black reviewer croaked at Keats—so hard it is to be just to one's contemporaries. The bobolink was indeed singing out of season, and it was impossible to say whether he really belonged most to this summer or to the next. He might have been delayed on his northward journey; at any rate, he had a light heart now, to judge from his song, and I wished that I could ask him a few questions—how he liked being the last man among the bobolinks, and where he had taken singing lessons in the South.

Presently I left the lower fields, and took a path that led higher, where I could look beyond the village to the northern country mountainward. Here the sweet fern grew thick and fragrant, and I also found myself heedlessly treading on pennyroyal. Nearby, in a field corner, I long ago made a most comfortable seat by putting a stray piece of board and bit of rail across the angle of the fences. I have spent many a delightful hour there, in the shade and shelter of a young pitch pine and a wild cherry tree, with a lovely outlook toward the village, just far enough away beyond the green slopes and tall elms of the lower meadows. But that day I still had the feeling of being outward bound, and did not turn aside nor linger. The high pasture land grew more and more enticing.

I stopped to pick some blackberries that twinkled at me like beads among their dry vines, and two or three yellowbirds fluttered up from the leaves of a thistle and then came back again, as if they had complacently discovered that I was only an overgrown yellowbird, in strange disguise but perfectly harmless. They made me feel as if I were an intruder, though they did not offer to peck at me, and we parted company very soon. It was good to stand at last on the great shoulder of the hill. The wind was coming in from the sea, there was a fine fragrance from the pines, and the air grew sweeter every moment. I took new pleasure in the thought that in a piece of wild pasture land like this one may get closest to Nature, and subsist upon what she gives of her own free will. There have been no drudging, heavy-shod ploughmen to overturn the soil, and vex it into yielding artificial crops. Here one has to take just what Nature is pleased to give, whether one is a yellowbird or a human being. It is very good entertainment for a summer wayfarer, and I am asking my reader now to share the winter provision which I harvested that day. Let us hope that the small birds are also faring well after their fashion, but I give them an anxious thought while the snow goes hurrying in long waves across the buried fields, this windy winter night.

I next went farther down the hill, and got a drink of fresh cool water from the brook, and pulled a tender sheaf of sweet flag beside it. The mossy old fence just beyond was the last barrier between me and the pasture which had sent an invisible messenger earlier in the day, but I saw that somebody else had come first to the rendezvous: there was a brown gingham cape-bonnet and a sprigged shoulder-shawl bobbing up and down, a little way off among the junipers. I had taken such uncommon pleasure in being alone that I instantly felt a sense of disappointment; then a warm glow of pleasant satisfaction rebuked my selfishness. This could be no one but dear old Mrs. Goodsoe, the friend of my childhood and fond dependence of my maturer years. I had not seen her for many weeks, but here she was, out on one of her famous campaigns for herbs, or perhaps just returning from a blueberrying expedition. I approached with care, so as not to startle the gingham bonnet; but she heard the rustle of the bushes against my dress, and looked up quickly, as she knelt, bending over the turf. In that position she was hardly taller than the luxuriant junipers themselves.

"I'm a-gittin' in my mulleins," she said briskly, "an' I've been thinking o' you these twenty times since I come out o' the house. I begun to believe you must ha' forgot me at last."

"I have been away from home," I explained. "Why don't you get in your pennyroyal too? There's a great plantation of it beyond the next fence but one."

"Pennyr'yal!" repeated the dear little old woman, with an air of compassion for inferior knowledge; "'tain't the right time, darlin'. Pennyr'yal's too rank now. But for mulleins this day is prime. I've got a dreadful graspin' fit for 'em this year; seems if I must be goin' to need 'em extry. I feel like the squirrels must when they know a hard winter's comin'." And Mrs. Goodsoe bent over her work again, while I stood by and watched her carefully cut the best full-grown leaves with a clumsy pair of scissors, which might have served through at least half a century of herb-gathering. They were fastened to her apron strings by a long piece of list.

"I'm going to take my jack-knife and help you," I suggested, with some fear of refusal. "I just passed a flourishing family of six or seven heads that must have been growing on purpose for you."

"Now be keerful, dear heart," was the anxious response; "choose 'em well. There's odds in mulleins same's there is in angels. Take a plant that's all run up to stalk, and there ain't but little goodness in the leaves. This one I'm at now must ha' been stepped on by some creatur and blighted of its bloom, and the leaves is han'some! When I was small I used to have a notion that Adam an' Eve must ha' took mulleins fer their winter wear. Ain't they just like flannel, for all the world? I've had experience, and I know there's plenty of sickness might be saved to folks if they'd quit horse-radish and such fiery, exasperating things, and use mullein drarves in proper season. Now I shall spread these an' dry 'em nice on my spare floor in the garrit, an' come to steam 'em for use along in the winter there'll be the valley of the whole summer's goodness in 'em, sartin." And she snipped away with the dull scissors while I listened respectfully, and took great pains to have my part of the harvest present a good appearance.

"This is most too dry a head," she added presently, a little out of breath. "There! I can tell you there's win'rows o' young doctors, bilin' over with book-larnin', that is truly ignorant of what to do for the sick, or how to p'int out those paths that well people foller toward sickness. Book-fools I call 'em, them young men, an' some on 'em never'll live to know much better, if they git to be Methuselahs. In my time every middle-aged woman who had brought up a family had some proper ideas of dealin' with complaints. I won't say but there was some fools amongst *them*, but I'd rather take my chances, unless they'd forsook herbs and gone to dealin' with patent stuff. Now my mother really did sense the use of herbs and roots. I never see anybody that come up to her. She was a meek-looking woman, but very understandin', mother was."

"Then that's where you learned so much yourself, Mrs. Goodsoe," I ventured to say.

"Bless your heart, I don't hold a candle to her; 'tis but little I can recall of what she used to say. No, her larnin' died with her," said my friend, in a self-deprecating tone. "Why, there was as many as twenty kinds of roots alone that she used to keep by her, that I forgot the use of; an' I'm sure I shouldn't know where to find the most of 'em, any. There was a herb"—*airb* she called it—"an herb called Pennsylvany; and she used to think everything of nobleliver-wort, but I never could seem to get the right effects from it, as she could. Though I don't know as she ever really did use masterwort where somethin' else wouldn't ha' served. She had a cousin married out in Pennsylvany that used to take pains to get it to her every year or two, and so she felt 'twas important to have it. Some set more by such things as come from a distance, but I rec'lect mother always used to maintain that folks was meant to be doctored with the stuff that grew right about 'em; 'twas sufficient, an' so ordered. That was before the whole population took to livin' on wheels, the way they do now. 'Twas never my idee that we was meant to know what's goin' on all over the world to once. There's goin' to be some sort of a set-back one o' these days, with these telegraphs an' things, an' letters comin' every hand's turn, and folks leavin' their proper work to answer 'em. I may not live to see it. 'Twas allowed to be difficult for folks to git about in old times, or to git word across the country, and they stood in their lot an' place, and weren't all just alike, either, same as pine-spills."

We were kneeling side by side now, as if in penitence for the march of progress, but we laughed and we turned to look at each other.

"Do you think it did much good when everybody brewed a cracked quart mug of herb-tea?" I asked, walking away on my knees to a new mullein.

"I've always lifted my voice against the practice, far's I could," declared Mrs. Goodsoe; "an' I won't deal out none o' the herbs I save for no such nonsense. There was three houses along our road—I call no names—where you couldn't go into the livin' room without findin' a mess o' herb-tea drorin' on the stove or side o' the fireplace, winter or summer, sick or well. One was thoroughwut, one would be camomile, and the other, like as not, yellow dock; but they all used to put in a little new rum to git out the goodness, or keep it from spilin'."." (Mrs. Goodsoe favored me with a knowing smile.) "Land, how mother used to laugh! But, poor creatures, they had to work hard, and I guess it never done 'em a mite o' harm; they was all good herbs. I wish you could hear the quawkin' there used to be when they was indulged with a real case o' sickness. Everybody would collect from far an' near; you'd see 'em coming along the road and across the pastures then; everybody clamorin' that nothin' would do no kind o' good but her choice o' teas or drarves to the feet. I wonder there was a babe lived to grow up in the whole lower part o' the town; an' if nothin' else 'peared to ail 'em, word was passed about that 'twas likely Mis' So-and-So's last young one was goin' to be foolish. Land, how they'd gather! I know one day the doctor come to Widder Peck's and the house was crammed so't he could scercely git inside the door; and he says, just as polite, 'Do send for some of the neighbors!' as if there wa'n't a soul to turn to, right or left. You'd ought to seen 'em begin to scatter."

"But don't you think the cars and telegraphs have given people more to interest them, Mrs. Goodsoe? Don't you believe people's lives were narrower then, and more taken up with little things?" I asked, unwisely, being a product of modern times.

"Not one mite, dear," said my companion stoutly. "There was as big thoughts then as there is now; these times was born o' them. The difference is in folks themselves; but now, instead o' doin' their own housekeepin' and watchin' their own neighbors—though that was carried to excess—they git word that a niece's child is ailin' the other side o' Massachusetts, and they drop everything and git on their best clothes, and off they jiggit in the cars. 'Tis a bad sign when folks wear out their best clothes faster 'n they do their everyday ones. The other side o' Massachusetts has got to look after itself by rights. An' besides that, Sunday-keepin's all gone out o' fashion. Some lays it to one thing an' some another, but some o' them old ministers that folks are all a-sighin' for did preach a lot o' stuff that wa'n't nothin' but chaff; 'twa'n't the word o' God out o' either Old Testament or New. But everybody went to meetin' and heard it, and come home, and was set to fightin' with their next door neighbor over it. Now I'm a believer, and I try to live a Christian life, but I'd as soon hear a surveyor's book read out, figgers an' all, as try to get any simple truth out o' most sermons. It's them as is most to blame."

"What was the matter that day at Widow Peck's?" I hastened to ask, for I knew by experience that the good, clear minded soul beside me was apt to grow unduly vexed and distressed when she contemplated the state of religious teaching.

"Why, there wa'n't nothin' the matter, only a gal o' Miss Peck's had met with a dis'pintment and had gone into screechin' fits. 'Twas a rovin' creatur that had come along hayin' time, and he'd gone off an' forsook her betwixt two days; nobody ever knew what become of him. Them Pecks was 'Good Lord, anybody!' kind o' gals, an' took up with whoever they could get. One of 'em married Heron, the Irishman; they lived in that little house that was burnt this summer, over the edge o' the plains. He was a good-hearted creatur, with a laughin' eye and a clever word for everybody. He was the first Irishman that ever came this way, and we was all for gettin' a look at him, when he first used to go by. Mother's folks was what they call Scotch-Irish, though; there was an old race of 'em settled about here. They could foretell events, some on 'em, and had second-sight. I know folks used to say mother's grandmother had them gifts, but mother was never free to speak about it to us. She remembered her well, too."

"I suppose that you mean old Jim Heron, who was such a famous fiddler?" I asked with great interest, for I am always delighted to know more about that rustic hero, parochial Orpheus that he must have been!

"Now, dear heart, I suppose you don't remember him, do you?" replied Mrs. Goodsoe, earnestly. "Fiddle! He'd about break your heart with them tunes of his, or else set your heels flyin' up the floor in a jig, though you was minister o' the First Parish and all wound up for a funeral prayer. I tell ye there win't no tunes sounds like them used to. It used to seem to me summer nights when I was comin' along the plains road, and he set by the window playin', as if there was a bewitched human creatur in that old red fiddle o' his. He could make it sound just like a woman's voice tellin' somethin' over and over, as if folks could help her out o' her sorrows if she could only make 'em understand. I've set by the stone wall and cried as if my heart was broke, and dear knows it wa'n't in them days. How he would twirl off them jigs and dance tunes! He used to make somethin' han'some out of 'em in fall an' winter, playin' at huskins and dancin' parties; but he was unstiddy by spells, as he got along in years, and never knew what it was to be forehanded. Everybody felt bad when he died; you couldn't help likin' the creatur. He'd got the gift— that's all you could say about it.

"There was a Mis' Jerry Foss, that lived over by the brook bridge, on the plains road, that had lost her husband early, and was left with three child'n. She set the world by 'em, and was a real pleasant, ambitious little woman, and was workin' on as best she could with that little farm, when there come a rage o' scarlet fever, and her boy and two girls was swept off and laid dead within the same week. Everyone o' the neighbors did what they could, but she'd had no sleep since they was taken sick, and after the funeral she set there just like a piece o' marble, and would only shake her head when you spoke to her. They all thought her reason would go; and 'twould certain, if she couldn't have shed tears. An' one o' the neighbors—'twas like mother's sense, but it might have been somebody else—spoke o' Jim Heron. Mother an' one or two o' the women that knew her best was in the house with her. 'T was right in the edge o' the woods and some of us younger ones was over by the wall on the other side of the road where there was a couple of old willows—I remember just how the brook damp felt—and we kept quiet's we could, and some other folks come along down the road, and stood waitin' on the little bridge, hopin' somebody'd come out, I suppose, and they'd git news. Everybody was wrought up, and felt a good deal for her, you know. By an' by Jim Heron come stealin' right out o' the shadows an' set down on the doorstep, an' 'twas a good while before we heard a sound; then, oh, dear me! 'twas what the whole neighborhood felt for that mother all spoke in the notes, an' they told me afterwards that Mis' Foss's face changed in a minute, and she come right over an' got into my mother's lap—she was a little woman—an' laid her head down, and there she cried herself into a blessed sleep. After awhile one o' the other women stole out an' told the folks, and we all went home. He only played that one tune.

"But there!" resumed Mrs. Goodsoe, after a silence, during which my eyes were filled with tears. "His wife always complained that the fiddle made her nervous. She never 'peared to think nothin' o' poor Heron after she'd once got him."

"That's often the way," I said, with harsh cynicism though I had no guilty person in my mind at the moment; and we went straying off, not very far apart, up through the pasture. Mrs. Goodsoe cautioned me that we must not get so far off that we could not get back the same day. The sunshine began to feel very hot on our backs, and we both turned toward the shade. We had already collected a large bundle of mullein leaves, which were carefully laid into a clean, calico apron, held together by the four corners, and proudly carried by me, though my companion regarded them with anxious eyes. We sat down together at the edge of the pine woods, and Mrs. Goodsoe proceeded to fan herself with her limp cape-bonnet.

"I declare, how hot it is! The east wind's all gone again," she said. "It felt so cool this afternoon that I overburdened myself with as thick a petticoat as any I've got. I'm despri't afeared of having a chill, now that I ain't so young as once. I hate to be housed up."

"It's only August, after all," I assured her unnecessarily, confirming my statement by taking two peaches out of my pocket, and laying them side by side on the brown pine needles between us.

"Dear sakes alive!" exclaimed the old lady, with evident pleasure. "Where did you get them, now? Doesn't anything taste twice better our-o'-doors? I ain't had such a peach for years. Do le's keep the stones, an' I'll plant 'em; it only takes four years for a peach pit to come to bearing, an' I guess I'm good for four years, 'thout I meet with some accident."

I could not help agreeing, or taking a fond look at the thin little figure, and her wrinkled brown face and kind, twinkling eyes. She looked as if she had properly dried herself, by mistake, with some of her mullein leaves, and was likely to keep her goodness, and to last the longer in consequence. There never was a truer, simple-hearted soul made out of the old-fashioned country dust than Mrs. Goodsoe. I thought, as I looked away from her across the wide country, that nobody was left in any of the farmhouses so original, so full of rural wisdom and reminiscence, so really able and dependable, as she. And nobody had made better use of her time in a world foolish enough to sometimes undervalue medicinal herbs.

When we had eaten our peaches we still sat under the pines, and I was not without pride when I had poked about in the ground with a little twig, and displayed to my crony a long fine root, bright yellow to the eye, and a wholesome bitter to the taste.

"Yis, dear, goldthread," she assented indulgently. "Seems to me there's more of it than anything except grass an' hardtack. Good for canker, but no better than two or three other things I can call to mind; but I always lay in a good wisp of it, for old times' sake. Now, I want to know why you should ha' bit it, and took away all the taste o' your nice peach? I was just thinkin' what a han'some entertainment we've had. I've got so I 'sociate certain things with certain folks, and goldthread was somethin' Lizy Wisby couldn't keep house without, no ways whatever. I believe she took so much it kind o' puckered her disposition."

"Lizy Wisby?" I repeated inquiringly.

"You knew her, if ever, by the name of Mis' Deacon Brimblecom," answered my friend, as if this were only a brief preface to further information, so I waited with respectful expectation. Mrs. Goodsoe had grown tired out in the sun, and a good story would be an excuse for sufficient rest. It was a most lovely place where we sat, halfway up the long hillside; for my part, I was perfectly contented and happy. "You've often heard of Deacon Brimblecom?" she asked, as if a great deal depended upon his being properly introduced.

"I remember him," said I. "They called him Deacon Brimfull, you know, and he used to go about with a witch-hazel branch to show people where to dig wells."

"That's the one," said Mrs. Goodsoe, laughing. "I didn't know's you could go so far back. I'm always divided between whether you can remember everything I can, or are only a babe in arms."

"I have a dim recollection of there being something strange about their marriage," I suggested, after a pause, which began to appear dangerous. I was so much afraid the subject would be changed.

"I can tell you all about it," I was quickly answered. "Deacon Brimblecom was very pious accordin' to his lights in his early years. He lived way back in the country then, and there come a rovin' preacher along, and set everybody up that way all by the ears. I've heard the old folks talk it over, but I forget most of his doctrine, except some of his followers was persuaded they could dwell among the angels while yet on airth, and this Deacon Brimfull, as you call him, felt sure he was called by the voice of a spirit bride. So he left a good, deservin' wife he had, an' four children, and built him a new house over to the other side of the land he'd had from his father. They didn't take much pains with the buildin', because they expected to be translated before long, and then the spirit brides and them folks was goin' to appear and divide up the airth amongst 'em, and the world's folks and on-believers was goin' to serve 'em or be sent to torments. They had meetin's about in the schoolhouses, an' all sorts o' goin's on; some of 'em went crazy, but the deacon held on to what wits he had, an' by an' by the spirit bride didn't turn out to be much of a housekeeper, an' he had always been used to good livin', so he sneaked home ag'in. One o' mother's sisters married up to Ash Hill, where it all took place; that's how I come to have the particulars."

"Then how did he come to find his Eliza Wisby?" I inquired. "Do tell me the whole story; you've got mullein leaves enough."

"There's all yesterday's at home, if I haven't," replied Mrs. Goodsoe. "The way he come a-courtin' o' Sister Wisby was this: she went a-courtin' o' him.

"There was a spell he lived to home, and then his poor wife died, and he had a spirit bride in good earnest, an' the child'n was placed about with his folks and hers, for they was both out o' good families; and I don't know what come over him, but he had another pious fit that looked for all the world like the real thing. He hadn't no family cares, and he lived with his brother's folks, and turned his land in with theirs. He used to travel to every meetin' an' conference that was within reach of his old sorrel hoss's feeble legs; he j'ined the Christian Baptists that was just in their early prime, and he was a great exhorter, and got to be called deacon, though I guess he wa'n't deacon, 'less it was for a spare hand when deacon times was scercer'n usual. An' one time there was a four-days' protracted meetin' to the church in the lower part of the town. 'Twas a real solemn time; somethin' more'n usual was goin' forward, an' they collected from the whole country round. Women folks liked it, an' the men too; it gave 'em a change, an' they was quartered round free, same as conference folks now. Some on 'em, for a joke, sent Silas Brimblecom up to Lizy Wisby's, though she'd give out she couldn't accommodate nobody, because of expectin' her cousin's folks. Everybody knew 'twas a lie; she was amazin' close considerin' she had plenty to do with. There was a streak that wa'n't just right somewheres in Lizy's wits, I always thought. She was very kind in case o' sickness, I'll say that for her.

"You know where the house is, over there on what they call Windy Hill? There the deacon went, all unsuspectin', and 'stead o' Lizy's resentin' of him she put in her own hoss, and they come back together to evenin' meetin'. She was prominent among the sect herself, an' he bawled and talked, and she bawled and talked, an' took up more'n the time allotted in the exercises, just as if they was showin' off to each what they was able to do at expoundin'. Everybody was laughin' at 'em after the meetin' broke up, and the next day an' the next, an' all through, they was constant, and seemed to be havin' a beautiful occasion. Lizy had always give out she scorned the men, but when she got a chance at a particular one 'twas altogether different, and the deacon seemed to please her somehow or 'nother, and—There! you don't want to listen to this old stuff that's past an' gone?"

"Oh, yes, I do," said I.

"I run on like a clock that's onset her striking hand," said Mrs. Goodsoe mildly. "Sometimes my kitchen timepiece goes on half the forenoon, and I says to myself the day before yisterday I would let it be a warnin', and keep it in mind for a check on my own speech. The next news that was heard was that the deacon an' Lizy—well, opinions differed which of 'em had spoke first, but them fools settled it before the protracted meetin' was over, and give away their hearts before he started for home. They considered 'twould be wise, though, considerin' their short acquaintance, to take one another on trial a spell; 'twas Lizy's notion, and she asked him why he wouldn't come over and stop with her till spring, and then, if both continued to like, they could git married any time 'twas convenient. Lizy, she come and talked it over with mother, and mother disliked to offend her, but she spoke pretty plain; and Lizy felt hurt, an' thought they was showin' excellent judgment, so much harm come from hasty unions and folks comin' to a realizin' sense of each other's failin's when 'twas too late.

"So one day our folks saw Deacon Brimfull a-ridin' by with a gre't coopful of hens in the back o' his wagon, and bundles o' stuff tied to top and hitched to the exes underneath; and he riz a hymn just as he passed the house, and

was speedin' the old sorrel with a willer switch. 'Twas most
Thanksgivin' time, an' sooner'n she expected him. New
Year's was the time she set; but he thought he'd come while
the roads was fit for wheels. They was out to meetin' together
Thanksgivin' Day, an' that used to be a gre't season for marryin'; so the young folks nudged each other, and some on 'em
ventured to speak to the couple as they come down the aisle.
Lizy carried it off real well; she wa'n't afraid o' what nobody
said or thought, and so home they went. They'd got out her
yaller sleigh and her hoss; she never would ride after the deacon's poor old creatur, and I believe it died long o' the winter
from stiffenin' up.

"Yes," said Mrs. Goodsoe, emphatically, after we had
silently considered the situation for a short space of time,
"yes, there was consider'ble talk, now I tell you! The raskil
boys pestered 'em just about to death for a while. They used
to collect up there an' rap on the winders, and they'd turn
out all the deacon's hens 'long at nine o'clock o' night, and
chase 'em all over the dingle; an' one night they even lugged
the pig right out o' the sty, and shoved it into the back entry,
an' run for their lives. They'd stuffed its mouth full o' somethin', so it couldn't squeal till it got there. There wa'n't a sign
o' nobody to be seen when Lizy hasted out with the light, and
she an' the deacon had to persuade the creatur back as best
they could; 'twas a cold night, and they said it took 'em till
towards mornin'. You see the deacon was just the kind of a
man that a hog wouldn't budge for; it takes a masterful man
to deal with a hog. Well, there was no end to the works nor
the talk, but Lizy left 'em pretty much alone. She did 'pear
kind of dignified about it, I must say!"

"And then, were they married in the spring?"

"I was tryin' to remember whether it was just before Fast
Day or just after," responded my friend, with a careful look
at the sun, which was nearer the west then either of us had
noticed. "I think likely 'twas along in the last o' April, anyway some of us looked out o' the window one Monday
mornin' early, and says, 'For goodness' sake! Lizy's sent the
deacon home again!' His old sorrel havin' passed away, he
was ridin' in Ezry Welsh's hoss-cart, and his hen-coop and
more bundles than he had when he come, and looked as
meechin' as ever you see. Ezry was drivin', and he let a
glance fly swiftly round to see if any of us was lookin' out;
an' then I declare if he didn't have the malice to turn right in

towards the barn, where he see my oldest brother, Joshuay, an' says he real natural, 'Joshuay, just step out with your wrench. I believe I hear my kingbolt rattlin' kind o' loose.' Brother, he went out an' took in the sitooation, an' the deacon bowed kind of stiff. Joshuay was so full o' laugh, and Ezry Welsh, that they couldn't look one another in the face. There wa'n't nothing ailed the kingbolt, you know, an' when Josh riz up he says, 'Goin' up country for a spell, Mr. Brimblecom?'

" 'I be,' says the deacon, lookin' dreadful mortified and cast down.

" 'Ain't things turned out well with you an' Sister Wisby?' says Joshuay. 'You had ought to remember that the woman is the weaker vessel.'

" 'Hang her, let her carry less sail, then!' the deacon bu'st out, and he stood right up an' shook his fist there by the hencoop, he was so mad; an' Ezry's hoss was a young creatur, an' started up and set the deacon right over backwards into the chips. We didn't know but he'd broke his neck; but when he see the women folks runnin' out he jumped up quick as a cat, an' clim into the cart, an' off they went. Ezry said he told him that he couldn't git along with Lizy, she was so fractious in thundery weather; if there was a rumble in the daytime she must go right to bed an' screech, and 'twas night she must git right up an' go an' call him out of a sound sleep. But everybody knew he'd never gone home unless she'd sent him.

"Somehow they made it up ag'in, him an' Lizy, and she had him back. She's been countin' all along on not havin' to hire nobidy to work about the gardin' an' so on, an' she said she wa'n't goin' to let him have a whole winter's board for nothin'. So the old hens was moved back, and they was married right off fair an' square, an' I don't know but they got along well as most folks. He brought his youngest girl down to live with 'em after a while, an' she was a real treasure to Lizy; everybody spoke well o' Phoebe Brimblecom. The deacon got over his pious fit, and there was consider'ble work in him if you kept right after him. He was an amazin' cider-drinker, and he airnt the name you know him by in his latter days. Lizy never trusted him with nothin', but she kep' him well. She left everything she owned to Phoebe, when she died, 'cept somethin' to satisfy the law. There, they're all gone now; seems to me sometimes, when I get thinkin', as if I'd lived a thousand years!"

I laughed, but I found Mrs. Goodsoe's thoughts had taken a serious turn.

"There, I come by some old graves down here in the lower edge of the pasture," she said as we rose to go. "I couldn't help thinking how I should like to be laid right out in the pasture ground, when my time comes; it looked sort o' comfortable, and I have ranged these slopes so many summers. Seems as if I could see right up through the turf and tell when the weather was pleasant, and get the goodness o' the sweet fern. Now, dear, just hand me my apernful o' mulleins out o' the shade. I hope you won't come to need none this winter, but I'll dry some special for you."

"I'm going by the road," said I, "or else by the path across the meadows, so I will walk as far as the house with you. Aren't you pleased with my company?" for she demurred at my going the least bit out of the way.

So we strolled towards the little gray house, with our plunder of mullein leaves slung on a stick which we carried between us. Of course I went in to make a call, as if I had not seen my hostess before; she is the last maker of muster-gingerbread, and before I came away I was kindly measured for a pair of mittens.

"You'll be sure to come an' see them two peach trees after I get 'em well growin'?" Mrs. Goodsoe called after me when I had said good-by; and was almost out of hearing down the road.

SELMA LAGERLÖF was born at Marbocka, Sweden, in 1858. Along with Hans Christian Andersen she is among Sweden's most famous authors. Her literary preoccupation with miraculous transformations may have had their source in her own sudden return to health. Paralyzed as a child—all her life she walked with a limp—she experienced a dramatic recovery. All her novels are shot through with such wondrous happenings. Fairy tale, legend, and ghost story mingle with tales of ordinary affairs. But in the words of one critic, "Lagerlöf herself could never quite accept the marvels and mysteries she recounted; she has aptly been defined as the great seeker who never achieved and never claimed to have achieved certainty."

In the 1880s, after her father lost his money, she studied to be a teacher in order to support herself, all the while working on her first book, *The Story of Gosta Berling* (1891). It was her epic two-part novel *Jerusalem* (1901–1902) which established her as a writer of international importance. Its hero Ingmar Ingmarsson is her most well-known character; in his struggle for moral integrity is the universal motif that runs through all her work—i.e., the problem of combining happiness with goodness. Her best-known book is *The Wonderful Adventures of Nils*, a school reader describing a small boy's magic flight throughout Sweden. After she received the Nobel Prize for Literature in 1909, she bought back the family manor at Marbocka which later became the shrine of a worldwide Lagerlöf cult. She died in 1940.

Selma Lagerlöf
(1858—1940)

THE ECLIPSE

There were Stina of Ridgecôte and Lina of Birdsong and Kajsa of Littlemarsh and Maja of Skypeak and Beda of Finn-darkness and Elin, the new wife on the old soldier's place, and two or three other peasant women besides—all of them lived at the far end of the parish, below Storhöjden, in a region so wild and rocky none of the big farm owners had bothered to lay hands on it.

One had her cabin set up on a shelf of rock, another had hers put up at the edge of a bog, while a third had one that stood at the crest of a hill so steep it was a toilsome climb getting to it. If by chance any of the others had a cottage built on more favorable ground, you may be sure it lay so close to the mountain as to shut out the sun from autumn fair time clear up to Annunciation Day.

They each cultivated a little potato patch close by the cabin, though under serious difficulties. To be sure, there were many kinds of soil there at the foot of the mountain, but it was hard work to make the patches of land yield anything. In some places they had to clear away so much stone from their fields, it would have built a cow-house on a manorial estate; in some they had dug ditches as deep as graves, and in others they had brought their earth in sacks and spread it on the bare rocks. Where the soil was not so poor, they were forever fighting the tough thistle and pigweed which sprang up in such profusion you would have thought the whole potato land had been prepared for their benefit.

All the livelong day the women were alone in their cabins; for even where one had a husband and children, the man went off to his work every morning and the children went to school. A few among the older women had grown sons and daughters, but they had gone to America. And some there were with little children, who were always around, of course; but these could hardly be regarded as company.

Being so much alone, it was really necessary that they should meet sometimes over the coffee cups. Not that they got on so very well together, nor had any great love for each other; but some liked to keep posted on what the others were doing, and some grew despondent living like that, in the shadow of the mountain, unless they met people now and then. And there were those, too, who needed to unburden their hearts, and talk about the last letter from America, and those who were naturally talkative and jocular, and who longed for opportunity to make use of these happy God-given talents.

Nor was it any trouble at all to prepare for a little party. Coffee-pot and coffee cups they all had of course, and cream could be got at the manor, if one had no cow of one's own to milk; fancy biscuits and small cakes one could, at a pinch, get the dairy-man's driver to fetch from the municipal bakery, and country merchants who sold coffee and sugar were to be found everywhere. So, to get up a coffee party was the easiest thing imaginable. The difficulty lay in finding an occasion.

For Stina of Ridgecôte, Lina of Birdsong, Kajsa of Little-marsh, Maja of Skypeak, Beda of Finn-darkness, and Elin, the new wife at the old soldier's, were all agreed that it would never do for them to celebrate in the midst of the common everyday life. Were they to be that wasteful of the precious hours which never return, they might get a bad name. And to hold coffee parties on Sundays or great Holy Days was out of the question; for them the married women had husband and children at home, which was quite company enough. As for the rest—some liked to attend church, some wished to visit relatives, while a few preferred to spend the day at home, in perfect peace and stillness, that they might really feel it was a Holy Day.

Therefore they were all the more eager to take advantage of every possible opportunity. Most of them gave parties on their name-days, though some celebrated the great event when the wee little one cut its first tooth, or when it took its first steps. For those who received money-letters from America that was always a convenient excuse, and it was also in order to invite all the women of the neighborhood to come and help tack a quilt or stretch a web just off the loom.

All the same, there were not nearly as many occasions to meet as were needed. One year one of the women was at her wit's end. It was her turn to give a party, and she had no objection to carrying out what was expected of her; but she could not seem to hit upon anything to celebrate. Her own name-day she could not celebrate, being named Beda, as Beda had been stricken out of the almanac. Nor could she celebrate that of any member of her family, for all her dear ones were resting in the churchyard. She was very old, and the quilt she slept under would probably outlast her. She had a cat of which she was very fond. Truth to tell, it drank coffee just as well as she did; but she could hardly bring herself to hold a party for a cat!

Pondering, she searched her almanac again and again, for there she felt she must surely find the solution of her problem.

She began at the beginning, with "The Royal House" and "Signs and Forecasts," and read on, right through to "Markets and Postal Transmittances for 1912," without finding anything.

As she was reading the book for the seventh time, her glance rested on "Eclipses." She noted that that year, which was the year of our Lord nineteen-hundred twelve, on April seventeenth there would be a solar eclipse. It would begin at twenty minutes past high noon and end at 2:40 o'clock, and would cover nine-tenths of the sun's disk.

This she had read before, many times, without attaching any significance to it; but now, all at once, it became dazzlingly clear to her.

"Now I have it!" she exclaimed.

But it was only for a second or two that she felt confident; and then she put the thought away, fearing that the other women would just laugh at her.

The next few days, however, the idea that had come to her when reading her almanac kept recurring to her mind, until at last she began to wonder whether she hadn't better venture. For when she thought about it, what friend had she in all the world she loved better than the Sun? Where her hut lay not a ray of sunlight penetrated her room the whole winter long. She counted the days until the Sun would come back to her in the spring. The Sun was the only one she longed for, the only one who was always friendly and gracious to her and of whom she could never see enough.

She looked her years, and felt them, too. Her hands shook as if she were in a perpetual chill and when she saw herself in the looking-glass, she appeared so pale and washed out, as if she had been lying out to bleach. It was only when she stood in a strong, warm, down-pouring sunshine that she felt like a live human being and not a walking corpse.

The more she thought about it, the more she felt there was no day in the whole year she would rather celebrate than the one when her friend the Sun battled against darkness, and after a glorious conquest, came forth with new splendor and majesty.

The seventeenth of April was not far away, but there was ample time to make ready for a party. So, on the day of the eclipse Stina, Lina, Kajsa, Maja, and the other women all sat drinking coffee with Beda at Finn-darkness. They drank their second and third cups, and chatted about everything imaginable. For one thing, they said they couldn't for the life of them understand why Beda should be giving a party.

Meanwhile, the eclipse was under way. But they took little notice of it. Only for a moment, when the sky turned blackish gray, when all nature seemed under a leaden pall, and there came driving a howling wind with sounds as of the Trumpet of Doom and the lamentations of Judgment Day—only then did they pause and feel a bit awed. But here they each had a fresh cup of coffee, and the feeling soon passed.

When all was over, and the Sun stood out in the heavens so beamingly happy—it seemed to them it had not shone with such brilliancy and power the whole year—they saw old Beda go over to the window, and stand with folded hands. Looking out toward the sunlit slope, she sang in her quavering voice:

> "Thy shining sun goes up again,
> I thank Thee, O my Lord!
> With new-found courage, strength and hope,
> I raise a song of joy."

Thin and transparent, old Beda stood there in the light of the window, and as she sang the sunbeams danced about her, as if wanting to give her, also, of their life and strength and color.

When she had finished the old hymn-verse she turned and looked at her guests, as if in apology.

"You see," she said, "I haven't any better friend than the Sun, and I wanted to give her a party on the day of her eclipse. I felt that we should come together to greet her, when she came out of her darkness."

Now they understood what old Beda meant, and their hearts were touched. They began to speak well of the Sun. "She was kind to rich and poor alike, and when she came peeping into the hut on a winter's day, she was comforting as a flowing fire on the hearth. Just the sight of her smiling face made life worth living, whatever the troubles one had to bear."

The women went back to their homes after the party, happy and content. They somehow felt richer and more secure in the thought that they had a good, faithful friend in the Sun.

DOROTHY RICHARDSON was born in Oxfordshire, England, in 1873. She was the third in a family of four daughters. Her mother became emotionally unstable as her father piled up debts and longed for a son. (He sometimes called Dorothy "Charles," as she in her willful and undomesticated ways was the closest thing to a son he could hope for.) She worked as a governess and a teacher to help support her family, and then, after her mother's suicide and her father's bankruptcy, she moved out on her own to a flat in Bloomsbury and a clerking job in Harley Street. The attic room and her love of the freedom of living alone in London are described in the excerpt from *Pilgrimage* reprinted here.

She did not begin her sequence of thirteen novels until she was in her forties. The protagonist, Miriam Henderson, is Richardson's persona, through whom she gives the biographical data of her own first thirty years. She attempted to represent the effect of every experience on Miriam's sensibility. The narrative, most of which is set in London, provides descriptions of Miriam's jobs, of her membership in socialist and avant-garde intellectual groups, of her friendship with the prototype of H. G. Wells (with whom Richardson had a love affair that ended in pregnancy and miscarriage).

The subject of *Pilgrimage* is consciousness itself, though Richardson disliked the phrase "stream of consciousness" that was so often applied to her work. First used by novelist May Sinclair in an article she wrote on "The Novels of Dorothy Richardson," it comes from William James's *The Principles of Psychology*: "Consciousness . . . does not appear to itself chopped up in bits . . . It is nothing jointed; it flows. A 'river' or a 'stream' are the metaphors by which it is most naturally described. In telling of it hereafter, let us call it the stream of thought, of consciousness, or of subjective life." Dorothy Richardson's own use of this technique changed the course of the modern novel. Her place in the history of the genre is as the immediate precursor of the Joyce of *Ulysses,* of Virginia Woolf, and of Katherine Mansfield, and yet she is an obscure figure to many readers. Elizabeth Bowen once referred to her as the great unknown English novelist of the twentieth century.

Dorothy Richardson
(1873—1957)

From PILGRIMAGE

Miriam paused with her heavy bag dragging at her arm. It was a disaster. But it was the last of Mornington Road. To explain about it would be to bring Mornington Road here.

"It doesn't matter now," said Mrs. Bailey as she dropped her bag and fumbled for her purse.

"Oh, I'd better settle it at once or I shall forget about it. I'm so glad the things have come so soon."

When Mrs. Bailey had taken the half-crown they stood smiling at each other. Mrs. Bailey looked exactly as she had done the first time. It was exactly the same; there was no disappointment. The light coming through the glass above the front door made her look more shabby and worn. Her hair was more metallic. But it was the same girlish figure and the same smile triumphing over the badly fitting teeth. Miriam felt like an inmate returning after an absence. The smeariness of the marble-topped hall table did not offend her. She held herself in. It was better to begin as she meant to go on. Behind Mrs. Bailey the staircase was beckoning. There was something waiting upstairs that would be gone if she stayed talking to Mrs. Bailey.

Assuring Mrs. Bailey that she remembered the way to the room, she started at last on the journey up the many flights of stairs. The feeling of confidence that had come the first time she mounted them with Mrs. Bailey returned now. She could not remember noticing anything then but a large brown dinginess, one rich warm even tone everywhere in the house; a sharp contrast to the cold, harshly lit little bedroom in Mornington Road. The day was cold. But this house did not seem cold and, when she rounded the first flight and Mrs. Bailey was out of sight, the welcome of the place fell upon her. She knew it well, better than any place she had known in all her wanderings—the faded umbers and browns of the stair carpet, the gloomy heights of wall, a patternless sheen where

the staircase lights fell upon it and, in the shadowed parts, a
blurred scrolling pattern in dull madder on a brown background; the dark landings with lofty ceilings and high dark
polished doors surmounted by classical reliefs in grimed plaster, the high staircase windows screened by long smoke-
grimed lace curtains. On the third landing the ceiling came
down nearer to the tops of the doors. The light from above
made the little grained doors stare brightly. Patches of fresh
brown and buff shone here and there in the threadbare lino-
leum. The cracks of the flooring were filled with dust and
dust lay along the rim of the skirting. Two large tin trunks
standing one upon the other almost barred the passage way.
It was like a landing in a small suburban lodging-house, a
small silent afternoon brightness, shut in and smelling of dust.
Silence flooded up from the lower darkness. The hall where
she had stood with Mrs. Bailey was far away below, and below that were basements deep in the earth. The outside of the
house, with its first-floor balcony, the broad shallow flight of
steps leading to the dark green front door, the little steep
flight running sharply down into the railed area, seemed as
far away as yesterday.

　　The little landing was a bright plateau. Under the skylight,
shut off by its brightness from the rest of the house, the
rooms leading from it would be bright and flat and noisy
with light compared with the rest of the house. From above
came the tap-tap of a door swinging gently in a breeze and
behind the sound was a soft faint continuous murmur. She
ran up the short twisting flight of bare stairs into a blaze of
light. Would her room be a bright suburban bedroom? Had it
been a dull day when she first called? The skylight was blue
and gold with light, its cracks threads of bright gold. Three
little glaring yellow-grained doors opened on to the small
strip of uncovered dusty flooring; to the left the little box-loft,
to the right the empty garret behind her own and, in front of
her, her own door ajar; tapping in the breeze. The little brass
knob rattled loosely in her hand and the hinge ran up the
scale to a high squeak as she pushed open the door, and
down again as it closed behind her neatly with a light wooden
sound. The room was half dark shadow and half brilliant
light.

　　She closed the door and stood just inside it looking at the
room. It was smaller than her memory of it. When she had
stood in the middle of the floor with Mrs. Bailey, she had

looked at nothing but Mrs. Bailey, waiting for the moment to ask about the rent. Coming upstairs she had felt the room was hers and barely glanced at it when Mrs. Bailey opened the door. From the moment of waiting on the stone steps outside the front door, everything had opened to the movement of her impulse. She was surprised now at her familiarity with the detail of the room . . . that idea of visiting places in dreams. It was something more than that . . . all the real part of your life has a real dream in it; some of the real dream part of you coming true. You know in advance when you are really following your life. These things are familiar because reality is here. Coming events cast *light*. It is like dropping everything and walking backwards to something you know is there. However far you go out, you come back. . . . I am back now where I was before I began trying to do things like other people. I left home to get here. None of those things can touch me here.

. . . The room asserted its chilliness. But the dark yellow graining of the wall-paper was warm. It shone warmly in the stream of light pouring through the barred lattice window. In the further part of the room, darkened by the steep slope of the roof, it gleamed like stained wood. The window space was a little square wooden room, the long low double lattice breaking the roof, the ceiling and walls warmly reflecting its oblong of bright light. Close against the window was a firm little deal table covered with a thin, brightly coloured printed cotton table-cloth. When Miriam drew her eyes from its confusion of rich fresh tones, the bedroom seemed very dark. The bed, drawn in under the slope, showed an expanse of greyish white counterpane, the carpet was colourless in the gloom. She opened the door. Silence came in from the landing. The blue and gold had gone from the skylight. Its sharp grey light shone in over the dim colours of the threadbare carpet and on to the black bars of the little grate and the little strip of tarnished yellow-grained mantelpiece, running along to the bedhead where a small globeless gas bracket stuck out at an angle over the head of the bed. The sight of her luggage piled up on the other side of the fireplace drew her forward into the dimness. There was a small chest of drawers, battered and almost paintless, but with two long drawers and two small ones and a white cover on which stood a little looking-glass framed in polished pine . . . and a small yellow wardrobe with a deep drawer under the hanging part, and a little drawer in the rickety little washstand and another above the dusty cupboard of the little mahogany sideboard. I'll paint the bright part of the ceiling; scrolls of leaves. . . . Shutting the quiet door she went into the brilliance of the window space. The outside world appeared; a long row of dormer windows and the square tops of the larger windows below them, the windows black or sheeny grey in the light, cut out against the dinginess of smoke-grimed walls. The long strip of roof sloping back from the dormers was a pure even dark grey. She bent to see the sky, clear soft heavy grey, striped by the bars of her window. Behind the top rim of the iron framework of the bars was a discoloured roll of window blind. Then the bars must move. . . . Shifting the table she pressed close to the barred window. It smelt strongly of rust and dust. Outside she saw grey tiles sloping steeply from the window to a cemented gutter, beyond which was a little stone parapet about two feet high. A soft wash of madder lay along the grey tiles. There must be an afterglow somewhere, just out of sight. Her hands went through the bars and lifted the little rod which held the lattice half open. The little square four-paned frame swung free and flattened itself back against the fixed panes, out of reach, its bar sticking out over the leads. Drawing back grimed fingers and wrists striped with grime, she grasped the iron bars and pulled. The heavy framework left the window frame with a rusty creak and the sound of paint peeling and cracking. It was very heavy, but it came up and up until her arms were straight above her head, and looking up she saw a stout iron ring in a little trapdoor in the wooden ceiling and a hook in the centre of the endmost bar in the iron framework.

Kneeling on the table to raise the frame once more and fix it to the ceiling, she saw the whole length of the top row of windows across the way and wide strips of grimy stucco placed across the house fronts between the windows.

The framework of the freed window was cracked and blistered, but the little square panes were clean. There were four little windows in the row, each with four square panes. The outmost windows were immovable. The one next to the open one had lost its bar, but a push set it free and it swung wide. She leaned out, holding back from the dusty sill, and met a soft fresh breeze streaming straight in from the west. The distant murmur of traffic changed into the clear plonk plonk and rumble of swift vehicles. Right and left at the far end of the vista were glimpses of bare trees. The cheeping of birds came faintly from the distant squares and clear and sharp from neighboring roofs. To the left the trees were black against pure grey, to the right they stood spread and bunched in front of the distant buildings blocking the vista. Running across the rose-washed façade of the central mass she could just make out "Edwards's Family Hotel" in large black letters. That was the distant view of the courtyard of Euston Station. . . . In between that and the square of trees ran the Euston Road, by day and by night, her unsleeping guardian, the rim of the world beyond which lay the northern suburbs, banished.

From a window somewhere down the street out of sight came the sound of an unaccompanied violin, clearly attacking and dropping and attacking a passage of half a dozen bars. The music stood serene and undisturbed in the air of the quiet street. The man was following the phrase, listening; strengthening and clearing it, completely undisturbed and unconscious of his surroundings. "Good heavens," she breathed quietly, feeling the extremity of relief, passing some boundary, emerging strong and equipped in a clear medium. . . . She turned back into the twilight of the room. Twenty-one and only one room to hold the richly renewed consciousness, and a living to earn, but the self that was with her in the room was the untouched tireless self of her seventeenth year and all the earlier time. The familiar light moved within the twilight, the old light. . . . She might as well wash the grime from her wrists and hands. There was a scrap of soap in the soap dish, dry and cracked and seamed with dirt. The washstand rocked as she washed her hands; the toilet things did not match, the towel-horse held one small thin face-towel and fell sideways against the wardrobe as she drew off the towel. When the gas was on she would be visible from the opposite dormer window. Short skimpy faded Madras muslin curtains screened a few inches of the endmost windows and were caught back and tied up with tape. She untied the tape and disengaged with the curtains a strong smell of dust. The curtains would cut off some of the light. She tied them firmly back and pulled at the edge of the rolled-up blind. The blind, streaked and mottled with ironmould, came down in a stifling cloud of dust. She rolled it up again and washed once more. She must ask for a bath towel and do something about the blind, sponge it or something; that was all.

A light had come in the dormer on the other side of the street. It remained unscreened. Watching carefully she could see only a dim figure moving amongst motionless shapes. No need to trouble about the blind. London could come freely in day and night through the unscreened happy little panes; light and darkness and darkness and light.

London, just outside all the time, coming in with the light, coming in with the darkness, always present in the depths of the air in the room.

The gas flared out into a wide bright flame. The dingy ceiling and counterpane turned white. The room was a square of bright light and had a rich brown glow, shut brightly in by the straight square of level white ceiling and thrown up by the oblong that sloped down, white, at the side of the big bed almost to the floor. She left her things half unpacked about the floor and settled herself on the bed under the gas jet with *The Voyage of the Beagle*. Unpacking had been a distraction from the glory, very nice, getting things straight. But there was no *need* to do anything or think about anything . . . ever, here. No interruption, no one watching or speculating or treating one in some particular way that had to be met. Mrs. Bailey did not speculate. She knew, everything. Every evening here would have a glory, but not the same kind of glory. Reading would be more of a distraction than unpacking. She read a few lines. They had a fresh attractive *meaning*. Reading would be real. The dull adventures of the *Beagle* looked real, coming along through reality. She put the book on her knee and once more met the clear brown shock of her room. . . .

When she turned out the gas the window spaces remained faintly alight with a soft light like moonlight. At the window she found a soft bluish radiance cast up from below upon the opposite walls and windows. It went up into the clear blue darkness of the sky.

When she lay down the bed smelt faintly of dust. The air about her head under the sharply sloping ceiling was still a little warm with the gas. It was full of her untrammelled thoughts. Her luggage was lying about, quite near. She thought of washing in the morning in the bright light on the other side of the room . . . leaves crowding all round the lat-

tice and here and there a pink rose . . . *several pink roses*
. . . the lovely air chilling the water . . . the basin quite up
against the lattice . . . dew splashing off the rose bushes in
the little garden almost dark with trellises and trees, crowding
with Harriett through the little damp stiff gate, the sudden
lineny smell of Harriett's pinafore and the thought of Harriett in it, feeling the same, sudden bright sunshine, two shouts,
great cornfields going up and up with a little track between
them . . . up over Blewburton . . . *Whittenham Clumps*. Before I saw Whittenham Clumps I had always known them.
But we saw them before we knew they were called Whittenham Clumps. It was a surprise to know anybody who had
seen them and that they had a name.

St. Pancras bells were clamouring in the room; rapid
scales, beginning at the top, coming with a loud full thump
on to the fourth note and finishing with a rush to the lowest
which was hardly touched before the top note hung again in
the air, sounding outdoors clean and clear while all the other
notes still jangled together in her room. Nothing had
changed. The night was like a moment added to the day; like
years going backwards to the beginning; and in the brilliant
sunshine the unchanging things began again, perfectly new.
She leaped out of bed into the clamorous stillness and stood
in the window rolling up the warm hair that felt like a shawl
round her shoulders. A cup of tea and then the bus to Harriett's. A bus somewhere just out there beyond the morning
stillness of the street. What an *adventure* to go out and take
a bus without having to face anybody. They were all out
there, away somewhere, the very thought and sight of them,
disapproving and deploring her surroundings. She listened.
There they were. There were their very voices, coming
plaintive and reproachful with a held-in indignation, intona-
tions that she knew inside and out, coming on bells from
somewhere beyond the squares—another church. She withdrew the coloured cover and set her spirit lamp on the
inkstained table. Strong bright light was standing outside the
window. The clamour of the bells had ceased. From far away
down in the street a loud hoarse voice came thinly up.
"*Referee—Lloyd's—Sunday Times—People*—pypa. . . ." A
front door opened with a loud crackle of paint. The voice
dropped to speaking tones that echoed clearly down the street
and came up clear and soft and confidential. "*Referee?*

Lloyd's?" The door closed with a large firm wooden sound
and the harsh voice went on down the street.

St. Pancras bells burst forth again. Faintly interwoven with
their bright headlong scale were the clear sweet delicate contralto of the more distant bells playing very swiftly and
reproachfully a five-finger exercise in a minor key. That must
be a very high-Anglican church; with light coming through
painted windows on to carvings and decorations.

As she began on her solid slice of bread and butter, St.
Pancras bells stopped again. In the stillness she could hear
the sound of her own munching. She stared at the surface of
the table that held her plate and cup. It was like sitting up to
the nursery table. "How frightfully happy I am," she thought
with bent head. Happiness streamed along her arms and from
her head. St. Pancras bells began playing a hymn tune, in
single firm beats with intervals between that left each note
standing for a moment gently in the air. The first two lines
were playing carefully through to the distant accompaniment
of the rapid weaving and interweaving in a regular unbroken
pattern of the five soft low contralto bells of the other
church. The third line of the hymn ran through Miriam's
head, a ding-dong to and fro from tone to semitone. The
bells played it out, without the semitone, with a perfect, satisfying falsity. Miriam sat hunched against the table listening
for the ascending stages of the last line. The bells climbed
gently up, made a faint flat dab at the last top note, left it in
the air askew above the decorous little tune and rushed away
down their scale as if to cover the impropriety. They clam-
oured recklessly mingling with Miriam's shout of joy as
they banged against the wooden walls of the window space.

DOROTHY CANFIELD FISHER was born in Laurence, Kansas, in 1879, the daughter of a university-president father and an artist mother. She received a doctorate in French from Columbia University in 1905, preparing for the academic career which she eventually abandoned for writing.

After her marriage, she and her husband moved to one of the Canfield farms, near Arlington, Vermont (the Canfields have been Vermonters for two hundred years). During World War I she worked in the Basque country of France setting up a home for the starving children of the northern districts invaded by Germany. During and after the war she traveled so much in Europe that her own children forgot their English.

A prolific writer (thirty-five published books), editor (a member of the Book-of-the-Month Club selection committee for twenty-five years), and educator (an early discoverer of Maria Montessori), Dorothy Canfield attributed her decision to be a writer to the influence of her unconventional, impetuous mother. In her essay "What My Mother Taught Me," Canfield remembers looking at one of the Velasquez court dwarfs in the Prado, and connects the conception of the story reprinted here and her own commitment to art with that experience:

> The subject of one of the first stories I wrote, "The Bedquilt," was as helplessly starved as the Spanish dwarf of what all human beings need for growth . . . was as humbled before her fellow-men through no fault of hers . . . as defenselessly given over to the careless mockery of those luckier than she. This by no glandular lack . . . by the social code of her time which decreed that plain women without money, who did not have husbands, who had never been admired by men, were only outcasts from the normal group . . . grotesque deformities, so

33

that to look at them was to laugh at them! I had never known, had never before thought, what had been the impulse which in my youth had inexplicably detached me from the study of phonetic changes in Old French, to which I had been set as part of the training to earn my living; the impulse which had lifted me away from my textbooks to gaze, deeply sorrowing with her, into the patient remembered eyes of an insignificant old maid whom I had known in my careless childhood; the impulse which had forced me into facing the enormous difficulties of story telling, often enough too great for my powers to cope with. Well, now I had a clue to that impulse. A message received from the marvelously painted, dark, tragic eyes of Sebastian de Morra had forced me to look deep into the faded blue eyes of Aunt Mehetabel. With that look the walls which keep a scholar's room windless and still had fallen, leaving me in the heartsick turmoil of a compulsion to imagine and desperately to try to portray a human being not as what she seemed, but what she was . . . to convince people who in life hardly even noticed her existence that she shared in the human dignity of the instinct to create. . . .

Dorothy Canfield Fisher
(1879—1958)

THE BEDQUILT

Of all the Elwell family Aunt Mehetabel was certainly the most unimportant member. It was in the old-time New England days, when an unmarried woman was an old maid at twenty, at forty was everyone's servant, and at sixty had gone through so much discipline that she could need no more in the next world. Aunt Mehetabel was sixty-eight.

She had never for a moment known the pleasure of being important to anyone. Not that she was useless in her brother's family; she was expected, as a matter of course, to take upon herself the most tedious and uninteresting part of the household labors. On Mondays she accepted as her share the washing of the men's shirts, heavy with sweat and stiff with dirt from the fields and from their own hard-working bodies. Tuesdays she never dreamed of being allowed to iron anything pretty or even interesting, like the baby's white dresses or the fancy aprons of her young lady nieces. She stood all day pressing out a monotonous succession of dish-cloths and towels and sheets.

In preserving-time she was allowed to have none of the pleasant responsibility of deciding when the fruit had cooked long enough, nor did she share in the little excitement of pouring the sweet-smelling stuff into the stone jars. She sat in a corner with the children and stoned cherries incessantly, or hulled strawberries until her fingers were dyed red.

The Elwells were not consciously unkind to their aunt, they were even in a vague way fond of her; but she was so insignificant a figure in their lives that she was almost invisible to them. Aunt Mehetabel did not resent this treatment; she took it quite as unconsciously as they gave it. It was to be expected when one was an old-maid dependent in a busy family. She gathered what crumbs of comfort she could from their occasional careless kindnesses and tried to hide the hurt which even yet pierced her at her brother's rough joking. In the winter when they all sat before the big hearth, roasted apples, drank mulled cider, and teased the girls about their beaux and the boys about their sweethearts, she shrank into a dusky corner with her knitting, happy if the evening passed without her brother saying, with a crude sarcasm, "Ask your Aunt Mehetabel about the beaux that used to come a-sparkin' her!" or, "Mehetabel, how was't when you was in love with Abel Cummings?" As a matter of fact, she had been the same at twenty as at sixty, a mouselike little creature, too shy for anyone to notice, or to raise her eyes for a moment and wish for a life of her own.

Her sister-in-law, a big hearty housewife, who ruled indoors with as autocratic a sway as did her husband on the farm, was rather kind in an absent, offhand way to the shrunken little old woman, and it was through her that Mehetabel was able to enjoy the one pleasure of her life. Even as a girl she had been clever with her needle in the way of patching bedquilts. More than that she could never learn to do. The garments which she made for herself were lamentable affairs, and she was humbly grateful for any help in the bewildering business of putting them together. But in patchwork she enjoyed a tepid importance. She could really do that as well as anyone else. During years of devotion to this one art she had accumulated a considerable store of quilting patterns. Sometimes the neighbors would send over and ask "Miss Mehetabel" for the loan of her sheaf-of-wheat design, or the double-star pattern. It was with an agreeable flutter at being able to help someone that she went to the dresser, in her bare little room under the eaves, and drew out from her crowded portfolio the pattern desired.

She never knew how her great idea came to her. Sometimes she thought she must have dreamed it, sometimes she even wondered reverently, in the phraseology of the weekly prayer-meeting, if it had not been "sent" to her. She never admitted to herself that she could have thought of it without other help. It was too great, too ambitious, too lofty a project for her humble mind to have conceived. Even when she finished drawing the design with her own fingers, she gazed at it incredulously, not daring to believe that it could indeed be her handiwork. At first it seemed to her only like a lovely but unreal dream. For a long time she did not once think of putting an actual quilt together following that pattern, even though she herself had invented it. It was not that she feared the prodigious effort that would be needed to get those tiny, oddly shaped pieces of bright-colored material sewed together with the perfection of fine workmanship needed. No, she thought zestfully and eagerly of such endless effort, her heart uplifted by her vision of the mosaic-beauty of the whole creation as she saw it, when she shut her eyes to dream of it—that complicated, splendidly difficult pattern—good enough for the angels in heaven to quilt.

But as she dreamed, her nimble old fingers reached out longingly to turn her dream into reality. She began to think adventurously of trying it out—it would perhaps not be too selfish to make one square—just one unit of her design to see how it would look. She dared do nothing in the household where she was a dependent, without asking permission. With a heart full of hope and fear thumping furiously against her old ribs, she approached the mistress of the house on churning-day, knowing with the innocent guile of a child that the country woman was apt to be in a good temper while working over the fragrant butter in the cool cellar.

Sophia listened absently to her sister-in-law's halting petition. "Why, yes, Mehetabel," she said, leaning far down into the huge churn for the last golden morsels—"why, yes, start another quilt if you want to. I've got a lot of pieces from the spring sewing that will work in real good." Mehetabel tried honestly to make her see that this would be no common quilt, but her limited vocabulary and her emotion stood between her and expression. At last Sophia said, with a kindly impatience: "Oh, there! Don't bother me. I never could keep track of your quiltin' patterns, anyhow. I don't care what pattern you go by."

Mehetabel rushed back up the steep attic stairs to her room, and in a joyful agitation began preparations for the work of her life. Her very first stitches showed her that it was even better than she hoped. By some heaven-sent inspiration she had invented a pattern beyond which no patchwork quilt could go.

She had but little time during the daylight hours filled with the incessant household drudgery. After dark she did not dare to sit up late at night lest she burn too much candle. It was weeks before the little square began to show the pattern. Then Mehetabel was in a fever to finish it. She was too conscientious to shirk even the smallest part of her share of the

housework, but she rushed through it now so fast that she
was panting as she climbed the stairs to her little room.

Every time she opened the door, no matter what weather
hung outside the one small window, she always saw the little
room flooded with sunshine. She smiled to herself as she bent
over the innumerable scraps of cotton cloth on her work
table. Already—to her—they were ranged in orderly, complex, mosaic-beauty.

Finally she could wait no longer, and one evening ventured
to bring her work down beside the fire where the family sat,
hoping that good fortune would give her a place near the tal-
low candles on the mantelpiece. She had reached the last corner of that first square and her needle flew in and out, in and
out, with nervous speed. To her relief no one noticed her. By
bedtime she had only a few more stitches to add.

As she stood up with the others, the square fell from her
trembling old hands and fluttered to the table. Sophia glanced
at it carelessly. "Is that the new quilt you said you wanted to
start?" she asked, yawning. "Looks like a real pretty pattern.
Let's see it."

Up to that moment Mehetabel had labored in the purest
spirit of selfless adoration of an ideal. The emotional shock
given her by Sophia's cry of admiration as she held the work
towards the candle to examine it, was as much astonishment
as joy to Mehetabel.

"Land's sakes!" cried her sister-in-law. "Why, Mehetabel
Elwell, where did you git that pattern?"

"I made it up," said Mehetabel. She spoke quietly but she
was trembling.

"No!" exclaimed Sophia. "Did you! Why, I never see such
a pattern in my life. Girls, come here and see what your
Aunt Mehetabel is doing."

The three tall daughters turned back reluctantly from the
stairs. "I never could seem to take much interest in patchwork quilts," said one. Already the old-time skill born of
early pioneer privation and the craving for beauty had gone
out of style.

"No, nor I neither!" answered Sophia. "But a stone image
would take an interest in this pattern. Honest, Mehetabel, did
you really think of it yourself?" She held it up closer to her
eyes and went on, "And how under the sun and stars did you
ever git your courage up to start in a-making it? Land! Look
at all those tiny squinchy little seams! Why, the wrong side

ain't a thing *but* seams! Yet the good side's just like a picture, so smooth you'd think 'twas woven that way. Only nobody could."

The girls looked at it right side, wrong side, and echoed their mother's exclamations. Mr. Elwell himself came over to see what they were discussing. "Well, I declare!" he said, looking at his sister with eyes more approving than she could ever remember. "I don't know a thing about patchwork quilts, but to my eye that beats old Mis' Andrew's quilt that got the blue ribbon so many times at the County Fair."

As she lay that night in her narrow hard bed, too proud, too excited to sleep, Mehetabel's heart swelled and tears of joy ran down from her old eyes.

The next day her sister-in-law astonished her by taking the huge pan of potatoes out of her lap and setting one of the younger children to peeling them. "Don't you want to go on with that quiltin' pattern?" she said. "I'd kind o' like to see how you're goin' to make the grapevine design come out on the corner."

For the first time in her life the dependent old maid contradicted her powerful sister-in-law. Quickly and jealously she said, "It's not a grapevine. It's a sort of curlicue I made up."

"Well, it's nice-looking anyhow," said Sophia pacifyingly. "I never could have made it up."

By the end of the summer the family interest had risen so high that Mehetabel was given for herself a little round table in the sitting room, for *her*, where she could keep her pieces and use odd minutes for her work. She almost wept over such kindness and resolved firmly not to take advantage of it. She went on faithfully with her monotonous housework, not neglecting a corner. But the atmosphere of her world changed. Now things had a meaning. Through the longest task of washing milk-pans, there rose a rainbow of promise. She took her place by the little table and put the thimble on her knotted, hard finger with the solemnity of a priestess performing a rite.

She was even able to bear with some degree of dignity the honor of having the minister and the minister's wife comment admiringly on her great project. The family felt quite proud of Aunt Mehetabel as Minister Bowman had said it was work as fine as any he had ever seen, "and he didn't know but finer!" The remark was repeated verbatim to the neighbors in the following weeks when they dropped in and examined in a perverse Vermontish silence some astonishingly difficult tour de force which Mehetabel had just finished.

The Elwells especially plumed themselves on the slow progress of the quilt. "Mehetabel has been to work on that corner for six weeks, come Tuesday, and she ain't half done yet," they explained to visitors. They fell out of the way of always expecting her to be the one to run on errands, even for the children. "Don't bother your Aunt Mehetabel," Sophia would call. "Can't you see she's got to a ticklish place on the quilt?" The old woman sat straighter in her chair, held up her head. She was a part of the world at last. She joined in the conversation and her remarks were listened to. The children were even told to mind her when she asked them to do some service for her, although this she ventured to do but seldom.

One day some people from the next town, total strangers, drove up to the Elwell house and asked if they could inspect the wonderful quilt which they had heard about even down in their end of the valley. After that, Mehetabel's quilt came little by little to be one of the local sights. No visitor to town, whether he knew the Elwells or not, went away without having been to look at it. To make her presentable to strangers, the Elwells saw to it that their aunt was better dressed than she had ever been before. One of the girls made her a pretty little cap to wear on her thin white hair.

A year went by and a quarter of the quilt was finished. A second year passed and half was done. The third year Mehetabel had pneumonia and lay ill for weeks and weeks, horrified by the idea that she might die before her work was completed. A fourth year and one could really see the grandeur of the whole design. In September of the fifth year, the entire family gathered around her to watch eagerly, as Mehetabel quilted the last stitches. The girls held it up by the four corners and they all looked at it in hushed silence.

Then Mr. Elwell cried as one speaking with authority. "By ginger! That's goin' to the County Fair!"

Mehetabel blushed a deep red. She had thought of this herself, but never would have spoken aloud of it.

"Yes, indeed!" cried the family. One of the boys was dispatched to the house of a neighbor who was Chairman of the Fair Committee for their village. He came back beaming,

"Of course he'll take it. Like's not it may git a prize, he says. But he's got to have it right off because all the things from our town are going tomorrow morning."

Even in her pride Mehetabel felt a pang as the bulky package was carried out of the house. As the days went on she felt lost. For years it had been her one thought. The little round stand had been heaped with a litter of bright-colored scraps. Now it was desolately bare. One of the neighbors who took the long journey to the Fair reported when he came back that the quilt was hung in a good place in a glass case in "Agricultural Hall." But that meant little to Mehetabel's ignorance of everything outside her brother's home. She drooped. The family noticed it. One day Sophia said kindly, "You feel sort o' lost without the quilt, don't you, Mehetabel?"

"They took it away so quick!" she said wistfully. "I hadn't hardly had one good look at it myself."

The Fair was to last a fortnight. At the beginning of the second week Mr. Elwell asked his sister how early she could get up in the morning.

"I dunno. Why?" she asked.

"Well, Thomas Ralston has got to drive to West Oldton to see a lawyer. That's four miles beyond the Fair. He says if you can git up so's to leave here at four in the morning he'll drive you to the Fair, leave you there for the day, and bring you back again at night." Mehetabel's face turned very white. Her eyes filled with tears. It was as though someone had offered her a ride in a golden chariot up to the gates of heaven. "Why, you can't *mean* it!" she cried wildly. Her brother laughed. He could not meet her eyes. Even to his easy-going unimaginative indifference to his sister this was a revelation of the narrowness of her life in his home. "Oh, 'tain't so much—just to go to the Fair," he told her in some confusion, and then "Yes, sure I mean it. Go git your things ready, for it's tomorrow morning he wants to start."

A trembling, excited old woman stared all that night at the rafters. She who had never been more than six miles from home—it was to her like going into another world. She who had never seen anything more exciting than a church supper was to see the County Fair. She had never dreamed of doing it. She could not at all imagine what it would be like.

The next morning all the family rose early to see her off.

Perhaps her brother had not been the only one to be shocked by her happiness. As she tried to eat her breakfast they called out conflicting advice to her about what to see. Her brother said not to miss inspecting the stock, her nieces said the fancywork was the only thing worth looking at, Sophia told her to be sure to look at the display of preserves. Her nephews asked her to bring home an account of the trotting races.

The buggy drove up to the door, and she was helped in. The family ran to and fro with blankets, woolen tippet, a hot soapstone from the kitchen range. Her wraps were tucked about her. They all stood together and waved goodby as she drove out of the yard. She waved back, but she scarcely saw them. On her return home that evening she was ashy pale, and so stiff that her brother had to lift her out bodily. But her lips were set in a blissful smile. They crowded around her with questions until Sophia pushed them all aside. She told them Aunt Mehetabel was too tired to speak until she had had her supper. The young people held their tongues while she drank her tea, and absent-mindedly ate a scrap of toast with an egg. Then the old woman was helped into an easy chair before the fire. They gathered about her, eager for news of the great world, and Sophia said, "Now, come, Mehetabel, tell us all about it!"

Mehetabel drew a long breath. "It was just perfect!" she said. "Finer even than I thought. They've got it hanging up in the very middle of a sort o' closet made of glass, and one of the lower corners is ripped and turned back so's to show the seams on the wrong side."

"What?" asked Sophia, a little blankly.

"Why, the quilt!" said Mehetabel in surprise. "There are a whole lot of other ones in that room, but not one that can hold a candle to it, if I do say it who shouldn't. I heard lots of people say the same thing. You ought to have heard what the women said about that corner, Sophia. They said—well, I'd be ashamed to *tell* you what they said. I declare if I wouldn't!"

Mr. Elwell asked, "What did you think of that big ox we've heard so much about?"

"I didn't look at the stock," returned his sister indifferently. She turned to one of her nieces. "That set of pieces you gave me, Maria, from your red waist, come out just lovely! I heard one woman say you could 'most smell the red roses."

"How did Jed Burgess' bay horse place in the mile trot?" asked Thomas.

"I didn't see the races."

"How about the preserves?" asked Sophia.

"I didn't see the preserves," said Mehetabel calmly.

Seeing that they were gazing at her with astonished faces she went on, to give them a reasonable explanation, "You see I went right to the room where the quilt was, and then I didn't want to leave it. It had been so long since I'd seen it. I had to look at it first real good myself, and then I looked at the others to see if there was any that could come up to it. Then the people begun comin' in and I got so interested in hearin' what they had to say I couldn't think of goin' anywheres else. I ate my lunch right there too, and I'm glad as can be I did, too; for what do you think?"—she gazed about her with kindling eyes. "While I stood there with a sandwich in one hand, didn't the head of the hull concern come in and open the glass door and pin a big bow of blue ribbon right in the middle of the quilt with a label on it, 'First Prize.' "

There was a stir of proud congratulation. Then Sophia returned to questioning, "Didn't you go to see anything else?"

"Why, no," said Mehetabel. "Only the quilt. Why should I?"

She fell into a reverie. As if it hung again before her eyes she saw the glory that shone around the creation of her hand and brain. She longed to make her listeners share the golden vision with her. She struggled for words. She fumbled blindly for unknown superlatives. "I tell you it looked like—" she began, and paused.

Vague recollections of hymnbook phrases came into her mind. They were the only kind of poetic expression she knew. But they were dismissed as being sacrilegious to use for something in real life. Also as not being nearly striking enough.

Finally, "I tell you it looked real *good*," she assured them and sat staring into the fire, on her tired old face the supreme content of an artist who has realized his ideal.

SIGRID UNDSET was born at Kalundborg, Denmark, in 1882. Her father was a well-known Norwegian archaeologist who inspired in her an interest in the past, especially in Norway's Roman Catholic Middle Ages. After her father's death (when she was eleven years old), Undset had to leave school and go to work as an office clerk for ten years. The subsequent financial success of her first novel enabled her to devote herself to full-time writing. Undset's early novels and short stories are concerned with the question of woman's role in marriage and in the complex contemporary world. In their day they were considered daring because of their descriptions of the erotic lives of their heroines. Indeed the sexual impulse plays a prominent part in all her novels.

In 1912 Undset married the painter Anders Svarstad. They were divorced in 1924, the year of her conversion to Roman Catholicism. Between 1920 and 1922 she published the three volumes of her great medieval epic *Kristin Lavransdatter* which made her world-famous. The trilogy is the single most important work of historical fiction in all Norwegian literature. The action of the story spans fifty years. Volume I, *The Bridal Wreath,* is about Kristin's girlhood. The account of her intitial meetings with Erland, at first her lover and then her husband, contains some of the most marvelous erotic passages in the history of the novel. Volume II, *The Mistress of Husaby,* is about Kristin as a married woman and the mother of eight sons. In the third volume, *The Cross,* the lifelong struggle between Kristin's rich, passionate earthly life and her longing for transcendence ends in her realization that "one must seek God rather than men." She enters a monastery and dies after giving decent burial to the rotting corpse of a promiscuous woman, a plague victim, whom no one else will touch. On Kristin's deathbed the memories of Erland and her marriage come before her for final judgment.

After the publication of her second medieval epic, *The Master of Hestvikken* (which has been compared to Ibsen's *The Master Builder* and *When We Dead Awaken*), Undset was awarded the Nobel Prize for Literature in 1928. (Both of her epic novels were written after her three children and three stepchildren were in bed at night; with the help of cigarettes and black coffee she would write until two or three o'clock in the morning.) Her strong moral consciousness and her encyclopedic knowledge of history are widely acknowledged; other than Ibsen and the composer Edvard Grieg no Norwegian artist has been as famous as Undset. But her work has not received much critical attention, perhaps, some would say, because it is heavy with Catholic propaganda, others because her religious world-view is an embarrassment to critics who have established that nihilism is the only accurate description of the way things are in the post-Christian era. Above all, her belief in the old virtues of loyalty, moderation, and a sense of responsibility seems decidedly out of step in a narcissistic age.

When the Germans invaded Norway in 1940, they burned her books. She fled to the United States and spent the war years working for the liberation of her homeland. She became the friend of Willa Cather and Marjorie Kinnan Rawlings. She died at Lillehammer, Norway, in 1949.

Sigrid Undset
(1882—1949)

From KRISTIN LAVRANSDATTER

The farmers' guild of Aker had St. Margaret for their pa-
troness, and they began their festival each year on the twentieth of July, the day of St. Margaret's Mass. On that day the
guild brothers and sisters, with their children, their guests and
their serving-folk, gathered at Aker's church and heard mass
at St. Margaret's altar there; after that they wended their way
to the hall of the guild, which lay near the Hofvin Hospital—there they were wont to hold a drinking-feast lasting five
days.

But since both Aker's church and the Hofvin spital belonged to Nonneseter, and as, besides, many of the Aker farmers were tenants of the convent, it had come to be the
custom that the Abbess and some of the elder Sisters should
honour the guild by coming to the feasting on the first day.
And those of the young maids who were at the convent only
to learn, and were not to take the veil, had leave to go with
them and to dance in the evening; therefore at this feast they
wore their own clothes and not the convent habit.

And so there was great stir and bustle in the novices' sleeping rooms on the eve of St. Margaret's Mass; the maids who
were to go to the guild feast ransacking their chests and making ready their finery, while the others, less fortunate, went
about something moodily and looked on. Some had set small
pots in the fireplace and were boiling water to make their
skin white and soft; others were making a brew to be
smeared on their hair—then they parted the hair into strands
and twisted them tightly round strips of leather, and this gave
them curling, wavy tresses.

Ingebjörg brought out all the finery she had, but could not
think what she should wear—come what might, not her best,
leaf-green velvet dress; that was too good and too costly for
such a peasant rout. But a little, thin sister who was not to go
with them; Helga was her name; she had been vowed to the

convent by her father and mother while still a child—took Kristin aside and whispered: she was sure Ingebjörg would wear the green dress and her pink silk shift too.

"You have ever been kind to me, Kristin," said Helga. "It beseems me little to meddle in such doings—but I will tell you none the less. The knight who brought you home that evening in the spring—I have seen and heard Ingebjörg talking with him since—they spoke together in the church, and he has tarried for her up in the hollow when she hath gone to Ingunn at the commoners' house. But 'tis you he asks for, and Ingebjörg has promised him to bring you there along with her. But I wager you have not heard aught of this before!"

"True it is that Ingebjörg has said naught of this," said Kristin. She pursed up her mouth that the other might not see the smile that would come out. So this was Ingebjörg's way. " 'Tis like she knows I am not of such as run to trysts with strange men round house-corners and behind fences," said she proudly.

"Then I might have spared myself the pains of bringing you tidings whereof 'twould have been but seemly I should say no word," said Helga, wounded, and they parted.

But the whole evening Kristin was put to it not to smile when any one was looking at her.

Next morning, Ingebjörg went dallying about in her shift, till Kristin saw she meant not to dress before she herself was ready.

Kristin said naught, but laughed as she went to her chest and took out her golden-yellow silken shift. She had never worn it before, and it felt so soft and cool as it slipped down over her body. It was broidered with goodly work, in silver and blue and brown silk, about the neck and down upon the breast, as much as should be seen above the low-cut gown. There were sleeves to match, too. She drew on her linen hose, and laced up the small, purple-blue shoes which Haakon, by good luck, had saved that day of commotion. Ingebjörg gazed at her—then Kristin said laughing:

"My father ever taught me never to show disdain of those beneath us—but 'tis like you are too grand to deck yourself in your best for poor tenants and peasant-folk—"

Red as a berry, Ingebjörg slipped her woollen smock down over her white hips and hurried on the pink silk shift. Kristin threw over her own head her best velvet gown—it was violet-blue, deeply cut out at the bosom, with long slashed sleeves flowing well-nigh to the ground. She fastened the gilt belt about her waist, and hung her grey squirrel cape over her shoulders. Then she spread her masses of yellow hair out over her shoulders and back, and fitted the golden fillet, chased with small roses, upon her brow.

She saw that Helga stood watching them. Then she took from her chest a great silver clasp. It was that she had on her cloak the night Bentein met her on the highway, and she had never cared to wear it since. She went to Helga, and said in a low voice:

"I know 'twas your wish to show me goodwill last night; think me not unthankful—" and with that she gave her the clasp.

Ingebjörg was a fine sight, too, when she stood fully decked in her green gown, with a red silk cloak over her shoulders and her fair, curly hair waving behind her. They had ended by striving to outdress each other, thought Kristin, and she laughed.

The morning was cool and fresh with dew as the procession went forth from Nonneseter and wound its way westward toward Frysja. The hay-making was near at an end here on the lowlands, but along the fences grew blue-bells and yellow crowsfoot in clumps; in the fields the barley was in ear, and bent its heads in pale silvery waves just tinged with pink. Here and there, where the path was narrow and led through the fields, the corn all but met about folks' knees.

Haakon walked at the head, bearing the convent's banner with the Virgin Mary's picture upon the blue silken cloth. After him walked the servants and the commoners, and then came the Lady Groa and four old Sisters on horseback, while behind these came the young maidens on foot; their many-hued holiday attire flaunted and shone in the sunlight. Some of the commoners' women-folk and a few armed serving-men closed the train.

They sang as they went over the bright fields, and the folk they met at the byways stood aside and gave them reverent greeting. All round, out on the fields, they could see small groups of men coming, walking and riding, for folks were drawing toward the church from every house and every farm. Soon they heard behind them the sound of hymns chanted in men's deep voices, and the banner of the Hovedö monastery rose above a hillock—the red silk shone in the sun, swaying and bending to the step of the bearer.

The mighty, metal voice of the bells rang out above the neighing and screaming of stallions as the procession climbed the last slope to the church. Kristin had never seen so many horses at one time—a heaving, restless sea of horses' backs round about the green before the church door. Upon the sward stood and sat lay folk dressed in all their best—but all rose in reverence as the Virgin's flag from Nonneseter was borne in amongst them, and all bowed deeply before the Lady Groa.

It seemed as though more folk had come than the church could hold, but for those from the convent room had been kept in front near the altar. Straightway after them the Cistercian monks from Hovedö marched in and went up into the choir—and forthwith song burst from the throats of men and boys and filled the church.

Soon after the mass had begun, when the services brought all to their feet, Kristin caught sight of Erlend Nikulaussön. He was tall, and his head rose above those about him—she saw his face from the side. He had a high, steep, and narrow forehead, and a large, straight nose—it jutted, triangle-like, from his face, and was strangely thin about the fine, quivering nostrils—something about it reminded Kristin of a restless, high-strung stallion. His face was not as comely as she had thought it—the long-drawn lines running down to his small, weak, yet well-formed mouth gave it as 'twere a touch of joylessness—ay, but yet he *was* comely.

He turned his head and saw her. She knew not how long they stood thus, looking into each other's eyes. From that time she thought of naught but the end of the mass; she waited, intent on what would then befall.

There was some pressing and thronging as the folks made their way out from the overcrowded church. Ingebjörg held Kristin back till they were at the rear of the throng; she gained her point—they were quite cut off from the nuns, who went out first—the two girls were among the last in coming to the offertory-box and out of the church.

Erlend stood without, just by the door, beside the priest from Gerdarud and a stoutish, red-faced man, spendid in blue velvet. Erlend himself was clad in silk, but of a sober hue—a long coat of brown, figured with black, and a black cloak with a pattern of small yellow hawks inwoven.

They greeted each other and crossed the green together to where the men's horses stood tethered. While they spoke of the fine weather, the goodly mass and the great crowd of folk that were mustered, the fat, ruddy knight—he bore golden spurs and was named Sir Munan Baardsön—took Ingebjörg by the hand; 'twas plain he was mightily taken with the maid. Erlend and Kristin fell behind—they were silent as they walked.

There was a great to-do upon the church-green as folk began to ride away—horses jostled one another, people shouted—some angry, others laughing. Many sat in pairs upon the horses; men had their wives behind them, or their children in front upon the saddle; youths swung themselves up beside a friend. They could see the church banners, the nuns and the priests far down the hill already.

Sir Munan rode by; Ingebjörg sat in front of him, his arm about her. Both of them called out and waved. Then Erlend said:

"My serving-men are both with me—they could ride one horse and you have Haftor's—if you would rather have it so?"

Kristin flushed as she replied: "We are so far behind the others already—I see not your serving-men hereabouts, and—" Then she broke into a laugh, and Erlend smiled.

He sprang to the saddle and helped her to a seat behind him. At home Kristin had often sat thus sidewise behind her father, after she had grown too big to ride astride the horse. Still, she felt a little bashful and none too safe as she laid a hand upon Erlend's shoulder; the other she put on the horse's back to steady herself. They rode slowly down towards the bridge.

In a while Kristin thought she must speak, since he was silent, so she said:

"We looked not, sir, to meet you here to-day."

"Looked you not to meet me?" asked Erlend, turning his head. "Did not Ingebjörg Filippusdatter bear you my greeting, then?"

"No," said Kristin. "I heard naught of any greeting—she hath not named you once since you came to our help last May," said she guilefully. She was not sorry that Ingebjörg's falseness should come to light.

Erlend did not look back again, but she could hear by his voice that he was smiling when he asked again:

"But the little dark one—the novice—I mind not her name—her I even fee'd to bear you my greeting."

Kristin blushed, but she had to laugh too: "Ay, 'tis but Helga's due I should say that she earned her fee," she said.

Erlend moved his head a little—his neck almost touched her hand. Kristin shifted her hand at once farther out on his shoulder. Somewhat uneasily she thought, maybe she had been more bold than was fitting, seeing she had come to this feast after a man had, in a manner, made tryst with her there.

Soon after Erlend asked:

"Will you dance with me to-night, Kristin?"

"I know not, sir," answered the maid.

"You think, mayhap, 'tis not seemly?" he asked, and, as she did not answer, he said again: "It may well be it is not so. But I thought now maybe you might deem you would be none the worse if you took my hand in the dance to-night. But, indeed, 'tis eight years since I stood up to dance."

"How may that be, sir?" asked Kristin. "Mayhap you are wedded?" But then it came into her head that had he been a wedded man, to have made tryst with her thus would have been no fair deed of him. On that she tried to mend her speech, saying: "Maybe you have lost your betrothed maid or your wife?"

Erlend turned quickly and looked on her with strange eyes.

"Hath not Lady Aashild . . . ? Why grew you so red when you heard who I was that evening?" he asked a little after.

Kristin flushed red once more, but did not answer; then Erlend asked again:

"I would fain know what my mother's sister said to you of me."

"Naught else," said Kristin quickly, "but in your praise. She said you were so comely and so great of kin that—she said that beside such as you and her kin we were of no such great account—my folk and I—"

"Doth she still talk thus, living the life she lives," said Erlend, and laughed bitterly. "Ay, ay—if it comfort her. . . . Said she naught else of me?"

"What should she have said?" asked Kristin; she knew not why she was grown so strangely heavy-hearted.

"Oh, she might have said—" he spoke in a low tone, looking down, "she might have said that I had been under the

Church's ban, and had to pay dear for peace and atonement—"

Kristin was silent a long time. Then she said softly:

"There is many a man who is not master of his own fortunes—so have I heard said. 'Tis little I have seen of the world—but I will never believe of you, Erlend, that 'twas for any—dishonourable—deed."

"May God reward you for those words, Kristin," said Erlend, and bent his head and kissed her wrist so vehemently that the horse gave a bound beneath them. When Erlend had it in hand again, he said earnestly: "Dance with me to-night then, Kristin. Afterward I will tell how things are with me—will tell you all—but to-night we will be happy together?"

Kristin answered: "Ay," and they rode a while in silence.

But ere long Erlend began to ask of Lady Aashild, and Kristin told all she knew of her; she praised her much.

"Then all doors are not barred against Björn and Aashild?" asked Erlend.

Kristin said they were thought much of, and that her father and many with him deemed that most of the tales about these two were untrue.

"How liked you my kinsman, Munan Baardsön?" asked Erlend, laughing slyly.

"I looked not much upon him," said Kristin, "and methought, too, he was not much to look on."

"Knew you not," asked Erlend, "that he is her son?"

"Son to Lady Aashild!" said Kristin, in great wonder.

"Ay, her children could not take their mother's fair looks, though they took all else," said Erlend.

"I have never known her first husband's name," said Kristin.

"They were two brothers who wedded two sisters," said Erlend. "Baard and Nikulaus Munansön. My father was the elder, my mother was his second wife, but he had no children by his first. Baard, whom Aashild wedded, was not young either, nor, I trow, did they ever live happily together—ay, I was a little child when all this befell, they hid from me as much as they could. . . . But she fled the land with Sir Björn and married him against the will of her kin—when Baard was dead. Then folk would have had the wedding set aside—they made out that Björn had sought her bed while her first husband was still living, and that they had plotted together to put away my father's brother. 'Tis clear they could not bring this home to them, since they had to leave them together in wedlock. But to make amends, they had to forfeit all their estate—Björn had killed their sister's son, too—my mother's and Aashild's, I mean—"

Kristin's heart beat hard. At home her father and mother had kept strict watch that no unclean talk should come to the ears of their children or of young folk—but still, things had happened in their own parish and Kristin had heard of them—a man had lived in adultery with a wedded woman. That was whoredom, one of the worst of sins; 'twas said they plotted the husband's death, and that brought with it outlawry and the Church's ban. Lavrans had said no woman was bound to stay with her husband, if he had had to do with another's wife; the state of a child gotten in adultery could never be mended, not even though its father and mother were free to wed afterward. A man might bring into his family and make his heir his child by any wanton or strolling beggar-woman, but not the child of his adultery—not if its mother came to be a knight's lady. She thought of the misliking she had ever felt for Sir Björn, with his bleached face and fat, yet shrunken body. She could not think how Lady Aashild could be so good and yielding at all times to the man who had led her away into such shame; how such a gracious woman could have let herself be beguiled by him. He was not even good to her; he let her toil and moil with all the farmwork; Björn did naught but drink beer. Yet Aashild was ever mild and gentle when she spoke with her husband. Kristin wondered if her father could know all this, since he had asked Sir Björn to their home. Now she came to think, too, it seemed strange Erlend should think fit to tell such tales of his near kin. But like enough he deemed she knew of it already.

"I would like well," said Erlend in a while, "to visit her, Moster* Aashild, some day—when I journey northwards. Is he comely still, Björn, my kinsman?"

"No," said Kristin. "He looks like hay that has lain the winter through upon the fields."

"Ay, ay, it tells upon a man, I trow," said Erlend, with the same bitter smile. "Never have I seen so fair a man—'tis twenty years since, I was but a lad then—but his like have I never seen—"

---

* Moster = mother's sister.

A little after they came to the hospital. It was an exceeding great and fine place, with many houses both of stone and of wood—houses for the sick, almshouses, hostels for travellers, a chapel and a house for the priest. There was great bustle in the courtyard, for food was being made ready in the kitchen of the hospital for the guild feast, and the poor and sick too, that were dwelling in the place, were to be feasted on the best this day.

The hall of the guild was beyond the garden of the hospital, and folks took their way thither through the herb-garden, for this was of great renown. Lady Groa had had brought hither plants that no one had heard of in Norway before, and, moreover, all plants that else folks were used to grow in gardens, throve better in her herbaries, both flowers and pot-herbs and healing herbs. She was a most learned woman in all such matters, and had herself put into the Norse tongue the herbals of the Salernitan school. . . . Lady Groa had been more than ever kind to Kristin since she had marked that the maid knew somewhat of herb-lore, and was fain to know yet more of it.

So Kristin named for Erlend what grew in the beds on either side the grassy path they walked on. In the midday sun there was a warm and spicy scent of dill and celery, garlic and roses, southernwood and wallflower. Beyond the shade-less, baking herb-garden, the fruit orchards looked cool and enticing—red cherries gleamed amid the dark leafy tops, and the apple trees drooped their branches heavy with green fruit.

About the garden was a hedge of sweet briar. There were some flowers on it still—they looked the same as other briar roses, but in the sun the leaves smelt of wine and apples. Folk plucked sprays to deck themselves as they went past. Kristin, too, took some roses and hung them on her temples, fixed under her golden fillet. One she kept in her hand. . . . After a time Erlend took it, saying no word. A while he bore it in his hand as they walked, then fastened it with the brooch upon his breast—he looked awkward and bashful as he did it, and was so clumsy that he pricked his fingers till they bled.

Broad tables were spread in the loft-room of the guild's hall—two by the main walls, for the men and the women; and two smaller boards out on the floor, where children and young folk sat side by side.

At the women's board Lady Groa was in the high-seat, the nuns and the chief of the married women sat on the inner bench along the wall, and the unwedded women on the outer benches, the maids from Nonneseter at the upper end. Kristin knew that Erlend was watching her, but she durst not turn her head even once, either when they rose or when they sat down. Only when they got up at last to hear the priest read the names of the dead guild-brothers and sisters, she stole a hasty glance at the men's table—she caught a glimpse of him where he stood by the wall, behind the candles burning on the board. He was looking at her.

The meal lasted long, with all the toasts in honour of God, the Virgin Mary, and St. Margaret and St. Olav and St. Halvaad, and prayers and song between.

Kristin saw through the open door that the sun was gone; sounds of fiddling and song came in from the green without, and all the young folks had left the tables already when Lady Groa said to the convent maidens that they might go now and play themselves for a time if they listed.

Three red bonfires were burning upon the green; around them moved the many-coloured chains of dancers. The fiddlers sat aloft on heaped-up chests and scraped their fiddles—they played and sang a different tune in every ring; there were too many folk for *one* dance. It was nearly dark already—northward the wooded ridge stood out coal-black against the yellow-green sky.

Under the loft-balcony folk were sitting drinking. Some men sprang forward, as soon as the six maids from Nonneseter came down the steps. Munan Baardsön flew to meet Ingebjörg and went off with her, and Kristin was caught by the wrist—Erlend, she knew his hand already. He pressed her hand in his so that their rings grated on one another and bruised the flesh.

He drew her with him to the outermost bonfire. Many children were dancing there; Kristin gave her other hand to a twelve-year-old lad, and Erlend had a little, half-grown maid on his other side.

No one was singing in the ring just then—they were swaying in and out to the tune of the fiddle as they moved round. Then some one shouted that Sivord the Dane should sing them a new dance. A tall, fair-haired man with huge fists stepped out in front of the chain and struck up his ballad:

> "Fair goes the dance at Munkolm
>   On silver sand.
> There danceth Ivar Sir Alfsön—
>   Holds the Queen's own hand.
>   *Know ye not Ivar Sir Alfsön?*"

The fiddlers knew not the tune, they thrummed their strings a little, and the Dane sang alone—he had a strong, tuneful voice:

> "Mind you, Queen of the Danemen,
>   That summer fair,
> They led you out of Sweden,
>   To Denmark here?
>
> They led you out of Sweden,
>   To Denmark here,
> All with a crown of the red gold
>   And many a tear.
>
> All with a crown of the red gold
>   And tear-filled eyne—
> —Mind you, Queen of the Danemen
>   You first were mine?"

The fiddles struck in again, the dancers hummed the new-learned tune and joined in the burden:

> "And are you, Ivar Sir Alfsön,
>   Sworn man to me,
> Then shall you hang to-morrow
>   On the gallows tree!"
>
> But 'twas Ivar Sir Alfsön,
>   All unafraid
> He leaped into the gold-bark
>   In harness clad.
>
> "God send you, oh Dane-Queen,
>   So many a good night,
> As in the high heavens
>   Are stars alight.

God send you, oh Dane-King,
    So many ill years
    As be leaves on the linden—
    Or the hind hath hairs."
        Know ye not Ivar Sir Alfsön?

It was far on in the night, and the fires were but heaps of embers growing more and more black. Kristin and Erlend stood hand in hand under the trees by the garden fence. Behind them the noise of the revellers was hushed—a few young lads were hopping round the glowing mounds singing softly, but the fiddlers had sought their resting-places, and most of the people were gone. One or two wives went round seeking their husbands, who were lying somewhere out of doors overcome by the beer.

"Where think you I can have laid my cloak?" whispered Kristin. Erlend put his arm about her waist and drew his mantle round them both. Close pressed to one another they went into the herb-garden.

A lingering breath of the day's warm spicy scents, deadened and damp with the chill of the dew, met them in there. The night was very dark, the sky overcast, with murky grey clouds close down upon the tree-tops. But they could tell that there were other folks in the garden. Once Erlend pressed the maiden close to him and asked in a whisper:

"Are you not afraid, Kristin?"

In her mind she caught a faint glimpse of the world outside this night—and knew that this was madness. But a blessed strengthlessness was upon her. She only leaned closer to the man and whispered softly—she herself knew not what.

They came to the end of the path; a stone wall divided them from the woods. Erlend helped her up. As she jumped down on the other side, he caught her and held her lifted in his arms a moment before he set her on the grass.

She stood with upturned face to take his kiss. He held her head between his hands—it was so sweet to her to feel his fingers sink into her hair—she felt she must repay him, and so she clasped his head and sought to kiss him, as he had kissed her.

When he put his hands upon her breast, she felt as though he drew her heart from out her bosom; he parted the folds of silk ever so little and laid a kiss betwixt them—it sent a glow into her inmost soul.

"You I could never harm," whispered Erlend. "You should never shed a tear through fault of mine. Never had I dreamed a maid might be so good as you, my Kristin—"

He drew her down into the grass beneath the bushes; they sat with their backs against the wall. Kristin said naught, but when he ceased from caressing her, she put up her hand and touched his face.

In a while Erlend asked: "Are you not weary, my dear one?" And when Kristin nestled in to his breast, he folded his arms around her, and whispered: "Sleep, sleep, Kristin, here in my arms—"

She slipped deeper and deeper into darkness and warmth and happiness upon his breast.

When she came to herself again, she was lying outstretched in the grass with her cheek upon the soft brown silk above his knees. Erlend was sitting as before with his back to the stone wall, his face looked grey in the grey twilight, but his wide opened eyes were marvellously clear and fair. She saw he had wrapped his cloak all about her—her feet were so warm and snug with the fur lining around them.

"Now have you slept in my lap," said he, smiling faintly. "May God bless you, Kristin—you slept as safe as a child in its mother's arms—"

"Have *you* not slept, Sir Erlend?" asked Kristin; and he smiled down into her fresh opened eyes.

"Maybe the night will come when you and I may lie down to sleep together—I know not what you will think when you have weighed all things. I have watched by you to-night—there is still so much betwixt us two that 'tis more than if there had lain a naked sword between you and me. Tell me if you will hold me dear, when this night is past?"

"I will hold you dear, Sir Erlend," said Kristin. "I will hold you dear, so long as you will—and thereafter I will love none other."

"Then," said Erlend slowly, "may God forsake me if any maid or woman come to my arms ere I may make you mine in law and honour. Say you this, too," he prayed. Kristin said:

"May God forsake me if I take any other man to my arms so long as I live on earth."

"We must go now," said Erlend, a little after, "before folk waken."

They passed along without the wall among the bushes.

"Have you bethought you," asked Erlend, "what further must be done in this?"

" 'Tis for you to say what we must do, Erlend," answered Kristin.

"Your father," he asked in a little, "they say at Gerdarud he is a mild and a righteous man. Think you he will be so exceeding loth to go back from what he hath agreed with Andres Darre?"

"Father has said so often, he would never force us, his daughters," said Kristin. "The chief thing is that our lands and Simon's lie so fitly together. But I trow father would not that I should miss all my gladness in this world for the sake of that." A fear stirred within her that so simple as this perhaps it might not prove to be—but she fought it down.

"Then maybe 'twill be less hard than I deemed in the night," said Erlend. "God help me, Kristin—methinks I *cannot* lose you now—unless I win you now, never can I be glad again."

They parted among the trees, and in the dawning light Kristin found her way to the guest-chamber where the women from Nonneseter were to lie. All the beds were full, but she threw a cloak upon some straw on the floor and laid her down in all her clothes.

When she awoke, it was far on in the day. Ingebjörg Filippusdatter was sitting on a bench near by, stitching down an edge of fur that had been torn loose on her cloak. She was full of talk as ever.

"Were you with Erlend Nikulaussön the whole night?" she asked. " 'Twere well you went warily with that lad, Kristin—how think you Simon Andressön would like it if you came to be dear friends with him?"

Kristin found a hand-basin and began to wash herself.

"And your betrothed—think you he would like that you danced with Dumpy Munan last night? Surely we must dance with him who chooses us out on such a night of merry-making—and Lady Groa had given us leave."

Ingebjörg pshawed:

"Einar Einarssön and Sir Munan are friends—and, besides, he is wedded and old. Ugly he is to boot for that matter—but likeable and hath becoming ways—see what he gave me for a remembrance of last night," and she held forth a gold clasp which Kristin had seen in Sir Munan's hat the day before. "But this Erlend—'tis true he was freed of the ban at Easter last year, but they say Eline Ormsdatter has been with him at Husaby since—Sir Munan says Erlend hath fled to Sira Jon at Gerdarud, and he deems 'tis because he cannot trust himself not to fall back into sin, if he meet her again—"

Kristin crossed over to the other—her face was white.

"Knew you not this?" said Ingebjörg. "That he lured a woman from her husband somewhere in Haalogaland in the North—and held her with him at his manor in despite of the King's command and the Archbishop's ban—they had two children together—and he was driven to fly to Sweden, and hath been forced to pay in forfeit so much of his lands and goods, Sir Munan says he will be a poor man in the end unless he mend his ways the sooner."

"Think not but that I know all this," said Kristin, with a set face. "But 'tis known the matter is ended now."

"Ay, but as to that Sir Munan said there had been an end between them so many times before," said Ingebjörg pensively. "But all these things can be nothing to you—you that are to wed Simon Darre. But a comely man is Erlend Nikulaussön, sure enough."

The company from Nonneseter was to set out for home that same day after nones. Kristin had promised Erlend to meet him by the wall where they had sat the night before, if she could but find a way to come.

He was lying face downwards in the grass with his head upon his hands. As soon as he saw her, he sprang to his feet and held out both his hands, as she was about jumping from the wall.

Kristin took them, and the two stood a little, hand in hand. Then said Kristin:

"Why told you me that of Sir Björn and Lady Aashild yesterday?"

"I can see you know it all," said Erlend, and let go her hands suddenly. "What think you of me now, Kristin?"

"I was eighteen then," he went on vehemently, " 'tis ten years since that the King, my kinsman, sent me with the mission to Vargöyhus, and we stayed the winter at Steigen. . . . She was wife to the Lagmand, Sigurd Saksulvsön. . . . I thought pity of her, for he was old and ugly beyond belief. I know not how it came to pass—ay, but I loved her too. I bade Sigurd crave what amends he would; I would fain have done right by him—he is a good and doughty man in many ways—but he would have it that all must go by law; he took the matter to the Thing—I was to be branded for whoredom with the wife of him whose guest I had been, you understand . . .

"Then it came to my father's ears, and then to King Haakon's . . . he—he drove me from his court. And if you must know the whole—there is naught more now betwixt Eline and me save the children, and she cares not much for them. They are in Österdal, upon a farm I owned there; I have given it to Orm, the boy—but she will not stay with them. Doubtless she reckons that Sigurd cannot live for ever—but I know not what she would be at.

"Sigurd took her back again—but she says she fared like a dog and a bondswoman in his house—so she set a tryst with me at Nidaros. 'Twas little better for me at Husaby with my father. I sold all I could lay hands on, and fled with her to Holland—Count Jacob stood my friend. Could I do aught else?—she was great with my child. I knew many a man had lived even so with another's wife and had got off cheap enough—if he were rich, that is. But so it is with King Haakon, he is hardest upon his own kin. We were away from one another for a year, but then my father died and then she came back. Then there were other troubles. My tenants denied me rent and would have no speech with my bailiffs because I lay under ban—I, on my side, dealt harshly with them, and so they brought suit against me for robbery; but I had not the money to pay my household withal; and you can see I was too young to meet these troubles wisely, and my kinsfolk would not help me—save Munan—he did all his wife would let him. . . .

"Ay, now you know it, Kristin: I have lost much both of lands and goods and of honour. True it is; you would be better served if you held fast to Simon Andressön."

Kristin put her arms about his neck.

"We will abide by what we swore to each other yesternight, Erlend—if so be you think as I do."

Erlend drew her close to him, kissed her and said:

"You will see too, trust me, that all things will be changed with me now—for none in the world has power on me now but you. Oh, my thoughts, were many last night, as you slept upon my lap, my fairest one. So much power the devil cannot have over a man that I should ever work you care and woe—you, my dearest life. . . ."

KATHARINE PRICHARD, Australian novelist, dramatist, and short story writer, was born in the Fiji Islands, in 1883. She was educated at the University of Melbourne and worked for the Melbourne *Herald* in London, reporting, in particular, on topics related to the employment and interests of women. The theories of Marx and Engels made a lasting impression on her. She was one of the founders of the Australian Communist party and remained a lifelong, although anguished, member. Her political convictions insured that her critics often either overpraised or dismissed her writing for ideological, rather than artistic reasons. She is remembered for having helped lay the foundation for a native Australian literature, one free from the dominating influence of the English literary establishment: "Although there were more opportunities for a writer in London at that time, I wanted to write about Australia and the Australian people and have never regretted devoting my life to them and interpreting them to the people of other countries." She is the author of twelve novels and three volumes of short stories which have been translated into nineteen foreign languages. "The Cooboo" is her most famous story.

Prichard was married and the mother of one son. She died in 1969.

Katharine Prichard
(1883—1969)

THE COOBOO

They had been mustering all day on the wide plains of Murndoo station. Over the red earth, black with ironstone pebbles, through mulga and curari bush, across the ridges which make a blue wall along the horizon. And the rosy, garish light of sunset was on plains, hills, moving cattle, men and horses.

Through red dust the bullocks mooched, restless and scary still, a wild mob from the hills. John Gray, in the rear with Arra, the boy who was his shadow; Wongana, on the right with his gin, Rose; Frank, the half-caste, on the left with Minni.

A steer breaking from the mob before Rose, she wheeled and went after him. Faint and wailing, a cry followed her, as though her horse had stepped on and crushed some small creature. But the steer was getting away. Arra went after him, stretched along his horse's neck, rounded the beast and rode him back to the mob, sulky and blethering. The mob swayed; it had broken three times that day, but was settling to the road.

John Gray called: "Yienda (you) damn fool, Rosey. Finish!"

The gin, on her slight, rough-haired horse, pulled up scowling.

"Tell Meetchie, Thirty Mile, to-morrow," John Gray said. "Miah, new moon."

Rose slewed her horse away from the mob of men and cattle. That wailing, thin and hard as hair-string, moved with her.

"Minni!"

John Gray jerked his head towards Rose. Minni's bare heels struck her horse's belly; with a turn of the wrist she swung her horse off from the mob, turned, leaned forward, rising in her stirrups, and came up with Rose.

63

Thin, dark figures on their wiry station-bred horses, the gins rode into the haze of sunset towards the hills. The dull, dirty blue of the trousers wrapped round their legs was torn; their short, fairish hair tousled by the wind. But the glitter and tumult of Rose's eyes, Minni looked away from them.

At a little distance, when men and cattle were a moving cloud of red dust, Rose's anger gushed after them.

"Koo!"

Fierce as the cry of a hawk flew her last note of derision and defiance.

A far-away rattle of laughter drifted back across country. Alone they would have been afraid, as darkness coming up behind, was hovering near them, secreting itself among the low, writhen trees and bushes; afraid of the evil spirits who wander over the plains and stony ridges when the light of day is withdrawn. But together they were not so afraid. Twenty miles away, over there, below that dent in the hills where Nyedee Creek made a sandy bed for itself among white-bodied gums, was Murndoo homestead and the uloo of their people.

There was no track; and in the first darkness, which would be thick as wool after the glow of sunset faded, only their instinct would keep them moving in the direction of the homestead and their own low, round huts of bagging, rusty tin and dead boughs.

Both were Wongana's women: Rose, tall, gaunt and masterful; Minni, younger, fat and jolly. Rose had been a good stockman in her day: one of the best. Minni did not ride or track nearly as well as Rose.

And yet, as they rode along, Minni pattered complacently of how well she had worked that day; of how she was flashed, this way and that, heading-off breakaways, dashing after them, turning them back to the mob so smartly that John had said, "Good man, Minni!" There was the white bullock—he had rushed near the yards. Had Rose seen the chestnut mare stumble in a crab-hole and send Arra flying? But Minni had chased the white bullock, chased him for a couple of miles, and brought him back to the yards. No doubt there would be nammery for her and a new gina-gina when the men came in from the muster.

She pulled a pipe from her belt, shook the ashes out, and with reins looped over one arm stuffed the bowl with tobacco from a tin tied to her belt. Stooping down, she struck a match on her stirrup-iron, guarded the flame to the pipe between her short, white teeth, and smoked contentedly.

The scowl on Rose's face deepened, darkened. That thin, fretted wailing came from her breast.

She unslung from her neck the rag rope by which the baby had been held against her body, and gave him a sagging breast to suck. Holding him with one arm, she rode slowly, her horse picking his way over the rough, stony earth.

It had been a hard day. The gins were mustering with the men at sunrise. Camped at Nyedee well the night before, in order to get a good start, they had been riding through the timbered ridges all the morning, rounding up wild cows, calves and young bullocks, and driving them down to the yards at Nyedee, where John Gray cut out the fats, left old Jimmy and a couple of boys to brand calves, turn the cows and calves back to the ridge again while he took on the mob for trucking at Meekatharra. The bullocks were as wild as birds: needed watching all day. And all the time that small, whimpering bundle against her breast had hampered Rose's movements.

There was nothing the gins liked better than a muster, riding after cattle. And they could ride, were quicker in their movements, more alert than the men; sharper at picking up tracks. They did not go mustering very often nowadays when there was work to do at the homestead. Since John Gray had married, and there was a woman on Murndoo, she found plenty of washing, scrubbing and sweeping for the gins to do; would not spare them often to go after cattle. But John was short-handed. He had said he must have Rose and Minni to muster Nyedee. And all day her baby's crying had irritated Rose. The cooboo had wailed and wailed as she rode with him tied to her body.

The cooboo was responsible for the wrong things she had done all day. Stupid things. Rose was furious. The men had yelled at her. Wongana, her man, blackguarding her before everybody, had called her "a hen who did not know where she laid her eggs." And John Gray, with his "Yienda, damn fool, Rosey, Finish!" had sent her home like a naughty child.

Now, here was Minni jabbering of the tobacco she would get and the new gina-gina. How pleased Wongana would be with her! And the cooboo, wailing, wailing. He wailed as he chewed Rose's empty breast, squirming, against her; wailed and gnawed.

She cried out with hurt and impatience. Rage, irritated to madness, rushed through her; rushed like waters coming down the dry creek-beds after heavy rain. Rose wrenched the cooboo from her breast and flung him from her to the ground. There was a crack as of twigs breaking.

Minni glanced aside. "Wiah!" she gasped with widening eyes. But Rose rode on, gazing ahead over the rosy, garish plains and wall of the hills, darkening from blue to purple and indigo.

When the women came into the station kitchen, earth, hills and trees were dark; the sky heavy with stars. Minni gave John's wife his message; that he would be home with the new moon, in about a fortnight.

Meetchie, as the blacks called Mrs. John Gray, could not make out why the gins were so stiff and quiet: why Rose stalked, scowling and sulky-fellow, sombre eyes just glancing, and away again. Meetchie wanted to ask about the muster, what sort of condition the bullocks had on; how many were on the road; if many calves had been branded at Nyedee. But she knew them too well to ask questions when they looked like that.

Only when she had given them bread and a tin of jam, cut off hunks of corned beef for them, filled their billies with strong black tea, put sugar in their empty tins, and they were going off to the uloo, she was surprised to see Rose without her baby.

"Why, Rose," she exclaimed, "where's the cooboo?"

Rose stalked off into the night. Minni glanced back with scared eyes, and followed Rose.

In the dawn, when a cry, remote and anguished flew through the clear air, Meetchie wondered who was dead in the camp by the creek. She remembered Rose: how she had looked the night before. And the cooboo—where was he?

Then she knew that it was Rose wailing for her cooboo in the dawn: Rose cutting herself with stones until her body bled: Rose screaming in a fury of unavailing grief.

ISAK DINESEN was born Karen Dinesen in 1885 at Rungstedlund, Denmark. As a young woman she published short stories under the pseudonym "Osceola." After her marriage in 1914 to a Swedish cousin she was known as Baroness Karen Blixen-Finecke. The couple went to East Africa and took a 6,000-acre farm near Nairobi. After seventeen years of running the farm (all recorded in *Out of Africa*), she returned to Denmark, bankrupt, divorced, and dedicated henceforth to the vocation of writer under the name of Isak Dinesen.

"All sorrows can be borne," she once remarked, "if you put them into a story or tell a story about them." Her childhood was unhappy. Her father, a colorful and adventurous man whom Karen admired deeply, hanged himself when she was ten years old, leaving his wife to bring up their five children alone. Mrs. Dinesen was helped by her mother and unmarried sister, neither of whom understood or liked Karen, who took after her father's family. Isak Dinesen's marriage to Bror Blixen, a big-game hunter, safari-leader, and friend of Hemingway, was never happy. She once remarked that Blixen didn't know whether the Crusades dated from before or after the French Revolution. He was unfaithful to her from the beginning, and as a result of his promiscuity, she contracted a venereal disease that gave her long hard years of illness in later life.

Because of debts she had to sell her farm and leave Africa, which she loved; in 1931 she returned to her mother's home in Denmark, without money or future. She became a professional writer under very difficult circumstances—she lived in Denmark and wrote in English. ("Nothing is more difficult and unwelcome than to write without confidence of finding readers," wrote Shelley.) She finished the short stories she had begun in Kenya ("to amuse myself in the rainy season"), and they were published with great success as *Seven Gothic Tales* in 1934. She has received high praise as an aristocratic writer and a born narrator whose writing is full of subtle irony and an unusual elegance and sensitivity. "Sorrow-Acre," based on a Danish folk-tale, is one of her finest stories. (If you visit the village of Ballum on the west coast of Jutland, you can find what is said to be Anne-Marie's grave in the churchyard and see the field which is still called "Sorrow-Acre.")

During a visit to New York in 1959, her menu was always the same—a half dozen oysters, a split of champagne, a few grapes. When asked which poet she would have chosen to have been loved by, she replied unhesitatingly, "Robert Burns."

Isak Dinesen
(1885—1962)

SORROW-ACRE

The low, undulating Danish landscape was silent and serene, mysteriously wide-awake in the hour before sunrise. There was not a cloud in the pale sky, not a shadow along the dim, pearly fields, hills and woods. The mist was lifting from the valleys and hollows, the air was cool, the grass and the foliage dripping wet with morning-dew. Unwatched by the eyes of man, and undisturbed by his activity, the country breathed a timeless life, to which language was inadequate.

All the same, a human race had lived on this land for a thousand years, had been formed by its soil and weather, and had marked it with its thoughts, so that now no one could tell where the existence of the one ceased and the other began. The thin grey line of a road, winding across the plain and up and down hills, was the fixed materialisation of human longing, and of the human notion that it is better to be in one place than another.

A child of the country would read this open landscape like a book. The irregular mosaic of meadows and cornlands was a picture, in timid green and yellow, of the people's struggle for its daily bread; the centuries had taught it to plough and sow in this way. On a distant hill the immovable wings of a windmill, in a small blue cross against the sky, delineated a later stage in the career of bread. The blurred outline of thatched roofs—a low, brown growth of the earth—where the huts of the village thronged together, told the history, from his cradle to his grave, of the peasant, the creature nearest to the soil and dependent on it, prospering in a fertile year and dying in years of drought and pests.

A little higher up, with the faint horizontal line of the white cemetery-wall round it, and the vertical contour of tall poplars by its side, the red-tiled church bore witness, as far as the eye reached, that this was a Christian country. The child of the land knew it as a strange house, inhabited only for a few hours every seventh day, but with a strong, clear voice in it to give out the joys and sorrows of the land; a plain, square embodiment of the nation's trust in the justice and mercy of heaven. But where, amongst cupular woods and groves, the lordly, pyramidal silhouette of the cut lime avenues rose in the air, there a big country house lay.

The child of the land would read much within these elegant, geometrical ciphers on the hazy blue. They spoke of power, the lime trees paraded round a stronghold. Up here was decided the destiny of the surrounding land and of the men and beasts upon it, and the peasant lifted his eyes to the green pyramids with awe. They spoke of dignity, decorum and taste. Danish soil grew no finer flower than the mansion to which the long avenue led. In its lofty rooms life and death bore themselves with stately grace. The country house did not gaze upward, like the church, nor down to the ground like the huts; it had a wider earthly horizon than they, and was related to much noble architecture all over Europe. Foreign artisans had been called in to panel and stucco it, and its own inhabitants travelled and brought back ideas, fashions and things of beauty. Paintings, tapestries, silver and glass from distant countries had been made to feel at home here, and now formed part of Danish country life.

The big house stood as firmly rooted in the soil of Denmark as the peasants' huts, and was as faithfully allied to her four winds and her changing seasons, to her animal life, trees and flowers. Only its interests lay in a higher plane. Within the domain of the lime trees it was no longer cows, goats and pigs on which the minds and the talk ran, but horses and dogs. The wild fauna, the game of the land, that the peasant shook his fist at, when he saw it on his young green rye or in his ripening wheat field, to the residents of the country houses were the main pursuit and the joy of existence.

The writing in the sky solemnly proclaimed continuance, a worldly immortality. The great country houses had held their ground through many generations. The families who lived in them revered the past as they honoured themselves, for the history of Denmark was their own history.

A Rosenkrantz had sat at Rosenholm, a Juel at Hverringe, a Skeel at Gammel-Estrup as long as people remembered. They had seen kings and schools of style succeed one another and, proudly and humbly, had made over their personal existence to that of their land, so that amongst their equals and

with the peasants they passed by its name: Rosenholm, Hverringe, Gammel-Estrup. To the King and the country, to his
family and to the individual lord of the manor himself it was
a matter of minor consequence which particular Rosenkrantz,
Juel or Skeel, out of a long row of fathers and sons, at the
moment in his person incarnated the fields and woods, the
peasants, cattle and game of the estate. Many duties rested on
the shoulders of the big landowners—towards God in
heaven, towards the King, his neighbour and himself—and
they were all harmoniously consolidated into the idea of his
duties towards his land. Highest amongst these ranked his
obligation to uphold the sacred continuance, and to produce
a new Rosenkrantz, Juel or Skeel for the service of Rosenholm, Hverringe and Gammel-Estrup.

Female grace was prized in the manors. Together with
good hunting and fine wine it was the flower and emblem of
the higher existence led there, and in many ways the families
prided themselves more on their daughters than on their sons.

The ladies who promenaded in the lime avenues, or drove
through them in heavy coaches with four horses, carried the
future of the name in their laps and were, like dignified and
debonair caryatides, holding up the houses. They were themselves conscious of their value, kept up their price, and
moved in a sphere of pretty worship and self-worship. They
might even be thought to add to it, on their own, a graceful,
arch, paradoxical haughtiness. For how free were they, how
powerful! Their lords might rule the country, and allow
themselves many liberties, but when it came to that supreme
matter of legitimacy which was the vital principle of their
world, the centre of gravity lay with them.

The lime trees were in bloom. But in the early morning
only a faint fragrance drifted through the garden, an airy
message, an aromatic echo of the dreams during the short
summer night.

In a long avenue that led from the house all the way to the
end of the garden, where, from a small white pavilion in the
classic style, there was a great view over the fields, a young
man walked. He was plainly dressed in brown, with pretty
linen and lace, bare-headed, with his hair tied by a ribbon.
He was dark, a strong and sturdy figure with fine eyes and
hands; he limped a little on one leg.

The big house at the top of the avenue, the garden and the
fields had been his childhood's paradise. But he had travelled

and lived out of Denmark, in Rome and Paris, and he was at present appointed to the Danish Legation to the Court of King George, the brother of the late, unfortunate young Danish Queen. He had not seen his ancestral home for nine years. It made him laugh to find, now, everything so much smaller than he remembered it, and at the same time he was strangely moved by meeting it again. Dead people came towards him and smiled at him; a small boy in a ruff ran past him with his hoop and kite, in passing gave him a clear glance and laughingly asked: "Do you mean to tell me that you are I?" He tried to catch him in the flight, and to answer him: "Yes, I assure you that I am you," but the light figure did not wait for a reply.

The young man, whose name was Adam, stood in a particular relation to the house and the land. For six months he had been heir to it all; nominally he was so even at this moment. It was this circumstance which had brought him from England, and on which his mind was dwelling, as he walked along slowly.

The old lord up at the manor, his father's brother, had had much misfortune in his domestic life. His wife had died young, and two of his children in infancy. The one son then left to him, his cousin's playmate, was a sickly and morose boy. For ten years the father travelled with him from one watering place to another, in Germany and Italy, hardly ever in other company than that of his silent, dying child, sheltering the faint flame of life with both hands, until such time as it could be passed over to a new bearer of the name. At the same time another misfortune had struck him: he fell into disfavour at Court, where till now he had held a fine position. He was about to rehabilitate his family's prestige through the marriage which he had arranged for his son, when before it could take place the bridegroom died, not yet twenty years old.

Adam learned of his cousin's death, and his own changed fortune, in England, through his ambitious and triumphant mother. He sat with her letter in his hand and did not know what to think about it.

If this, he reflected, had happened to him while he was still a boy, in Denmark, it would have meant all the world to him. It would be so now with his friends and schoolfellows, if they were in his place, and they would, at this moment, be congratulating or envying him. But he was neither covetous nor vain by nature; he had faith in his own talents and had been content to know that his success in life depended on his personal ability. His slight infirmity had always set him a little apart from other boys; it had, perhaps, given him a keener sensibility of many things in life, and he did not, now, deem it quite right that the head of the family should limp on one leg. He did not even see his prospects in the same light as his people at home. In England he had met with greater wealth and magnificence than they dreamed of; he had been in love with, and made happy by, an English lady of such rank and fortune that to her, he felt, the finest estate of Denmark would look but like a child's toy farm.

And in England, too, he had come in touch with the great new ideas of the age: of nature, of the right and freedom of man, of justice and beauty. The universe, through them, had become infinitely wider to him; he wanted to find out still more about it and was planning to travel to America, to the new world. For a moment he felt trapped and imprisoned, as if the dead people of his name, from the family vault at home, were stretching out their parched arms for him.

But at the same time he began to dream at night of the old house and garden. He had walked in these avenues in dream, and had smelled the scent of the flowering limes. When at Ranelagh an old gypsy woman looked at his hand and told him that a son of his was to sit in the seat of his fathers, he felt a sudden, deep satisfaction, queer in a young man who till now had never given his sons a thought.

Then, six months later, his mother again wrote to him that his uncle had himself married the girl intended for his dead son. The head of the family was still in his best age, not over sixty, and although Adam remembered him as a small, slight man, he was a vigorous person; it was likely that his young wife would bear him sons.

Adam's mother in her disappointment lay the blame on him. If he had returned to Denmark, she told him, his uncle might have come to look upon him as a son, and would not have married; nay, he might have handed the bride over to him. Adam knew better. The family estate, differing from the neighbouring properties, had gone down from father to son ever since a man of their name first sat there. The tradition of direct succession was the pride of the clan and a sacred dogma to his uncle; he would surely call for a son of his own flesh and bone.

But at the news the young man was seized by a strange, deep, aching remorse towards his old home in Denmark. It was as if he had been making light of a friendly and generous gesture, and disloyal to someone unfailingly loyal to him. It would be but just, he thought, if from now the place should disown and forget him. Nostalgia, which before he had never known, caught hold of him; for the first time he walked in the streets and parks of London as a stranger.

He wrote to his uncle and asked if he might come and stay with him, begged leave from the Legation and took ship for Denmark. He had come to the house to make his peace with it; he had slept little in the night, and was up so early and walking in the garden, to explain himself, and to be forgiven.

While he walked, the still garden slowly took up its day's work. A big snail, of the kind that his grandfather had brought back from France, and which he remembered eating in the house as a child, was already, with dignity, dragging a silver train down the avenue. The birds began to sing; in an old tree under which he stopped a number of them were worrying an owl; the rule of the night was over.

He stood at the end of the avenue and saw the sky lightening. An ecstatic clarity filled the world; in half an hour the sun would rise. A rye field here ran along the garden; two roe-deer were moving in it and looked roseate in the dawn. He gazed out over the fields, where as a small boy he had ridden his pony, and towards the wood where he had killed his first stag. He remembered the old servants who had taught him; some of them were now in their graves.

The ties which bound him to this place, he reflected, were of a mystic nature. He might never again come back to it, and it would make no difference. As long as a man of his own blood and name should sit in the house, hunt in the fields and be obeyed by the people in the huts, wherever he travelled on earth, in England or amongst the red Indians of America, he himself would still be safe, would still have a home, and would carry weight in the world.

His eyes rested on the church. In old days, before the time of Martin Luther, younger sons of great families, he knew, had entered the Church of Rome, and had given up individual wealth and happiness to serve the greater ideals. They, too, had bestowed honour upon their homes and were remembered in its registers. In the solitude of the morning half in jest he let his mind run as it listed; it seemed to him that he might speak to the land as to a person, as to the mother of his race. "Is it only my body that you want," he asked her, "while you reject my imagination, energy and emotions? If the world might be brought to acknowledge that the virtue of our name does not belong to the past only, will it give you no satisfaction?" The landscape was so still that he could not tell whether it answered him yes or no.

After a while he walked on, and came to the new French rose garden laid out for the young mistress of the house. In England he had acquired a freer taste in gardening, and he wondered if he could liberate these blushing captives, and make them thrive outside their cut hedges. Perhaps, he meditated, the elegantly conventional garden would be a floral portrait of his young aunt from Court, whom he had not yet seen.

As once more he came to the pavilion at the end of the avenue his eyes were caught by a bouquet of delicate colours which could not possibly belong to the Danish summer morning. It was in fact his uncle himself, powdered and silk-stockinged, but still in a brocade dressing-gown, and obviously sunk in deep thought. "And what business, or what meditations," Adam asked himself, "drags a connoisseur of the beautiful, but three months married to a wife of seventeen, from his bed into his garden before sunrise?" He walked up to the small, slim, straight figure.

His uncle on his side showed no surprise at seeing him, but then he rarely seemed surprised at anything. He greeted him, with a compliment of his matunality, as kindly as he had done on his arrival last evening. After a moment he looked to the sky, and solemnly proclaimed: "It will be a hot day." Adam, as a child, had often been impressed by the grand, ceremonial manner in which the old lord would state the common happenings of existence; it looked as if nothing had changed here, but all was what it used to be.

The uncle offered the nephew a pinch of snuff. "No, thank you, Uncle," said Adam, "it would ruin my nose to the scent of your garden, which is as fresh as the Garden of Eden, newly created." "From every tree of which," said his uncle, smiling, "thou, my Adam, mayest freely eat." They slowly walked up the avenue together.

The hidden sun was now already gilding the top of the tallest trees. Adam talked of the beauties of nature, and of the greatness of Nordic scenery, less marked by the hand of man than that of Italy. His uncle took the praise of the landscape as a personal compliment, and congratulated him because he had not, in likeness to many young travellers in foreign countries, learned to despise his native land. No, said Adam, he had lately in England longed for the fields and woods of his Danish home. And he had there become acquainted with a new piece of Danish poetry which had enchanted him more than any English or French work. He named the author, Johannes Ewald, and quoted a few of the mighty, turbulent verses.

"And I have wondered, while I read," he went on after a pause, still moved by the lines he himself had declaimed, "that we have not till now understood how much our Nordic mythology in moral greatness surpasses that of Greece and Rome. If it had not been for the physical beauty of the ancient gods, which has come down to us in marble, no modern mind could hold them worthy of worship. They were mean, capricious and treacherous. The gods of our Danish forefathers are as much more divine than they as the Druid is nobler than the Augur. For the fair gods of Asgaard did possess the sublime human virtues; they were righteous, trustworthy, benevolent and even, within a barbaric age, chivalrous." His uncle here for the first time appeared to take any real interest in the conversation. He stopped, his majestic nose a little in the air. "Ah, it was easier to them," he said.

"What do you mean, Uncle?" Adam asked. "It was a great deal easier," said his uncle, "to the northern gods than to those of Greece to be, as you will have it, righteous and benevolent. To my mind it even reveals a weakness in the souls of our ancient Danes that they should consent to adore such divinities." "My dear uncle," said Adam, smiling, "I have always felt that you would be familiar with the modes of Olympus. Now please let me share your insight, and tell me why virtue should come easier to our Danish gods than to those of milder climates." "They were not as powerful," said his uncle.

"And does power," Adam again asked, "stand in the way of virtue?" "Nay," said his uncle gravely. "Nay, power is in itself the supreme virtue. But the gods of which you speak were never all-powerful. They had, at all times, by their side those darker powers which they named the Jotuns, and who worked the suffering, the disasters, the ruin of our world. They might safely give themselves up to temperance and kindness. The omnipotent gods," he went on, "have no such facilitation. With their omnipotence they take over the woe of the universe."

They had walked up the avenue till they were in view of the house. The old lord stopped and ran his eyes over it. The stately building was the same as ever; behind the two tall front windows, Adam knew, was now his young aunt's room. His uncle turned and walked back.

"Chivalry," he said, "chivalry, of which you were speaking, is not a virtue of the omnipotent. It must needs imply mighty rival powers for the knight to defy. With a dragon inferior to him in strength, what figure will St. George cut? The knight who finds no superior forces ready to hand must invent them, and combat wind-mills; his knighthood itself stipulates dangers, vileness, darkness on all sides of him. Nay, believe me, my nephew, in spite of his moral worth, your chivalrous Odin of Asgaard as a Regent must take rank below that of Jove who avowed his sovereignty, and accepted the world which he ruled. But you are young," he added, "and the experience of the aged to you will sound pedantic."

He stood immovable for a moment and then with deep gravity proclaimed: "The sun is up."

The sun did indeed rise above the horizon. The wide landscape was suddenly animated by its splendour, and the dewy grass shone in a thousand gleams.

"I have listened to you, Uncle," said Adam, "with great interest. But while we have talked you yourself have seemed to me preoccupied; your eyes have rested on the field outside the garden, as if something of great moment, a matter of life and death, was going on there. Now that the sun is up, I see the mowers in the rye and hear them whetting their sickles. It is, I remember you telling me, the first day of the harvest. That is a great day to a landowner and enough to take his mind away from the gods. It is very fine weather, and I wish you a full barn."

The elder man stood still, his hands on his walking-stick. "There is indeed," he said at last, "something going on in that field, a matter of life and death. Come, let us sit down here, and I will tell you the whole story." They sat down on the seat that ran all along the pavilion, and while he spoke the old lord of the land did not take his eyes off the rye field.

"A week ago, on Thursday night," he said, "someone set fire to my barn at Rødmosegaard—you know the place, close to the moor—and burned it all down. For two or three days we could not lay hands on the offender. Then on Monday morning the keeper at Rødmose, with the wheelwright over there, came up to the house; they dragged with them a boy, Goske Piil, a widow's son, and they made their Bible oath that he had done it; they had themselves seen him sneaking round the barn by nightfall on Thursday. Goske had no good name on the farm; the keeper bore him a grudge upon an old matter of poaching, and the wheelwright did not like him either, for he did, I believe, suspect him with his young wife. The boy, when I talked to him, swore to his innocence, but he could not hold his own against the two old men. So I had him locked up, and meant to send him in to our judge of the district, with a letter.

"The judge is a fool, and would naturally do nothing but what he thought I wished him to do. He might have the boy sent to the convict prison for arson, or put amongst the soldiers as a bad character and a poacher. Or again, if he thought that that was what I wanted, he could let him off.

"I was out riding in the fields, looking at the corn that was soon ripe to be mowed, when a woman, the widow, Goske's mother, was brought up before me, and begged to speak to me. Anne-Marie is her name. You will remember her; she lives in the small house east of the village. She has not got a good name in the place either. They tell as a girl she had a child and did away with it.

"From five days' weeping her voice was so cracked that it was difficult for me to understand what she said. Her son, she told me at last, had indeed been over at Rødmose on Thursday, but for no ill purpose; he had gone to see someone. He was her only son, she called the Lord God to witness on his innocence, and she wrung her hands to me that I should save the boy for her.

"We were in the rye field that you and I are looking at now. That gave me an idea. I said to the widow: 'If in one day, between sunrise and sunset, with your own hands you can mow this field, and it be well done, I will let the case drop and you shall keep your son. But if you cannot do it, he must go, and it is not likely that you will then ever see him again.'

"She stood up then and gazed over the field. She kissed my riding boot in gratitude for the favour shown to her."

The old lord here made a pause, and Adam said: "Her son

meant much to her?" "He is her only child," said his uncle. "He means to her her daily bread and support in old age. It may be said that she holds him as dear as her own life. As," he added, "within a higher order of life, a son to his father means the name and the race, and he holds him as dear as life everlasting. Yes, her son means much to her. For the mowing of that field is a day's work to three men, or three days' work to one man. Today, as the sun rose, she set to her task. And down there, by the end of the field, you will see her now, in a blue head-cloth, with the man I have set to follow her and to ascertain that she does the work unassisted, and with two or three friends by her, who are comforting her."

Adam looked down, and did indeed see a woman in a blue head-cloth, and a few other figures in the corn.

They sat for a while in silence. "Do you yourself," Adam then said, "believe the boy to be innocent?" "I cannot tell," said his uncle. "There is no proof. The word of the keeper and the wheelwright stand against the boy's word. If indeed I did believe the one thing or the other, it would be merely a matter of chance, or maybe of sympathy. The boy," he said after a moment, "was my son's playmate, the only other child that I ever knew him to like or to get on with." "Do you," Adam again asked, "hold it possible to her to fulfill your condition?" "Nay, I cannot tell," said the old lord. "To an ordinary person it would not be possible. No ordinary person would ever have taken it on at all. I chose it so. We are not quibbling with the law, Anne-Marie and I."

Adam for a few minutes followed the movement of the small group in the rye. "Will you walk back?" he asked. "No," said his uncle, "I think that I shall stay here till I have seen the end of the thing." "Until sunset?" Adam asked with surprise. "Yes," said the old lord. Adam said: "It will be a long day." "Yes," said his uncle, "a long day. But," he added, as Adam rose to walk away, "if, as you said, you have got that tragedy of which you spoke in your pocket, be as kind as to leave it here, to keep me company." Adam handed him the book.

In the avenue he met two footmen who carried the old lord's morning chocolate down to the pavilion on large silver trays.

As now the sun rose in the sky, and the day grew hot, the lime trees gave forth their exuberance of scent, and the garden was filled with unsurpassed, unbelievable sweetness.

Towards the still hour of midday the long avenue reverberated like a soundboard with a low, incessant murmur: the humming of a million bees that clung to the pendulous, thronging clusters of blossoms and were drunk with bliss.

In all the short lifetime of Danish summer there is no richer or more luscious moment than that week wherein the lime trees flower. The heavenly scent goes to the head and to the heart; it seems to unite the fields of Denmark with those of Elysium; it contains both hay, honey and holy incense, and is half fairy-land and half apothecary's locker. The avenue was changed into a mystic edifice, a dryad's cathedral, outward from summit to base lavishly adorned, set with multitudinous ornaments, and golden in the sun. But behind the walls the vaults were benignly cool and sombre, like ambrosial sanctuaries in a dazzling and burning world, and in here the ground was still moist.

Up in the house, behind the silk curtains of the two front windows, the young mistress of the estate from the wide bed stuck her feet into two little high-heeled slippers. Her lace-trimmed nightgown had slid up above her knee and down from the shoulder; her hair, done up in curling-pins for the night, was still frosty with the powder of yesterday, her round face flushed with sleep. She stepped out to the middle of the floor and stood there, looking extremely grave and thoughtful, yet she did not think at all. But through her head a long procession of pictures marched, and she was unconsciously endeavouring to put them in order, as the pictures of her existence had used to be.

She had grown up at Court; it was her world, and there was probably not in the whole country a small creature more exquisitely and innocently drilled to the stately measure of a palace. By favour of the old Dowager Queen she bore her name and that of the King's sister, the Queen of Sweden: Sophie Magdalena. It was with a view to these things that her husband, when he wished to restore his status in high places, had chosen her as a bride, first for his son and then for himself. But her own father, who held an office in the Royal Household and belonged to the new Court aristocracy, in his day had done the same thing the other way round, and had married a country lady, to get a foothold within the old nobility of Denmark. The little girl had her mother's blood in her veins. The country to her had been an immense surprise and delight.

To get into her castle-court she must drive through the farm yard, through the heavy stone gateway in the barn itself, wherein the rolling of her coach for a few seconds re-echoed like thunder. She must drive past the stables and the timber-mare, from which sometimes a miscreant would follow her with sad eyes, and might here startle a long string of squalling geese, or pass the heavy, scowling bull, led on by a ring in his nose and kneading the earth in dumb fury. At first this had been to her, every time, a slight shock and a jest. But after a while all these creatures and things, which belonged to her, seemed to become part of herself. Her mothers, the old Danish country ladies, were robust persons, undismayed by any kind of weather; now she herself had walked in the rain and had laughed and glowed in it like a green tree.

She had taken her great new home in possession at a time when all the world was unfolding, mating and propagating. Flowers, which she had known only in bouquets and festoons, sprung from the earth round her; birds sang in all the trees. The new-born lambs seemed to her daintier than her dolls had been. From her husband's Hanoverian stud, foals were brought to her to give names; she stood and watched as they poked their soft noses into their mothers' bellies to drink. Of this strange process she had till now only vaguely heard. She had happened to witness, from a path in the park, the rearing and screeching stallion on the mare. All this luxuriance, lust and fecundity was displayed before her eyes, as for her pleasure.

And for her own part, in the midst of it, she was given an old husband who treated her with punctilious respect because she was to bear him a son. Such was the compact; she had known of it from the beginning. Her husband, she found, was doing his best to fulfill his part of it, and she herself was loyal by nature and strictly brought up. She would not shirk her obligation. Only she was vaguely aware of a discord or an incompatibility within her majestic existence, which prevented her from being as happy as she had expected to be.

After a time her chagrin took a strange form: as the consciousness of an absence. Someone ought to have been with her who was not. She had no experience in analysing her feelings; there had not been time for that at Court. Now, as she was more often left to herself, she vaguely probed her own mind. She tried to set her father in that void place, her sisters, her music master, an Italian singer whom she had admired; but none of them would fill it for her. At times she felt lighter at heart, and believed the misfortune to have left her. And then again it would happen, if she were alone, or in her husband's company, and even within his embrace, that everything round her would cry out: Where? Where? so that she let her wild eyes run about the room in search for the being who should have been there, and who had not come.

When, six months ago, she was informed that her first young bridegroom had died and that she was to marry his father in his place, she had not been sorry. Her youthful suitor, the one time she had seen him, had appeared to her infantile and insipid; the father would make a statelier consort. Now she had sometimes thought of the dead boy, and wondered whether with him life would have been more joyful. But she soon again dismissed the picture, and that was the sad youth's last recall to the stage of this world.

Upon one wall of her room there hung a long mirror. As she gazed into it new images came along. The day before, driving with her husband, she had seen, at a distance, a party of village girls bathing in the river, and the sun shining on them. All her life she had moved amongst naked marble deities, but it had till now never occurred to her that the people she knew should themselves be naked under their bodices and trains, waistcoats and satin breeches, that indeed she herself felt naked within her clothes. Now, in front of the looking-glass, she tardily untied the ribbons of her nightgown, and let it drop to the floor.

The room was dim behind the drawn curtains. In the mirror her body was silvery like a white rose; only her cheeks and mouth, and the tips of her fingers and breasts had a faint carmine. Her slender torso was formed by the whalebones that had clasped it tightly from her childhood; above the slim, dimpled knee a gentle narrowness marked the place of the garter. Her limbs were rounded as if, at whatever place they might be cut through with a sharp knife, a perfectly circular transverse incision would be obtained. The side and belly were so smooth that her own gaze slipped and glided, and grasped for a hold. She was not altogether like a statue, she found, and lifted her arms above her head. She turned to get a view of her back, the curves below the waistline were still blushing from the pressure of the bed. She called to mind a few tales about nymphs and goddesses, but they all seemed a long way off, so her mind returned to the peasant girls in the river. They were, for a few minutes, idealized into play-mates, or sisters even, since they belonged to her as did the meadow and the blue river itself. And within the next moment the sense of forlornness once more came upon her, a *horror vaccui* like a physical pain. Surely, surely someone should have been with her now, her other self, like the image in the glass, but nearer, stronger, alive. There was no one, the universe was empty round her.

A sudden, keen itching under her knee took her out of her reveries, and awoke in her the hunting instincts of her breed. She wetted a finger on her tongue, slowly brought it down and quickly slapped it to the spot. She felt the diminutive, sharp body of the insect against the silky skin, pressed the thumb to it, and triumphantly lifted up the small prisoner between her fingertips. She stood quite still, as if meditating upon the fact that a flea was the only creature risking its life for her smoothness and sweet blood.

Her maid opened the door and came in, loaded with the attire of the day—shift, stays, hoop and petticoats. She remembered that she had a guest in the house, the new nephew arrived from England. Her husband had instructed her to be kind to their young kinsman, disinherited, so to say, by her presence in the house. They would ride out on the land together.

In the afternoon the sky was no longer blue as in the morning. Large clouds slowly towered up on it, and the great vault itself was colourless, as if diffused into vapours round the white-hot sun in zenith. A low thunder ran along the western horizon; once or twice the dust of the roads rose in tall spirals. But the fields, the hills and the woods were as still as a painted landscape.

Adam walked down the avenue to the pavilion, and found his uncle there, fully dressed, his hands upon his walking-stick and his eyes on the rye field. The book that Adam had given him lay by his side. The field now seemed alive with people. Small groups stood here and there in it, and a long row of men and women were slowly advancing towards the garden in the line of the swath.

The old lord nodded to his nephew, but did not speak or change his position. Adam stood by him as still as himself.

The day to him had been strangely disquieting. At the meeting again with old places the sweet melodies of the past had filled his senses and his mind, and had mingled with new, bewitching tunes of the present. He was back in Denmark, no longer a child but a youth, with a keener sense of the beautiful, with tales of other countries to tell, and still a true son of his own land and enchanted by its loveliness as he had never been before.

But through all these harmonies the tragic and cruel tale which the old lord had told him in the morning, and the sad contest which he knew to be going on so near by, in the corn field, had re-echoed, like the recurrent, hollow throbbing of a muffled drum, a redoubtable sound. It came back time after time, so that he had felt himself to change colour and to answer absently. It brought with it a deeper sense of pity with all that lived than he had ever known. When he had been riding with his young aunt, and their road ran along the scene of the drama, he had taken care to ride between her and the field, so that she should not see what was going on there, or question him about it. He had chosen the way home through the deep, green wood for the same reason.

More dominantly even than the figure of the woman struggling with her sickle for her son's life, the old man's figure, as he had seen it at sunrise, kept him company through the day. He came to ponder on the part which that lonely, determinate form had played in his own life. From the time when his father died, it had impersonated to the boy law and order, wisdom of life and kind guardianship. What was he to do, he thought, if after eighteen years these filial feelings must change, and his second father's figure take on to him a horrible aspect, as a symbol of the tyranny and oppression of the world? What was he to do if ever the two should come to stand in opposition to each other as adversaries?

At the same time an unaccountable, a sinister alarm and dread on behalf of the old man himself took hold of him. For surely here the Goddess Nemesis could not be far away. This man had ruled the world round him for a longer period than Adam's own lifetime and had never been gainsaid by anyone. During the years when he had wandered through Europe with a sick boy of his own blood as his sole companion he had learned to set himself apart from his surroundings, and to close himself up to all outer life, and he had become insusceptible to the ideas and feelings of other human beings. Strange fancies might there have run in his mind, so that in the end he had seen himself as the only person really existing, and the world as a poor and vain shadow-play, which had no substance to it.

Now, in senile wilfullness, he would take in his hand the life of those simpler and weaker than himself, of a woman, using it to his own ends, and he feared of no retributive justice. Did he not know, the young man thought, that there were powers in the world, different from and more formidable than the short-lived might of a despot?

With the sultry heat of the day this foreboding of impending disaster grew upon him, until he felt ruin threatening not the old lord only, but the house, the name and himself with him. It seemed to him that he must cry out a warning to the man he had loved, before it was too late.

But as now he was once more in his uncle's company, the green calm of the garden was so deep that he did not find his voice to cry out. Instead a little French air which his aunt had sung to him up in the house kept running in his mind.— *"C'est un trop doux effort . . ."* He had good knowledge of music; he had heard the air before, in Paris, but not so sweetly sung.

After a time he asked: "Will the woman fulfill her bargain?" His uncle unfolded his hands. "It is an extraordinary thing," he said animatedly, "that it looks as if she might fulfill it. If you count the hours from sunrise till now, and from now till sunset, you will find the time left her to be half of that already gone. And see! She has now mowed two-thirds of the field. But then we will naturally have to reckon with her strength declining as she works on. All in all, it is an idle pursuit in you or me to bet on the issue of the matter; we must wait and see. Sit down, and keep me company in my watch." In two minds Adam sat down.

"And here," said his uncle, and took up the book from the seat, "is your book, which has passed the time finely. It is great poetry, ambrosia to the ear and the heart. And it has, with our discourse on divinity this morning, given me stuff for thought. I have been reflecting upon the law of retributive justice." He took a pinch of snuff, and went on. "A new age," he said, "has made to itself a god in its own image, an emotional god. And now you are already writing a tragedy on your god."

Adam had no wish to begin a debate on poetry with his uncle, but he also somehow dreaded a silence, and said: "It may be, then, that we hold tragedy to be, in the scheme of life, a noble, a divine phenomenon."

"Aye," said his uncle solemnly, "a noble phenomenon, the noblest on earth. But of the earth only, and never divine. Tragedy is the privilege of man, his highest privilege. The God of the Christian Church Himself, when He wished to experience tragedy, had to assume human form. And even at that," he added thoughtfully, "the tragedy was not wholly valid, as it would have become had the hero of it been, in very truth, a man. The divinity of Christ conveyed to it a divine note, the moment of comedy. The real tragic part, by the nature of things, fell to the executors, not to the victim. Nay, my nephew, we should not adulterate the pure elements of the cosmos. Tragedy should remain the right of human beings, subject, in their conditions or in their own nature, to the dire law of necessity. To them it is salvation and beatification. But the gods, whom we must believe to be unacquainted with and incomprehensive of necessity, can have no knowledge of the tragic. When they are brought face to face with it they will, according to my experience, have the good taste and decorum to keep still, and not interfere.

"No," he said after a pause, "the true art of the gods is the comic. The comic is a condescension of the divine to the world of man; it is the sublime vision, which cannot be studied, but must ever be celestially granted. In the comic the gods see their own being reflected as in a mirror, and while the tragic poet is bound by strict laws, they will allow the comic artist a freedom as unlimited as their own. They do not even withhold their own existence from his sports. Jove may favour Lucianos of Samosata. As long as your mockery is in true godly taste you may mock at the gods and still remain a sound devotee. But in pitying, or condoling with your god, you deny and annihilate him, and such is the most horrible of atheisms.

"And here on earth, too," he went on, "we, who stand in lieu of the gods and have emancipated ourselves from the tyranny of necessity, should leave to our vassals their monopoly of tragedy, and for ourselves accept the comic with grace. Only a boorish and cruel master—a parvenu, in fact—will make a jest of his servants' necessity, or force the comic upon them. Only a timid and pedantic ruler, a *petit-maître*, will fear the ludicrous on his own behalf. Indeed," he finished his long speech, "the very same fatality, which, in striking

the burgher or peasant, will become tragedy, with the aristo-
crat is exalted to the comic. By the grace and wit of our
acceptance hereof our aristocracy is known."

Adam could not help smiling a little as he heard the
apotheosis of the comic on the lips of the erect, ceremonious
prophet. In this ironic smile he was, for the first time, estrang-
ing himself from the head of his house.

A shadow fell across the landscape. A cloud had crept over
the sun; the country changed colour beneath it, faded and
bleached, and even all sounds for a minute seemed to die out
of it.

"Ah, now," said the old lord, "if it is going to rain, and
the rye gets wet, Anne-Marie will not be able to finish in
time. And who comes there?" he added, and turned his head
a little.

Preceded by a lackey a man in riding boots and a striped
waistcoat with silver buttons, and with his hat in his hand,
came down the avenue. He bowed deeply, first to the old lord
and then to Adam.

"My bailiff," said the old lord. "Good afternoon, Bailiff.
What news have you to bring?" The bailiff made a sad gesture. "Poor news only, my lord," he said. "And how poor
news?" asked his master. "There is," said the bailiff with
weight, "not a soul at work on the land, and not a sickle going except that of Anne-Marie in this rye field. The mowing
has stopped; they are all at her heels. It is a poor day for a
first day of the harvest." "Yes, I see," said the old lord. The
bailiff went on. "I have spoken kindly to them," he said, "and
I have sworn at them; it is all one. They might as well all be
deaf."

"Good bailiff," said the old lord, "leave them in peace; let
them do as they like. This day may, all the same, do them
more good than many others. Where is Goske, the boy,
Anne-Marie's son?" "We have set him in the small room by
the barn," said the bailiff. "Nay, let him be brought down,"
said the old lord; "let him see his mother at work. But what
do you say—will she get the field mowed in time?" "If you
ask me, my lord," said the bailiff, "I believe that she will.
Who would have thought so? She is only a small woman. It is
as hot a day today as, well, as I do ever remember. I myself,
you yourself, my lord, could not have done what Anne-Marie
has done today." "Nay, nay, we could not, Bailiff," said the
old lord.

The bailiff pulled out a red handkerchief and wiped his brow, somewhat calmed by venting his wrath. "If," he remarked with bitterness, "they would all work as the widow works now, we would make a profit on the land." "Yes," said the old lord, and fell into thought, as if calculating the profit it might make. "Still," he said, "as to the question of profit and loss, that is more intricate than it looks. I will tell you something that you may not know: The most famous tissue ever woven was ravelled out again every night. But come," he added, "she is close by now. We will go and have a look at her work ourselves." With these words he rose and set his hat on.

The cloud had drawn away again; the rays of the sun once more burned the wide landscape, and as the small party walked out from under the shade of the trees the dead-still heat was heavy as lead; the sweat sprang out on their faces and their eyelids smarted. On the narrow path they had to go one by one, the old lord stepping along first, all black, and the footman, in his bright livery, bringing up the rear.

The field was indeed filled with people like a market-place; there were probably a hundred or more men and women in it. To Adam the scene recalled pictures from his Bible: the meeting between Esau and Jacob in Edom, or Boas' reapers in his barley field near Bethlehem. Some were standing by the side of the field, others pressed in small groups close to the mowing woman, and a few followed in her wake, binding up sheaves where she had cut the corn, as if thereby they thought to help her, or as if by all means they meant to have part in her work. A younger woman with a pail on her head kept close to her side, and with her a number of half-grown children. One of these first caught sight of the lord of the estate and his suite, and pointed to him. The binders let their sheaves drop, and as the old man stood still many of the onlookers drew close round him.

The woman on whom till now the eyes of the whole field had rested—a small figure on the large stage—was advancing slowly and unevenly, bent double as if she were walking on her knees, and stumbling as she walked. Her blue head-cloth had slipped back from her head; the grey hair was plastered to the skull with sweat, dusty and stuck with straw. She was obviously totally unaware of the multitude round her; neither did she now once turn her head or her gaze towards the new arrivals.

Absorbed in her work she again and again stretched out her left hand to grasp a handful of corn, and her right hand with the sickle in it to cut it off close to the soil, in wavering, groping pulls, like a tired swimmer's strokes. Her course took her so close to the feet of the old lord that his shadow fell on her. Just then she staggered and swayed sideways, and the woman who followed her lifted the pail from her head and held it to her lips. Anne-Marie drank without leaving her hold on her sickle, and the water ran from the corners of her mouth. A boy, close to her, quickly bent one knee, seized her hands in his own and, steadying and guiding them, cut off a gripe of rye. "No, no," said the old lord, "you must not do that, boy. Leave Anne-Marie in peace to her work." At the sound of his voice the woman, falteringly, lifted her face in his direction.

The bony and tanned face was streaked with sweat and dust; the eyes were dimmed. But there was not in its expression the slightest trace of fear or pain. Indeed amongst all the grave and concerned faces of the field hers was the only one perfectly calm, peaceful and mild. The mouth was drawn together in a thin line, a prim, keen, patient little smile, such as will be seen in the face of an old woman at her spinning-wheel or her knitting, eager on her work, and happy in it. And as the younger woman lifted back the pail, she immediately again fell to her mowing, with an ardent, tender craving, like that of a mother who lays a baby to the nipple. Like an insect that bustles along in high grass, or like a small vessel in a heavy sea, she butted her way on, her quiet face once more bent upon her task.

The whole throng of onlookers, and with them the small group from the pavilion, advanced as she advanced, slowly and as if drawn by a string. The bailiff, who felt the intense silence of the field heavy on him, said to the old lord: "The rye will yield better this year than last," and got no reply. He repeated his remark to Adam, and at last to the footman, who felt himself above a discussion on agriculture, and only cleared his throat in answer. In a while the bailiff again broke the silence. "There is the boy," he said and pointed with his thumb. "They have brought him down." At that moment the woman fell forward on her face and was lifted up by those nearest to her.

Adam suddenly stopped on the path, and covered his eyes with his hand. The old lord without turning asked him if he felt incommoded by the heat. "No," said Adam, "but stay. Let me speak to you." His uncle stopped, with his hand on the stick and looking ahead, as if regretful of being held back.

"In the name of God," cried the young man in French, "force not this woman to continue." There was a short pause. "But I force her not, my friend," said his uncle in the same language. "She is free to finish at any moment." "At the cost of her child only," again cried Adam. "Do you not see that she is dying? You know not what you are doing, or what it may bring upon you."

The old lord, perplexed by this unexpected animadversion, after a second turned all round, and his pale, clear eyes sought his nephew's face with stately surprise. His long, waxen face, with two symmetrical curls at the sides, had something of the mien of an idealized and ennobled old sheep or ram. He made sign to the bailiff to go on. The footman also withdrew a little, and the uncle and nephew were, so to say, alone on the path. For a minute neither of them spoke.

"In this very place where we now stand," said the old lord, then, with hauteur, "I gave Anne-Marie my word."

"My uncle!" said Adam. "A life is a greater thing even than a word. Recall that word, I beseech you, which was given in caprice, as a whim. I am praying you more for your sake than for my own, yet I shall be grateful to you all my life if you will grant me my prayer."

"You will have learned in school," said his uncle, "that in the beginning was the word. It may have been pronounced in caprice, as a whim, the Scripture tells us nothing about it. It is still the principle of our world, its law of gravitation. My own humble word has been the principle of the land on which we stand, for an age of man. My father's word was the same, before my day."

"You are mistaken," cried Adam. "The word is creative— it is imagination, daring and passion. By it the world was made. How much greater are these powers which bring into being than any restricting or controlling law! You wish the land on which we look to produce and propagate; you should not banish from it that forces which cause, and which keep up life, nor turn it into a desert by dominance of law. And when you look at the people, simpler than we and nearer to the heart of nature, who do not analyse their feelings, whose life is one with the life of the earth, do they not inspire in you tenderness, respect, reverence even? This woman is ready to die for her son; will it ever happen to you or me that a woman willingly gives up her life for us? And if it did indeed come to pass, should we make so light of it as not to give up a dogma in return?"

"You are young," said the old lord. "A new age will undoubtedly applaud you. I am old-fashioned, I have been quoting to you texts a thousand years old. We do not, perhaps, quite understand one another. But with my own people I am, I believe, in good understanding. Anne-Marie might well feel that I am making light of her exploit, if now, at the eleventh hour, I did nullify it by a second word. I myself should feel so in her place. Yes, my nephew, it is possible, did I grant you your prayer and pronounce such an amnesty, that I should find it void against her faithfulness, and that we would still see her at her work, unable to give it up, as a shuttle in the rye field, until she had it all mowed. But she would then be a shocking, a horrible sight, a figure of unseemly fun, like a small planet running wild in the sky, when the law of gravitation had been done away with."

"And if she dies at her task," Adam exclaimed, "her death, and its consequences will come upon your head."

The old lord took off his hat and gently ran his hand over his powdered head. "Upon my head?" he said. "I have kept up my head in many weathers. Even," he added proudly, "against the cold wind from high places. In what shape will it come upon my head, my nephew?" "I cannot tell," cried Adam in despair. "I have spoken to warn you. God only knows." "Amen," said the old lord with a little delicate smile. "Come, we will walk on." Adam drew in his breath deeply.

"No," he said in Danish. "I cannot come with you. This field is yours; things will happen here as you decide. But I myself must go away. I beg you to let me have, this evening, a coach as far as town. For I could not sleep another night under your roof, which I have honoured beyond any on earth." So many conflicting feelings at his own speech thronged in his breast that it would have been impossible for him to give them words.

The old lord, who had already begun to walk on, stood still, and with him the lackey. He did not speak for a minute, as if to give Adam time to collect his mind. But the young man's mind was in uproar and would not be collected.

"Must we," the old man asked, in Danish, "take leave here,

in the rye field? I have held you dear, next to my own son. I have followed your career in life from year to year, and have been proud of you. I was happy when you wrote to say that you were coming back. If now you will go away, I wish you well." He shifted his walking-stick from the right hand to the left and gravely looked his nephew in the face.

Adam did not meet his eyes. He was gazing out over the landscape. In the late mellow afternoon it was resuming its colours, like a painting brought into proper light; in the meadows the little black stacks of peat stood gravely distinct upon the green sward. On this same morning he had greeted it all, like a child running laughingly to its mother's bosom; now already he must tear himself from it, in discordance, and forever. And at the moment of parting it seemed infinitely dearer than any time before, so much beautified and solemnized by the coming separation that it looked like the place in a dream, a landscape out of paradise, and he wondered if it was really the same. But, yes—there before him was, once more, the hunting-ground of long ago. And there was the road on which he had ridden today.

"But tell me where you mean to go from here," said the old lord slowly. "I myself have travelled a good deal in my days. I know the word of leaving, the wish to go away. But I have learned by experience that, in reality, the word has a meaning only to the place and the people which one leaves. When you have left my house—although it will see you go with sadness—as far as it is concerned the matter is finished and done with. But to the person who goes away it is a different thing, and not so simple. At the moment that he leaves one place he will be already, by the laws of life, on his way to another, upon this earth. Let me know, then, for the sake of our old acquaintance, to which place you are going when you leave here. To England?"

"No," said Adam. He felt in his heart that he could never again go back to England or to his easy and care-free life there. It was not far enough away; deeper waters than the North Sea must now be laid between him and Denmark. "No, not to England," he said. "I shall go to America, to the new world." For a moment he shut his eyes, trying to form to himself a picture of existence in America, with the gray Atlantic Ocean between him and these fields and woods.

"To America?" said his uncle and drew up his eyebrows. "Yes, I have heard of America. They have got freedom there, a big waterfall, savage red men. They shoot turkeys, I have read, as we shoot partridges. Well, if it be your wish, go to America, Adam, and be happy in the new world."

He stood for some time, sunk in thought, as if he had already sent off the young man to America, and had done with him. When at last he spoke, his words had the character of a monologue, enunciated by the person who watches things come and go, and himself stays on.

"Take service, there," he said, "with the power which will give you an easier bargain than this: That with your own life you may buy the life of your son."

Adam had not listened to his uncle's remarks about America, but the conclusive, solemn words caught his ear. He looked up. As if for the first time in his life, he saw the old man's figure as a whole, and conceived how small it was, so much smaller than himself, pale, a thin black anchorite upon his own land. A thought ran through his head: "How terrible to be old!" The abhorrence of the tyrant, and the sinister dread on his behalf, which had followed him all day, seemed to die out of him, and his pity with all creation to extend even to the sombre form before him.

His whole being had cried out for harmony. Now, with the possibility of forgiving, of a reconciliation, a sense of relief went through him; confusedly he bethought himself of Anne-Marie drinking the water held to her lips. He took off his hat, as his uncle had done a moment ago, so that to a beholder at a distance it would seem that the two dark-clad gentlemen on the path were repeatedly and respectfully saluting one another, and brushed the hair from his forehead. Once more the tune of the garden-room rang in his mind:

> *"Mourir pour ce qu'on aime*
> *C'est un trop doux effort . . ."*

He stood for a long time immobile and dumb. He broke off a few ears of rye, kept them in his hand and looked at them.

He saw the ways of life, he thought, as a twined and tangled design, complicated and mazy; it was not given him or any mortal to command or control it. Life and death, happiness and woe, the past and the present, were interlaced within the pattern. Yet to the initiated it might be read as easily as our ciphers—which to the savage must seem confused and incomprehensible—will be read by the schoolboy. And out of the contrasting elements concord rose. All that lived must suffer; the old man, whom he had judged hardly, had suffered, as he had watched his son die, and had dreaded the obliteration of his being. He himself would come to know ache, tears and remorse, and, even through these, the fullness of life. So might now, to the woman in the rye field, the ordeal be a triumphant procession. For to die for the one you loved was an effort too sweet for words.

As now he thought of it, he knew that all his life he had sought the unity of things, the secret which connects the phenomena of existence. It was this strife, this dim presage, which had sometimes made him stand still and inert in the midst of the games of his play-fellows, or which had, at other moments—on moonlight nights, or in his little boat on the sea—lifted the boy to ecstatic happiness. Where other young people, in their pleasures of their amours, had searched for contrast and variety, he himself had yearned only to comprehend in full the oneness of the world. If things had come differently, if his young cousin had not died, and the events that followed his death had not brought him to Denmark, his search for understanding and harmony might have taken him to America, and he might have found them there, in the virgin forests of a new world. Now they have been disclosed to him today, in the place where he had played as a child. As the song is one with the voice that sings it, as the road is one with the goal, as lovers are made one in their embrace, so is man one with his destiny, and he shall love it as himself.

He looked up again, towards the horizon. If he wished to, he felt, he might find out what it was that had brought to him, here, the sudden conception of the unity of the universe. When this same morning he had philosophized, lightly and for his own sake, on his feeling of belonging to this land and soil, it had been the beginning of it. But since then it had grown; it had become a mightier thing, a revelation to his soul. Some time he would look into it, for the law of cause and effect was a wonderful and fascinating study. But not now. This hour was consecrated to greater emotions, to a surrender to fate and to the will of life.

"No," he said at last. "If you wish it I shall not go. I shall stay here."

At that moment a long, loud roll of thunder broke the

stillness of the afternoon. It re-echoed for a while amongst the low hills, and it reverberated within the young man's breast as powerfully as if he had been seized and shaken by hands. The landscape had spoken. He remembered that twelve hours ago he had put a question to it, half in jest, and not knowing what he did. Here it gave him its answer.

What it contained he did not know; neither did he inquire. In his promise to his uncle he had given himself over to the mightier powers of the world. Now what must come must come.

"I thank you," said the old lord, and made a little stiff gesture with his hand. "I am happy to hear you say so. We should not let the difference in our ages, or of our views, separate us. In our family we have been wont to keep peace and faith with one another. You have made my heart lighter."

Something within his uncle's speech faintly recalled to Adam the misgivings of the afternoon. He rejected them; he would not let them trouble the new, sweet felicity which his resolution to stay had brought him.

"I shall go on now," said the old lord. "But there is no need for you to follow me. I will tell you tomorrow how the matter has ended." "No," said Adam, "I shall come back by sunset, to see the end of it myself."

All the same he did not come back. He kept the hour in his mind, and all through the evening the consciousness of the drama, and the profound concern and compassion with which, in his thoughts, he followed it, gave to his speech, glance and movements a grave and pathetic substance. But he felt that he was, in the rooms of the manor, and even by the harpsichord on which he accompanied his aunt to her air from *Alceste*, as much in the centre of things as if he had stood in the rye field itself, and as near to those human beings whose fate was now decided there. Anne-Marie and he were both in the hands of destiny, and destiny would, by different ways, bring each to the designated end.

Later on he remembered what he had thought that evening.

But the old lord stayed on. Late in the afternoon he even had an idea; he called down his valet to the pavilion and made him shift his clothes on him and dress him up in a brocaded suit that he had worn at Court. He let a lace-trimmed shirt be drawn over his head and stuck out his slim legs to have them put into thin silk stockings and buckled shoes. In this majestic attire he dined alone, of a frugal meal, but took a bottle of Rhenish wine with it, to keep up his strength. He sat on for a while, a little sunk in his seat; then, as the sun neared the earth, he straightened himself, and took the way down to the field.

The shadows were now lengthening, azure blue along all the eastern slopes. The lonely trees in the corn marked their site by narrow blue pools running out from their feet, and as the old man walked a thin, immensely elongated reflection stirred behind him on the path. Once he stood still; he thought he heard a lark singing over his head, a spring-like sound; his tired head held no clear perception of the season; he seemed to be walking, and standing, in a kind of eternity.

The people in the field were no longer silent, as they had been in the afternoon. Many of them talked loudly among themselves, and a little farther away a woman was weeping.

When the bailiff saw his master, he came up to him. He told him, in great agitation, that the widow would, in all likelihood, finish the mowing of the field within a quarter of an hour.

"Are the keeper and the wheelwright here?" the old lord asked him. "They have been here," said the bailiff, "and have gone away, five times. Each time they have said that they would not come back. But they have come back again, all the same, and they are here now." "And where is the boy?" the old lord asked again. "He is with her," said the bailiff. "I have given him leave to follow her. He has walked close to his mother all the afternoon, and you will see him now by her side, down there."

Anne-Marie was now working her way up towards them more evenly than before, but with extreme slowness, as if at any moment she might come to a stand-still. This excessive tardiness, the old lord reflected, if it had been purposely performed, would have been an inimitable, dignified exhibition of skilled art; one might fancy the Emperor of China advancing in like manner on a divine procession or rite. He shaded his eyes with his hand, for the sun was now just beyond the horizon, and its last rays made light, wild, many-coloured specks dance before his sight. With such splendour did the sunset emblazon the earth and the air that the landscape was turned into a melting-pot of glorious metals. The meadows and the grasslands became pure gold; the barley field near by, with its long ears, was a live lake of shining silver.

There was only a small patch of straw standing in the rye field, when the woman, alarmed by the change in the light, turned her head a little to get a look at the sun. The while she did not stop her work, but grasped one handful of corn and cut it off, then another, and another. A great stir, and a sound like a manifold, deep sigh, ran through the crowd. The field was now mowed from one end to the other. Only the mower herself did not realize the fact; she stretched out her hand anew, and when she found nothing in it, she seemed puzzled or disappointed. Then she let her arms drop, and slowly sank to her knees.

Many of the women burst out weeping, and the swarm drew close round her, leaving only a small open space at the side where the old lord stood. Their sudden nearness frightened Anne-Marie; she made a slight, uneasy movement, as if terrified that they should put their hands on her.

The boy, who had kept by her all day, now fell on his knees beside her. Even he dared not touch her, but held one arm low behind her back and the other before her, level with her collar-bone, to catch hold of her if she should fall, and all the time he cried aloud. At that moment the sun went down.

The old lord stepped forward and solemnly took off his hat. The crowd became silent, waiting for him to speak. But for a minute or two he said nothing. Then he addressed her, very slowly.

"Your son is free, Anne-Marie," he said. He again waited a little, and added: "You have done a good day's work, which will long be remembered."

Anne-Marie raised her gaze only as high as his knees, and he understood that she had not heard what he said. He turned to the boy. "You tell your mother, Goske," he said, gently, "what I have told her."

The boy had been sobbing wildly, in raucous, broken moans. It took him some time to collect and control himself. But when at last he spoke, straight into his mother's face, his voice was low, a little impatient, as if he were conveying an everyday message to her. "I am free, Mother," he said. "You have done a good day's work that will long be remembered."

At the sound of his voice she lifted her face to him. A faint, bland shadow of surprise ran over it, but still she gave no sign of having heard what he said, so that the people round them began to wonder if the exhaustion had turned her deaf. But after a moment she slowly and waveringly raised her hand, fumbling in the air as she aimed at his face, and with her fingers touched his cheek. The cheek was wet with tears, so that at the contact her fingers lightly stuck to it, and she seemed unable to overcome the infinitely slight resistance, or to withdraw her hand. For a minute the two looked each other in the face. Then softly and lingeringly, like a sheaf of corn that falls to the ground, she sank forward onto the boy's shoulder, and he closed his arms round her.

He held her thus, pressed against him, his own face buried in her hair and head-cloth, for such a long time that those nearest to them, frightened because her body looked so small in his embrace, drew closer, bent down and loosened his grip. The boy let them do so without a word or a movement. But the woman who held Anne-Marie, in her arms to lift her up, turned her face to the old lord. "She is dead," she said.

The people who had followed Anne-Marie all through the day kept standing and stirring in the field for many hours, as long as the evening light lasted, and longer. Long after some of them had made a stretcher from branches of the trees and had carried away the dead woman, others wandered on, up and down the stubble, imitating and measuring her course from one end of the rye field to the other, and binding up the last sheaves, where she had finished her mowing.

The old lord stayed with them for a long time, stepping along a little, and again standing still.

In the place where the woman had died the old lord later on had a stone set up, with a sickle engraved in it. The peasants on the land then named the rye field "Sorrow-Acre." By this name it was known a long time after the story of the woman and her son had itself been forgotten.

JEAN RHYS was born on the island of Dominica in the West Indies in 1894. Her father was a Welsh doctor, her mother a Creole. She still remembers the beautiful place of her childhood: "I think it does something to one to be brought up in such a beautiful place, to know nothing but that." Though she was one of five children, she was lonely. In secret she wrote poetry and plays. "At that early age I learned that you can write out a sadness, and then it isn't so bad. It is the only lucky thing about being a writer. Since then, I have had glimpses of happiness and wealth in my life, but during those periods, I never wanted to write." When she was sixteen, she came to England and took up studies at the Royal Academy of Dramatic Art in London, but had to quit school when her father died. She worked as a chorus girl, joined a touring acting company, and at the end of World War I, after marrying a Dutch poet, moved to the Continent. She had a daughter, Maryvonne. Her husband abandoned her suddenly and her fiction reverberates with the pain of being alone and poor, unable to achieve economic stability. All her heroines are victims; embitterment is a recurring theme.

In Paris she met Stein and Hemingway and Joyce, and Ford Madox Ford launched her writing career in the *Transatlantic Review*. The first to recognize her passion, insight, and what another critic has called her "acid elegance," he later wrote an enthusiastic introduction to her first book, *The Left Bank* (1927). After the publication of *Good Morning, Midnight* (1939) twenty-seven years passed before her next book appeared, *Wide Sargasso Sea*, the well-known and widely praised novel about Bertha Mason, Rochester's mad Creole first wife in *Jane Eyre*. The publication of this book marked the rise of a Jean Rhys cult. She now lives alone, without television or telephone, in a small bungalow in Devon.

Some critics say her books insist that sin is glamorous and sadness rather fine. Others agree that she is one of the most original and memorable writers of our time. "Terrible, but superb," wrote Rebecca West of an early novel. All her work is "years ahead of its time in style, thought, and attitude," wrote Hannah Carter in the *Guardian*. Another reviewer in the same publication wrote, "I rate her higher than Colette." Rhys told an interviewer: "If you want to write the truth, you *must* write about yourself. It must go out from yourself. I don't see what else you can do. I am the only real truth I know."

Jean Rhys
(1894—   )

OUTSIDE THE MACHINE

I

The big clinic near Versailles was run on strictly English lines, so every morning the patients in the women's general ward were woken up at six. They had tea and bread-and-butter. Then they lay and waited while the nurses brought tin basins and soap. When they had washed they lay and waited again.

There were fifteen beds in the tall, narrow room. The walls were painted grey. The windows were long but high up, so that you could see only the topmost branches of the trees in the grounds outside. Through the glass the sky had no colour.

At half-past ten the matron, attended by a sister, came in to inspect the ward, walking as though she were royalty opening a public building. She stopped every now and again, glanced at a patient's temperature chart here, said a few words there. The young woman in the last bed but one on the left-hand side was a newcomer. "Best, Inez," the chart said.

"You came last evening, didn't you?"

"Yes."

"Quite comfortable?"

"Oh yes, quite."

"Can't you do without all those things while you are here?" the matron asked, meaning the rouge, powder, lipstick and hand mirror on the bed table.

"It's so that I shouldn't look too awful, because then I always feel much worse."

But the matron shook her head and walked on without smiling, and Inez drew the sheets up to her chin, feeling bewildered and weak. *I'm cold, I'm tired.*

"Has anyone ever told you that you've very much like Raquel Meller?" the old lady in the next bed said. She was sitting up, wrapped in a black shawl embroidered with pink and yellow flowers.

"Am I? Oh, am I really?"

"Yes, very much like."

"Do you think so?" Inez said.

The tune of *La Violetera*, Raquel Meller's song, started up in her head. She felt happier—then quite happy and rather gay. "Why should I be so damned sad?" she thought. "It's ridiculous. The day after I come out of this place something lucky might happen."

And it was not so bad lying there and having everything done for you. It was only when you moved that you got frightened because you couldn't imagine ever moving again without hurting yourself.

She looked at the row of beds opposite and sighed. "It's rum here, isn't it?"

"Oh, you'll feel different tomorrow," the old lady said. She spoke English hesitatingly—not with an accent, but as if her tongue were used to another language.

The two talked a good deal that day, off and on.

". . . And how was I to know," Inez complained, "that, on top of everything else, my inside would go *kaput* like this? And of course it must happen at the wrong time."

"Now, shut up," she told herself, "shut up. Don't say, 'Just when I haven't any money.' Don't give yourself away. What a fool you are!" But she could not stop the flood of words.

At intervals the old lady clicked her tongue compassionately or said "Poor child." She had a broad, placid face. Her hair was black—surely dyed, Inez thought. She wore two rings with coloured stones on the third finger of her left hand and one—a thick gold ring carved into an indistinguishable pattern—on the little finger. There was something wrong with her knee, it appeared, and she had tried several other hospitals.

"French hospitals are more easy-going, but I was very lucky to get into this place; it has quite a reputation. There's nothing like English nursing. And, considering what you get, you pay hardly anything. An English matron, a resident English doctor, several of the nurses are English. I believe the private rooms are *most* luxurious, but of course they are very expensive."

Her name was Tavernier. She had left England as a young girl and had never been back. She had been married twice. Her first husband was a bad man, her second husband was a good man. Just like that. Her second husband was a good man who had left her a little money.

When she talked about the first husband you could tell that she still hated him, after all those years. When she talked about the good one tears came into her eyes. She said that they were perfectly happy, completely happy, never an unkind word and tears came into her eyes.

"Poor old mutt," Inez thought, "she really has persuaded herself to believe that."

Madame Tavernier said in a low voice, "Do you know what he said in the last letter he wrote to me? 'You are everything to me.' Yes, that's what he said in the last letter I had."

"Poor old mutt," Inez thought again.

Madame Tavernier wiped her eyes. Her face looked calm and gentle, as if she were repeating to herself, "Nobody can say this isn't true, because I've got the letter and I can show it."

The fat, fair woman in the bed opposite was also chatting with her neighbour. They were both blonde, very clean and aggressively respectable. For some reason they fitted in so well with their surroundings that they made everyone else seem dubious, out of place. The fat one discussed the weather, and her neighbour's answers were like an echo. "Hot . . . oh yes, very hot . . . hotter than yesterday . . . yes, much hotter . . . I wish the weather would break . . . yes, I wish it would, but no chance of that . . . no, I suppose not . . . oh, I rather fancy so. . . ."

Under cover of this meaningless conversation the fair woman's stare at Inez was sharp, sly and inquisitive. "An English person? English, what sort of English? To which of the seven divisions, sixty-nine subdivisions, and thousand-and-three subsubdivisions do you belong? (*But only one sauce, damn you.*) My world is a stable, decent world. If you withhold information, or if you confuse me by jumping from one category to another, I can be extremely disagreeable, and I am not without subtlety and inventive powers when I want to be disagreeable. Don't underrate me. I have set the machine in motion and crushed many like you. Many like you . . ."

Madame Tavernier shifted uneasily in her bed, as if she sensed this clash of personalities—stares meeting in mid-air, sparks flying. . . .

"Those two ladies just opposite are English," she whispered.

"Oh, are they?"

"And so is the one in the bed on the other side of you."

"The sleepy one they make such a fuss about?"

"She's a dancer—a 'girl,' you know. One of the Yetta Kauffman girls. She's had an operation for appendicitis."

"Oh, has she?"

"The one with the screen round her bed," Madam Tavernier chattered on, "is very ill. She's not expected to—And the one . . ."

Inez interrupted after a while. "They seem to have stuck all the English down this end, don't they? I wish they had mixed us up a bit more."

"They never do," Madame Tavernier answered. "I've often noticed it."

"It's mistake," said Inez. "English people are usually pleasanter to foreigners than they are to each other."

After a silence Madame Tavernier inquired politely, "Have you travelled a lot?"

"Oh, a bit."

"And do you like it here?"

"Yes, I like Paris much the best."

"I suppose you feel at home," Madame Tavernier said. Her voice was ironical. "Like many people. There's something for every taste."

"No, I don't feel particularly at home. That's not why I like it."

She turned away and shut her eyes. She knew the pain was going to start again. And, sure enough, it did. They gave her an injection and she went to sleep.

Next morning she woke feeling dazed. She lay and watched two nurses charging about, very brisk and busy and silent. They did not even say "Come along," or "Now, now," or "Drink that up."

They moved about surely and quickly. They did everything in an impersonal way. They were like parts of a machine, she thought that was working smoothly. The women in the beds bobbed up and down and in and out. They were parts of a machine. They had a strength, a certainty, because all their lives they had belonged to the machine and worked smoothly, in and out, just as they were told. Even if the machine got out of control, even if it went mad, they would still work in and out, just as they were told, whirling smoothly, faster and faster, to destruction.

She lay very still, so that nobody should know she was afraid. Because she was outside the machine they might come along any time with a pair of huge iron tongs and pick her up and put her on the rubbish heap, and there she would lie and rot. "Useless, this one," they would say; and throw her away before she could explain. "It isn't like you think it is, not at all. It isn't like they say it is. Wait a bit and let me explain. You must listen; it's very important."

But in the evening she felt better.

The girl in the bed on the right, who was sitting up, said she wanted to write to a friend at the theatre.

"In French," she said. "Can anybody write the letter for me, because I don't know French?"

"I'll write it for you," Madame Tavernier offered.

" 'Dear Lili . . . L-i-l-i. Dear Lili . . .' well, say: 'I'm getting all right again. Come and see me on Monday or Thursday. Any time from two to four. And when you come will you bring me some notepaper and stamps? I hope it won't be long before I get out of this place. I'll tell you about that on Monday. Don't forget the stamps. Tell the others that they can come to see me, and tell them how to get here. Your affectionate friend, and so on, Pat.' Give it to me and I'll sign it. . . . Thanks."

The girl's voice had two sounds in it. One was clear and light, the other heavy and ruthless.

"You seem to be having a rotten time, you in the next bed," she said.

"I feel better now."

"Have you been in Paris long?"

"I live here."

"Ah, then you'll be having your pals along to cheer you up."

"I don't think so. I don't expect anybody."

The girl stared. She was not much over twenty and her clear blue eyes slanted upwards a little. She looked as if, standing up, she would be short with sturdy dancer's legs. Stocky, like a little pony.

Oh God, let her go on talking about herself and not looking at me, or sizing me up, or anything like that.

"This French girl, this friend of mine, she's a perfect scream," Pat said. "But she's an awfully obliging girl. If I say, 'Turn up with stamps,' she will turn up with stamps. That's why I'm writing to her and not to one of our lot. Our lot might turn up or they might not. You know. But she's a perfect scream, really. . . . As a matter of fact, she's not bad-looking, but the way she walks is too funny. She's a *femme nue*, and they've taught her to walk like that. It's all right without shoes, but with shoes it's—well . . . you'll see when she comes here. They only get paid half what we do, too. Anyway, she's an awfully obliging kid; she's a sweet kid, poor devil."

A nurse brought in supper.

"The girls are nice and the actors are nice," Pat went on, "but the stage hands hate us. Isn't it funny? You see, one of them tried to kiss one of our lot and she smacked his face. He looked sort of surprised, she said. And then do you know what he did? He hit her back! Well, and do you know what we did? We said to the stage manager, 'If that man doesn't get the sack, we won't go on.' They tried one show without us and then they gave in. The principals whose numbers were spoilt made a hell of a row. The French girls can't do our stuff because they can't keep together. They're all right alone—very good sometimes, but they don't understand team work. . . . And now, my God, the stage hands don't half hate us. We have to go in twos to the lavatory. And yet, the girls and the actors are awfully nice; it's only the stage hands who hate us."

The fat woman opposite—her name was Mrs. Wilson—listened to all this, at first suspiciously, then approvingly. Yes, this is permissible; it has its uses. Pretty English chorus girl—north country—with a happy, independent disposition and bright, teasing eyes. Placed! All correct.

Pat finished eating and then went off to sleep again very suddenly, like a child.

"A saucy girl, isn't she?" Madame Tavernier said. Her eyes were half-shut, the corners of her mouth turned downwards.

Through the windows the light turned from dim yellow to mauve, from mauve to grey, from grey to black. Then it was dark except for the unshaded bulbs tinted red all along the ward. Inez put her arm round her head and turned her face to the pillow.

"Good night," the old lady said. And after a long while she said, "Don't cry, don't cry."

Inez whispered, "They kill you so slowly. . . ."

The ward was a long, grey river; the beds were ships in a mist. . . .

The next day was Sunday. Even through those window panes the sky looked blue, and the sun made patterns on the highly polished floor. The patients had breakfast half an hour later—seven instead of half-past six.

"Only milk for you today," the nurse said. Inez was going to ask why; then she remembered that her operation was fixed for Monday. *Don't think of it yet. There's still quite a long time to go.*

After the midday meal the matron told them that an English clergyman was going to visit the ward and hold a short service if nobody minded. Nobody did mind, and after a while the parson came in through an unsuspected door, looking as if he felt very cold, as if he had never been warm in his life. He had grey hair and a shy, shut-in face.

He stood at the end of the ward and the patients turned their heads to look at him. The screen round the bed on the other side had been taken away and the yellow-faced, shrunken woman who lay there turned her head like the others and looked.

The clergyman said a prayer and most of the patients said "Amen." ("Amen," they said. "We are listening," they said. . . . I am poor bewildered unhappy comfort me I am dying console me of course I don't let on that I know I'm dying but I know I know Don't talk about life as it is because it has nothing to do with me now Say something go on say something because I'm so darned sick of women's voices Christ how I hate women Say something funny that I can laugh at but anything you say will be funny you old geezer you Never mind say something . . . "We are listening," they said, "we are listening. . . .") But the parson was determined to stick to life as it is, for his address was a warning against those vices which would antagonize their fellows and make things worse for them. Self-pity, for instance. Where does that lead you? Ah, where? Cynicism. So cheap. . . . Rebellion. So useless. . . . "Let us remember," he ended, "that God is a just God and that man, made in His image, is also just. On the whole. And so, dear sisters, let us try to

live useful, righteous and God-fearing lives in that state to
which it has pleased Him to call us. Amen."

He said another prayer and then went round shaking
hands. "How do you do, how do you do, how do you do?"
All along the two lines. Then he went out again.

After he had gone there was silence in the ward for a few
seconds, then somebody sighed.

Madame Tavernier remarked, "Poor little man, he was so
nervous."

"Well, it didn't last long, anyway," Pat said. "On and off
like the Demon King. . . ."

She began to sing:

"Oh, he doesn't look much like a lover,
But you can't tell a book by its cover."

Then she sang *The Sheik of Araby*. She tied a towel round
her head for a turban and began again: "Over the desert wild
and free . . . Sing up, girls, chorus. I'm the Sheik of
Arabee. . . ."

Everybody looked at Pat and laughed; the dying woman's
small yellow face was convulsed with laughter.

"There's lots of time before tomorrow," Inez thought. "I
needn't bother about it yet."

"I'm the Sheik of Arabee. . . ." Somebody was singing it
in French—"*Je cherche Antinéa*." It was a curious translation—significant when you came to think of it.

Pat shouted, "Listen to this. Anybody recognize it? Old but
good. 'Who's that knocking at my door? said the fair young
ladye. . . .'"

The tall English sister came in. She had a narrow face,
small deep-set eyes of an unusual reddish-brown colour and a
large mouth. Her pale lips lay calmly one on the other, as if
she were very good-tempered, or perhaps very self-controlled.
She smiled blandly and said, "Now then, Pat, you must stop
this," arranged the screen round the bed on the other side
and pulled down the blind of the window at the back.

It was really very hot after she had gone out again most of
the women lay in a coma, but Pat went on talking. The
sound of her own voice seemed to excite her. She became
emphatic, as if someone was arguing with her.

She talked about love and the difference between glamour
and dirt. The real difference was £—s—d, she said. If there

was some money about there could be some glamour; otherwise, say what you liked, it was simply dirty—as well as foolish.

"Plenty of survival value there," Inez thought. She lay with her eyes closed, trying to see trees and smooth water. But the pictures she made slipped through her mind too quickly, so that they became distorted and malignant.

That night everybody in the ward was wakeful. Somebody moaned. The nurse rushed about with a bed pan, grumbling under her breath.

II

At nine o'clock on Monday morning the tall English sister was saying, "You'll be quite all right. I'm going to give you a morphine injection now."

After this Inez was still frightened, but in a much duller way.

"I hope you'll be there," she said drowsily. But there was another nurse in the operating room. She was wearing a mask and she looked horrible, Inez thought—like a torturer.

Floating in the air, which was easy and natural after the morphine—*Of course, I've always been able to do this. Why did I ever forget? How stupid of me!*—she watched herself walking across the floor with tears streaming down her cheeks, supported by the terrifying stranger.

"Now, don't be silly," the nurse said irritably.

Inez sat down on the edge of the couch, not floating now, not divided. One, and heavy as lead.

"You don't know why I'm crying," she thought.

She tried to look at the sky, but there was a mist before her eyes and she could not see it. She felt hands pressing hard on her shoulders.

"No, no, no, leave her alone," somebody said in French.

The English doctor was not there—only this man, who was also wearing a mask.

"They're so stupid," Inez said in a high, complaining voice. "It's terrible. Oh, what's going to happen, what's going to happen?"

"Don't be afraid," the doctor said. His brown eyes looked kind. "*N'ayez pas peur, n'ayez pas peur.*"

"All right," Inez said, and lay down.

The English doctor's voice said, "Now breathe deeply. Count slowly. One—two—three—four—five—six. . . ."

III

"Do you feel better today?" the old lady asked.

"Yes, much better."

The blind at the back of her bed was down. It tapped a bit. She was sleepy; she felt as if she could sleep for weeks.

"Hullo," said Pat, "come to life again?"

"I'm much better now."

"You've been awfully bad," Pat said. "You were awfully ill on Monday, weren't you?"

"Yes, I suppose I was."

The screen which had been up round her bed for three days had shut her away even from her hand mirror; and now she took it up and looked at herself as if she were looking at a stranger. She had lain seeing nothing but a succession of pictures of the past, always sinister, always too highly coloured, always distorted. She had heard nothing but the incoherent, interminable conversations in her head.

"I look different," she thought.

"I look awful," she thought, staring anxiously at her thin, grey face and the hollows under her eyes. This was very important; her principal asset was threatened.

"I must rest," she thought. "Rest, not worry."

She passed her powder puff over her face and put some rouge on.

Pat was watching her. "D'you know what I've noticed? People who look ghastly oughtn't to put makeup on. You only look worse if you aren't all right underneath—much older. My pal Lili came along on Monday. You should have seen how pretty she looked. I will say for these Paris girls they do know how to make up. . . ."

Yap, yap, yap. . . .

"Even if they aren't anything much—and often they aren't, mind you—they know how to make themselves look all right. I mean, you see prettier girls in London, but in my opinion. . . ."

The screen round the bed on the opposite side had been taken away. The bed was empty. Inez looked at it and said nothing. Madame Tavernier, who saw her looking at it, also said nothing, but for a moment her eyes were frightened.

IV

The next day the ward sister brought in some English novels.

"You'll find these very soothing," she said, and there was a twinkle in her eye. A splendid nurse, that one; she knew her job. What they call a born nurse.

A born nurse, as they say. Or you could be a born cook, or a born clown or a born fool, a born this, a born that . . .

"What's the joke now?" Pat asked suspiciously.

"Oh, nothing. I was thinking how hard it is to believe in free will."

"I suppose you know what you're talking about," Pat answered coldly. She had become hostile for some reason. Not that it mattered. . . .

"Everything will be all right; I needn't worry," Inez assured herself. "There's still heaps of time."

And soon she believed it. Lying there, being looked after and waking obediently at dawn, she began to feel like a child, as if the future would surely be pleasant, though it was hardly conceivable. It was as if she had always lain there and had known everyone else in the ward all her life—Madame Tavernier, her shawl, her rings, her crochet and her travel books, Pat and her repertoire of songs, the two fair, fat women who always looked so sanctimonious when they washed.

The room was wide and the beds widely spaced, but now she knew something of the others too. There was a mysterious girl with long plaits and a sullen face who sometimes helped the nurse to make the beds in the morning—mysterious because there did not seem to be anything the matter with her. She ought to have been pretty, but she always kept her head down and if by chance you met her eyes she would blink and glance away. And there was the one who wore luxury pyjamas, the one who knitted, the other constant reader—watching her was sometimes a frightening game—the one who had a great many visitors, the ugly one, rather like a monkey, who all day sewed something that looked like a pink crêpe-de-chine chemise.

But her dreams were uneasy, and if a book fell or a door banged her heart would jump—a painful echo. And she found herself disliking some of the novels the sister brought.

One day when she was reading her face reddened with anger. *Why, it's not a bit like that. My Lord, what liars these people are! And nobody to stand up and tell them so. Yah, Judas! Thinks it's the truth! You're telling me.*

She glanced sideways. Pat, who was staring at her, laughed, raised her eyebrows and tapped her forehead. Inez laughed back, also tapped her forehead and a moment afterwards was reading again, peacefully.

The days were like that, but when night came she burrowed into the middle of the earth to sleep. "Never wake up, never wake up," her wise heart told her. But the morning always came, the tin basins, the smell of soap, the long, sunlit, monotonous day.

At last she was well enough to walk into the bathroom by herself. Going there was all right, but coming back her legs gave way and she had to put her hand on the wall of the passage for support. There was a weight round the middle of her body which was dragging her to earth.

She got back into bed again. Darkness, quiet, safety—all the same, it was time to face up to things, to arrange them neatly. "One, I feel much worse than I expected; two, I must ask the matron tomorrow if I can stay for another week; they won't want me to pay in advance; three, as soon as I know that I'm all right for another week, I must start writing round and trying to raise some money. Fifty francs when I get out! What's fifty francs when you feel like this?"

That night she lay awake for a long time, making plans. But next morning, when the matron came round, she became nervous of a refusal. "I'll ask her tomorrow for certain." However, the whole of the next day passed and she did not say a word.

She ate and slept and read soothing English novels about the respectable and the respected and she did not say a word nor write a letter. Any excuse was good enough: "She doesn't look in a good temper today. . . . Oh, the doctor's with her; I don't think he liked me much. (Well, I don't like you much either, old cock; your eyes are too close together.) Today's Friday, not my lucky day. . . . I'll write when my head is clear. . . ."

A long brown passage smelling of turpentine led from the ward to the washroom. There were rows of basins along either whitewashed wall, three water closets and two bath-rooms at the far end.

Inez went to one of the washbasins. She was carrying a sponge bag. She took out of it soap, a toothbrush, toothpaste and peroxide.

Somebody opened the door stealthily, hesitated for a moment, then walked past and stood over one of the basins at the far end. It was the sullen girl, the one with the long plaits. She was wearing a blue kimono.

"She does look fed up," Inez thought.

The girl leant over the basin with both hands on its edge. Was she going to be sick? Then she gave a long, shivering sigh and opened her sponge bag.

Inez turned away without speaking and began to clean her teeth.

The door opened again and a nurse came in and glanced round the washroom. It was curious to see the expression on her plump, pink face change in a few moments from indifference to inquisitiveness, to astonishment, to shocked anger.

Then she ran across the room, shouting, "Stop that. Come along, Mrs. Murphy. Give it up."

Inez watched them struggling. Something metallic fell to the floor. Mrs. Murphy was twisting like a snake.

"Come on, help me, can't you? Hold her arms," the nurse said breathlessly.

"Oh, leave me alone, leave me alone," Mrs. Murphy wailed. "Do for God's sake leave me alone. What do you know about it anyway?"

"Go and call the sister. She's in the ward."

"She's speaking to me," Inez thought.

"Oh, leave me alone, leave me alone. Oh, please, please, please, please, please," Mrs. Murphy sobbed.

"What's she done?" Inez said. "Why don't you leave her alone?"

As she spoke two other nurses rushed in at the door and flung themselves on Mrs. Murphy, who began to scream loudly, with her mouth open and her head back.

Inez held on to the basins, one by one, and got to the door. Then she held on to the door post, then to the wall of the passage. She reached her bed and lay down shaking.

"What's up? What's the matter?" Pat asked excitedly.

"I don't know."

"Was it Murphy? You're all right, aren't you? We were wondering if it was Murphy, or . . ."

" 'Or you,' she means," Inez thought. " 'Or you . . .' "

All that evening Pat and the fair woman, Mrs. Wilson, who had become very friendly, talked excitedly. It seemed that they knew all about Mrs. Murphy. They knew that she had tried the same thing on before. Suddenly, by magic, they seemed to know all about her. And what a thing to do, to try to kill yourself! If it had been a man, now, you might have been a bit sorry. You might have said, "Perhaps the poor devil has had a rotten time." But a woman!

"A married woman with two sweet little kiddies."

"The fool," said Pat. "My God, what would you do with a fool like that?"

Mrs. Wilson, who had been in the clinic for some time, explained that there was a medicine cupboard just outside the ward.

"It must have been open," she said. "In *which* case, somebody will get into a row. Perhaps Murphy got hold of the key. That's where she might get the morphine tablets."

But Pat was of the opinion—she said she knew it for a fact, a nurse had told her—that Mrs. Murphy had had the hypodermic syringe and the tablets hidden for weeks, ever since she had been in the clinic.

"She's one of these idiotic neurasthenics, neurotics, or whatever you call them. She says she's frightened of life, I ask you. That's why she's here. Under observation. And it only shows you how cunning they are, that she managed to hide the things. . . ."

"I'm so awfully sorry for her husband," said Mrs. Wilson. "And her children. So sorry. The poor kiddies, the poor sweet little kiddies. . . . Oughtn't a woman like that to be hung?"

Even after the lights had been put out they still talked.

"What's she got to be neurasthenic and neurotic about, anyway?" Pat demanded. "If she has a perfectly good husband and kiddies, what's she got to be neurasthenic and neurotic about?"

Stone and iron, their voices were. One was stone and one was iron. . . .

Inez interrupted the duet in a tremulous voice. "Oh, she's neurasthenic, and they've sent her to a place like this to be cured? That was a swell idea. What a place for a cure for neurasthenia! Who thought that up? The perfectly good, kind husband, I suppose."

Pat said, "For God's sake! You get on my nerves. Stop always trying to be different from everybody else."

"Who's everybody else?"

Nobody answered her.

"What a herd of swine they are!" she thought, but no heat of rage came to warm or comfort her. Sized her up, Pat had. *Why should you care about a girl like that? She's as stupid as a foot. But not when it comes to sizing people up, not when it comes to knowing who is done for. I'm cold, I'm tired, I'm tired, I'm cold.*

The next morning Mrs. Murphy appeared in time to help make the beds. As usual she walked with her head down and her eyes down and her shoulders stooped. She went very slowly along the opposite side of the ward, and everybody stared at her with hard, inquisitive eyes.

"What are you muttering about, Inez?" Pat said sharply.

Mrs. Murphy and the nurse reached the end of the row opposite. Then they began the other row. Slowly they were coming nearer.

"Shut up, it's nothing to do with you," Inez told herself, but her cold hands were clenched under the sheet.

The nurse said, "Pat, you're well enough to give a hand, aren't you? I won't be a moment."

"Idiot," Inez thought. "She oughtn't to have gone away. But they never know what's happening. But yes, they know. The machine works smoothly, that's all."

In silence Pat and Mrs. Murphy started pulling and stretching and patting the sheets and pillows.

"Hullo, Pat," Mrs. Murphy said at last in a low voice.

Pat closed her lips with a righteously disgusted expression.

They turned the sheet under at the bottom. They smoothed it down at the top. They began to shake the pillows.

Mrs. Murphy's face broke up and she started to cry. "Oh God," she said, "they won't let me get out. They won't."

Pat said, "Don't snivel over my pillow. People like you make me sick," and Mrs. Wilson laughed like a horse neighing.

The voice and the laughter were so much alike that they might have belonged to the same person. *Greasy and cold,*

*silly and raw, coarse and thin; everything unutterably horri-
ble.*

"Well, here's bad luck to you," Inez burst out, "you pair of bitches. Behaving like that to a sad woman! What do you know about her? . . . You hold your head up and curse them back, Mrs. Murphy. It'll do you a lot of good."

Mrs. Murphy rushed out of the room sobbing.

"Who was speaking to you?" Pat said.

Inez heard words coming round and full and satisfying out of her mouth—exactly what she thought about them, exactly what they were, exactly what she hoped would happen to them.

"Disgusting," said Mrs. Wilson. "I *told* you so," she added triumphantly. "I knew it, I knew the sort she was from the first."

At this moment the door opened and the doctor came in accompanied, not as usual by the matron, but by the tall ward sister.

Once more, for a gesture, Inez shouted, "This and that to the lot of you!"—"Not the nurse," she whispered to the pillow, "I don't mean her."

Mrs. Wilson announced in a loud, clear voice, "I think that people who use filthy language oughtn't to be allowed to associate with decent people. I think it's a shame that some women are allowed to associate with ladies at all—a shame. It oughtn't to be allowed."

The doctor blinked, but the sister's long, narrow face was expressionless. The two went round the beds glancing at the temperature charts here, saying a few words there. Best, Inez . . .

The doctor asked, "Does this hurt you?"

"No."

"When I press here does it hurt you?"

"No."

They were very tall, thin and far away. They turned their heads a little and she could not hear what they said. And when she began, "I wanted to . . ." she saw that they could not hear her either, and stopped.

v

"You can dress in the washroom after lunch," the sister said next morning.

"Oh, yes?"

There was nothing to be surprised about. So much time had been paid for and now the time was up and she would have to go. There was nothing to be surprised about.

Inez said, "Would it be possible to stay two or three days longer? I wanted to make some arrangements. It would be more convenient. I was idiotic not to speak about it before."

The sister's raised eyebrows were very thin—like two thin new moons.

She said, "I'm sorry, I'm afraid it's not possible. Why didn't you ask before? I told the doctor yesterday that I don't think you are very strong yet. But we are expecting four patients this evening and several others tomorrow afternoon. Unfortunately we are going to be very full up and he thinks you are well enough to go. You must rest when you get back home. Move as little as possible."

"Yes, of course," Inez said; but she thought, "No, this time I won't be able to pull it off, this time I'm done." *"We wondered if it was Murphy—or you. . . ."* Well, it's both of us.

Then her body relaxed and she lay and did not think of anything, for there is peace in despair in exactly the same way as there is despair in peace. Everything in her body relaxed. She did not make any more plans, she just lay there.

They had their midday dinner—roast beef, potatoes and beans, and then a milk pudding. Just like England. Inez ate and enjoyed it, and then lay back with her arm over her eyes. She knew that Pat was watching her but she lay still, peaceful, and thought of nothing.

"Here are your things," the nurse said. "Will you get dressed now?"

"All right."

"I'm afraid you're not feeling up to much. Well, you'll have some tea before you go, won't you? And you must go straight to bed as soon as you get back."

"Get back where?" Inez thought. "Why should you always take it for granted that everybody has somewhere to get back to?"

"Oh yes," she said, "I will."

And all the time she dressed she saw the street, the 'buses and taxis charging at her, the people jostling her. She heard their voices, saw their eyes. . . . When you fall you don't ever get up; they take care of that. . . .

She leant against the wall thinking of Mrs. Murphy's voice when she said, "Please, please, please, please, please. . . ."

After a while she wiped the tears off her face. She did not put any powder on, and when she got into the ward she could only see the bed she was going to lie on and wait till they came with the tongs to throw her out.

"Will you come over here for a moment?"

"There was a chair at the head of each bed. She sat down and looked at the fan-shaped wrinkles under Madame Tavernier's small, dark, melancholy eyes, the swollen blue veins on her hands and the pattern of the gold ring—two roses, the petals touching each other. She read a sentence of the open book lying on the bed: *"De là-haut le paysage qu'on découvre est d'une indescriptible beauté . . ."*

Madame Tavernier said, "That's a charming dress, and you look very nice—very nice indeed."

"My God!" Inez said. "That's funny."

Madame Tavernier whispered, "S-sh, listen! Turn the chair round. I want to talk to you."

Inez turned the chair so that her back was towards the rest of the room.

Madame Tavernier took a handkerchief from under her pillow—a white, old-fashioned handkerchief, not small, of very fine linen trimmed with lace. She put it into Inez' hands. "Here," she said. "S-sh . . . here!"

Inez took the handkerchief. It smelt of vanilla. She felt the notes inside it.

"Take care. Don't let the others see. Don't let them notice you crying. . . ." She whispered. "You mustn't mind these people; they don't know anything about life. You mustn't mind them. So many people don't know anything about life . . . so many of them . . . and sometimes I wonder if it isn't getting worse instead of better." She sighed. "You hadn't any money, had you?"

Inez shook her head.

"I thought you hadn't. There's enough there for a week or perhaps two. If you are careful."

"Yes, yes," Inez said. "Now I'll be quite all right."

She stopped crying. She felt tired, rested and rather degraded. She had never taken money from a woman before. She did not like women, she had always told herself, or trust them.

Madame Tavernier went on talking. "That is quite a lot of

money if you use it carefully," she meant. But that was not what she said.

"Thank you," Inez said, "oh, thank you."

"You'd like some tea before you go, wouldn't you?" the nurse said.

Inez drank the tea, went into the washroom and made up her face. She went back to the old lady's bed.

"Will you give me a kiss?" Madame Tavernier said.

Her powdered skin was soft and flabby as used elastic; it smelt, like her handkerchief, of vanilla. When Inez said, "I'll never forget your kindness, it's made such a difference to me," she closed her eyes in a way that meant, "All right, all all right, all right."

"I'll have a taxi to the station," Inez decided.

But in the taxi she could only wonder what Madame Tavernier would say if she were suddenly asked what it is like to be old—perhaps she would answer, "Sometimes it's peaceful"—and remember the gold ring carved into two roses, and above all wish she were back in her bed in the ward with the sheets drawn over her head. Because you can't die and come to life again for a few hundred francs. It takes more than that. It takes more, perhaps, than anybody is ever willing to give.

CAROLINE GORDON was born in Todd County, Kentucky, in 1895. Her father ran a classical school for boys in Clarksville, Tennessee, and she got her early education there from him. The setting of her first novels is this region—the environs of the Cumberland River near Clarksville which includes a part of Kentucky. In 1924 she married Allen Tate.

Her subject matter is the American Southern experience. Like a number of Southern writers (Flannery O'Connor, Katherine Anne Porter, Eudora Welty), her work reflects her dislike of the liberal-urban society of the North and her admiration for the stable, aristocratic world of the old South. Her Civil War novel *None Shall Look Back* was published soon after *Gone with the Wind* and, as a result, was ignored in the marketplace. But her work has been recognized within the literary establishment. Ford Madox Ford called it "a classical phenomenon . . . an achievement at once of erudition and of sombre and smouldering passion." Andrew Lytle in the *Sewanee Review* wrote: "I know of no writer of fiction that other writers can study with greater profit. Her tension at times seems too severe, as if her image as mask penetrates the passion and, instead of objectifying, freezes it. It causes her characters at times to appear immobile or cold. . . . But certainly she is one of the few distinguished writers of fiction, in the shorter pieces as well as the novels."

Gordon has spoken about her work with the composure and tranquillity Ford admired in her fiction: "I wrote my first novel on my husband's Guggenheim fellowship in 1928. In those days one was required to go abroad in order to receive the award. In France, where living was cheaper than in the United States, I was able to hire a nurse for my child. Otherwise I would not have been able to write the novel. I have never received any honors except an honorary degree from my college, Bethany, in 1946, a Guggenheim fellowship in 1932, and the second O. Henry prize in 1934. My novels do not sell well and hence have received no serious critical consideration. . . ." She now lives and writes in Texas.

Caroline Gordon
(1895—   )

THE PETRIFIED WOMAN

We were sitting on the porch at the Fork—it is where two creeks meet—after supper, talking about our family reunion. It was to be held at a place called Arthur's Cave that year (it has the largest entrance in the world, though it is not so famous as Mammoth), and there was to be a big picnic dinner, and we expected all our kin and connections to come, some of them from as far off as California.

Hilda and I had been playing in the creek all afternoon and hadn't had time to wash our legs before we came in to supper, so we sat on the bottom step where it was dark. Cousin Eleanor was in the porch swing with Cousin Tom. She had on a long white dress. It brushed the floor a little every time the swing moved. But you had to listen hard to hear it, under the noise the creek made. Wherever you were in that house you could hear the creek running over the rocks. Hilda and I used to play in it all day long. I liked to stay at her house better than at any of my other cousins'. But they never let me stay there long at a time. That was because she didn't have any mother, just her old mammy, Aunt Rachel— till that spring, when her father, Cousin Tom, married a lady from Birmingham named Cousin Eleanor.

A mockingbird started up in the juniper tree. It was the same one sang all night long that summer; we called him Sunny Jim. Cousin Eleanor got up and went to the end of the porch to try to see him.

"Do they always sing when there's a full moon?" she asked.

"They're worse in August," Cousin Tom said. "Got their crops laid by and don't give a damn if they do stay up all night."

"And in August the Fayerlees repair to Arthur's Cave," she said. "Five hundred people repairing *en masse* to the womb—what a sight it must be."

Cousin Tom went over and put his arm about her waist.

"Do they look any worse than other folks, taking them by and large?" he asked.

The mockingbird burst out as if he was the one who would answer, and I heard Cousin Eleanor's dress brushing the floor again as she walked back to the swing. She had on tiny diamond earrings that night and a diamond cross that she said her father had given her. My grandmother said that she didn't like her mouth. I thought that she was the prettiest person ever lived.

"I'd rather not take them by and large," she said. "Do we *have* to go, Tom?"

"Hell!" he said. "I'm contributing three carcasses to the dinner. I'm going, to get my money's worth."

"One thing, I'm not going to let Cousin Edward Barker kiss me tomorrow," Hilda said. "He's got tobacco juice on his mustaches."

Cousin Tom hadn't sat down in the swing when Cousin Eleanor did. He came and stood on the step above us. "I'm going to shave off my mustache," he said, "and then the women won't have any excuse."

"Which one will you start with?"

"Marjorie Wrenn. She's the prettiest girl in Gloversville. No, she isn't. I'm going to start with Sally. She's living in town now. . . . Sally, you ever been kissed?"

"She's going to kiss me good night right this minute," Cousin Eleanor said and got up from the swing and came over and bent down and put her hand on each of our shoulders and kissed us, French fashion, she said, first on one cheek and then on the other. We said good night and started for the door. Cousin Tom was there. He put his arm about our waists and bumped our heads together and kissed Hilda first, on the mouth, and then he kissed me and he said, "What about Joe Larrabee now?"

After we got in bed Hilda wanted to talk about Joe Larrabee. He was nineteen years old and the best dancer in town. That was the summer we used to take picnic suppers to the cave, and after supper the band would play and the young people would dance. Once, when we were sitting there watching, Joe Larrabee stopped and asked Hilda to dance, and after that she always wanted to sit on that same bench and when he went past, with Marjorie Wrenn or somebody, she would squeeze my hand tight, and I knew that she thought that maybe he would stop and ask her again. But I didn't think he ever would, and anyway I didn't feel like talking about him that night, so I told her I had to go to sleep.

I dreamed a funny dream. I was at the family reunion at the cave. There were a lot of other people there, but when I'd look into their faces it would be somebody I didn't know and I kept thinking that maybe I'd gone to the wrong picnic, when I saw Cousin Tom. He saw me too, and he stood till I got to where he was and he said, "Sally, this is Tom." He didn't say Cousin Tom, just Tom. I was about to say something but somebody came in between us, and then I was in another place that wasn't like the cave and I was wondering how I'd ever get back when I heard a *knock, knock, knock,* and Hilda said, "Come on, let's get up."

The knocking was still going on. It took me a minute to know what it was: the old biscuit block was on the downstairs back porch right under our room, and Jason, Aunt Rachel's grandson, was pounding the dough for the beaten biscuits that we were going to take on the picnic.

We got to the cave around eleven o'clock. They don't start setting the dinner out till noon, so we went on down into the hollow, where Uncle Jack Dudley and Richard were tending the fires in the barbecue pits. A funny-looking wagon was standing over by the spring, but we didn't know what was in it, then, so we didn't pay any attention, just watched them barbecuing. Thirteen carcasses were roasting over the pits that day. It was the largest family reunion we ever had. There was a cousin named Robert Dale Owen Fayerlee who had gone off to St. Louis and got rich and he hadn't seen any of his kin in a long time and wanted everybody to have a good time, so he had chartered the cave and donated five cases of whisky. There was plenty of whisky for the Negroes too. Every now and then Uncle Jack would go off into the bushes and come back with tin cups that he would pass around. I like to be around Negroes, and so does Hilda. We were just sitting there watching them and not doing a thing, when Cousin Tom came up.

There are three or four Cousin Toms. They keep them straight by their middle names, usually, but they call him Wild Tom. He is not awfully old and has curly brown hair. I don't think his eyes would look so light if his face wasn't so red. He is out in the sun a lot.

He didn't see us at first. He went up to Uncle Jack and asked, "Jack, how you fixed?" Uncle Jack said, "Mister Tom,

I ain't fooling you. I done already fixed." "I ain't going to fool with you, then," Cousin Tom said, and he was pulling a bottle out of his pocket when he saw us. He is a man that is particular about little girls. He said, "Hilda, what are you doing here?" and when we said we weren't doing a thing he said, "You go right on up the hill."

The first person I saw up there was my father. I hadn't expected to see him because before I left home I heard him say, "All those mediocre people getting together to congratulate themselves on their mediocrity! I ain't going a step." But I reckon he didn't want to stay home by himself and, besides, he likes to watch them making fools of themselves.

My father is not connected. He is Professor Aleck Maury and he had a boys' school in Gloversville then. There was a girls' school there too, Miss Robinson's, but he said that I wouldn't learn anything if I went there till I was blue in the face, so I had to go to school with the boys. Sometimes I think that that is what makes me so peculiar.

It takes them a long time to set out the dinner. We sat down on a top rail of one of the benches with Susie McIntyre and watched the young people dance. Joe Larrabee was dancing with Marjorie Wrenn. She had on a tan coat-suit, with buttons made out of brown braid. Her hat was brown straw, with a tan ribbon. She held it in her hand, and it flopped up and down when she danced. It wasn't twelve o'clock but Joe Larrabee already had whisky on his breath. I smelled it when they went past.

Susie said for us to go out there and dance too. She asked me first, and I started to, and then I remembered last year when I got off on the wrong foot and Cousin Edward Barker came along and stepped on me, and I thought it was better not to try than to fail, so I let Hilda go with Susie.

I was still sitting there on top of the bench when Cousin Tom came along. He didn't seem to remember that he was mad at us. He said, "Hello, Bumps." I am not Bumps. Hilda is Bumps, so I said, "I'm just waiting for Hilda . . . want me to get her?"

He waved his hand and I smelled whisky on his breath. "Well, hello, anyhow," he said, and I thought for a minute that he was going to kiss me. He is a man that you don't so much mind having him kiss you, even when he has whisky on his breath. But he went on to where Cousin Eleanor was helping Aunt Rachel set out the dinner. On the way he knocked into a lady and when he stepped back he ran into another one, so after he asked them to excuse him he went off on tiptoe. But he lifted his feet too high and put one of them down in a basket of pies. Aunt Rachel hollered out before she thought, "Lord God, he done ruint my pies!"

Cousin Eleanor just stood there and looked at him. When he got almost up to her and she still didn't say anything, he stopped and looked at her a minute and then he said, "All right!" and went off down the hill.

Susie and Hilda came back and they rang a big bell and Cousin Sidney Grassdale (they call them by the names of their places when there are too many of the same name) said a long prayer, and they all went in.

My father got his plate helped first and then he turned around to a man behind him and said, "You stick to me and you can't go wrong. I know the ropes."

The man was short and fat and had on a cream-colored Palm Beach suit and smiled a lot. I knew he was Cousin Robert Dale Owen Fayerlee, the one that gave all the whisky.

I didn't fool with any of the barbecue, just ate ham and chicken. And then I had some chicken salad, and Susie wanted me to try some potato salad, so I tried that too, and then we had a good many hot rolls and some stuffed eggs and some pickles and some cocoanut cake and some chocolate cake. I had been saving myself up for Aunt Rachel's chess pies and put three on my plate when I started out, but by the time I got to them I wasn't really hungry and I let Susie eat one of mine.

After we got through, Hilda said she had a pain in her stomach and we sat down on a bench till it went away. My grandmother and Aunt Maria came and sat down too. They had on white shirtwaists and black skirts and they both had their palmleaf fans.

Cousin Robert D. Owen got up and made a speech. It was mostly about his father. He said that he was one of nature's noblemen. My grandmother and Aunt Maria held their fans up before their faces when he said that, and Aunt Maria said, "Chh! *Jim* Fayerlee!" and my grandmother said that all that branch of the family was boastful.

Cousin Robert D. Owen got through with his father and started on back. He said that the Fayerlees were descended from Edward the Confessor and *Philippe le Bel* of France and the grandfather of George Washington.

My father was sitting two seats down, with Cousin Edward Barker. "Now ain't that tooting?" he said.

Cousin Edward Barker hit himself on the knee. "I be damn if I don't write to the *Tobacco Leaf* about that," he said. "The Fayerlees have been plain, honest countrymen since 1600. Don't that fool know anything about his own family?"

Susie touched me and Hilda on the shoulder, and we got up and squeezed past my grandmother and Aunt Maria. "Where you going?" my grandmother asked.

"We're just going to take a walk, Cousin Sally," Susie said.

We went out to the gate. The cave is at the foot of a hill. There are some long wooden steps leading up to the top of the hill, and right by the gate that keeps people out if they haven't paid is a refreshment stand. I thought that it would be nice to have some orange pop, but Susie said, "No, let's go to the carnival."

"There isn't any carnival," Hilda said.

"There is, too," Susie said, "but it costs a quarter."

"I haven't got but fifteen cents," Hilda said.

"Here comes Giles Allard," Susie said. "Make out you don't see him."

Cousin Giles Allard is a member of our family connection who is not quite right in the head. He doesn't have any special place to live, just roams around. Sometimes he will come and stay two or three weeks with you and sometimes he will come on the place and not come up to the house, but stay down in the cabin with some darky that he likes. He is a little, warped-looking man with pale blue eyes. I reckon that before a family reunion somebody gives him one of their old suits. He had on a nice gray suit that day and looked just about like the rest of them.

He came up to us and said, "You all having a good time?" and we said, "Fine," and thought he would go on, but he stood and looked at us. "My name is Giles Allard," he said.

We couldn't think of anything to say to that. He pointed his finger at me. "You're named for your grandmother," he said, "but your name ain't Fayerlee."

"I'm Sally Maury," I said, "Professor Maury's daughter." My father being no kin to us, they always call me and my brother Sally Maury and Frank Maury, instead of plain Sally and Frank, the way they would if our blood was pure.

"Let's get away from him," Susie whispered and she said out loud, "We've got to go down to the spring, Cousin Giles," and we hurried on as fast as we could. We didn't realize at first that Cousin Giles was coming with us.

"There comes Papa," Hilda said.

"He looks to me like he's drunk," Susie said.

Cousin Tom stood still till we got up to him, just as he did in my dream. He smiled at us then and put his hand on Hilda's head and said, "How are you, baby?" Hilda said, "I'm all right," and he said, "You are three, sweet, pretty little girls. I'm going to give each one of you fifty cents," and he stuck his hand in his pocket and took out two dollar bills, and when Hilda asked how we were going to get the change out, he said, "Keep the change."

"Whoopee!" Susie said. "Now we can go to the carnival. You come, too, Cousin Tom," and we all started out toward the hollow.

The Negroes were gone, but there were still coals in the barbecue pits. That fat man was kneeling over one, cooking something.

"What you cooking for, fellow?" Cousin Tom asked. "Don't you know this is the day everybody eats free?"

The fat man turned around and smiled at us.

"Can we see the carnival?" Susie asked.

The fat man jumped up. "Yes, *ma'am*," he said, "you sure can see the carnival," and he left his cooking and we went over to the wagon.

On the way the fat man kept talking, kind of singsong: "You folks are in luck. . . . Wouldn't be here now but for a broken wheel . . . but one man's loss is another man's gain . . . I've got the greatest attraction . . . yes, sir. Behind them draperies of pure silk lies the world's greatest attraction."

"Well, what is it?" Cousin Tom asked.

The fat man stopped and looked at us and then he began shouting:

> "Stell-a, Stell-a, the One and Only Stella!
> Not flesh, not bone,
> But calkypyrate stone,
> Sweet Sixteen a Hundred Years Ago
> And Sweet Sixteen Today!"

A woman sitting on a chair in front of the wagon got up and ducked around behind it. When she came out again she had on a red satin dress, with ostrich feathers on the skirt, and a red satin hat. She walked up to us and smiled and said, "Will the ladies be seated?" and the man got some little stools down, quick, from where they were hooked onto the end of the wagon, and we all sat down, except Cousin Giles Allard, and he squatted in the grass.

The wagon had green curtains draped at each end of it. Gold birds were on the sides. The man bent down and pushed a spring or something, and one side of the wagon folded back, and there, lying on a pink satin couch, was a girl.

She had on a white satin dress. It was cut so low that you could see her bosom. Her head was propped on a satin pillow. Her eyes were shut. The lashes were long and black, with a little gold on them. Her face was dark and shone a little. But her hair was gold. It waved down on each side of her face and out over the green pillow. *The pillow had gold fringe on it! . . . lightly prest . . . in palace chambers . . . far apart. . . . The fragrant tresses are not stirred . . . that lie upon her charmèd heart. . . .*

The woman went around to the other side of the wagon. The man was still shouting:

"Stell-a, Stell-a,
The One and Only Stell-a!"

Cousin Giles Allard squeaked like a rabbit. The girl's eyes had opened. Her bosom was moving up and down.

Hilda got hold of my hand and held it tight. I could feel myself breathing. . . . But *her* breathing *is not heard . . . in palace chambers, far apart.* Her eyes were no color you could name. There was a veil over them.

The man was still shouting:

"You see her now
As she was then,
Sweet Sixteen a Hundred Years Ago,
And Sweet Sixteen Today!"

"How come her bubbies move if she's been dead so long?" Cousin Giles Allard asked.

Cousin Tom stood up, quick. "She's a pretty woman," he said, "I don't know when I've seen a prettier woman . . . lies quiet, too. . . . Well, thank you, my friend," and he gave the man two or three dollars and started off across the field.

I could tell that Susie wanted to stay and watch the girl some more, and it did look like we could, after he had paid all that money, but he was walking straight off across the field and we had to go after him. Once, before we caught up with him, he put his hand into his pocket, and I saw the bottle flash in the sun as he tilted it, but he had it back in his pocket by the time we caught up with him.

"You reckon she is sort of mummied, Cousin Tom, or is she just turned to pure rock?" Susie asked.

He didn't answer her. He was frowning. All of a sudden he opened his eyes wide, as if he had just seen something he hadn't expected to see. But there wasn't anybody around or anything to look at, except that purple weed that grows all over the field. He turned around. He hollered, the way he hollers at the hands on the place: "You come on here, Giles Allard!" and Cousin Giles came running. Once he tried to turn back, but Cousin Tom wouldn't let him go till we were halfway up to the cave. He let him slip off into the bushes then.

The sun was in all our eyes. Hilda borrowed Susie's handkerchief and wiped her face. "What made you keep Cousin Giles with us, Papa?" she asked. "I'd just as soon not have him along."

Cousin Tom sat down on a rock. The sun's fiery glare was full on his face. You could see the pulse in his temple beat. A little red vein was spreading over one of his eyeballs. He pulled the bottle out of his pocket. "I don't want him snooping around Stella," he said.

"How could he hurt her, Papa, if she's already dead?" Hilda asked.

Cousin Tom held the bottle up and moved it so that it caught the sun. "Maybe she isn't dead," he said.

Susie laughed out.

Cousin Tom winked his red eye at Susie and shook the bottle. "Maybe she isn't dead," he said again. "Maybe she's just resting."

Hilda stamped her foot on the ground. "*Papa!* I believe you've had too much to drink."

He drank all there was in the bottle and let it fall to the ground. He stood up. He put his hand out, as if he could push the sun away. "And what business is that of yours?" he asked.

"I just wondered if you were going back to the cave, where everybody is," Hilda said.

He was faced toward the cave then, but he shook his head. "No," he said, "I'm not going up to the cave," and he turned around and walked off down the hill.

We stood there a minute and watched him. "Well, anyhow, he isn't going up there where everybody is," Susie said.

"Where Mama is," Hilda said. "It just drives her crazy when he drinks."

"She better get used to it," Susie said. "All the Fayerlee men drink."

The reunion was about over when we got up to the cave. I thought I had to go back to my grandmother's—I was spending the summer there—but Hilda came and said I was to spend the night at the Fork.

"But you got to behave yourselves," Aunt Rachel said. "Big doings tonight."

We rode back in the spring wagon with her and Richard and the ice-cream freezers and what was left of the dinner. Cousin Robert D. Owen and his wife, Cousin Marie, were going to spend the night at the Fork too, and they had gone on ahead in the car with the others.

Hilda and I had long-waisted dimity dresses made just alike that summer. I had a pink sash and she had a blue one. We were so excited while we were dressing for supper that night that we couldn't get our sashes tied right. "Let's get Mama to do it," Hilda said, and we went to Cousin Eleanor's room. She was sitting at her dressing table, putting rouge on her lips. Cousin Marie was in there, too, sitting on the edge of the bed. Cousin Eleanor tied our sashes—she had to do mine twice before she got it right—and then gave me a little spank and said, "Now! You'll be the belles of the ball."

They hadn't told us to go out, so we sat down on the edge of the bed too. "Mama, where is Papa?" Hilda asked.

"I have *no* idea, darling," Cousin Eleanor said. "Tom is a law unto himself." She said that to Cousin Marie. I saw her looking at her in the mirror.

Cousin Marie had bright black eyes. She didn't need to use any rouge, her face was so pink. She had a dimple in one cheek. She said, "It's a *world* unto itself. Bob's been telling me about it ever since we were married, but I didn't believe him, till I came and saw for myself. . . . These little girls, now, how are they related?"

"In about eight different ways," Cousin Eleanor said.

Cousin Marie gave a kind of little yip. "It's just like an English novel," she said.

"They are mostly Scottish people," Cousin Eleanor said, "descended from Edward the Confessor and *Philippe le Bel* of France . . ."

"And the grandfather of George Washington!" Cousin Marie said and rolled back on the bed in her good dress and giggled. "Isn't Bob priceless? But it *is* just like a book."

"I never was a great reader," Cousin Eleanor said. "I'm an outdoor girl."

She stood up. I never will forget the dress she had on that night. It was black but thin and it had a rose-colored bow right on the hip. She sort of dusted the bow off, though there wasn't a thing on it, and looked around the room as if she never had been there before. "I was, too," she said. "I was city champion for three years."

"Well, my dear, you could have a golf course here," Cousin Marie said. "Heaven knows there's all the room in creation."

"And draw off to swing, and a mule comes along and eats your golf ball up!" Cousin Eleanor said, "No, thank you, I'm through with all that."

They went down to supper. On the stairs Cousin Marie put her arm around Cousin Eleanor's waist, and I heard her say, "Wine for dinner. We don't need it." But Cousin Eleanor kept her face straight ahead. "There's no use for us to deny ourselves just because Tom can't control himself," she said.

Cousin Tom was already at the table when we got into the dining room. He had on a clean white suit. His eyes were bloodshot, and you could still see that vein beating in his temple. He sat at the head of the table, and Cousin Eleanor and Cousin Marie sat on each side of him. Cousin Sidney Grassdale and his daughter, Molly, were there. Cousin Sidney sat next to Cousin Marie, and Molly sat next to Cousin Eleanor. They had to do it that way on account of the overseer, Mr. Turner. He sat at the foot of the table, and Hilda and I sat on each side of him.

We usually played a game when we were at the table. It was keeping something going through a whole meal, without the grown folks knowing what it was. Nobody knew we did it except Aunt Rachel, and sometimes when she was passing things she would give us a dig in the ribs, to keep us quiet.

That night we were playing Petrified Woman. With everything we said we put in something from the fat man's song; like Hilda would say, "You want some butter?" and I would come back with, "No, thank you, calkypyrate bone."

Cousin Marie was asking who the lady with the white hair in the blue flowered dress was.

"That is Cousin Olivia Bradshaw," Cousin Eleanor said.

"She has a pretty daughter," Cousin Robert D. Owen said.

"*Mater pulcher, filia pulchrior,*" Cousin Sidney Grassdale said.

"And they live at Summer Hill?" Cousin Marie asked.

Cousin Tom laid his fork down. "I never could stand those Summer Hill folks," he said. "Pretentious."

"But the daughter has a great deal of charm," Cousin Marie said.

"Sweet Sixteen a Hundred Years Ago," Hilda said. "Give me the salt."

"And Sweet Sixteen Today," I said. "It'll thin your blood."

Cousin Tom must have heard us. He raised his head. His bloodshot eyes stared around the table. He shut his eyes. I knew that he was trying to remember.

"I saw a woman today that had real charm," he said.

Cousin Eleanor heard his voice and turned around. She looked him straight in the face and smiled, slowly. "In what did her charm consist, Tom?"

"She was petrified," Cousin Tom said.

I looked at her and then I wished I hadn't. She had blue eyes. I always thought that they were like violets. She had a way of opening them wide whenever she looked at you.

"Some women are just petrified in spots," Cousin Tom said. "She was petrified all over."

It was like the violets were freezing, there in her eyes. We all saw it. Molly Grassdale said something, and Cousin Eleanor's lips smiled and she half bent toward her and then her head gave a little shake and she straightened up so that she faced him. She was still smiling.

"In that case, how did she exert her charm?"

I thought, "Her eyes, they will freeze him, too." But he seemed to like for her to look at him like that. He was smiling, too.

"She just lay there and looked sweet," he said. "I like a

woman to look sweet. . . . Hell, they ain't got anything else to do!"

Cousin Sidney's nose was working up and down, like a squirrel I had once, named Adji-Daumo. He said, "Harry Crenfew seems to be very much in love with Lucy Bradshaw."

"*I'm* in love!" Cousin Tom shouted. "I'm in love with a petrified woman."

She was still looking at him. I never saw anything as cold as her eyes.

"What is her name, Tom?"

"Stell-a!" he shouted. "The One and Only Stell-a!" He pushed his chair back and stood up, still shouting. "I'm going down to Arthur's Cave and take her away from that fellow."

He must have got his foot tangled up in Cousin Marie's dress, for she shrieked and stood up, too, and he went down on the floor, with his wineglass in his hand. Somebody noticed us after a minute and sent us out of the room. He was still lying there when we left, his arms flung out and blood on his forehead from the broken glass. . . . I never did even see him get up off the floor.

We moved away that year and so we never went to another family reunion. And I never went to the Fort again. It burned down that fall. They said that Cousin Tom set it on fire, roaming around at night, with a lighted lamp in his hand. That was after he and Cousin Eleanor got divorced. I heard that they both got married again but I never knew who it was they married. I hardly ever think of them any more. If I do, they are still there in that house. The mockingbird has just stopped singing. Cousin Eleanor, in her long white dress, is walking over to the window, where, on moonlight nights, we used to sit, to watch the water glint on the rocks . . . But Cousin Tom is still lying there on the floor. . . .

ELIZABETH BOWEN was born in Dublin in 1899, and spent her childhood at Bowen's Court in Kildorrery, County Cork. Bowen attended school in England and married in 1923. She spent the years of World War II in London working days for the Ministry of Information, nights as an air-raid warden, and writing continuously—"the only interruption being the necessity to clean up my house from time to time when it had been blasted." Many of her novels of the period 1929–1949 deal with the same theme—a young sensitive person, hopeful and eager for experience, is repulsed, disenchanted and forced to confront the separateness and evil of others. They are stories of disillusionment and loss of innocence.

With *The Heat of the Day* (1949), the last of what one critic has called her major "trilogy" (it began with *The House in Paris* and *The Death of the Heart*), David Daiches says that she moved "out of the ranks of interesting minor writers to become a major modern novelist. Essentially she is, and has always been, a woman's novelist: a term too often used disparagingly to suggest thinness and sentimentality—charges which can never be brought against Elizabeth Bowen's work. But she is a woman's novelist in the sense that she has been concerned primarily with affairs of the heart, with 'the simple love story,' told not in conventional terms, but with a delicacy and sensitivity that raises some of her writings to the level of those of Virginia Woolf, Katherine Mansfield, and Henry James."

In *Why Do I Write,* Bowen (along with V. S. Pritchett and Graham Greene) has written with characteristic grace and intelligence on the art of fiction. As the following remarks indicate, writing to her was a matter of life and breath. "I wrote my first short stories when I was twenty. From the moment that my pen touched paper, I thought of nothing but writing and since then I have thought of practically nothing else. I have been idle for months, or even for a year, at a time; but when I have nothing to write, I feel only half alive."

She died in 1973.

Elizabeth Bowen
(1899—1973)

SUNDAY AFTERNOON

"So here you are!" exclaimed Mrs. Vesey to the newcomer who joined the group on the lawn. She reposed for an instant, her light, dry fingers on his. "Henry has come from London," she added. Acquiescent smiles from the others round her showed that the fact was already known—she was no more than indicating to Henry the role that he was to play. "What are your experiences?—Please tell us. But nothing dreadful: we are already feeling a little sad."

"I am sorry to hear that," said Henry Russel, with the air of one not anxious to speak of his own affairs. Drawing a cane chair into the circle, he looked from face to face with concern. His look traveled on to the screen of lilac, whose dark purple, pink-silver, and white plumes sprayed out in the brilliance of the afternoon. The late May Sunday blazed, but was not warm: something less than a wind, a breath of coldness, fretted the edge of things. Where the lilac barrier ended, across the sun-polished meadows, the Dublin mountains continued to trace their hazy, today almost colorless line. The coldness had been admitted by none of the seven or eight people who, in degrees of elderly beauty, sat here full in the sun, at this sheltered edge of the lawn: they continued to master the coldness, or to deny it, as though with each it were some secret *malaise*. An air of fastidious, stylized melancholy, an air of being secluded behind glass, characterized for Henry these old friends in whose shadow he had grown up. To their pleasure at having him back among them was added, he felt, a taboo or warning—he was to tell a little, but not much. He could feel with a shock, as he sat down, how insensibly he had deserted, these last years, the æsthetic of living that he had got from them. As things were, he felt over him their suspended charm. The democratic smell of the Dublin bus, on which he had made the outward journey to join them, had evaporated from his person by the time he was

half-way up Mrs. Vesey's chestnut avenue. Her house, with
its fanlights and tall windows, was a villa in the Italian sense,
just near enough to the city to make the country's sweetness
particularly acute. Now, the sensations of wartime, that
locked his inside being, began as surely to be dispelled—in
the influence of this eternalized Sunday afternoon.

"Sad?" he said, "that is quite wrong."

"These days, our lives seem unreal," said Mrs. Vesey—
with eyes that penetrated his point of view. "But, worse than
that, this afternoon we discover that we all have friends who
have died."

"Lately?" said Henry, tapping his fingers together.

"Yes, in all cases," said Ronald Cuffe—with just enough
dryness to show how much the subject had been beginning to
tire him. "Come, Henry, we look to you for distraction. To
us, these days, you are quite a figure. In fact, from all we
have heard of London, it is something that you should be
alive. Are things there as shocking as they say—or are they
more shocking?" he went on, with distaste.

"Henry's not sure," said someone, "he looks pontifical."

Henry, in fact, was just beginning to twiddle this far-off
word "shocking" round in his mind, when a diversion caused
some turning of heads. A young girl stepped out of a window
and began to come their way across the lawn. She was Maria,
Mrs. Vesey's niece. A rug hung over her bare arm: she
spread out the rug and sat down at her aunt's feet. With
folded arms, and her fingers on her thin pointed elbows, she
immediately fixed her eyes on Henry Russel. "Good afternoon," she said to him, in a mocking but somehow intimate
tone.

The girl, like some young difficult pet animal, seemed in a
way to belong to everyone there. Miss Ria Store, the pa-
troness of the arts, who had restlessly been refolding her fur
cape, said: "And where have *you* been Maria?"

"Indoors."

Someone said, "On this beautiful afternoon?"

"Is it?" said Maria, frowning impatiently at the grass.

"Instinct," said the retired judge, "now tells Maria it's time
for tea."

"No, this does," said Maria, nonchalantly showing her
wrist with the watch on it. "It keeps good time, thank you,
Sir Isaac." She returned her eyes to Henry. "What have you
been saying?"

"You interrupted Henry. He had been just going to speak."

"*Is* it so frightening?" Maria said.

"The bombing?" said Henry. "Yes. But as it does not connect with the rest of life, it is difficult, you know, to know what one feels. One's feelings seem to have no language for anything so preposterous. As for thoughts—"

"At that rate," said Maria, with a touch of contempt, "your thoughts would not be interesting."

"Maria," said somebody, "that is no way to persuade Henry to talk."

"About what is important," announced Maria, "it seems that no one can tell one anything. There is really nothing, till one knows it oneself."

"Henry is probably right," said Ronald Cuffe, "in considering that this—this outrage is *not* important. There is no place for it in human experience; it apparently cannot make a place of its own. It will have no literature."

"Literature!" said Maria. "One can see, Mr. Cuffe, that *you* have always been safe!"

"Maria," said Mrs. Vesey, "you're rather pert."

Sir Isaac said. "What does Maria expect to know?"

Maria pulled off a blade of grass and bit it. Something calculating and passionate appeared in her: she seemed to be crouched up inside herself. She said to Henry sharply: "But you'll go back, of course?"

"To London? Yes—this is only my holiday. Anyhow, one cannot stay long away."

Immediately he had spoken Henry realized how subtly this offended his old friends. Their position was, he saw, more difficult than his own, and he could not have said a more cruel thing. Mrs. Vesey, with her adept smile that was never entirely heartless, said: "Then we must hope your time here will be pleasant. Is it so very short?"

"And be careful, Henry," said Ria Store, "or you will find Maria stowed away in your baggage. And there would be an embarrassment, at an English port! We can feel her planning to leave us at any time."

Henry said, rather flatly: "Why should not Maria travel in the ordinary way?"

"Why should Maria travel at all? There is only one journey now—into danger. We cannot feel that that is necessary for her."

Sir Isaac added: "We fear, however, that that is the journey Maria wishes to make."

Maria, curled on the lawn with the nonchalance of a feline creature, through this kept her eyes cast down. Another cold puff came through the lilac, soundlessly knocking the blooms together. One woman, taken quite unawares, shivered—then changed this into a laugh. There was an aside about love from Miss Store, who spoke with a cold, abstracted knowledge—"Maria has no experience, none whatever; she hopes to meet heroes—she meets none. So now she hopes to find heroes across the sea. Why, Henry, she might make a hero of you."

"It is not that," said Maria, who had heard. Mrs. Vesey bent down and touched her shoulder; she sent the girl into the house to see if tea were ready. Presently they all rose and followed—in twos and threes, heads either erect composedly or else deliberately bowed in thought. Henry knew the idea of summer had been relinquished: they would not return to the lawn again. In the dining-room—where the white walls and the glass of the pictures held the reflections of summers—burned the log fire they were so glad to see. With her shoulder against the mantelpiece stood Maria, watching them take their places at the round table. Everything Henry had heard said had fallen off her—in these few minutes all by herself she had started in again on a fresh phase of living that was intact and pure. So much so, that Henry felt the ruthlessness of her disregard for the past, even the past of a few minutes ago. She came forward and put her hands on two chairs—to show she had been keeping a place for him.

Lady Ottery, leaning across the table, said: "I must ask you—we heard you had lost everything. But that cannot be true?"

Henry said, unwillingly: "It's true that I lost my flat, and everything in my flat."

"*Henry,*" said Mrs. Vesey, "all your beautiful things?"

"Oh dear," said Lady Ottery, overpowered, "I thought that could not be possible. I ought not to have asked."

Ria Store looked at Henry critically. "You take this too calmly. What has happened to you?"

"It was some time ago. And it happens to many people."

"But not to everyone," said Miss Store. "I should see no reason, for instance, why it should happen to me."

"One cannot help looking at you," said Sir Isaac. "You

must forgive our amazement. But there was a time, Henry, when I think we all used to feel that we knew you well. If this is not a painful question, at this juncture, why did you not send your valuables out of town? You could have even shipped them over to us."

"I was attached to them. I wanted to live with them."

"And now," said Miss Store, "you live with nothing, forever. Can you really feel that that is life?"

"I do. I may be easily pleased. It was by chance I was out when the place was hit. You may feel—and I honor your point of view—that I should have preferred, at my age, to go into eternity with some pieces of glass and jade and a dozen pictures. But, in fact, am very glad to remain. To exist."

"On what level?"

"On any level."

"Come, Henry," said Ronald Cuffe, "that is a cynicism one cannot like in you. You speak of your age: to us, of course that is nothing. You are at your maturity."

"Forty-three."

Maria gave Henry an askance look, as though, after all, he were not a friend. But she then said: "Why should he wish he was dead?" Her gesture upset some tea on the lace cloth, and she idly rubbed it up with her handkerchief. The tug her rubbing gave to the cloth shook a petal from a Chinese peony in the center bowl onto a plate of cucumber sandwiches. This little bit of destruction was watched by the older people with fascination, with a kind of appeasement, as though it were a guarantee against something worse.

"Henry is not young and savage, like you are. Henry's life is—or was—an affair of attachments," said Ria Store. She turned her eyes, under their lids, on Henry. "I wonder how much of you *has* been blown to blazes."

"I have no way of knowing," he said. "Perhaps you have?"

"Chocolate cake?" said Maria.

"Please."

For chocolate layer cake, the Vesey cook had been famous since Henry was a boy of seven or eight. The look, then the taste, of the brown segment linked him with Sunday afternoons when he had been brought here by his mother; then, with a phase of his adolescence when he had been unable to eat, but only to look round. Mrs. Vesey's beauty, at that time approaching its last lunar quarter, had swum on him when he was about nineteen. In Maria, child of her brother's late marriage, he now saw that beauty, or sort of physical genius, at the start. In Maria, this was without hesitation, without the halting influence that had bound Mrs. Vesey up—yes, and bound Henry up, from his boyhood, with her—in a circle of quizzical half-smiles. In revenge, he accused the young girl who moved him—who seemed framed, by some sort of antic-ipation, for the new catastrophic *outward* order of life—of brutality, of being without spirit. At his age, between two generations, he felt cast out. He felt Mrs. Vesey might not forgive him for having left her for a world at war.

Mrs. Vesey blew out the blue flame under the kettle, and let the silver trapdoor down with a snap. She then gave ex-actly one of those smiles—at the same time, it was the smile of his mother's friend. Ronald Cuffe picked the petal from the sandwiches and rolled it between his fingers, waiting for her to speak.

"It is cold, *indoors*," said Mrs. Vesey. "Maria, put another log on the fire—Ria, you say the most unfortunate things. We must remember Henry has had a shock—Henry, let us talk about something better. You work in an office, then, since the war?"

"In a Ministry—in an office, yes."

"Very hard?—Maria, that is all you would do if you went to England: work in an office. This is not like a war in his-tory, you know."

Maria said: "It is not in history yet." She licked round her lips for the rest of the chocolate taste, then pushed her chair a little back from the table. She looked secretively at her wrist-watch. Henry wondered what the importance of time could be.

He learned what the importance of time was when, on his way down the avenue to the bus, he found Maria between two chestnut trees. She slanted up to him and put her hand on the inside of his elbow. Faded dark-pink stamen from the flowers above them had molted down onto her hair. "You have ten minutes more, really," she said. "They sent you off ten minutes before your time. They are frightened someone would miss the bus and come back; then everything would have to begin again. As it is always the same, you would not think it would be so difficult for my aunt."

"Don't talk like that; it's unfeeling; I don't like it," said Henry, stiffening his elbow inside Maria's grasp.

"Very well, then: walk to the gate, then back. I shall be

able to hear your bus coming. It's true what they said—I'm intending to go away. They will have to make up something without me."

"Maria, I can't like you. Everything you say is destructive and horrible."

"Destructive?—I thought you didn't mind."

"I still want the past."

"Then how weak you are," said Maria. "At tea I admired you. The past—things done over and over again with more trouble than they were ever worth?—However, there's no time to talk about that. Listen, Henry: I must have your address. I suppose you *have* an address now?" She stopped him, just inside the white gate with the green drippings: here he blew stamen off a page of his notebook, wrote on the page and tore it out for her. "Thank you," said Maria, "I might turn up—if I wanted money, or anything. But there will be plenty to do: I can drive a car."

Henry said: "I want you to understand that I won't be party to this—*in any way*."

She shrugged and said: "You want *them* to understand"— and sent a look back to the house. Whereupon, on his entire being, the suspended charm of the afternoon worked. He protested against the return to the zone of death, and perhaps never ever seeing all this again. The cruciform lilac flowers, in all their purples, and the colorless mountains behind Mrs. Vesey's face besought him. The moment he had been dreading, returning desire, flooded him in this tunnel of avenue, with motors swishing along the road outside and Maria standing staring at him. He adored the stoicism of the group he had quitted—with their little fears and their great doubts— the grace of the thing done over again. He thought, with nothing left but our brute courage, we shall be nothing but brutes.

"What is the matter?" Maria said. Henry did not answer: they turned and walked to and fro inside the gates. Shadow played over her dress and hair: feeling the disenchantedness of his look at her she asked again, uneasily, "What's the matter?"

"You know," he said, "when you come away from here, no one will care any more that you are Maria. You will no longer be Maria, as a matter of fact. Those looks, those things that are said to you—they make you, you silly little girl. You are you only inside their spell. You may think action is better—but who will care for you when you only act? You will have an identity number, but no identity. Your whole existence has been in contradistinction. You may think you want an ordinary fate—but there is no ordinary fate. And that extraordinariness in the fate of each of us is only recognized by your aunt. I admit that her view of life is too much for me—that is why I was so stiff and touchy today. But where shall we be when nobody has a view of life?"

"You don't expect me to understand you, do you?"

"Even your being a savage, even being scornful—yes, even that you have got from them. Is that my bus?"

"At the other side of the river: it has still got to cross the bridge. Henry—" she put her face up. He touched it with kisses thoughtful and cold. "Good-by," he said, "Miranda."

"—Maria—"

"Miranda. This is the end of *you*. Perhaps it is just as well."

"I'll be seeing you—"

"You'll come round my door in London—with your little new number chained to your wrist."

"The trouble with you is, you're half old."

Maria ran out through the gates to stop the bus, and Henry got on to it and was quickly carried away.

ZORA NEALE HURSTON was born at Eatonville, Florida, in 1903, the daughter of a Baptist preacher and a seamstress. She writes: "I went to grammar school in the village and was generally considered a bright pupil, but impudent and a bit stubborn. There were many beatings, both at home and at school, and a great deal of talk at both places about 'breaking my spirit.' One mile away was a white village, mostly inhabited by white people from Wisconsin, Michigan, and upper New York State. They often visited our village school, and they found me and I found them. They gave me books to read and sent me more when they went North in the summer. I played with their children on their estates. I felt no fear of white faces. The Southern whites in the neighborhood were very friendly and kind, and so I failed to realize that I was any different from them, in spite of the fact that my own village had done its best to impress upon me that white faces were something to fear and be awed by. So I have never been able to achieve race prejudice. I just see people. I see the *man* first, and his race as just another detail of his description."

A recipient of a fellowship in anthropology, she returned to the South after graduating from Barnard to do research in folklore. "While I was working I began to think of writing. I saw that what was being written by Negro authors was all on the same theme—the race problem, and saturated with our sorrows. By the time I graduated from college, I had sensed the falsity of the picture, because I did not find that sorrow. We talk about the race problem a great deal, but go on living and laughing and striving like everybody else. So I saw that what was being written and declaimed was a pose. A Negro writer or speaker was supposed to say those things. It has such a definite pattern as to become approximately folklore.

So I made up my mind to write about my people as they are, and not to use the traditional lay figures."

Hurston became a writer and a much loved teacher at North Carolina College for Negroes. She died in 1960. The first of her many short stories—the one reprinted here—was included in Martha Foley's collection *Two Hundred Years of the Best American Short Stories.*

Zora Neale Hurston
(1903—1960)

THE GILDED SIX-BITS

It was a Negro yard around a Negro house in a Negro settlement that looked to the payroll of the G and G Fertilizer works for its support. But there was something happy about the place. The front yard was parted in the middle by a sidewalk from gate to door-step, a sidewalk edged on either side by quart bottles driven neck down into the ground on a slant. A mess of homey flowers planted without a plan but blooming cheerily from their helter-skelter places. The fence and house were whitewashed. The porch and steps scrubbed white.

The front door stood open to the sunshine so that the floor of the front room could finish drying after its weekly scouring. It was Saturday. Everything clean from the front gate to the privy house. Yard raked so that the strokes of the rake would make a pattern. Fresh newspaper cut in fancy edge on the kitchen shelves.

Missy May was bathing herself in the galvanized washtub in the bedroom. Her dark-brown skin glistened under the soapsuds that skittered down from her wash rag. Her stiff young breasts thrust forward aggressively like broad-based cones with the tips lacquered in black.

She heard men's voices in the distance and glanced at the dollar clock on the dresser.

"Humph! Ah'm way behind time t'day! Joe gointer be heah 'fore Ah git mah clothes on if Ah don't make haste."

She grabbed the clean meal sack at hand and dried herself hurriedly and began to dress. But before she could tie her slippers, there came the ring of singing metal on wood. Nine times.

Missie May grinned with delight. She had not seen the big tall man come stealing in the gate and creep up the walk

© 1933 Story Magazine

grinning happily at the joyful mischief he was about to commit. But she knew that it was her husband throwing silver dollars in the door for her to pick up and pile beneath her plate at dinner. It was this way every Saturday afternoon. The nine dollars hurled into the open door, he scurried to a hiding place behind the cape jasmine bush and waited.

Missie May promptly appeared at the door in mock alarm.

"Who dat chuckin' money in mah do'way?" she demanded. No answer from the yard. She leaped off the porch and began to search the shrubbery. She peeped under the porch and hung over the gate to look up and down the road. While she did this, the man behind the jasmine darted to the china berry tree. She spied him and gave chase.

"Nobody ain't gointer be chuckin' money at me and Ah not do 'em nothin'," she shouted in mock anger. He ran around the house with Missie May at his heels. She overtook him at the kitchen door. He ran inside but could not close it after him before she crowded in and locked with him in a rough and tumble. For several minutes the two were a furious mass of male and female energy. Shouting, laughing, twisting, turning, tussling, tickling each other in the ribs; Missie May clutching Joe and Joe trying, but not too hard, to get away.

"Missie May, take yo' hand out mah pocket!" Joe shouted out between laughs.

"Ah ain't, Joe, not lessen you gwine gimme whateve' it is good you got in you' pocket. Turn it go, Joe, do Ah'll tear yo' clothes."

"Go on tear 'em. You de one dat pushes de needles around heah. Move yo' hand, Missie May."

"Lemme git dat paper sack out yo' pocket. Ah bet it's candy kisses."

"Tain't. Move yo' hand. Woman ain't got no business in a man's clothes nohow. Go way."

"Unhhunh! Ah got it. It 'tis so candy kasses. Ah knowed you had somethin' for me in yo' clothes. Now Ah got to see whut's in every pocket you got."

Joe smiled indulgently and let his wife go through all of his pockets and take out the things that he had hidden there for her to find. She bore off the chewing gum, the cake of sweet soap, the pocket handkerchief as if she had wrested them from him, as if they had not been bought for the sake of this friendly battle.

"Whew! dat play-fight done got me all warmed up," Joe exclaimed. "Got me some water in de kittle?"

"Yo' water is on de fire and yo' clean things is cross de bed. Hurry up and wash yo'self and git changed so we kin eat. Ah'm hongry." As Missie said this, she bore the steaming kettle into the bedroom.

"You ain't hongry, sugar," Joe contradicted her. "Youse jes' a little empty. Ah'm de one whut's hongry. Ah could eat up camp meetin', back off 'ssociation, and drink Jurdan dry. Have it on de table when Ah git out de tub."

"Don't you mess wid mah business, man. You git in yo' clothes. Ah'm a real wife, not no dress and breath. Ah might not look lak one, but if you burn me, you won't git a thing but wife ashes."

Joe splashed in the bedroom and Missie May fanned around in the kitchen. A fresh red and white checked cloth on the table. Big pitcher of buttermilk beaded with pale drops of butter from the churn. Hot fried mullet, crackling bread, ham hock atop a mound of string beans and new potatoes, and perched on the window-sill a pone of spicy potato pudding.

Very little talk during the meal but that little consisted of banter that pretended to deny affection but in reality flaunted it. Like when Missie May reached for a second helping of the tater pone. Joe snatched it out of her reach.

After Missie May had made two or three unsuccessful grabs at the pan, she begged, "Aw, Joe, gimme some mo' dat tater pone."

"Nope, sweetenin' is for us men-folks. Y'all pritty lil frail eels don't need nothin' lak dis. You too sweet already."

"Please, Joe."

"Naw, naw. Ah don't want you to git no sweeter than whut you is already. We goin' down de road a lil piece t'night so you go put on yo' Sunday-go-to-meetin' things."

Missie May looked at her husband to see if he was playing some prank. "Sho nuff, Joe?"

"Yeah. We goin' to de ice cream parlor."

"Where de ice cream parlor at, Joe?"

"A new man done come heah from Chicago and he done got a place and took and opened it up for a ice cream parlor, and bein' as it's real swell, Ah wants you to be one de first ladies to walk in dere and have some set down."

"Do Jesus, Ah ain't knowed nothin' 'bout it. Who de man done it?"

"Mister Otis D. Slemmons, of spots and places—Memphis, Chicago, Jacksonville, Philadelphia and so on."

"Dat heavy-set man wid his mouth full of gold teethes?"

"Yeah. Where did you see 'im at?"

"Ah went down to de sto' tuh git a box of lye and Ah seen 'im standin' on de corner talkin' to some of de mens, and Ah come on back and went to scrubbin' de floor, and he passed and tipped his hat whilst Ah was scourin' de steps. Ah thought Ah never seen *him* befo'."

Joe smiled pleasantly. "Yeah, he's up to date. He got de finest clothes Ah ever seen on a colored man's back."

"Aw, he don't look no better in his clothes than you do in yourn. He got a puzzle gut on 'im and he so chuckle-headed, he got a pone behind his neck."

Joe looked down at his own abdomen and said wistfully, "Wisht Ah had a build on me lak he got. He ain't puzzle-gutted, honey. He jes' got a corperation. Dat make 'm look lak a rich white man. All rich mens is got some belly on 'em."

"Ah seen de pitchers of Henry Ford and he's a spare-built man and Rockefeller look lak he ain't got but one gut. But Ford and Rockefeller and dis Slemmons and all de rest kin be as many-gutted as dey please, Ah'm satisfied wid you jes' lak you is, baby. God took pattern after a pine tree and built you noble. Youse a pritty man, and if Ah knowed any way to make you mo' pritty still Ah'd take and do it."

Joe reached over gently and toyed with Missie May's ear. "You jes' say dat cause you love me, but Ah know Ah can't hold no light to Otis D. Slemmons. Ah ain't never been nowhere and Ah ain't got nothin' but you."

Missie May got on his lap and kissed him and he kissed back in kind. Then he went on. "All de womens is crazy 'bout 'im everywhere he go."

"How do you know dat, Joe?"

"He tole us so hisself."

"Dat don't make it so. His mouf is cut cross-ways, ain't it? Well, he kin lie jes' lak anybody else."

"Good Lawd, Missie! You womens sho is hard to sense into things. He's got a five-dollar gold piece for a stick-pin and he got a ten-dollar gold piece on his watch chain and his mouf is jes' crammed full of gold teethes. Sho wisht it wuz mine. And whut make it so cool, he got moncy 'cumulated. And womens give it all to 'im."

"Ah don't see whut de womens see on 'im. Ah wouldn't give 'im a wink if de sheriff wuz after 'im."

"Well, he tole us how de white womens in Chicago give 'im all dat gold money. So he don't 'low nobody to touch it at all. Not even put dey finger on it. Dey tole 'im not to. You kin make 'miration at it, but don't tetch it."

"Whyn't he stay up dere where dey so crazy 'bout 'im?"

"Ah reckon dey done made 'im vast-rich and he wants to travel some. He says dey wouldn't leave 'im hit a lick of work. He got mo' lady people crazy 'bout him than he kin shake a stick at."

"Joe, Ah hates to see you so dumb. Dat stray nigger jes' tell y'all anything and y'all b'lieve it."

"Go 'head on now, honey and put on yo' clothes. He takin' 'bout his pritty womens—Ah want 'im to see *mine*."

Missie May went off to dress and Joe spent the time trying to make his stomach punch out like Slemmons' middle. He tried the rolling swagger of the stranger, but found that his tall bone-and-muscle stride fitted ill with it. He just had time to drop back into his seat before Missie May came in dressed to go.

On the way home that night Joe was exultant. "Didn't Ah say ole Otis was swell? Can't he talk Chicago talk? Wuzn't dat funny whut he said when great big fat ole Ida Armstrong come in? He asted me, 'Who is dat broad wid de forte shake?' Dat's a new word. Us always thought forty was a set of figgers but he showed us where it means a whole heap of things. Sometimes he don't say forty, he jes' says thirty-eight and two and dat mean de same thing. Know whut he tole me when Ah wuz payin' for our ice cream? He say, 'Ah have to hand it to you, Joe. Dat wife of yours is jes' thirty-eight and two. Yessuh, she's forte!' Ain't he killin'?"

"He'll do in case of a rush. But he sho is got uh heap uh gold on 'im. Dats de first time Ah ever seed gold money. It lookted good on him sho nuff, but it'd look a whole heap better on you."

"Who, me? Missie May youse crazy! Where would a po' man lak me git gold money from?"

Missie May was silent for a time, then she said, "Us might find some goin' long de road some time. Us could."

"Who would be losin' gold money round heah? We ain't

ever seen none dese white folks wearin' no gold money on dey watch chain. You must be figgerin' Mister Packard or Mister Cadillac goin' pass through heah."

"You don't know whut been lost 'round heah. Maybe somebody way back in memorial times lost they gold money and went on off and it ain't never been found. And then if we wuz to find it, you could wear some 'thout havin' no gang of womens lak dat Slemmons say he got."

Joe laughed and hugged her. "Don't be so wishful 'bout me. Ah'm satisfied de way Ah is. So long as Ah be yo' husband, Ah don't keer 'bout nothin' else. Ah'd ruther all de other womens in de world to be dead than for you to have de toothache. Less we go to bed and git our night rest."

It was Saturday night once more before Joe could parade his wife in Slemmons' ice cream parlor again. He worked the night shift and Saturday was his only night off. Every other evening around six o'clock he left home, and dying dawn saw him hustling home around the lake where the challenging sun flung a flaming sword from east to west across the trembling water.

That was the best part of life—going home to Missie May. Their white-washed house, the mock battle on Saturday, the dinner and ice cream parlor afterwards, church on Sunday nights when Missie outdressed any other woman in town— all, everything was right.

One night around eleven the acid ran out at the G. and G. The foreman knocked off the crew and let the steam die down. As Joe rounded the lake on his way home, a lean moon rode the lake in a silver boat. If anybody had asked Joe about the moon on the lake, he would have said he hadn't paid it any attention. But he saw it with his feelings. It made him yearn painfully for Missie. Creation obsessed him. He thought about children. They ought to be making little feet for shoes. A little boy child would be about right.

He saw a dim light in the bedroom and decided to come in through the kitchen door. He could wash the fertilizer dust off himself before presenting himself to Missie May. It would be nice for her not to know that he was there until he slipped into his place in bed and hugged her back. She always liked that.

He eased the kitchen door open slowly and silently, but when he went to set his dinner bucket on the table he bumped it into a pile of dishes, and something crashed to the floor. He heard his wife gasp in fright and hurried to reassure her.

"Iss me, honey. Don't git skeered."

There was a quick, large movement in the bedroom. A rustle, a thud and a stealthy silence. The light went out.

What? Robbers? Murderers? Some varmit attacking his helpless wife, perhaps. He struck a match, threw himself on guard and stepped over the door-sill into the bedroom.

The great belt on the wheel of Time slipped and eternity stood still. By the match light he could see the man's legs fighting with his breeches in his frantic desire to get them on. He had both chance and time to kill the intruder in his helpless condition—half in and half out of his pants— but he was too weak to take action. The shapeless enemies of humanity that live in the hours of Time had waylaid Joe. He was assaulted in his weakness. Like Samson awakening after his haircut. So he just opened his mouth and laughed.

The match went out and he struck another and lit the lamp. A howling wind raced across his heart, but underneath its fury he heard his wife sobbing and Slemmons pleading for his life. Offering to buy it with all that he had. "Please, suh, don't kill me. Sixty-two dollars at de sto'. Gold money."

Joe just stood. Slemmons looked at the window, but it was screened. Joe stood like a rough-backed mountain between him and the door. Barring him from escape, from sunrise, from life.

He considered a surprise attack upon the big clown that stood there laughing like a chessy cat. But before his fist could travel an inch, Joe's own rushed out to crush him like a battering ram. Then Joe stood over him.

"Git into yo' damn rags, Slemmons, and dat quick."

Slemmons scrambled to his feet and into his vest and coat. As he grabbed his hat, Joe's fury overrode his intentions and he grabbed at Slemmons with his left hand and struck at him with his right. The right landed. The left grazed the front of his vest. Slemmons was knocked a somersault into the kitchen and fled through the open door. Joe found himself alone with Missie May, with the golden watch charm clutched in his left fist. A short bit of broken chain dangled between his fingers.

Missie May was sobbing. Wails of weeping without words. Joe stood, and after awhile he found out that he had something in his hand. And then he stood and felt without thinking and without seeing with his natural eyes. Missie May kept on crying and Joe kept on feeling so much and not knowing what to do with all his feelings, he put Slemmons watch charm in his pants pocket and took a good laugh and went to bed.

"Missie May, whut you cryin' for?"

"Cause Ah love you so hard and Ah know you don't love *me* no mo'."

Joe sank his face into the pillow for a spell then he said huskily, "You don't know de feelings of dat yet, Missie May."

"Oh Joe, honey, he said he wuz gointer give me dat gold money and he jes' kept on after me—"

Joe was very still and silent for a long time. Then he said, "Well, don't cry no mo', Missie May. Ah got yo' gold piece for you."

The hours went past on their rusty ankles. Joe still and quiet on one bed-rail and Missie May wrung dry of sobs on the other. Finally the sun's tide crept upon the shore of night and drowned all its hours. Missie May with her face stiff and streaked towards the window saw the dawn come into her yard. It was day. Nothing more. Joe wouldn't be coming home as usual. No need to fling open the front door and sweep off the porch, making it nice for Joe. Never no more breakfast to cook; no more washing and starching of Joe's jumper-jackets and pants. No more nothing. So why get up?

With this strange man in her bed, she felt embarrassed to get up and dress. She decided to wait till he had dressed and gone. Then she would get up, dress quickly and be gone forever beyond reach of Joe's looks and laughs. But he never moved. Red light turned to yellow, then white.

From beyond the no-man's land between them came a voice. A strange voice that yesterday had been Joe's.

"Missie May, ain't you gonna fix me no breakfus'?"

She sprang out of bed. "Yeah, Joe. Ah didn't reckon you wuz hongry."

No need to die today. Joe needed her for a few more minutes anyhow.

Soon there was a roaring fire in the cook stove. Water bucket full and two chickens killed. Joe loved fried chicken and rice. She didn't deserve a thing and good Joe was letting her cook him some breakfast. She rushed hot biscuits to the table as Joe took his seat.

He ate with his eyes in his plate. No laughter, no banter.

"Missie May, you ain't eatin' yo' breakfus'."

"Ah don't choose none, Ah thank yuh."

His coffee cup was empty. She sprang to refill it. When she turned from the stove and bent to set the cup beside Joe's plate, she saw the yellow coin on the table between them.

She slumped into her seat and wept into her arms.

Presently Joe said calmly, "Missie May, you cry too much. Don't look back lak Lot's wife and turn to salt."

The sun, the hero of every day, the impersonal old man that beams as brightly on death as on birth, came up every morning and raced across the blue dome and dipped into the sea of fire every evening. Water ran down hill and birds nested.

Missie knew why she didn't leave Joe. She couldn't. She loved him too much, but she could not understand why Joe didn't leave her. He was polite, even kind at times, but aloof.

There were no more Saturday romps. No ringing silver dollars to stack beside her plate. No pockets to rifle. In fact the yellow coin in his trousers was like a monster hiding in the cave of his pockets to destroy her.

She often wondered if he still had it, but nothing could have induced her to ask nor yet to explore his pockets to see for herself. Its shadow was in the house whether or no.

One night Joe came home around midnight and complained of pains in the back. He asked Missie to rub him down with liniment. It had been three months since Missie had touched his body and it all seemed strange. But she rubbed him. Grateful for the chance. Before morning, youth triumphed and Missie exulted. But the next day, as she joyfully made up their bed, beneath her pillow she found the piece of money with the bit of chain attached.

Alone to herself, she looked at the thing with loathing, but look she must. She took it into her hands with trembling and saw first thing that it was no gold piece. It was a gilded half dollar. Then she knew why Slemmons had forbidden anyone to touch his gold. He trusted village eyes at a distance not to recognize his stick-pin as a gilded quarter, and his watch charm as a for-bit piece.

She was glad at first that Joe had left it there. Perhaps he was through with her punishment. They were man and wife again. Then another thought came clawing at her. He had come home to buy from her as if she were any woman in the long house. Fifty cents for her love. As if to say that he could pay as well as Slemmons. She slid the coin into his Sunday pants pocket and dressed herself and left his house.

Half way between her house and the quarters she met her husband's mother, and after a short talk she turned and went back home. Never would she admit defeat to that woman who prayed for it nightly. If she had not the substance of marriage she had the outside show. Joe must leave *her*. She let him see she didn't want his old gold four-bits too.

She saw no more of the coin for some time though she knew that Joe could not help finding it in his pocket. But his health kept poor, and he came home at least every ten days to be rubbed.

The sun swept around the horizon, trailing its robes of weeks and days. One morning as Joe came in from work, he found Missie May chopping wood. Without a word he took the ax and chopped a huge pile before he stopped.

"You ain't got no business choppin' wood, and you know it."

"How come? Ah been choppin' it for de last longest."

"Ah ain't blind. You makin' feet for shoes."

"Won't you be glad to have a lil baby chile, Joe?"

"You know dat 'thout astin' me."

"Iss gointer be a boy chile and de very spit of you."

"You reckon, Missie May?"

"Who else could it look lak?"

Joe said nothing, but he thrust his hand deep into his pocket and fingered something there.

It was almost six months later Missie May took to bed and Joe went and got his mother to come wait on the house.

Missie May was delivered of a fine boy. Her travail was over when Joe came in from work one morning. His mother and the old women were drinking great bowls of coffee around the fire in the kitchen.

The minute Joe came into the room his mother called him aside.

"How did Missie May make out?" he asked quickly.

"Who, dat gal? She strong as a ox. She gointer have plenty mo'. We done fixed her wid de sugar and lard to sweeten her for de nex' one."

Joe stood silent awhile.

"You ain't ast 'bout de baby, Joe. You oughter be mighty proud cause he sho is de spittin' imagine of yuh, son. Dat's yourn all right, if you never git another one, dat un is yourn.

And you know Ah'm mighty proud too, son, cause Ah never thought well of you marryin' Missie May cause her ma used tuh fan her foot round right smart and Ah been mighty skeered dat Missie May wuz gointer git misput on her road."

Joe said nothing. He fooled around the house till late in the day then just before he went to work, he went and stood at the foot of the bed and asked his wife how she felt. He did this every day during the week.

On Saturday he went to Orlando to make his market. It had been a long time since he had done that.

Meat and lard, meal and flour, soap and starch. Cans of corn and tomatoes. All the staples. He fooled around town for a while and bought bananas and apples. Way after while he went around to the candy store.

"Hello, Joe," the clerk greeted him. "Ain't seen you in a long time."

"Nope, Ah ain't been heah. Been round in spots and places."

"Want some of them molasses kisses you always buy?"

"Yessuh." He threw the gilded half dollar on the counter. "Will dat spend?"

"Whut is it, Joe? Well, I'll be doggone! A gold-plated four-bit piece. Where'd you git it, Joe?"

"Offen a stray nigger dat come through Eatonville. He had it on his watch chain for a charm—goin' round making out iss gold money. Ha ha! He had a quarter on his tie pin and it wuz all golded up too. Tryin' to fool people. Makin' out he so rich and everything. Ha! Ha! Tryin' to tole off folkses wives from home."

"How did you git it, Joe? Did he fool you, too?"

"Who, me? Naw suh! He ain't fooled me none. Know what Ah done? He come round me wid his smart talk. Ah hauled off and knocked 'im down and took his old four-bits way from 'im. Gointer buy my wife some good ole lasses kisses wid it. Gimme fifty cents worth of dem candy kisses."

"Fifty cents buys a mighty lot of candy kisses, Joe. Why don't you split it up and take some chocolate bars, too. They eat good, too."

"Yessuh, dey do, but Ah wants all dat in kisses. Ah got a lil boy chile home now. Tain't a week old yet, but he kin suck a sugar tit and maybe eat one them kisses hisself."

Joe got his candy and left the store. The clerk turned to

the next customer. "Wist I could be like these darkies. Laughin' all the time. Nothin' worries 'em."

Back in Eatonville, Jo reached his own front door. There was the ring of singing metal on wood. Fifteen times. Missie May couldn't run to the door, but she crept there as quickly as she could.

"Joe Banks, Ah hear you chuckin' money in mah do'way. You wait till Ah get mah strength back and Ah'm gointer fix you for dat."

M(ary) F(rances) K(ennedy) FISHER was born in California in 1908. She attended a private school for girls in California, colleges in that state and in Illinois, and also the University of Dijon, France, from which she graduated in 1931. She has written many books on the subject of food: *Serve It Forth, How to Cook a Wolf, Consider the Oyster, The Gastronomical Me*, and most recently she translated and annotated *The Physiology of Taste* by Jean Anthelme Brillat-Savarin. These books were well-received, but Clifton Fadiman remarked that Mrs. Fisher was really born to write novels. Her first novel, *Not Now But* Now, defied the ordinary rules of structure and like her many short stories, deserved attention, in the words of one critic, "as the product of a richly civilized and fearless mind." She lives on a California ranch that has an herb garden and a "vineyard." Her favorite authors are Thackeray and Virginia Woolf.

M. F. K. Fisher
(1908—   )

THE WIND-CHILL FACTOR
OR, A PROBLEM OF MIND AND MATTER

There was some doubt in the woman's mind about whether it would be wise to try to make notes on her experience at once or let the long blizzard go through a fifth noisy night. Perhaps putting onto paper what had happened to her could make things worse, invite another such experience, and she was not sure how well she would handle it or, more truthfully, if she could survive.

Her name was Mrs. Thayer, and she was living alone in a friend's cottage, ideally installed for a solitary good few months on wild dunes toward the tip of Long Island. The house faced the ocean, and except for the earth's rounding she could have looked east to Portugal and south to Cuba. In the rooms heated by electricity, things were cozy and fine until an uncommonly sustained blizzard moved onto that part of the planet and onto that tiny spit of sand, like a bull covering and possessing the cow, the warm shelter.

On the fourth night of the storm, Mrs. Thayer was used to adjusting the thermostats in each of the five heated rooms, turning the one in the bathroom up when she could no longer put off a shower and the one in her bedroom down once the electric pad had warmed her guts. The house had a kind of private weather station on one wall, and the barometer and thermometer worked among all the other gadgets that did not: meters for wind velocity and wind direction, a tide clock, something called a durotherm hygrometer. The ship's bells that were part of it sounded later and later, and finally went silent. Now and then a delicate needle spun meaninglessly in one of the brass puddings with their crystal crusts as the blizzard yowled above and around. Mrs. Thayer found that she looked at them fairly often, as if to keep track of what might really be happening, and noticed blandly when the barometer dropped in a few hours from 30.15 to 29.60—whatever that might mean.

She also accustomed herself to listen through the static on the kitchen radio to mysteriously progressing reports about ice conditions on New York and Boston streets, about the amount of garbage that lay on their sidwalks. She herself had no such problems, for the car in her friend's garage would not start, and she made so little rubbish that it was all right to put it neatly in an unheated corridor until the wind stopped. Another problem in the cities was animals, the radio reported. Mrs. Thayer was, for the first time in her many lives, without a four-legged friend, a fact that may have added to the severity of her experience on the fourth night.

The wind, which during the first two days had shifted capriciously this way and that, settled into a northwest blow, fiercely insistent. It bent the grasses almost flat on the dunes, and when occasional dry snow piled up in corners it soon soiled the sculptured drifts with yellowish sand from the implacable surf. Waves changed from long piling rollers to mighty beasts wearing spume four times their height.

Mrs. Thayer found after the third night that as she slipped into good sleep it would seem for a few minutes as if she were being rocked, moved, gently tipped by what was happening outside the tight little shelter. She knew that she did not actually feel this, but she accepted it as a part of being so intimately close to the majesty she lay beside.

The air grew steadily colder, and along there in the dunes (the natives knew better than to build anywhere but inland in such brutal country) Mrs. Thayer closed off rooms she did not need and limited herself to the kitchen, the bedroom, the toilet. Everything stayed cozy for her, with no apprehensions: if the electricity went off, she would wait for people who knew she was there to get her to somehow, before the place grew too cold. Almost nonchalantly she tried not to think about such things, even when the telephone failed. It would ring clearly, but when she answered there would be only a wild squawk on the line. She suspected that her own voice might be heard, and would say in a high, firm way, "This is Mrs. Thayer. Everything is all right. I am all right. Thank you." It was childish to feel rather pleased and excited about the game, but she did.

The night of the fourth day, she ate a nice supper at the table in the warm kitchen, adjusted thermostats, and tidied herself, with parts of at least six books to read first. In bed, she turned on the electric warmer and succumbed late but easily to sleep, at one o'clock in the morning. She felt well fed, warm, and serene.

A little after four, an extraordinary thing happened to her. From deep and comfortable dreamings she was wrenched into the conscious world, as cruelly as if she had been grabbed by the long hairs of her head. Her heart had changed its slow, quiet beat and bumped in her rib cage like a rabbit's. Her breath was caught in a kind of net in her throat, not going in and down fast enough. She touched her body and it was hot, but her palms felt clammy and stuck to her.

Within a few seconds she knew that she was in a state— perhaps dangerous—of pure panic. It had nothing to do with physical fear, as far as she could tell. She was not afraid of being alone, or of being on the dunes in a storm. She was not afraid of bodily attack, rape, all that. She was simply in panic, or what Frenchmen home from the Sahara used to call *le cafard affolé.*

This is amazing, she said. This is indescribable. It is here. I shall survive it or else run out howling across the dunes and die soon in the waves and the wind. Such a choice seemed very close and sweet, for her feeling was almost intolerably wishful of escape from the noise. It was above and against and around her, and she felt that it was invading her spirit. This is dangerous indeed, she said, and I must try not to run outside. That is a suicide wish, and weak. I must try to breathe more slowly, and perhaps swallow something to get back my more familiar rhythms. She was speaking slowly to her whole self, with silent but precise enunciation.

She waited for some minutes to see if she could manage the breathing in bed, but her heart and lungs were almost out of control when she got unsteadily to her feet, tied her night robe around her, and went into the little toilet. There it took a minute to get her hand to turn on the light, for she was racked with a kind of chill that made her lower back and thighs ache as if she were in labor, and her jaws click together like bare bones. She remembered that in her friend's mirror cabinet was a bottle of aspirin, and with real difficulty, almost as if she were spastic, she managed to shake two into her hand, fill a mug with water, and swallow the pills. If you cannot swallow, she said flatly, you are afraid of your enemy. She felt sick, and won this tiny battle of holding down the medicine at great moral cost, for by now in the astounding

onslaught she was as determined as an apparently insensate
animal not to submit to the roaring all around her.

She dared not look at herself for a time but walked in a
staggering way about the bedroom and kitchen, recalling
methods she had studied, and even practiced, for self-preser-
vation. There was one, taught to her during a period of deep
stress, in which one takes three slow sips of almost any liquid, then waits a set period—from five to fifteen minutes—
and takes three more, and so on. She devoted her whole
strength to this project. She carefully heated some milk, and
when she could not open the bottle of angostura, which might
have taken the curse off the potion's insipidity, she poured in
two big spoonfuls of sugar. It was a revolting brew, but she
drank about half a mugful of it over the next period of carefully repulsed frenzy.

The wind had become different. Its steady pressure of
sound had changed to a spasmodic violence. Snow was sting-
ing against the northern and western storm windows, and
Mrs. Thayer already knew that the doors on those sides of
the cottage were frozen shut. It did not matter. A door to the
outside place where people changed bathing suits in the summer began to bang hard, in irregular patterns. It is unhinged,
she said with a sly grin. That did not matter, either. Nothing
mattered except to keep herself inside her own skin, and with
real sweat she did.

She pulled every trick out of the bagful she had collected
during her long life with neurotics. She brushed her hair
firmly, and all the while her heart kept ticking against her
ribs and she felt so sick that she could scarcely lift her arm.
She tried to say some nursery rhymes and the Twenty-third
Psalm, but with no other result than an impatient titter. She
sipped the dreadful sweet milk. She prayed to those two pills
she had swallowed.

If I permit myself to think in my present terms, I am done
for. It is a question of moral energy, she said in rounded
words and clearly punctuated sentences, in a silent voice that
rang in her head like Teacher's, like Father Joseph's, like Dr.
Rab's. Subconsciously I am admitting that the storm is great
and I am small, and for a time or possibly forever I have lost
the balance that human beings must maintain between their
own inner force and that of Nature. I was unaware of what
the wind and the ocean were doing to me. I have been respectful and awed, but naïve. Now I am being told. Told off.

Yes, she said, I am admitting it. But do I have to bow any deeper, cry "uncle," lose everything?

She went on like this as she walked feebly about the rooms. Heavy curtains moved in the fierce air, and she added long woollen socks and a leather coat to her coverings, then as part of her dogged rescue work she focussed on a mirror enough to arrange her hair nicely and put on firm eyebrows and a mouth that looked poutish instead of hard, as she had intended. This is simply going on too long, she said like a woman on the delivery table, and added more lipstick.

For a time, as the aspirin and the warm milk seemed to slow down her limitless dread (Dread of what? Not that the roof would fly off, that she was alone, that she might die . . .), she made herself talk resonably to what was pulling and trembling and flickering in her spirit. She was a doctor—or, rather, an unwitting bystander caught in some kind of disaster, forced to be cool and wise with one of the victims, perhaps a child bleeding toward death or an old man pinned under a truck wheel. She talked quietly to this helpless, shocked soul fluttering in its poor body. She was strong and calm. All the while, she knew cynically that she was nonexistent except in the need thrust upon her, and that the victim would either die or recover and forget her dramatic saintliness before the ambulance had come.

"Listen to your breathing," she said coolly. "You are not badly hurt. Soon you will feel all right. Sip this. It will make the pain go away. Lift your head now, and breathe slowly. You are not really in trouble." And so on. Whenever the other part of Mrs. Thayer, the threatened part, let her mind slip back to the horror of an imminent breaking with all reason—and then, so then, out the door it would be final—the kindly stranger seemed to sense it in the eyeballs and the pulse as she bent over the body and spoke more firmly: "Now hold the cup. You can. I know you can. You will be all right."

This became monotonous, and in fact it was embarrassing to have the two things floating inside her as she tried deliberately to go with the sounds of the gale instead of letting her consciousness accept them and undermine her. At last she said rudely to the creature who had been trying to give her some help, "Go away. I *will* be all right." And the kindly-stranger part of her shrugged and withdrew, knowing there was nothing more to do, knowing she would not have been dismissed if Mrs. Thayer depended on her any further.

The next step was to try to read. But she found it hard to concentrate on the print, and when she did it was on sentences picked hit or miss from this page or that. There was one from an anonymous book called "Streetwalker": ". . . to admit fear and weakness to any living soul . . . would be to reveal my unfitness for the life I have chosen, and, since no other is now possible for me, to reach the limits of despair—and God knows what would happen then."

I am being played with, Mrs. Thayer said angrily, and with care put the book back in its shelf place and then was reading in a controlled way while her heart thugged along and she felt wambly all over "This is the day for each of us to assess our own strength, in utter silence to plumb the depth of our own spirit." What in God's name was she looking at? She saw coldly the title "Second Thoughts," by old man Mauriac, and all her admiration of a lot of things in him turned into fuming jelly, and she tossed the book on the floor and started to walk about the little house again.

Mrs. Thayer's secret balance, the stuff like the fluid of the inner ear, was centered now a little below her diaphragm, and she walked with special care, in order to keep the whole place from crushing like an egg as the giant thrashed.

Her father had talked often about a couple of years he'd spent as a reporter in North Dakota. He said that farm women went stark mad there because in their lonely cabins, when they looked out the window, the snow would always be blowing horizontally. Always. It sent them mad. For them, it was not the wind. The sideways snow did it.

Mrs. Thayer knew. The sound of the wind, for her, had been going sideways exactly on a line with the far horizon of the Atlantic for days, nights—too long. It was in her bowels, and suddenly they were loosened, and later, again to her surprise, she threw up. She told herself dizzily that the rhythm of the wind had bound her around, and that now she was defying it, but it kept on howling.

The pills worked, helped by the warm drink. The human parts of her body helped. The mind did not fail her, and she knew all the time—or, at least, brought herself by degrees to believe so—that she would never have run out like a beast, to die quickly on the dunes. Once, she stopped roaming and lay down, feeling purged and calmer, but the minute she was flat on the bed she heard the wind pressing against the wall beyond her head, and it was as if she were locked in a cell and in the next one a giant lay in his last agony, breathing with a terrible rage and roar. She got up and brushed at her hair again, and then walked with a decreasing stagger about the little rooms.

In another two hours everything was all right inwardly with her, except that she was languid, as if she had lain two weeks in a fever. The panic that had seized her bones and spirit faded fast, once routed. She was left wan and bemused. Never had she been afraid—that is, of tangibles like cold and sand and wind. She was not afraid, as far as she knew, of dying either fast or slowly. It was, she decided precisely, a question of sound. If the storm had not lasted so long, with its noise so much into her, into her brain and muscles . . . If this had been a kind of mating, it was without joy.

Gradually, she was breathing with deep but not worried rhythm as she lay under a cover on her bed. The wind still thrust at her, but she sensed that the giant was in that state of merciful lull that rewards old scoundrels in their final throes—he was not choking and hitting out at her. She got up carefully and did several small things, like polishing her finger-nails, and then she poached an egg in some beef broth and ate it. She felt as hollow as an old shell, and surprisingly trembly. She slept for two hours, out like a drunk.

The whole peculiar experience was still in her mind when she wakened. Why had it happened? Was it a question of decibels, of atmospheric pressure? Had her ears simply been too long assaulted by the pullulations of the violently moving air about her? Where was *she*, then? All of this puzzled her, and she found herself hoping like a child that the air would be calmer, and soon.

She permitted herself the weakness of one gentle tap on the barometer and felt no real dismay when its thin, fluttering indicator went down a little more. If there was any message in it, perhaps it said that since Mrs. Thayer had lived through the past hours she would never know them again. It is probable, she said, that if I must, I shall bow, succumb, admit great strength.

There was no point in thinking much about this in her weak, lackadaisical state, so she wrote a few notes to herself, not caring if they might bring on more wind or not, and went to bed. And during the late afternoon, while she dozed with a deep, soft detachment, the sound abated and then died, and she was lost in the sweet dream life of a delivered woman.

MARGUERITE YOUNG was born in Indianapolis in 1909. Educated at Midwestern universities, she had had two volumes of poetry published before embarking on *Miss MacIntosh, My Darling*, the eleven-hundred-and-ninety-seven-page epic which was to occupy her for eighteen years. The novel is Vera Cartwheel's account of her search for her old nurse. Vera's mother is the "beautiful opium lady," who lives among dreams in New England and rejects the very idea of certainty; everyone else that Vera recalls or encounters is possessed by illusion. Miss MacIntosh, long lost and presumed drowned, represents by contrast the principle of common-sense reality. But when she is at last discovered, she is hairless, incomplete, false. Life is seen to be "imagination even to the last tenth."

For some critics the novel was a failure—"self-indulgent," "amorphous," etc. Others were ecstatic. William Goyen in *The New York Times* wrote of Young's "masterwork": "The fluent, seminal passages . . . spurt forth in some of the richest, most expressive, most original and exhaustively revealing passages of prose that this reader has experienced in a long time. . . . In *Miss MacIntosh, My Darling* we have come upon a strong, deep loudness, a full-throated outcry, a literature of expanse and daring that makes most of our notable male writers look like a motorcycle gang trying to prove a kind of literary masculinity. . . ." In *The Novel of the Future*, Anaïs Nin writes: "Everything I have said about writing, every attitude, theory, technique, suggestions and indications, can be learned from the richest source of all, the work of Marguerite Young. Her work represents the nourishment which every young writer needs. It is endlessly fecund and fecundating, it develops free association, inner monologues, and psychological reality to the highest degree. It is a constant feast of images, both profound and comical. . . . I believe this book represents the nocturnal America just as *Don Quixote* became the spirit of Spain, and *Ulysses* that of Ireland. For Marguerite Young, herself a native Midwesterner, Americans are the wildest dreamers of all, and also the greatest poets."

Young lives in Greenwich Village in a small apartment crammed with sculptures and paintings, many of them of angels.

Marguerite Young
(1909—   )

From MISS MACINTOSH, MY DARLING

There was now no landscape but the soul's, and that is the inexactitude, the ever shifting and the distant. I would never know the man's name, the organization of this fleeting image, what were his hopes, what were his disappointments. Yet he would remain forever engraved on memory's whirling disc, that double-headed shape in curdled mist, as tantalizing as my ignorance of life. All my life I had been reaching for the tangible, and it had evaded me, much like the myth of Tantalus, much as if the tangible itself were an illusion. My life had been made up of just these disrelated, delusive images hovering only for a moment at the margin of consciousness, then passing like ships in the night, even ships manned by dead helmsmen, by ghostly crews, by one's own soul at large.

What was the organization of illusion, of memory? Who knew even his own divided heart? Who knew all hearts as his own? Among beings strange to each other, those divided by the long roarings of time, of space, those who have never met or, when they meet, have not recognized as their own the other heart and that heart's weakness, have turned stonily away, would there not be, in the vision of some omniscient eye, a web of spidery logic establishing the most secret relationships, deep calling to deep, illuminations of the eternal darkness, recognitions in the night world of voyager dreams, all barriers dissolving, all souls as one and united? Every heart is the other heart. Every soul is the other soul. Every face is the other face. The individual is the one illusion.

I had walked alone, searching, seeing only, though I sought for an ultimate harmony, the fleeting image, the disrelation, the chaos begetting the chaos, the truth as but another illusion, that which must perish, the rose which must fade, the heart which must stop. Nothing I had touched but that it had faded like a dream, there being no dream that would not fail, no life which would not cease, no soul which answered mine like deep calling to deep. I had walked alone, the seeker through mazes of sorrow, and none had answered me. That background of illusion from which I always fled like a drowning man who clutches at a straw, it was always that background of illusion confronting me again, even as the foreground, and there seemed no truth but what the erroneous mind provided, another dream which had nor purpose nor bearing. There were always the dead seagulls in the whirlwind, the brown leaves falling, an empty, resonant house of broken mirrors reflecting the light of the sea, my mother dead among her dreams, many others dead with her who had dreamed her life away and who still might be dreaming, for death might still be her life, and she had been already so much a part of the ethereal and of the abstract, of the things intangible, of the things unknown. I had peered into all faces, seeing none, only those who were already gone, only those who could not answer. My illness had been great, dead souls like the autumn leaves stirring where I walked, and could I have believed in that ultimate harmony, I could have been among them, but there had been only, in my narrow experience, the dream of chaos repeating chaos, so what I looked for always in the streets of those great harbor cities, was it not merely another illusion, that of the peace which should not be realized in heaven or on earth? Where should I go? Where should I turn? I had been too long half sleeping, cut off from communication with others, asking no more reasonable questions than a patient asks under the ether mask which seems to a train ride among the trackless stars or where there are no stars, no signposts any longer, and no one has ever seen the other person. All the other passengers, Negroes with white roosters crowing in their laps, beings unseen, merely sensed, each with his own dark and private heart, the darkness everlasting, their questions like my own, and no answer heard, for God is the loneliest of all, and there is perhaps no God but what we dreamed, and there is no train.

Long nights, searching for one who was dead, I, Vera Cartwheel, I, the imploring daughter of a mother under the sway of opium, a mother more beautiful than angels of light, I, Vera Cartwheel, had wandered through the streets of great, mysterious harbor cities, those which, at night, seemed all like each other, there where were the spectral faces appearing like foam, disappearing, faces as lost as mine, voices crying under

water, seaweed locked in the hair of the drowned swimmer. I
had slept in shelters for lost souls, those no one should miss,
searching for one who was lost, forever outside, alone, the
one person not dreaming and yet who had seemed, with the
passage of years since her disappearance from my life, the
central heart, the heart of all hearts, the face of all faces, the
dead steersman, Miss MacIntosh, my darling, an old, red-
headed nurse-maid with her face uplifted toward the watery
sky. I had walked through the desolate waterfront streets of
those dark and intricate harbor cities, the neighborhoods of
warehouses casting their shadows, shelters for old sailors, for
lost souls, darkened lighthouses, had turned down the un-
lighted alleys where the starved cats prowl among refuse,
gleaming fish, the drunken mariner lurches, the prostitute
screams, had looked into every muffled doorway, under every
dimmed, leering lamp, had searched for her among faceless
old beggar women huddled in empty parks, the ragged men
who sleep on fly-specked sidewalks, their mouths foaming
with homeless dreams, had searched for her in old-fashioned
saloons and bowling alleys and billiard parlors and under the
falling leaves, had walked in whirling crowds that I might
find her, had stopped at all corners where street preachers
preached of the golden tides of the future world and harvests
of dragons' teeth and reaping the whirlwind, had gone to
baseball games in those packed stadiums, watching the pitchers pitch the moons, the suns, the stars, had visited a plane-
tarium and an aquarium and a museum, had drifted with no
purpose but this, had followed everywhere, searching for her,
one so clear, thinking that, some day, just when I lost my
way in the absolute darkness or crossed a traffic-roaring avenue of obliterating head lights, screeching whistles, screaming
stars, I should surely find her, Miss MacIntosh, my darling,
only a step beyond, her whaler's hat dripping with water, her
plaid, faded water-proof flapping in the wind, her bent black
umbrella uplifted like some enormous, dark, scudding bird
against the clouded sky, the always overcast.

Long years, drifting without otherpurpose, I had searched
for that hale companion of my lost childhood, no one but a
fusty, busty old nursemaid, very simple-minded, very simple,
the salt of common sense, her red hair gleaming to show that
quick temper she always had, that impatience with which she
would dismiss all shades and phantoms, even herself should
she become one, for self-pity was not her meat, not her drink.
Long years, my heart a dry, imploring emptiness, my eyes

fixed on that one steady purpose, I had drifted from employment to employment, from hotel to hotel, searching re-
lentlessly and everywhere for that old, plain darling who was
lost, she who had cherished no illusions of noble grandeur,
she who had rejected an aura, a crown of gold, she whose
daily life had been unpresuming and hard, one not beloved
then so much as now in memory, the dead steersman, her
whaler's hat dripping with water, her boundless face
concealed by fog and wind, her heart the weakness of all
hearts, the strength. Where should I not find her again?
Where should I ever find her? The years of her death had
added to her stature, making her seem almost vague.

That she had only disappeared, I had always said, for hers
had been the face of every face, the heart of every heart, and
she had been the truest person ever I had seen, no one but a
poor old nursemaid walking along the seashore, taking her
constitutional, the salt crystals bearding her cheeks and her
pointed chin, nothing amazing her, no phantom accompany-
ing her in her morning or evening walks. She had no prince
charming, and she was a spinster, married not even to the
dream. We were always alone. We would sit under the storm
lamp in the evening, an old nursemaid and a child playing at
dominoes, two sentient beings alone in that great house of
shades and monsters, my mother's citadel of dreams and
visions and imaginary pretenders to vanished thrones, there
where my mother dreamed, when the sea blew high, that fifty
wild white horses had been struck dead by lightning in a ruined garden or that persons long drowned had walked out of
the sea, their locks dripping. There was no one, however, and
nothing had happened, Miss MacIntosh used to say, her knitting needles of ivory bone clicking like her false teeth, that
no one must dream of what was not, of what would never be,
that surely when I grew up, I must leave this realm of shades,
this old New England house with its privileges of the past,
those things which had been inherited, those which had been
stolen from the dead, that I must strike out on my own, that
I must lead a useful life and see America first, the broad interior, the spacious Middle West, that life which required no
medium of the evil imagination to stand between one's self
and the clear reality of simple things, for reality was very
good and could be found by those who lived, could be seen
even with the naked eye. Common sense is the finest sense,
she had always said, that the soul should not dream of those
things far distant and not to be realized, for the way was very

plain, quite direct. It was a granite road and not the sea road taken by the ships falling beyond a far horizon. But when no longer under the dimmed storm lamp in the long evenings we played at dominoes or Chinese puzzles, Miss MacIntosh and I, two living beings alone in that great, enchanted house which knew no time, when I was left alone, screaming and wild, then I had dreamed of her, my red-cheeked darling, for there had been no one else so true, so good, and, even in her unkindness, so kind.

Who now would recognize that background of illusion from which I had fled, so many years ago, seeking for her in all those places where she was not, where she might never be—that background from which I still was fleeing? After her disappearance or death, the sudden, terrible shock of that great loss which had divided my heart against my heart, there had been no one to turn to, no other sentient being of stable consciousness, and my mother, believing herself dead, that she had died long ago, had tried to kill me in order that I should be free of the influence of reality, had offered to me that poisonous compromise, my death pulsing rosily in the midst of my life, the world of dreams which would kill the dreamer and leave only the dream, the memories floating without purpose. Long ago, however, and by great effort, I had escaped my mother's darkened and secluded house that I might find the life which needed no dream of death, that life Miss MacIntosh had spoken of in no uncertain terms, and I had wandered from darkened harbor to darkened harbor and from employment to employment, always with one clear purpose in mind, the search for a lost companion who was, for all I knew, already dead, swept up upon the other shore. I had lived in ducal suites, in tenements like rabbit warrens—wearing my rags, had slept in fine hotels in the beds of dead emperors and false princes and banished dukes—wearing my regal jewels and ermine cape and long white gown, had slept in the beds of the poor, even where the subway roared, for I had been indifferent to my environment, and I had not always remembered where I was, and I had known no one. I had drifted from place to place, holding such little jobs as I could concentrate on and yet continue my dreams, beginning to study architecture, then giving it up because I could not plan a house if there was one soul which could not live in it, and finally, having tried all else, had been a poor fumbling typist in an insurance agency, typing mortality rates through

a blur of tears, the frequency or numbers of deaths in ratio
to population, age, sex, color, employment position in life.

No longer searching for her, the dead steersman, no longer
dreaming, I was following now, at last, her advice, for I had
come to this far place. No longer, by some momentary quiver
of the dreaming eyelid, should I find reality itself the banished, that surface phantoms had displaced it, that the world
had fled, that this was only its ghost blowing at the bus-window.

What motive in this quest but the search for life, for love,
for truth that does not fail? I had come because of my own
heart's need for an answer. I had come because of the search-
ings of other souls, the dead, the lost, because of a chance
remark overheard on the city streets, because of the encom-
passing darkness, because of my mind which had been filled
with nothing but the imaginary speakers, the endless dia-
logues of self with self, because I must find my way from the
darkness to the ultimate light. I had come because of a dead
girl's love letters scattered on the floor of her empty bedroom,
the palm leaves crossed above the marble mantel piece, her
rosary hanging on a brass bedpost, because of her suicide, because of a deaf musician, because of a drunkard's celestial
dream of childhood, because of the answers not heard, because of a blind man's groping for his coffee cup at an all-
night quick-lunch stand on the fog-shrouded waterfront of
that great harbor city as he had asked of his companion—
When shall the light, Peter, enter my soul? His eyes had been
withered in their sockets—the bare light bulb glaring only
three livid inches away from those burned-out hollows as he
had groped for a thick white coffee cup, asking his plaintive,
remorseless question—When shall the light, Peter, enter my
soul again? Should he never again be as he had been in the
old days, the world's greatest juggler, performing for the
Lord's sake and glory, keeping six coffee cups mid-air simultaneously as he skipped a rope or rode on a bicycle, a
sleight-of-hand artist who could pluck the playing cards off
any man's sleeve, produce a rabbit out of any man's hat,
make the invisible world visible as if an angel should be revealed?

Now as the bus groaned, each mile more laggard, the
world stretching out to an unseen horizon, the world flat, I
heard once more his question like my own—when shall the

light enter my soul—and when should the deprivation cease, and when should the body be restored, and when should the heart beat again? Travel-stained, my cheek against the cold bus-window, my head roaring with the memory of space, how should I ever know the land I passed through, the deep calling to the deep, the answer, for I was cut off, alone, seeing the fleeting image, the fragment beyond realization, the memory? I had come by many means of passage, by train and plane, by evening comet plane, that from where one could see the earth's abstract curvature in space, the dark mantle, the snowy dome lighted by stairlight, no human faces, by the morning star from where one saw the dreaming roof-tops, by day train which had jogged among steep hills of slag and burning eyes and coal-mining villages of bare-ribbed skeleton houses with their doors opened to the wind, the dust-colored rain, people blackened by coal dust, sweat, and sorrow, those who had gone down into the womb of mother earth, and now by this erratic bus which, plowing nowhere, suggested no landscape but the clouds, flight of angels drifting past the misted windows, no goal but something outside of time, some world more true than any that had been known, the beauty which would not be an aspect of the lie, the flesh and blood as organized, as complete, the hair, the lips, the eyes, the body organized, the human heart still beating.

And my search for this life was because of one already dead, she who had passed beyond, she who had been the moral guide, the unswerving, the true, her heart as stout as hickory or oak, her mind so sensible that she could not be deceived by any illusion or enchantment, she who was forever alone, outside, not taken in by all the sycophant luxuries of that opium paradise, a poor servant with patches on her best black cotton gloves, a fishnet reticule and rimless eye-glasses and no make-up, not even a touch of lip rouge, her face its natural color, her old black canvas umbrella lifted against the rain or sunlight as she had used to walk along the seashore, preferring that marginal estate to my mother's house where, though the roarings of the surf like the roarings of lions should fill it, the sea itself was but another dream and far away as if it were intangible. The great, sea-blackened house with golden spires and cornices and towers peeled by the salt air, dark allees, hidden interiors, the empty drawing rooms where the hostess had not set foot for many years, as many drawing rooms as tideless years, the rooms too many for mortal use, chambers within chambers, the gilded, mirroring ballrooms where no one danced, the hangings of scaly gold and rain-stained velvet, the heathen monsters everywhere, the painted, clouded ceilings illuminated by partial apparitions of the gods, the silken, padded walls, the ropes of rusted bells, the angels and the cherubim and the immortal rose, the dream of heaven, the lily-breasted virgins sporting in fields of asphodel, the water-gurgling gargoyles or those coated by dust, the interior and exterior fountains, the broken marble statues in ruined gardens sloping towards the sea, the disc throwers, the fat cupids, the thin psyches with flowing curls, the mute Apollo Belvedere, the king's horsemen, the life-sized chessmen seeming to move against the moving clouds that moved above the moving waters, the sea light lighting their wooden eyes, the seagulls perched like drifts of snow upon their heads.

What could Miss MacIntosh, a simple woman with a broken nose, find to admire in any broken marble statue, that which had been sculptured by man dreaming that he was other than he was or that he was man? Her religion was truth to nature, nothing else, as she would always say with a severity of good humor inviting no argument, no sad or meandering response. She disapproved quite heartily and firmly of all these unholy influences, these self-aggrandizements at the expense of common life which was the merest flesh and blood, her whole sensorium being repelled by the very dream of imagination which rejects reality, which flees from its bare face, for was she not sensible, the last person who would ever be taken in by what existed nowhere but in the dreaming mind, a plain, old-fashioned nursemaid, a red-headed and practical Middle Westerner, stoutly girded by her whale-boned corset, plainly clothed, visible to all, one who had kept her head above the waters in Chicago and elsewhere, one who, with her way clearly set and her heart not foolish, would submit to no luxurious temptation of this old crazy house on a desolate stretch of the primitive New England coast, there where, though all the ghosts of the universe wandered, shrieking like winds, like tides, like daft sea birds, she had seen nothing but what was plain, the desolation which was enough for her?

MARIA-LUISA BOMBAL, the Chilean writer, was born in 1910 and educated at the Sorbonne. As the story which follows shows, she is concerned with the subconscious and the reality of dream-life. Fittingly, she writes in a Proustian and poetic style. As one critic has written of "The Tree," "the profound psychological analysis of a woman is no less impressive than the contrapuntal technique followed in the story: point and counterpoint of a domestic drama and a concert. . . ." Bombal has lived in the United States and now lives in Buenos Aires.

Maria-Luisa Bombal
(1910—   )

THE TREE*

The pianist sits down, coughs affectedly and concentrates for a moment. The cluster of lights illuminating the hall slowly disminishes to a soft, warm glow, as a musical phrase begins to rise in the silence, and to develop, clear, restrained and judiciously capricious.

"Mozart, perhaps," thinks Brigida. As usual, she has forgotten to ask for the program. "Mozart, perhaps, or Scarlatti." She knew so little music! And it wasn't because she had no ear for it, or interest. As a child it was she who had demanded piano lessons; no one needed to force them on her, as with her sisters. Her sisters, however, played correctly now and read music at sight, while she . . . She had given up her studies the year she began them. The reason for her inconsistency was as simple as it was shameful; she had never succeeded in learning the key of F—never. "I don't understand; my memory only reaches to the key of G." How indignant her father was! "I'd given anyone this job of being a man alone with several daughters to bring up! Poor Carmen! She surely must have suffered because of Brigida. This child is retarded."

Brigida was the youngest of six girls, all different in character. When the father finally reached his sixth daughter, he was so perplexed and tired out by the first five that he preferred to simplify matters by declaring her retarded. "I'm not going to struggle any longer; it's useless. Let her be. If she won't study, all right. If she likes to spend time in the kitchen listening to ghost stories, that's up to her. If she likes dolls at sixteen, let her play with them." And Brigida had kept her dolls and remained completely ignorant.

* Reprinted from *Short Stories of Latin America*, edited by Zoila Nelken and Rosalie Torres-Rioseco, Las Americas Publishing Co., New York.

How pleasant it is to be ignorant! Not to know exactly who Mozart was, to ignore his origin, his influence, the details of his technique! To just let him lead one by the hand, as now.

And, indeed, Mozart is leading her. He leads her across a bridge suspended over a crystalline stream which runs in a bed of rosy sand. She is dressed in white, with a lace parasol—intricate and fine as a spider web—open over her shoulder.

"You look younger every day, Brigida. I met your husband yesterday, your ex-husband, I mean. His hair is all white."

But she doesn't answer, she doesn't stop, she continues to cross the bridge which Mozart has improvised for her to the garden of her youthful years when she was eighteen: tall fountains in which the water sings; her chestnut braids, which when undone reach her ankles, her golden complexion, her dark eyes opened wide and as if questioning: a small mouth with full lips, a sweet smile and the slenderest and most graceful body in the world. What was she thinking about as she sat on the edge of the fountain? Nothing. "She is as stupid as she is pretty," they said. But it never mattered to her that she was stupid, or awkward at dances. One by one, her sisters were asked to marry. No one proposed to her.

Mozart! Now he offers her a staircase of blue marble which she descends, between a double row of lilies of ice. And now he opens for her a gate of thick iron bars with gilded points so that she can throw herself on the neck of Luis, her father's close friend. Ever since she was a very small child, when they all abandoned her, she would run to Luis. He would pick her up and she would put her arms around his neck, laughing with little warbling sounds, and shower him with kisses like a downpour of rain, haphazardly, upon his eyes, forehead and hair, already gray (had he ever been young?).

"You are a garland," Luis would say to her. "You are like a garland of birds."

That is why she married him. Because, with that solemn and taciturn man, she didn't feel guilty of being as she was: silly, playful and lazy. Yes; now that so many years have passed she understands that she did not marry Luis for love; nevertheless, she doesn't quite understand why, why she went away one day, suddenly . . .

But at this point Mozart takes her nervously by the hand,

and dragging her along at a pace which becomes more urgent by the second, compels her to cross the garden in the opposite direction, to recross the bridge at a run, almost in headlong flight. And after having deprived her of the parasol and the transparent skirt, he closes the door of her past with a chord at once gentle and firm, and leaves her in a concert hall, dressed in black, mechanically applauding while the artificial lights are turned up.

Once more the half-shadow, and once more the foreboding silence.

And now Beethoven's music begins to surge under a spring moon. How far the sea has withdrawn! Brigida walks across the beach toward the sea now recoiled in the distance, shimmering and calm, but then, the sea swells, slowly grows, comes to meet her, envelops her, and with gentle waves, gradually pushes her, pushes her until it makes her rest her cheek upon the body of a man. And then it recedes, leaving her forgotten upon Luis' breast.

"You don't have a heart, you don't have a heart," she used to say to Luis. Her husband's heart beat so deep inside that she could rarely hear it, and then only in an unexpected way. "You are never with me when you are beside me," she protested in the bedroom when he ritually opened the evening papers before going to sleep. "Why did you marry me?"

"Because you have the eyes of a frightened little doe," he answered and kissed her. And she, suddenly happy, proudly received upon her shoulder the weight of his gray head. Oh, his shiny, silver hair!

"Luis, you have never told me exactly what color your hair was when you were a boy, and you have never told me either what your mother said when you began to get gray at fifteen. What did she say? Did she laugh? Did she cry? And were you proud or ashamed? And at school, your friends, what did they say? Tell me, Luis, tell me . . ."

"Tomorrow I'll tell you. I'm sleepy, Brigida. I'm very tired. Turn off the light."

Unconsciously he moved away from her to fall asleep, and she unconsciously pursued her husband's shoulder all night long, sought his breath. She tried to live beneath his breath, like a plant shut up and thirsty which stretches out its branches in search of a more favorable climate.

In the morning, when the maid opened the blinds, Luis was no longer at her side. He had got up cautiously and had left without saying good morning to her for fear of his "garland of birds," who insisted on vehemently holding him back by the shoulders. "Five minutes, just five minutes. Your office won't disappear because you stay five minutes longer with me, Luis."

Her awakenings. Ah, how sad her awakenings! But—it was strange—scarcely did she step into her dressing room than her sadness vanished, as if by magic.

Waves toss and break very far away, murmuring like a sea of leaves. Is it Beethoven? No.

It is the tree close to the window of the dressing room. It was enough for her to enter to feel a wonderfully pleasant sensation in the mornings! And what a harsh light! Here, on the other hand, in the dressing room, even one's eyes were rested, refreshed. The drab cretonnes, the tree that cast shadows on the walls like rippling, cold water, the mirrors that reflected the foliage and receded into an infinite, green forest. How pleasant that room was! It seemed like a world submerged in an aquarium. How that huge gum tree chattered! All the birds of the neighborhood came to take shelter in it. It was the only tree on that narrow, sloping street which dropped down directly to the river from one corner of the city.

"I'm busy. I can't accompany you. I have a lot to do, I won't make it for lunch. Hello, yes, I'm at the Club. An engagement. Have your dinner and go to bed. . . . No. I don't know. You better not wait for me, Brigida."

"If only I had some girl friends!" she sighed. But everybody was bored with her. If she only would try to be a little less stupid! But how to gain at one stroke so much lost ground! To be intelligent you should begin from childhood, shouldn't you?

Her sisters, however, were taken everywhere by their husbands, but Luis—why shouldn't she confess it to herself?—was ashamed of her, of her ignorance, her timidity and even her eighteen years. Had he not asked her to say that she was at least twenty-one, as if her extreme youth were a secret defect?

And at night, how tired he always was when he went to bed! He never listened to everything she said. He did smile at her, with a smile which she knew was mechanical. He showered her with caresses from which he was absent. Why do you suppose he had married her? To keep up a habit, perhaps to strenghten the friendly relationship with her father. Perhaps life consisted, for men, of a series of ingrained habits. If one should be broken, probably confusion, failure would result.

And then they would begin to wander through the streets of the city, to sit on the benches of the public squares, each day more poorly dressed and with longer beards. Luis' life, therefore, consisted in filling every minute of the day with some activity. Why hadn't she understood it before! Her father was right when he declared her backward.

"I should like to see it snow some time, Luis."

"This summer I'll take you to Europe, and since it will be winter there, you'll be able to see it snow."

"I know it is winter in Europe when it is summer here. I'm not that ignorant!"

Sometimes, as if to awaken him to the emotion of real love, she would throw herself upon her husband and cover him with kisses, weeping, calling him Luis, Luis, Luis . . .

"What? What's the matter with you? What do you want?"

"Nothing."

"Why do you call me that way then?"

"No reason, just to call you. I like to call you." And he would smile, taking kindly to that new game.

Summer arrived, her first summer since she was married. New duties kept Luis from offering her the promised trip.

"Brigida, the heat is going to be terrible this summer in Buenos Aires. Why don't you go to the farm with your father?"

"Alone?"

"I would go to see you every week on weekends."

She had sat down on the bed, ready to insult him. But she sought in vain for cutting words to shout at him. She didn't know anything, anything at all. Not even how to insult.

"What's the matter with you? What are you thinking about, Brigida?"

For the first time Luis had retraced his steps and bent over her, uneasy, letting the hour of arrival at his office pass by.

"I'm sleepy . . ." Brigida had replied childishly, while she hid her face in the pillows.

For the first time he had called her from the Club at lunchtime. But she had refused to go to the telephone, furiously wielding that weapon she had found without thinking: silence.

That same evening she ate opposite her husband without raising her eyes, all her nerves taut.

"Are you still angry, Brigida?"

But she did not break the silence.

"You certainly know that I love you, my garland. But I can't be with you all the time. I'm a very busy man. One reaches my age a slave to a thousand duties."

". . ."

"Do you want to go out tonight?"

". . ."

"You don't want to? Patience. Tell me, did Roberto call from Montevideo?"

". . ."

"What a pretty dress! Is it new?"

". . ."

"Is it new, Brigida? Answer, answer me . . ."

But she did not break the silence this time either. And immediately the unexpected, the astonishing, the absurd happened. Luis gets up from his chair, throws the napkin violently on the table and leaves the house, slamming doors behind him.

She had got up in her turn, stunned, trembling with indignation at such injustice. "And I, and I," she murmured confused; "I who for almost a year . . . when for the first time I allow myself one reproach . . . Oh, I'm going away, I'm going away this very night! I shall never set foot in this house again. . . ." And she furiously opened the closets of her dressing room, crazily threw the clothes on the floor.

It was then that someone rapped with his knuckles on the window panes.

She had run, she knew not how or with what unaccustomed courage, to the window. She had opened it. It was the tree, the gum tree which a great gust of wind was shaking, which was hitting the glass with its branches, which summoned her from outside as if she should see it writhing like an impetuous black flame beneath the fiery sky of that summer evening.

A heavy shower would soon beat against its cold leaves. How delightful! All night long she could hear the rain pattering, trickling through the leaves of the gum tree as if along the ducts of a thousand imaginary gutters. All night long she would hear the old trunk of the gum tree creak and groan, telling her of the storm, while she snuggled up very close to Luis, voluntarily shivering between the sheets of the big bed.

Handfuls of pearls that rain abundantly upon a silver roof. Chopin. *Etudes* by Frédéric Chopin.

How many weeks did she wake up suddenly, very early, when she scarcely perceived that her husband, now also stubbornly silent, had slipped out of bed?

The dressing room: the window wide open, an odor of river and pasture floating in that kindly room, and the mirrors veiled by a halo of mist.

Chopin and the rain that slips through the leaves of the gum tree with the noise of a hidden waterfall that seems to drench even the roses of the cretonnes, become intermingled in her agitated nostalgia.

What does one do in the summertime when it rains so much? Stay in one's room the whole day feigning convalescence or sadness? Luis had entered timidly one afternoon. He had sat down very stiffly. There was a silence.

"Brigida, then it is true? You no longer love me?"

She had become happy all of a sudden, stupidly. She might have cried out: "No, no; I love you, Luis; I love you," if he had given her time, if he had not added, almost immediately, with his habitual calm: "In any case, I don't think it is wise for us to separate, Brigida. It is necessary to think it over a great deal."

Her impulses subsided as abruptly as they had arisen. Why become excited uselessly! Luis loved her with tenderness and moderation; if some time he should come to hate her he would hate her justly and prudently. And that was life. She approached the window, rested her forehead against the icy glass. There was the gum tree clamly receiving the rain that struck it, softly and steadily. The room stood still in the shadow, orderly and quiet. Everything seemed to come to a stop, eternal and very noble. That was life. And there was a certain greatness in accepting it as it was, mediocre, as something definitive, irremediable. And from the depths of things there seemed to issue, and to rise, a melody of grave, slow words to which she stood listening: "Always." "Never" . . . And thus the hours, the days and the years go by. Always! Never! Life, life!

On regaining her bearings, she realized that her husband had slipped out of the room. Always! Never! . . .

And the rain, secretly and constantly, continued to murmur in the music of Chopin.

Summer tore the leaves from its burning calendar. Luminous and blinding pages fell like golden swords, pages of an unwholesome humidity like the breath of the swamps; pages of brief and violent storm, and pages of hot wind, of the wind that brings the "carnation of the air" and hangs it in the immense gum tree.

Children used to play hide-and-seek among the enormous twisted roots that raised the paving stones of the sidewalk, and the tree was filled with laughter and whispering. Then she appeared at the window and clapped her hands; the children dispersed, frightened, without noticing the smile of a girl who also wanted to take part in the game.

Alone, she would lean for a long time on her elbows at the window watching the trembling of the foliage—some breeze always blew along that street which ran straight to the river—and it was like sinking one's gaze in shifting water or in the restless fire of a hearth. One could spend one's idle hours this way, devoid of all thought, in a stupor of well-being.

Scarcely did the room begin to fill with the haze of twilight when she lit the first lamp, and the first lamp shone in the mirrors, multiplied like a firefly wishing to hurry the night.

And night after night she dozed next to her husband, suffering at intervals. But when her pain increased to the point of wounding her like a knife thrust, when she was beset by too urgent a desire to awaken Luis in order to hit him or caress him, she slipped away on tiptoe to the dressing room and opened the window. The room instantly filled with discreet sounds and presences, with mysterious footfalls, the fluttering of wings, the subtle crackling of vegetation, the soft chirping of a cricket hidden under the back of the gum tree submerged in the stars of a hot summer night.

Her fever passed as her bare feet gradually became chilled on the matting. She did not know why it was so easy for her to suffer in that room.

Chopin's melancholy linked one *étude* after another, linked one melancholy after another, imperturbably.

And autumn came. The dry leaves whirled about for a moment before rolling upon the grass of the narrow garden, upon the sidewalk of the sloping street. The leaves gave way and fell . . . The top of the gum tree remained green, but underneath, the tree turned red, darkened like the worn-out lining of a sumptuous evening cape. And the room now seemed to be submerged in a goblet of dull gold.

Lying upon the divan, she patiently waited for suppertime, for the improbable arrival of Luis. She had resumed speaking to him, she had become his wife again without enthusiasm and without anger. She no longer loved him. But she no longer suffered. On the contrary, an unexpected feeling of plenitude, of placidity had taken hold of her. Now no one or nothing could hurt her. It may be that true happiness lies in the conviction that one has irremediably lost happiness. Then we begin to move through life without hope or fear, capable of finally enjoying all the small pleasures, which are the most lasting.

A terrible din, then a flash of light throws her backward, trembling all over.

Is it the intermission? No. It is the gum tree; she knows it.

They had felled it with a single stroke of the ax. She could not hear the work that began very early in the morning. "The roots were raising the paving stones of the sidewalk and then, naturally, the neighbors' committee . . ."

Bewildered, she has lifted her hands to her eyes. When she recovers her sight she stands up and looks around her. What is she looking at? The hall suddenly lighted, the people who are dispersing? No. She has remained imprisoned in the web of her past, she cannot leave the dressing room. Her dressing room invaded by a white, terrifying light. It was as if they had ripped off the roof; a hard light came in everywhere, seeped through her pores, burned her with cold. And she saw everything in the light of that cold light; Luis, his wrinkled face, his hands crossed by coarse, discolored veins, and the cretonnes with gaudy colors. Frightened, she has run to the window. The window now opens directly on a narrow street, so narrow that her room almost strikes the front of an imposing skyscraper. On the ground floor, show windows and more show windows, full of bottles. On the street corner, a row of automobiles lined up in front of a service station painted red. Some boys in shirt sleeves are kicking a ball in the middle of the street.

And all that ugliness had entered her mirrors. Now in her mirrors there were nickel-plated balconies and shabby clotheslines and canary cages.

They had taken away her privacy, her secret; she found

herself naked in the middle of the street, naked beside an old husband who turned his back on her in bed, who had given her no children. She does not understand how until then she had not wanted to have children, how she had come to submit to the idea that she was going to live without children all her life. She does not understand how she could endure for a year Luis' laughter, that overcheerful laughter, that false laughter of a man who has become skilled in laughter because it is necessary to laugh on certain occasions.

A lie! Her resignation and her serenity were a lie; she wanted love, yes, love; and trips and madness, and love, love
. . .

"But, Brigida, why are you going? Why did you stay?" Luis had asked.

Now she would have known how to answer him.

"The tree, Luis, the tree! They have cut down the gum tree."

Translated by Rosalie Torres-Rioseco

GERTRUD FUSSENEGGER (pseudonym of Gertrud Dietz) is an Austrian novelist, poet, and dramatist who was born in 1912 in Pilsen. She grew up in Bohemia and the Tyrol and studied philosophy, history, and art history in Munich and Innsbruck. She is married to the sculptor Aloys Dorn.

Her novels and stories cover a wide span of time, from the ninth century, in the Carolingian period, to the post World War II urban present. Some of her stories of contemporary Germany have a bohemian background of nightmarish quality. These have been compared, of course, to the fictional nightmares of Kafka. Her work has been praised for its depth and for the richness of its characters and symbols. In most of her fiction, which is of a traditional mold, she treats the basic problems that beset people—guilt and suffering—and our often vain attempts to overcome them. Certainly this generalization is an accurate description of the story that follows. Yet "Woman Driver" has several layers of meaning. Fussenegger has lived in Munich and in Hall/Tyrol since 1944. She was awarded the Stifter Prize in 1951 and the Drama Prize of the Oldenburger Staatstheaters in 1956.

Gertrud Fussenegger
(1912—   )

WOMAN DRIVER

It's simply not true, as Fedja always maintains, that the devil's within me the moment I'm sitting behind the wheel. Admittedly I drive fast; fast, but well. Is it possible to drive well if one is driving fast?

The evening—clear after rain. In the west, far away, the pale yellow light, the sky swept clean and looking as cold as jade. The town is falling away now behind the slope. How boldly the road is climbing, curve after curve. Down there among the speckles of light, Fedja's house and mine is blinking away. He's sitting at home reading, reading and thinking and not saying a word, the clock is ticking away, its fingers are creeping round, from time to time Fedja flicks the ash off his cigarette and the ash will be mounting in the ash-tray.

There—in the rear-mirror, what's that? A great flat-looking bronze-brown ball—ah, the moon! Rises in the east, a dull, gleaming light, the September moon. They call it the Hunter's Moon, because September is the huntsman's season I suppose, "Tally-ho!" over moors and fields, the gun barks, and the deer hides trembling with fear in the wood.

What do you want, poor old star, your light is nothing, is nothing now in our nights which are bright with other and far stronger lights. You are no longer remote as you were once, no longer beyond our reach, old moon of lovers, friend of sighing poets. The rocket struck you, cut a wound in your icy skin, in your skin pock-marked with craters. Only yesterday I was talking to Fedja about it, and Fedja said: What's the point of it all? I don't understand human beings. And I in reply: Fedja, do you ever understand me? He narrowed his eyes and looked at me for a long time, and finally said: I don't always understand you, Barbara.

Not always? You've never understood me, Fedja; least of all when I drive off in the evening without rhyme or reason, drive like I'm driving now, just for the sake of steering the car, to avoid sitting with you in the room, where the clock is ticking away, the ash-tray filling with ash, where your silence is a silent appeal to the walls, so that they close in, close in more and more, till I feel as though they are going to smother me.

Then I *have to* go driving, Fedja. I'm not short of other excuses if you don't believe them any longer, these pitiful lies. I lied to you again today, saying I wanted to visit Ruth, my sister, who's ill. She's ill, all right; but all the same, I don't visit her, and you know it, know that I can't stand Ruth, that I really can't stand anyone, not even—you.

Ah, built-up area! Look out! The road's getting narrow here, damn! How I hate these narrow roads, chock-full with cyclists, pedestrians, children, and dogs. Dark and ponderous, some sort of vehicle is turning the corner, cart-horses, a cart-load of hay—ought to be banned on a road like this!

Old car, be patient, my beautiful old car, be patient, we'll be out of it soon, soon you'll be free again. There it is now at last—clearway. Houses and people are being left behind, the road is tearing towards us and the wind, the sweet sighing sound sweeping its leaves against the windows. Faster! Faster! The white line is running ahead of us, the red cat's-eyes on the kerb-stones, faster and faster the signs flash past: Cross-Roads, Bend, Steep Hill. Always the signposts call out: Danger! Danger! Who would want to drive but for the sense of danger?

Everything coming towards us goes swishing past like a ghostly apparition. Everything ahead of us is caught up, over-taken, obliterated to somewhere-behind-us. (Let none of them think he can drive faster than me, let none of them think: only a woman driver!) If you were beside me now, Fedja, you would be starting to curse: Are you crazy?—Over a hundred!—But you're not there, you're sitting at home in the room, turning the pages of your books, spinning a crazy web of memories of plans for later. Plan and memory: one and the same web designed to snare our life, life as you under-stand it. But I don't want it, this life-in-a-snare. I want the here-and-now, this here which is already there, clearway as far as the headlamps reach, tally-ho on the road, hunt and quarry. What is the quarry for a night such as this?

Time was when huntsmen hunted on horseback. The gun barked: a ball of fur and quivering flesh, glazed eyes, milky and unseeing, afterwards the meal served piping hot, and that was all. Now we hunt mounted on cars. The quarry: phantom and chimera, riding mounted on lights on the white cone of the headlamps, hurtling into the soot-black of night, a white clearing of light slicing its way through the dark. Conveyor-belt of scenery, woods and rocks like backdrops, come reeling towards us and past, bridges, walls, railings—somewhere a mountain torrent is raging, somewhere an abyss is roaring, out of some ghastly chasm a trail of water is blown, spray of colourless in the air.

All things dissolve into spray colourless in the air.

Yes, it's true, what Fedja said to me once: There is no love in you, only a yearning for the void.

Yes, it's true, true. But what is this void?

Does it not have a face? Is its face not our own? No. It is other than us and strange, out of our reach and beautiful.

Recently—how did it come about—when driving like this, or did I dream it? Yes, I dreamt it merely, this drive up into the mountains; and, as dreams always are, everything was larger than life and fantastic, giant scenery, giant-like the night, and the road, ever upwards, upwards, endless, spiraling, giddy viaducts towering one over the other. In front of me a blue car. Make? Not one I know. From some foreign country, I suppose, a foreigner on my road, keeping in front of me all the time, faster and faster still, going too fast to be overtaken, however hard I keep my foot down. Is he going to get away? No, I'll catch him, I will. Afraid that he may elude me, afraid because the road is getting so narrow, sweeping in tighter and tighter circles round ever narrower bends, and the stranger—not a cat at all—opens his silvery wings, smiles from behind his blue visor. . . .

Now the road has vanished into thin air—bottomless space is swallowing me up.

Over the edge of the road a tyre mark, and a young man travelling home from work, late, on his bicycle, has found and reported it.

The following morning a report in the paper: The death-a-day on the road and so on.

And so on for ever under the Hunter's Moon.

OLIVIA MANNING was born in Portsmouth, Hampshire. As she tells it, she wrote from the cradle—or at least the nursery. "Like most writers, I started writing down stories as soon as I could write at all. While I was still at school, I wrote four lurid serials which I sold to an agency for twelve pounds each. With the first twelve pounds I bought my first typewriter. My parents were pleased by my ability to make money, but they were less pleased when I began to discover the major writers in the public library and became more ambitious myself. My mother was horrified to find me reading the *Times Literary Supplement* and said, 'No one will ever marry you if you read papers like that.' I said it did not matter as I would prefer to write like Dostoievski. My first novel, written on Dostoievskian lines, was immensely long and I was broken by the cost of posting it to publishers. It was returned to me so quickly that I suspected no one tried to read it. One day someone typed a note on a rejection slip: 'Let me remind you of the words of a great writer: "Look in your heart and write."' I at once started another novel about the mysteries of living in a dismal provincial town where one never met any great writers. The hero escaped to Paris where he starved romantically to death. When this MS reached the publishing house of Cape, it was read by Edward Garnett who wrote an encouraging report. Cape wrote to say he would like to see my next novel and on the strength of this I decided to live and possibly, starve in London. I lived on less than it takes to feed a cat, but as I did not have to waste time on eating, I was able to spend all my free time writing. I completed another novel which I sent to Cape 'for the attention of Mr. Edward Garnett.' It was accepted. My advance was twenty-five pounds, which I badly needed as I had been sacked from my current job on the grounds that 'anyone who had time to write a novel could not be giving all her attention to her work.' "

Manning's Balkan trilogy (*The Great Fortune, The Spoilt City,* and *Friends and Heroes*) has been called "one of the outstanding achievements in postwar fiction." Its male protagonist, Guy Pringle, is, in the opinion of Walter Allen, "one of the most fascinating explorations of character in contemporary fiction."

Manning is married to a diplomat and lives in London.

Olivia Manning
(1914—   )

GIRLS TOGETHER

The first time I travelled anywhere alone was just after my sixteenth birthday. The following year I was to leave school and go to an art school, so I saw myself as practically grown up. I told my parents that I had been invited to visit a schoolfriend in Galway and though I went to Galway, I did not intend to stay there. I had been reading Yeats and Synge and was full of romantic excitement about the western islands where the language is Gaelic and they all speak poetry to each other.

It was a wild morning in Galway. Between the old warehouses with their crests of the Lynches and the O'Briens, the lanes were wind tunnels, warm, wet and salty, smelling of sea-wrack. I was thankful to see the steamer by the quayside. I had lost my way and thought I was late. The sea splashed up over the quay and the little barrel-bodied ship rocked and bumped as though impatient to be off. No one else was. The passengers were loitering ashore, indifferent to the soft drizzle which was everyday weather in the west. The minutes went by and I watched the swans blown over the grey choppy harbour like a fleet of sail.

"When do we go?" I asked the mate.

"We're going now," he said, but just then an American visitor found he had left his camera behind and wanted to go back for it. "Would there be time?" he wanted to know.

"Time enough," said the mate and another twenty minutes slid by. We could not see Clare or Connemara from the bay but the rain stopped and the clouds, swelling and shifting, were sometimes so thin that we could see the sun behind them, like a waxen moon. Whenever a glimmer of sun touched the deck, the mate told us it would be a fine day. We had been out an hour before we saw the islands strung across the horizon like a school of whales. The mate came round to tell us that we were calling first at the small islands to pick up beasts for the Galway market. This distressed the American who was on a day trip and feared he would have no time to see Inishmore.

"You will, of course," the mate assured him: "You'll have all the time in the world."

As we made for the smallest island, the sun broke free. The island, a rock crowned with a ruin, rose shimmering from the sea. There was no harbour, only a strand with cliffs rising on either side. The cliffs were limestone and blocks, big as coffins, had peeled off and fallen on each other at the water's edge, with here and there a block that had landed upright, standing like an idol looking out to sea. The sand had the creamy whiteness of pearl and all the movable life of the island was gathered on it, waiting for the day's work to begin. We had anchored so far out that the men pulling their curraghs down the sand were miniature figures, dark, distinct, busy, like the figures in a Flemish snow-scene.

On board, a crane was being got ready. The first curragh to reach us brought a cargo of pigs that lay trussed, on their backs, winking up at the ship with apprehensive little eyes. A hook was dropped down among the pigs and one by one they were hoisted up, screaming shamelessly in mid-air and subsiding, as they landed, into sobbing snuffles.

The captain watched the on-loading but took no part in it. The mate supervised everything. He was the only man on board who spoke Irish and English and it was clear he was in a powerful position. He took on a lordly manner, all the time shouting orders to the curraghs that waited in rows, sleek as seals, prows high from the water, filled with patient and frightened beasts.

The island men, wearing sleeveless frieze jackets over their navy blue jerseys, kept their heads shyly lowered but now and then raised their eyes to the passengers at the gunwale and, finding themselves observed, laughed self-consciously at each other.

After the pigs came the sheep. Because of their fragile legs, the sheep were handed up over the gunwale, feet tied, bodies crumpled and limp with nervous exhaustion.

On shore the cattle were being driven into the sea. A new fleet of curraghs came out, each with a man gripping the horns of the creature in the water. The cows seemed to swim with despairing terror. When hauled up, each was let hang in mid-air a minute so the water might stream from its flanks. A bullock was brought out, struggling and almost pulling its captor overboard. In the commotion it struck a horn against the curragh and the water was stained with blood. While it hung draining, it twisted and roared in protest and poured its ochre-colouring dung into the clear green sea. Last of all came a cow in calf that lay passive, like a drowned cow, buoyed on the surface by its swollen belly.

As all this happened, in the world beneath us a shoal of mackerel fry was making its way south. When we reached the middle island, the shoal was still passing, a vast band of tiny fish that flecked the sea with black and silver, all drifting in one direction, as close and numerous as the stars in the Milky Way.

The steamer could lie closer to the middle island and the scene was as large as life. There was a different spirit here. The men who came on board to supervise their own loading ignored the visitors and had no particular respect for the mate. They talked volubly among themselves. Their loud, galloping Gaelic would have sounded like abuse had they not been laughing so much. On this island the women dyed their skirts with madder and it seemed that the whole wide, bright shore was dotted with cardinals.

Still with the shoal beneath us, we went on to Inishmore and three dolphins escorted us into Killeany harbour, leaping just ahead of us as though in high spirits at our safe arrival. It was evening and the sun slanted across the faces of the crowd on the quayside.

I did not know where I was going when I landed. There was a hotel, but I had so little money that I confided my dilemma to the mate and he called to a man on the quayside. The man was Phelan, a thin fellow with a long, sad, drunkard's face, who had a room to let. Phelan hurried aboard and said it was a fine, large room. As it was "not in this city but the next one," I had to take his word for it. He had a horse and cart and hurried me on to the seat, eager to get me out of reach of rival establishments.

The road was a track between reaches of rock where there was a little grass and one or two precarious wind-bent trees. The island was long and narrow, a wedge rising steeply from the shore on our right to the cliffs on the Atlantic side. The sun was already below the cliff top and setting out in the shadowy evening, I was full of doubts and fears and realised that the mate had probably never seen Phelan's room; but I knew of no other. We caught up with the American who had started off briskly with his important-looking camera. He shouted to Phelan, "How far to the end of the island?"

"It's no distance at all," said Phelan. "Just up," but as the American jumped up, the steamer called to him from the harbour and he had to jump down again, leaving me alone with Phelan and his old, slow horse. We must have driven four miles before we reached a group of cottages that winked pale beside the road in the twilight. "Here's the city now," Phelan said and he stopped at his own house where the door stood open and chickens pecked indifferently from the muddy front to the earthen floor within. A woman looked out and Phelan shouted to her in Gaelic. "I've told her I've brought her a prize," he said. "You'll have to excuse her. She hasn't a word of the English."

Next morning it was wet again. I leaned from my bed to look out of the attic window and saw two sheep searching for grass through the misty rain. My room was certainly large but only the centre was high enough to allow me to stand up. The rafters were bare and on the bare, boarded floor stood a large bed, a wash-bowl and a chamber-pot. The chamber-pot marked my status. The Phelans themselves used the open fields.

I had misgivings the night before when I climbed a ladder to the attic and saw, by candlelight, the wrinkled sheets, grey-ish in colour, from which the damp rose like a miasma.

There was dust on the pillow and a smell of mildew came off the two grey blankets. I realised the bed had stood as it was, sheets and all, through the whole of the wet Aran winter and I called down to Phelan if I could have a hot-water bottle.

His red face appeared just above floor level and he suspiciously asked "What sort of a bottle would that be?"

"I thought the bed might be damp."

"Not at all," he scorned the idea: "Not at all," and he left me to make what I could of the situation.

I found when I got into it that the bed, a broken-down affair, had no mattress; but it had lace curtains looped at the head and between them hung a picture of Christ pointing to his burning heart. This did not save me. I rose aching in every muscle. I was sure I would not survive until the steamer came back on Thursday but when I heard the Phelan children laughing below, my spirits rose. I washed and dressed with an adventurous belief that dangers existed to be overcome.

Mrs. Phelan would not let me into the kitchen where the family lived their life. I was put into the other room which was filled with a wardrobe and two long tables. She shut the door on me. I had not even the hens for company.

On one of the tables the household treasures—odd cups and saucers, little cheap ornaments dabbed with gilt, holy statues—were crowded together. I saw among them a piece of dusty butter and a half-filled jar of marmalade stuck with dead flies. Both of these were put on my breakfast table with a pot of tea and a loaf of home-baked bread.

After breakfast I walked through the misty rain to the cliff-top. I followed a tunnel between dry stone walls where there were little drifts of earth, black as soot, and primroses, the size of florins, grew among grass and leaves of flashing green. Here the rain was no more than a cobweb on the skin but when I reached the open cliff-top the wind struck me like a blast, driving needles of water into my face.

Phelan had said it was not much of a wind. The winter, now, that was the time for gales. I could believe him for I came upon a tombstone that had been uprooted from a churchyard and now lay face down on the water-gleaming rock flats.

Phelan had a piece of ground boxed in with stones and filled with furrows of seaweed. Here, he told me, he could grow potatoes. There were a half a dozen of these potato patches between the road and the lower shore. But up here the wind swept everything away. The rock was polished smooth by wind. Yet I discovered an amazing thing. There were deep fissures where tongue ferns and maidenhair grew motionless as coral in a warm, damp conservatory air.

I was looking for the fort of Dun Aengus and found it on the highest point of the cliff. It was a great semi-circle of ancient stone that had been a circle until the waves ate the ground from under it. The wind deafened me so I was at the edge of the cliff before I could hear the sea. Crouching down I saw, some two hundred feet below, a narrow shore littered with fallen rock slabs round which the waves smacked and frothed with a sort of bad-tempered flippancy. There was nothing else to be seen. Mist hid the horizon and the next land was America. I thought of the sea, from which there was no cover for two thousand miles, every winter rushing like a battering-ram against the island, breaking the rock down and ingesting it so that half the island disappeared. One day there would be no island left.

While I sat contentedly watching the gulls sailing with the wind and watching the waves fall back green and veined like marble, someone yelled "Hey!" I turned in surprise. Two women were standing a few yards behind me. Their gestures, imperative and alarmed, required me to go to them. I went, bewildered.

"That was a foolish thing to do," the elder said when I was near enough to hear her.

"What was?"

"Sitting there on the overhang," said the younger. "No one with any sense goes to the edge of a cliff. It could break off and down you'd go and that would be the end of *you*."

The elder gravely adjured me: "Don't do it again." I knew at once what they were: teachers. English teachers. They too recognised me. I was one whose age and condition brought me under their authority. I said nothing. Having come here alone, as far as I could get from the tyranny of school, I resented this meeting with these all too familiar women. I wanted to walk away and could not. For all I knew they might have saved my life. As I was still standing there, the elder woman said, "I am Amanda Tucker. This is my friend, Miss Holt," so I introduced myself.

They stood looking around at the Dun Aengus wall and asking each other what it was. They had come on the fort by chance and knew nothing about it.

"I'd say," said the older woman, "it's some sort of Stone Age structure."

"It was built by the Fir-bolgs," I told them.

They looked at me startled, as though a rabbit had displayed powers of speech. I felt my old dangerous impulse to show off and said: "The Fir-bolgs were a very ancient people and after them came the Tuatha Dé Danann who understood magic."

The younger woman raised an ironical eyebrow at her companion and smiled: "Aren't we clever!" she said and they turned and went towards a break in the wall. I was going that way myself and as the wind blew me after them I felt I had asked for all I got. At school one was required to know what one had been taught. Any extraneous knowledge was felt to be a reflection upon the infallibility of the teacher. Miss

Tucker and Miss Holt might not have authority over me but they felt themselves my natural superiors. I had tried to impress them, and been snubbed as I deserved.

I followed them for about a mile, not certain whether I was with them or not. When we dropped below the noise of the wind, I could hear their conversation. The rain was falling harder and Miss Holt asked the heavens: "Do you think you can ever let up?"

"No good complaining, dear one," Miss Tucker mildly said: "You would come here."

"It's one place we're not likely to bump into some dismally familiar face. Still, we don't have to spend all our hols here. If this goes on, I vote we move."

"Where to?"

"We'll have to think about that."

Miss Tucker, whose voice was very deep, rumbled sadly: "Must we move? We haven't been here a week; and it was such a journey."

"We'll see," said Miss Holt lightly and I knew she was the one who made decisions. I was impressed by her because she was young and good-looking. She wore green pants and an Aran sweater and with her well-cut auburn hair she gave an impression of elegance. Miss Tucker, grey-haired, in old-fashioned tweeds, looked elderly and dull. But as the talk went on I discovered that Miss Tucker was a head mistress and I was awed to find myself in such august company. That was, if I were in their company. The matter was settled at the bottom of the hill when Miss Holt glanced back at me and said, "I suppose you're staying at the hotel?" Her tone suggested contempt for hotel visitors and I wondered where they could be staying themselves.

"I'm at the Phelans'," I said.

"The Phelans? You mean that fellow with the horse and cart?"

"Yes."

Miss Tucker looked startled while Miss Holt said with mock compassion, "Poor you."

I had an unnerving conviction that they knew something I did not know. I tried to defend myself: "They're all right. I know the place isn't very clean but . . ."

"You'll get typhoid," Miss Holt told me.

Miss Tucker glanced uncertainly at her friend but came to her support: "There is typhoid in these parts."

"You might pick up diphtheria. Have you been immunised?"

"I don't know."

"No," Miss Holt darkly agreed: "A lot of silly women don't get their babies done these days. Or you could be poisoned. You might even get botulism."

Miss Tucker protested: "That's not likely."

"We're in primitive parts," said Miss Holt: "Anything might happen here." She went on happily and I lagged behind contemplating, in lonely ignorance, these dire diseases of which I had never even heard. Could I, I wondered, afford one night at the hotel? It would have to be two nights because the steamer did not come till Thursday. Remembering Phelan's look of naïve cunning, remembering Mrs. Phelan, smiling, slovenly, with a face that seemed to have been old from the start, I wondered how I could bring myself to leave them. Phelan had told his wife he had brought her a prize. He had spoken with pride of his fine large room. If I went anywhere else, their feelings would be hurt.

Miss Holt and Miss Tucker were so far ahead I thought they had forgotten me. When they paused at the road, I did not imagine they were pausing for me. I was wandering away from them, absorbed in my fears, when Miss Holt called out, "You can come and see our house if you like."

I stopped, not over-eager to hear more from Miss Holt but too cast down to withstand her. For years I had been in the charge of women like these and they had wielded an authority much greater than that of my parents. I could argue angrily with my mother but only the most restrained form of argument had been permitted by the Miss Holts in my life. They gave advice as from the sanctum of an oracle and this Miss Holt who could name the dangers that surrounded me at the Phelans could probably also tell me what safeguards I might take.

Seeing me unnerved and yielding, Miss Holt said "This way," and I followed her, feeling a certain safety in her wake. Miss Holt's unpleasantness was familiar. The Phelans were not unpleasant but they were unknown.

A path led down to the strand. In the distance, built on the rock, there was a cottage that looked like any other cottage until I was near enough to see that, although simple, it had splendours unknown to the island houses. A terrace had been built before it and there were shrubs growing in pots. It was a double-fronted house and the windows on either side of the door were so wide they suggested there was something to be seen from them. Whatever it was, there was nothing now but rain and sea mist, an edge of sand and a frill of grey, cold sea.

"Is it your house?" I asked.

"In a manner of speaking," said Miss Holt.

The front door opened in to a large whitewashed room with a few pieces of dark cottage furniture and armchairs covered with the most brilliant Donegal tweed.

"Goodness," I said in admiration.

Miss Tucker said, "It's nicely done, isn't it? It's suitable."

I nodded. The Phelans with their plywood wardrobe would never have anything as suitable as this.

Miss Tucker said she was going to wash her hands. Nervous at being left with Miss Holt, I wandered around, looking at things. The fireplace was formed by three blocks of polished limestone and over it hung the room's only picture. I took it to be a Klee; not a real one, of course, because the colour key was all wrong. I thought it a poor reproduction but when I went closer, I saw it was a painting. As I stared at it, puzzled, Miss Holt said, "That was done by the man who owns the place."

"But it's a Klee."

"If you look in the corner, you'll see it's signed 'J. Dring.' "

It was signed "J. Dring"; I turned away, shocked by such an egregrious pastiche and then was more shocked to realise that Miss Holt was triumphant, imagining I had been made to look foolish. Her satisfaction was such that she invited me to eat with them, saying, "We're having boiled eggs. How do you like yours?"

"The Phelans are expecting me. I'd better go back."

"I wouldn't if I were you."

Disturbed again, I betrayed myself by asking, "What is botulism?"

"Ah!" Miss Holt was almost gleeful as she told nothing but implied much.

A woman with the same flat-featured, heavy look as Mrs. Phelan entered and stood smiling at us. Awaiting orders, she was like some gentle pack animal that had never learnt anything but obedience.

Miss Holt turned on me sharply: "Are you staying or aren't you?"

"Yes, thank you."

"Well, well, well!" When Miss Tucker returned, Miss Holt said, "Our young friend has kindly agreed to stay for luncheon."

The woman was told to set the table for three. When she came back with plates and cutlery, she brought with her a boy so like her, he could only be her son. She handed the things to him one by one and as he put them on the table, she spoke quietly to him in Gaelic, directing him to this place and that. He was only a year or two younger than I was and we glanced at each other, conscious of our affinity of age. Both mother and son had an air of good-natured willingness to please, but pleasing the Englishwomen was, I felt, a precarious business. The boy was clumsy. Whenever he tripped over his feet or let a plate rattle to the table, the mother glanced apprehensively towards Miss Holt who bore it in silence for some minutes then suddenly raised her head and said with venom, "If that boy breaks another plate, I'll murder him."

The woman, understanding the threat if not the words, shouted something at the boy and made to smack his head, but the gesture turned to a caress and they both smiled as though it were a joke. This did not please Miss Holt who grumbled, "Why do we have to have this oaf about the place?"

Miss Tucker felt a need to explain to me: "She is trying to train him to be a waiter. She hopes he'll get a job at the hotel. She seems to have persuaded herself he's not strong enough for outdoor work."

"Not strong enough! Look at him!" Miss Holt spoke with such disgust that his mother was frightened and motioned him to leave the room. As he went, Miss Holt shouted after him, "And shut the door." He left it open and his mother, muttering, "He does not understand," hurried to close it.

"How absurd it is," said Miss Tucker as though to excuse Miss Holt's exasperation, "All these children brought up to speak this useless language. Do you know the parents get a government grant for a child that speaks Irish, but only if it knows no English at all."

"They subsidise ignorance," Miss Holt summed up the situation and dismissed it, wishing to speak of a more immediate grievance. "That boy's tied to her apron strings. Training him to be a waiter! Whoever heard of such a thing! She just wants to have him with her all day. She can't let him out of her sight."

"I suppose, being a widow . . . the father drowned . . ."

"You think that's a reason why he should eat our food and break crockery that we have to pay for? Really, Amanda, you're always making excuses for people. I'm getting sick of it."

"Oh, Daphne!" Miss Tucker lost her dignity. Her voice, though it remained deep, became hollow as she pleaded: "Don't nag me, dearest. Please don't."

Miss Holt answered briskly: "Then don't be a fool."

The woman brought in our boiled eggs and we moved to the table, Miss Holt saying: "Let us see if she's managed to get them right this time." Breaking in the top of her egg, she gave a snort of annoyance.

"Hard?" asked Miss Tucker.

"Like a rock."

"After all the trouble we've had trying to teach her what we mean by a one-minute egg. Suppose we told her to coddle them!"

"*Coddle!* She's never heard of such a thing!"

As I had not answered the question about my egg, all three eggs had been parboiled. I could scarcely swallow the gluey albumen which I spooned out of my egg-shell.

"She doesn't know much English," said Miss Tucker.

"She doesn't listen. All she thinks about is that boy."

"Mothers are like that, I'm afraid."

"God, yes. When I think how my brother was spoilt." Miss Holt reflected glumly on her grievance, then seemed to reach a resolution: "If we have to have him here, he can earn his keep. There must be something he could do."

"He could row the boat."

"That's an idea!" Miss Holt laughed, becoming suddenly pleased and happy: "I don't see why we shouldn't keep this place on for the summer hols."

"Keep it on!" Miss Tucker smiled in indulgent wonder at her friend's vagaries. "Why, just now you were saying we should move."

"The weather should be better in July and August."

"Do we really want to spend a summer alone here?"

"We needn't be alone. I thought of inviting Elaine Lauderdale."

"Elaine Lauderdale! Oh *no*."

"At least she's decorative."

"Dearest!"

Miss Tucker spoke with an anguished growl that was absurd and pathetic. Miss Holt raised her brow quizzically at her, then giving a sudden giggle that astonished me, she said, "Girls together." Rising with dignity, Miss Tucker left the room. When she had gone, Miss Holt looked sulky, and I, feeling called upon to show tactful aplomb, said:

"This is a large house for the island."

"Quite large, but we aren't looking for a lodger."

A moment passed before this came home to me and I stammered: "I never thought . . ."

"Well, just in case you do get ideas, we may have a friend on the next boat."

"I'll go now. Thank you for lunch."

Miss Holt did not try to detain me. The Phelans had a fried mackerel ready for me and were astounded when they heard where I had eaten my meal. "You got your dinner at the Big House?" Phelan said in awe. He spoke to his wife and they both gazed at me as though some curious change had come over me.

"To think of it!" Phelan swayed his head and mused and murmured, and I thought he was making rather much of the Big House hospitality. Then he revealed the cause of his amazement, saying: "So you're just the same as they are!" I realised that what he meant was "socially the same." He discussed this with his wife who drew in her breath and opened her eyes, scarcely able to credit the fact that someone who could not afford the hotel could, nevertheless, be accepted at the Big House. Overwhelmed though they were, they remained what they had been: simple and kind. I knew that whatever the risks I was bound to them until I left the island, but my fears remained. I was full of cramps and thought I was feverish, but the only thing I caught was a heavy cold.

Next day, awaking again to foggy rain, I decided to return on Thursday's steamer, but on Thursday I changed my mind. The sun was shining and I threw myself out of bed in excitement.

The sun was the tender misty sun of the west. The whole island had taken on the look of the newly born. The wind had dropped and on the cliff-top I looked out on the glassy azure sea that stretched like a dew-pond between us and America. That morning I had learnt that Phelan had been to

America. So, for that matter, had half the male population of the islands. Phelan saw no reason for surprise. "Sure, it's just over the water," he said, and I felt the train journey to Dublin would hold more hazards for him.

I returned to the Phelans and ate a fried mackerel. The day before I had had fried mackerel at mid-day and fried mackerel for tea. Cooked food, I decided, would do no harm but I would not eat the butter and marmalade. I asked Phelan if I could buy fruit on the island.

"Fruit!" he murmured, as though naming an almost unimaginable delicacy: "I'm told they have fruit at the hotel," quickly adding: "But only a little glass, mind you."

In the afternoon I wandered down to the strand and for the first time saw the Connemara shore with the Twelve Pins rising into the delicate sky. It seemed the shore of an undiscovered country, exquisite, untouched, wild as it had been since the beginning of time.

I took off my shoes, rolled up my jeans and walked in the transparent, warmish sea. I had picked up a handful of sand and examining it, I found that the grains were not rock particles but shells so small that it was only for an instant of acute concentration I could make out their shape. So entranced was I by this discovery that I almost walked into Miss Holt who was directing the launching of a boat.

"Goodness!" I said, seeing the new honey-coloured rowing-boat that looked as light and fragile as a skiff compared with the heavy curraghs. "Is it yours?"

"It goes with the house." She was hot and irritable with the effort of getting Miss Tucker and the servant's son to behave as she wished them to behave. She shouted to Miss Tucker: "What does he think he's doing? He's only pretending to push. Tell him to put his weight behind it."

Miss Tucker leant near the boy's ear and growled "Push." He jerked his head round, startled and perplexed, and she gripped his shoulder and demonstrated that more was expected of him.

With Miss Holt on one side and her two weak assistants on the other, the boat was persuaded down to the water's edge. I stood with my shoes in one hand, the shells in the other, and benignly watched the keel cut into the firm white sand until, the boat half in the water, Miss Holt called a halt. Stepping back and brushing her hair from her face, she observed me with disapproval: "You wouldn't think of helping, would you?"

It was true: I had not thought of it and I was silent.

"But no doubt you expect to be invited along."

I shook my head: "I was just watching. I was really thinking about the sand. If you look at it carefully you'll see it isn't sand at all. It's made of tiny shells."

I held out my hand and Miss Holt let me trickle some of the sand into her palm. She squinted at it a moment then threw it away: "My sight's pretty good but I see no shells. I think you're imagining things. Now, if you're coming, jump in." When I was slow to obey, she said, "What's the matter? Afraid you'll be drowned? Get in, do."

I responded to a teacher's impatience and climbing aboard, took a seat in the stern.

"Now you," Miss Holt indicated the boy who stared and then, understanding, stepped back in alarm. He bumped into Miss Tucker. Miss Holt shouted, "Hold him," and Miss Tucker held his arm. He could have escaped her easily but was too mild of temperment to shake off a woman.

"Do you think we should take him without letting her know?" Miss Tucker doubtfully asked.

"What! Let her know we've got her pet lamb! Not likely. Come on, make him get in."

Miss Tucker could not make him get in. When she pulled on his sleeve, he remained where he was and shook his head.

"Here!" Running to the other side of the boat in a rage, Miss Holt gripped his shoulder and shouted instructions to Miss Tucker. The boy's resistance was merely passive. Between them they were able to bundle him aboard and he sat, drooping, on one of the two centre seats.

"Now you," Miss Holt commanded her friend. Miss Tucker sat in the bows. When we were all aboard, Miss Holt gave the boat a final shove and leapt in as it wobbled away.

She was an agile and capable woman and was, I felt, resentful of the fact that the boy, with all the advantages of his sex, could not, or would not, be as capable.

He was facing me. He crouched in his seat, his hands flat together between his knees, and looked, for all his weight and size, like a trapped, unhappy bird. His head was hanging but once or twice he glanced towards the house as though in hope that his mother would come and rescue him.

Miss Holt took the oars in a businesslike way and rowed us

northwards. As soon as we were out of sight of the house, she shipped the oars and said, "Now, let's see what mother's pet can do." She moved back and sat beside me.

The boy was puzzled by her behaviour and finding her eyes fixed on him, he smiled placatingly until she shouted and pointed and he realised what was expected of him; he gripped the seat as though afraid of being hauled out of it.

"Give him a dunt," said Miss Holt. Miss Fletcher touched his rear with her shoe and he gave his head a violent shake.

"It's no good," Miss Tucker said, quite happy to let the matter drop, but the boy's refusal seemed to rouse Miss Holt to masterful fury. "Give him a real kick. Don't be afraid. He can't hurt you. Let him know you mean it."

Miss Tucker was afraid but she was afraid of Miss Holt. Her foot gave a spasmodic jerk and unintentionally she caught the boy in some very tender spot. He cried out and whimpered a word that I had heard used by the Phelan children.

I said, "I think he said 'Father.' "

"Calling on Daddy, the great baby!" Miss Holt now showed a gleeful jocularity. "Well, he'll get no help from that quarter. Daddy's at the bottom of the briny. Go on," she returned to poor Miss Tucker. "Kick him again."

Feeling Miss Tucker's foot behind him the boy evaded it by sliding off the seat, then, wearying of the whole business, he crawled forward and sat between the rowlocks. When he began to row, he fell at once into an easy rhythm that carried the boat through the shadowed water below the cliff.

Miss Holt, who had watched him critically, seemed satisfied: "He can row all right. You can see he's had practice. What was mumsie going on about?"

Miss Tucker, though she had obeyed orders, did not seem as satisfied as Miss Holt. "She said he wasn't strong. I don't think we should let him row for long."

"He's doing fine. The trouble is, his mother spoils him. He's her little baby. I've seen it happen before. She thinks if she protects him and saves him from trouble, she'll keep him under her influence for ever. What that boy needs is a separate existence. If we can knock him into shape, he'll have cause to thank us."

Miss Tucker did not look too sure of this. Facing the boy, I wondered if Miss Holt might be right. Rowing with more effort than was necessary, he once or twice caught my eye

and half smiled as though to draw attention to his perform-
ance. Perhaps, after all, his mother protected him for her
own sake rather than his.

In the gloom under the headland, the air was cold and the
waters black beneath us. We passed through the channel between the cliff and the outlying rocks, then returned to sunlight. On the other side we skirted the shore that I had
glimpsed when I looked down from the heights of Dun Aengus.

The sun was dropping towards the horizon and its rich
light glowed on the great cliff face and the stone blocks that
lay tumbled together on the strip of beach. The shore seemed
a scene set for murderous combat and even Miss Holt sur-
veyed it doubtfully. Intent on his own efforts, the boy did not
notice where he was until we came to a row of caves where
the waves washed in with a booming noise. He glanced round
quickly and seeing the cliffs above him, he looked frightened
and began to pull on the oars as though to escape a pursuer.

Miss Tucker said: "I think that's enough for one day. We
ought to go back."

Miss Holt, ready to agree, said: "Yes. I'll take over.
Mother's pet can have a rest."

She motioned to him to move, and sliding forward on to her
knees, put her hands on the oars. Again he shook his head.
Holding to the oars with his large hands, he pulled on them
strongly, sending us at a good pace down the long, straight
coast. Looking anxiously over her shoulder, seeing the cliffs
stretching away out of sight, Miss Tucker asked fearfully:
"Where is he taking us? This is madness. No one ever comes
here. If we were to capsize, we'd never be found even if we
got ashore."

"It's not my fault he won't let me take over. We *won't* capsize, but if I were to struggle with him we *would*. So we'll
have to let him keep at it."

"Does he think he can reach the harbour? How far is it?"
"Miles."

The boy was making more effort now but achieving less
speed. I could hear him breathing through his teeth and his
face was damp and pallid. Catching my eye he grinned
tensely, but I looked away, refusing to encourage him, nervous for him and for the rest of us.

I tried to distract myself with the grandeur of the shore,
but all sorts of possibilities were going through my head. The

boy might collapse and drop the oars which could drift away before someone seized them. Or the boat could strike a rock and sink. Miss Tucker had been right. Even if we reached a patch of foreshore, we would not get up the cliffs and not a soul would know where we were. Perhaps Miss Holt was nervous, too, for she said suddenly, "I could kill him."

"He's slowing down," said Miss Tucker. "Perhaps if you had another try! But whatever you do, don't upset the boat."

"Do you think I want to upset the boat?"

Miss Holt slid forward on to her knees shouting "Give me the oars, you silly fool." Again he ignored her, and doubling her fist like a man, she gave him a blow in the chest. He lifted his head and stared at her blankly but that was all. He would not give up his seat and he went on rowing.

"Obstinate bloody imbecile," said Miss Holt. Sitting back beside me: "I hate the whole boiling. Give him another kick."

"What good would that do?" Miss Tucker asked in helpless misery.

He was obstinate and in his obstinacy there was a masculine resolution that probably disturbed Miss Holt more than his defiance or her own danger. I could see her fine, strong profile fixed in impotent rage and I felt she really could kill if it did not mean killing us all.

During the long, slow pull to the southern end of the island, Miss Holt watched the boy but said nothing. When we reached the southern point the mainland came into view and I could see the setting sun reflected on the glossy blackness of the Cliffs of Moher. We turned and there was the Connemara shore and the Twelve Pins fading into the amethyst haze of evening. It would all have been a delight and a comfort after peril had it not been for the white-faced boy panting and straining to keep the boat moving.

"Make him put in at the harbour," said Miss Tucker.

"You make him," said Miss Holt, but being the one who took action, she pointed to the quayside and gave an order that had no more effect than before. The harbour was left behind us and we followed the flat rocky shore that would bring us to the strand. The amethyst turned to grey, a gusty wind sprang up and disturbed the water. The boy hung heavily on the oars, gasping and pulling as though they were a great weight. His expression was fixed and his eyes looked glazed. Miss Holt, though concerned in spite of herself, twitched her lips with something like a smile because she would win in the end.

We dragged on through the long spring twilight. It was nearly dark when we saw the glimmer of the white crescent of sand and the white house on the rocks above it.

"Well, we've made it," said Miss Holt.

"Thank goodness for that." Miss Tucker began to collect herself.

The boy turned the boat and as he paused to let it run ashore, he gave a croak and fell backwards. Dropping the oars and catching at his chest, he slid to the bottom of the boat and crouched there, groaning.

"Damn," said Miss Holt and turning herself expertly into the vacant seat, she caught the trailing oars and brought them aboard. The keel ran smoothly into the sand.

"He's fainted," Miss Tucker whispered.

"I'm not surprised." Miss Holt jumped down to the shore and pointed to me: "You! You help Miss Tucker to get him over the side. I'll take him from you."

The boy was inert and heavy. We could not lift him but we managed to pull him up on to a seat and then roll him over the gunwale. Miss Holt, almost collapsing as his weight came down on her, lowered him to the sand where he lay, a black shape in the last of the light.

She said, "He'll have to say there until we get help."

"Is he dead?" Miss Tucker sounded tearful. "God, what will we tell that woman? You *would* go round there, Daphne. You *will* have your own way."

Miss Holt said: "Trust you to go to pieces. I don't suppose he is dead, but if he is you can blame yourself for it. It was your idea that he should row the boat."

"How could you, dearest? How could you be so cruel? I can't stand much more of it. I warn you my nerves are all anyhow. I sometimes feel I . . . I feel I . . . I feel I . . . feel . . ."

"Shut up, you silly fool. We're not alone. Pull yourself together." Miss Holt turned on me: "Here!" she gripped my arm as though I were the defecting Miss Tucker. "Run back to the house and prepare his mother. Tell her there's been an accident. Don't say we let him row, for goodness' sake. We don't want her with hysterics on top of everything else. Just say he's fainted."

She threw me from her and, regaining my balance, I ran

across the sand, ploughed through a ridge of shingle and made for the lights of the house. Away from the reflecting sea it was dark, and I tripped over rocks and brambles before I came to the terrace. Through a side window I could see the woman setting the supper table. Watching her slow, distracted movements, I knew I could not be the one to tell her of the boy's collapse. I turned to run and hearing me she threw some knives on the table and hurried to the window. She pulled it up. I pressed back against the wall. She called out urgently, "Cormac. Cormac," and I held my breath. She stood for a minute peering into the darkness, then drew in her head and I jumped down from the terrace. I thought I had escaped but Miss Holt was there and had seen the movement of my white sweater.

She whispered hoarsely, "Is that you? Did you see her? What did you say?"

I paused, aware of my disobedience, feeling the old uneasiness of school, and side-tracking her question, I asked, "How is the boy?"

"I don't know. She'll have to get some men to carry him up. You didn't say anything foolish, I hope."

"I didn't say anything at all. I saw her but I didn't speak to her."

"I told you to warn her."

"Well, I didn't. What happened was your fault. You should be the one to tell her." I began to feel my way up the rocks.

"What cheek!" Miss Holt, in the darkness, made a hissing noise of indignation. "And ingratitude. We fed you, we took you out in the boat. I can tell you this, if you were in my class—"

"But I'm not, I'm not, I'm not," I sang out boldly. Then, jumping up to the lane, I ran for the safety of the Phelans' cottage.

NATALIA GINZBURG, Italian novelist, short story writer, and dramatist, was born Natalia Levi in Palermo in 1916. She grew up in Turin where her father, a scientist, taught anatomy at the university. Both her parents were socialists. In *Family Sayings* (1967) she tells the story of her family in a way that in the words of one reviewer, "gives biography a new dimension, new possibilities, and the tired old form of the family chronicle an aspect that is entirely new." In 1938 she married Leone Ginzburg, a professor of Russian Literature and an active anti-Fascist. During the years 1940–1943 the couple were in compulsory residence in Abruzzi; they had three children and Mrs. Ginzburg's first novel, *The Road to the City*, was published. In 1943 her husband was arrested in Rome when working on an underground press and was handed over to the Germans. He died in the infirmary of the Nazi-controlled Regina Coeli prison in 1944.

Ginzburg's books have received various literary prizes and high critical praise. A reviewer in the *Times Literary Supplement* has described her "curious technique of omission, of felicitous gaps. . . . She writes conversationally (some say chattily), with an apparent simplicity that is in fact dense and suggestive. . . . It is this capacity to mean much while saying little—a kind of poetic compression, or metaphorical outlook, using the plainest, most 'anti-poetic' language—that her quality and above all her originality lie." Her stories of marriage and other relationships unfolded against a backdrop of historical events show her deep insight into states of anxiety, loneliness, and disappointment.

Natalia Ginzburg
(1916—   )

THE MOTHER

Their mother was small and thin, and slightly round-shoul-
dered; she always wore a blue skirt and a red woollen blouse.
She had short, curly black hair which she kept oiled to control
its bushiness; every day she plucked her eyebrows, making two
black fish of them that swam towards her temples; and she
used yellow powder on her face. She was very young; how
old, they didn't know, but she seemed much younger than the
mothers of the boys at school; they were always surprised to
see their friends' mothers, how old and fat they were. She
smoked a great deal and her fingers were stained with smoke;
she even smoked in bed in the evening, before going to sleep.
All three of them slept together, in the big double bed with
the yellow quilt; their mother was on the side nearest the
door, and on the bedside table she had a lamp with its shade
wrapped in red cloth, because at night she read and smoked;
sometimes she came in very late, and the boys would wake
up and ask her where she had been: she nearly always answered: "At the cinema," or else "With a girl friend of
mine"; who this friend was they didn't know, because no
woman friend had ever been to the house to see their mother.
She told them they must turn the other way while she
undressed, they heard the quick rustle of her clothes, and
shadows danced on the walls; she slipped into bed beside
them, her thin body in its cold silk nightdress, and they
moved away from her because she always complained that
they came too close and kicked while they slept; sometimes
she put out the light so that they should go to sleep and
smoked in silence in the darkness.

Their mother was not important. Granny, Grandpa, Aunt
Clementina who lived in the country and turned up now and
then with chestnuts and maize-flour were important; Diomira
the maid was important, Giovanni the tubercular porter who

214

made cane chairs was important; all these were very important to the two boys because they were strong people you could trust, strong people in allowing and forbidding, very good at everything they did and always full of wisdom and strength; people who could defend you from storms and robbers. But if they were at home with their mother the boys were frightened, just as if they had been alone; as for allowing or forbidding, she never allowed or forbade anything, at the most she complained in a weary voice: "Don't make such a row because I've got a headache," and if they asked permission to do something or other she answered at once: "Ask Granny," or she said no first and then yes and then no and it was all a muddle. When they went out alone with their mother they felt uncertain and insecure because she always took wrong turnings and had to ask a policeman the way, and then she had such a funny, timid way of going into shops to ask for things to buy, and in the shops she always forgot something, gloves or handbag or scarf, and had to go back to look and the boys were ashamed.

Their mother's drawers were untidy and she left all her things scattered about and Diomira grumbled about her when she did out the room in the morning. She even called Granny in to see and together they picked up stockings and clothes and swept up the ash that was scattered all over the place. In the morning their mother went to do the shopping: she came back and flung the string bag on the marble table in the kitchen and took her bicycle and dashed off to the office where she worked. Diomira looked at all the things in the string bag, touched the oranges one by one and the meat, and grumbled and called Granny to see what poor meat it was. Their mother came home at two o'clock when they had all eaten and ate quickly with the newspaper propped up against her glass and then rushed off again to the office on her bicycle and they saw her for a minute at supper again, but after supper she nearly always dashed off.

The boys did their homework in the bedroom. There was their father's picture, large at the head of the bed, with his square black beard and bald head and tortoiseshell-rimmed spectacles, and then another small portrait on the table, with the younger of the boys in his arms. Their father had died when they were very small, they remembered nothing about him: or rather in the older boy's memory there was the

shadow of a very distant afternoon, in the country at Aunt
Clementina's: his father was pushing him across the meadow
in a green wheelbarrow; afterwards he had found some pieces
of this wheelbarrow, a handle and a wheel, in Aunt Clementina's attic; when it was new it was a splendid wheelbarrow
and he was glad to have it; his father ran along pushing him
and his long beard flapped. They knew nothing about their
father but they thought he must be the sort of person who is
strong and wise in allowing and forbidding; when Grandpa or
Diomira got angry with their mother Granny said that they
should be sorry for her because she had been very unfortunate, and she said that if Eugenio, the boys' father, had been
there she would have been an entirely different woman,
whereas she had had the misfortune to lose her husband when
she was still young. For a time there had been their father's
mother as well, they never saw her because she lived in
France but she used to write and send Christmas presents:
then in the end she died because she was very old.

At tea-time they ate chestnuts, or bread with oil and vine-
gar, and then if they had finished their homework they could
go and play in the small piazza or among the ruins of the
public baths, which had been blown up in an air raid. In the
small piazza there were a great many pigeons and they took
them bread or got Diomira to give them a paper bag of leftover rice. There they met all the local boys, boys from school
and others they met in the youth clubs on Sundays when they
had football matches with Don Vigliani, who hitched up his
black cassock and kicked. Sometimes they played football in
the small piazza too or else cops and robbers. Their grandmother appeared on the balcony occasionally and called to
them not to get hurt: it was nice seeing the lighted windows
of their home, up there on the third floor, from the dark
piazza, and knowing that they could go back there, warm up
at the stove and guard themselves from the night. Granny
sat in the kitchen with Diomira and mended the linen;
Grandpa was in the dining-room with his cap on, smoking
his pipe. Granny was very fat, and wore black, and on her
breast a medal with a picture of Uncle Oreste who had died
in the war: she was very good at cooking pizzas and things.
Sometimes she took them on her knee, even now when they
were quite big boys; she was fat, she had a large soft bosom;
from under the neck of her black dress you could see the
thick white woollen vest with a scolloped edge which she had

made herself. She would take them on her knee and say tender and slightly pitiful-sounding words in dialect; then she would take a long iron hair-pin out of her bun and clean their ears, and they would shriek and try to get away and Grandpa would come to the door with his pipe.

Grandpa had taught Greek and Latin at the high school. Now he was pensioned off and was writing a Greek grammer: many of his old pupils used to come and see him now and then. Then Diomira would make coffee; in the lavatory there were exercise book pages with Latin and Greek unseens on them, and his corrections in red and blue. Grandpa had a small white beard, a sort of goatee, and they were not to make a racket because his nerves were tired after all those years at school; he was always rather alarmed because prices kept going up and Granny always had a bit of a row with him in the morning because he was always surprised at the money they needed; he would say that perhaps Diomira pinched the sugar and made coffee in secret and Diomira would hear and rush at him and yell that the coffee was for the students who kept coming; but these were small incidents that quietened down at once and the boys were not alarmed, whereas they were alarmed when there was a quarrel between Grandpa and their mother; this happened sometimes if their mother came home very late at night, he would come out of his room with his overcoat over his pyjamas and bare feet, and he and their mother would shout: he said: "I know where you've been, I know where you've been, I know what you are," and their mother said: "What do I care?" and then: "Look, now you've woken the children," and he said: "A fat lot you care what happens to your children. Don't say anything because I know what you are. You're a bitch. You run around at night like the mad bitch you are." And then Granny and Diomira would come out in their nightdresses and push him into his room and say: "Shush, shush," and their mother would get into bed and sob under the bedclothes, her deep sobs echoing in the dark room: the boys thought that Grandpa must be right, they thought their mother was wrong to go to the cinema and to her girl friends at night. They felt very unhappy, frightened and unhappy, and lay huddled close together in the deep, warm, soft bed, and the older boy who was in the middle pushed away so as not to touch his mother's body: there seemed to him something disgusting in his mother's tears, in the wet pillow: he thought: "It gives a chap the creeps when his mother cries." They never spoke between themselves of these rows their mother and Grandpa had, they carefully avoided mentioning them: but they loved each other very much and clung close together at night when their mother cried: in the morning they were faintly embarrassed, because they had hugged so tightly as if to protect themselves, and because there was that thing they didn't want to talk about; besides, they soon forgot that they had been unhappy, the day began and they went to school, and met their friends in the street, and played for a moment at the school door.

In the grey light of morning, their mother got up: with her petticoat wound round her waist she soaped her neck and arms standing bent over the basin: she always tried not to let them see her but in the looking glass they could make out her thin brown shoulders and small naked breasts: in the cold the nipples became dark and protruding, she raised her arms and powdered her armpits: in her armpits she had thick curly hair. When she was completely dressed she started plucking her eyebrows, staring at herself in the mirror from close to and biting her lips hard: then she smothered her face with cream and shook the pink swansdown puff hard and powdered herself: then her face became all yellow. Sometimes she was quite gay in the mornings and wanted to talk to the boys, she asked them about school and their friends and told them things about her time at school: she had a teacher called "Signorina Dirce" and she was an old maid who tried to seem young. Then she put on her coat and picked up her string shopping bag, leant down to kiss the boys and ran out with her scarf wound round her head and her face all perfumed and powdered with yellow powder.

The boys thought it strange to have been born of her. It would have been much less strange to have been born of Granny or Diomira, with their large warm bodies that protected you from fear, that defended you from storms and robbers. It was very strange to think she was their mother, that she had held them for a while in her small womb. Since they learnt that children are in their mother's tummy before being born, they had felt very surprised and also a little ashamed that that womb had once held them. And that she had given them milk from her breasts as well: this was even more unlikely. But now she no longer had small children to feed and cradle, and every day they saw her dash off on her bicycle when the shopping was done, her body jerking away, free and happy. She certainly didn't belong to them: they couldn't count on her. You couldn't ask her anything: there were other mothers, the mothers of their school friends, whom clearly you could ask about all sorts of things; their friends ran to their mothers when school was over and asked them heaps of things, got their noses blown and their overcoats buttoned, showed their homework and their comics: these mothers were pretty old, with hats and veils or fur collars and they came to talk to the master practically every day: they were people like Granny or like Diomira, large soft imperious bodies of people who didn't make mistakes: people who didn't lose things, who didn't leave their drawers untidy, who didn't come home late at night. But their mother ran off free after the shopping; besides, she was bad at shopping, she got cheated by the butcher and was often given wrong change: she went off and it was impossible to join her where she went, deep down they marvelled at her enormously when they saw her go off: who knows what that office of hers was like, she didn't talk about it much; she had to type and write letters in French and English: who knows, maybe she was pretty good at that.

One day when they were out for a walk with Don Vigliani and with other boys from the youth club, on the way back they saw their mother in a suburban café. She was sitting inside the café; they saw her through the window, and a man was sitting with her. Their mother had laid her tartan scarf on the table and the old crocodile handbag they knew well: the man had a loose light overcoat and a brown moustache and was talking to her and smiling: their mother's face was happy, relaxed and happy, as it never was at home. She was looking at the man and they were holding hands and she didn't see the boys: the boys went on walking beside Don Vigliani who told them all to hurry because they must catch the tram: when they were on the tram the younger boy moved over to his brother and said: "Did you see Mummy?" and his brother said: "No, I didn't." The younger one laughed softly and said: "Oh yes you did, it was Mummy and there was a man with her." The older boy turned his head away: he was big, nearly thirteen: his younger brother irritated him because he made him feel sorry for him, he couldn't understand why he felt sorry for him but he was sorry for himself as well and he didn't want to think of what he had seen, he wanted to behave as if he had seen nothing.

They said nothing to Granny. In the morning while their mother was dressing the younger boy said: "Yesterday when we were out for a walk with Don Vigliani we saw you and there was a man with you." Their mother jerked round, looking nasty: the black fish on her forehead quivered and met. She said: "But it wasn't me. What an idea. I've got to stay in the office till late in the evening, as you know. Obviously you made a mistake." The older boy then said, in a tired calm voice: "No, it wasn't you. It was someone who looked like you." And both boys realized that the memory must disappear: and they both breathed hard to blow it away.

But the man in the light overcoat once came to the house. He hadn't got his overcoat because it was summer, he wore blue spectacles and a light linen suit, he asked leave to take off his jacket while they had lunch. Granny and Grandpa had gone to Milan to meet some relations and Diomira had gone to her village, so they were alone with their mother. It was then the man came. Lunch was pretty good: their mother had bought nearly everything at the cooked meat shop: there was chicken with chips and this came from the shop: their mother had done the pasta, it was good, only the sauce was a bit burnt. There was wine, too. Their mother was nervous and gay, she wanted to say so much at once: she wanted to talk of the boys to the man and of the man to the boys. The man was called Max and he had been in Africa, he had lots of photographs of Africa and showed them: there was a photograph of a monkey of his, the boys asked him about this monkey a lot; it was so intelligent and so fond of him and had such a funny, pretty way with it when it wanted a sweet. But he had left it in Africa because it was ill and he was afraid it would die on the steamer. The boys became friendly with this Max. He promised to take them to the cinema one day. They showed him their books, they hadn't got many: he asked them if they had read *Saturnino Farandola* and they said no and he said he would give it to them, and *Robinson delle praterie* as well, as it was very fine. After lunch their mother told them to go and play in the recreation ground. They wished they could stay on with Max. They protested a bit but their mother, and Max too, said they must go; then in

the evening when they came home Max was no longer there.
Their mother hurriedly prepared the supper, coffee with milk
and potato salad: they were happy, they wanted to talk
about Africa and the monkey, they were extraordinarily
happy and couldn't really understand why: and their mother
seemed happy too and told them things, about a monkey she
had once seen dancing to a little street organ. And then she
told them to go to bed and said she was going out for a
minute, they mustn't be scared, there was no reason to be;
she bent down to kiss them and told them there was no point
in telling Granny and Grandpa about Max because they
never liked one inviting people home.

So they stayed on their own with their mother for a few
days: they ate unusual things because their mother didn't
want to cook, ham and jam and coffee with milk and fried
things from the cooked meat shop. Then they washed up together. But when Granny and Grandpa came back the boys
felt relieved: the tablecloth was on the dining-room table
again, and the glasses and everything there should be: Granny
was sitting in her rocking chair again, with her soft body and
her smell: Grandma couldn't dash off, she was too old and
too fat, it was nice having someone who stayed at home and
couldn't ever dash away.

The boys said nothing to Granny about Max. They waited
for the book *Saturnino Farandola* and waited for Max to
take them to the cinema and show them more photographs of
the monkey. Once or twice they asked their mother when
they'd be going to the cinema with signor Max. But their
mother answered harshly that signor Max had left now. The
younger boy asked if he'd gone to Africa. Their mother
didn't answer. But he thought he must have gone to Africa to
fetch the monkey. He imagined that someday or other he
would come and fetch them at school, with a black servant
and a monkey in his arms. School began again and Aunt
Clementina came to stay with them for a while; she had
brought a bag of pears and apples which they put in the oven
to cook with marsala and sugar. Their mother was in a very
bad temper and quarrelled continually with Grandpa. She
came home late and stayed awake smoking. She had got very
much thinner and ate nothing. Her face became even smaller
and yellower, she now put black on her eyelashes too, she spat
into a little box and picked up the black where she had spat

with a brush; she put on masses of powder, Granny tried to wipe it off her face with a handkerchief and she turned her face away. She hardly ever spoke and when she did it seemed an effort, her voice was so weak. One day she came home in the afternoon at about six o'clock: it was strange, usually she came home much later; she locked herself in the bedroom. The younger boy came and knocked because he needed an exercise book: their mother answered angrily from inside that she wanted to sleep and that they were to leave her in peace: the boy explained timidly that he needed the exercise book; then she came to open up and her face was all swollen and wet: the boy realized she was crying, he went back to Granny and said: "Mummy's crying," and Granny and Aunt Clementina talked quietly together for a long time, they spoke of their mother but you couldn't make out what they were saying.

One night their mother didn't come home. Grandpa kept coming to see, barefoot, with his overcoat over his pyjamas; Granny came too and the boys slept badly, they could hear Granny and Grandpa walking about the house, opening and shutting the windows. The boys were very frightened. Then in the morning, they rang up from the police station: their mother had been found dead in an hotel, she had taken poison, she had left a letter: Grandpa and Aunt Clementina went along, Granny shrieked, the boys were sent to an old lady on the floor below who said continually: "Heartless, leaving two babes like this." Their mother was brought home. The boys went to see her when they had her laid out on the bed: Diomira had dressed her in her patent leather shoes and red silk dress from the time she was married: she was small, a small dead doll.

It was strange to see flowers and candles in the same old room. Diomira and Aunt Clementina and Granny were kneeling and praying: they had said she took the poison by mistake, otherwise the priest wouldn't come and bless her, if he knew she had done it on purpose. Diomira told the boys they must kiss her: they were terribly ashamed and kissed her cold cheek one after the other. Then there was the funeral, it took ages, they crossed the entire town and felt very tired, Don Vigliani was there too and a great many children from school and from the youth club. It was cold, and very windy in the cemetery. When they went home again, Granny started crying and bawling at the sight of the bicycle in the passage:

because it was really just like seeing her dashing away, with her free body and her scarf flapping in the wind: Don Vigliani said she was now in heaven, perhaps because he didn't know she had done it on purpose, or he knew and pretended not to: but the boys didn't really know if heaven existed, because Grandpa said no, and Granny said yes, and their mother had once said there was no heaven, with little angels and beautiful music, but that the dead went to a place where they were neither well nor ill, and that where you wish for nothing you rest and are wholly at peace.

The boys went to the country for a time, to Aunt Clementina's. Everyone was very kind to them, and kissed and caressed them, and they were very ashamed. They never spoke together of their mother nor of signor Max either; in the attic at Aunt Clementina's they found the book of *Saturnino Farandola* and they read it over and over and found it very fine. But the older boy often thought of his mother, as he had seen her that day in the café with Max, holding her hands and with such a relaxed, happy face; he thought then that maybe their mother had taken poison because Max had gone back to Africa for good. The boys played with Aunt Clementina's dog, a fine dog called Bubi, and they learnt to climb trees, as they couldn't do before. They went bathing in the river, too, and it was nice going back to Aunt Clementina's in the evening and doing crosswords all together. The boys were very happy at Aunt Clementina's. Then they went back to Granny's and were very happy. Granny sat in the rocking chair, and wanted to clean their ears with her hairpins. On Sunday they went to the cemetery, Diomira came too, they bought flowers and on the way back stopped at a bar to have hot punch. When they were in the cemetery, at the grave, Granny prayed and cried, but it was very hard to think that the grave and the crosses and the cemetery had anything to do with their mother, who had been cheated by the butcher and dashed off on her bicycle, and smoked, and took wrong turnings, and sobbed at night. The bed was very big for them now and they had a pillow each. They didn't often think of their mother because it hurt them a little and made them ashamed to think of her. Sometimes they tried to remember how she was, each on his own in silence: and they found it harder and harder to reassemble her short curly hair and the fish on her forehead and her lips: she put on a lot of yellow powder, this they remembered quite well; little by little there was a yellow dot, it was impossible to get the shape of her cheeks and face. Besides, they now realized that they had never loved her much, perhaps she too hadn't loved them much, if she had loved them she wouldn't have taken poison, they had heard Diomira and the porter and the lady on the floor below and so many other people say so. The years went by and the boys grew and so many things happened and that face which they had never loved very much disappeared for ever.

JANE BOWLES was born in New York City in 1917. She married the composer and writer Paul Bowles in 1938. After a year's residence in the Brooklyn Heights boardinghouse also inhabited by Richard and Ellen Wright, Carson McCullers, W. H. Auden, Benjamin Britten, Gypsy Rose Lee, and a monkey trainer (with monkeys), they settled in Tangiers.

Ignored by the popular critics and anthologists, Bowles's work is revered by writers. Alan Sillitoe called her novel *Two Serious Ladies* (1943) "a landmark in twentieth century American literature." John Ashberry regards her as "one of the finest modern writers of fiction, in any language." Truman Capote in his introduction to *The Collected Works of Jane Bowles* wrote ". . . though the tragic view is central to her vision, Jane Bowles is a very funny writer, a humorist of sorts—but *not*, by the way, of the Black School. Black Comedy, as its perpetrators label it, is, when successful, all lovely artifice and lacking any hint of compassion. 'Camp Cataract,' to my mind the most complete of Mrs. Bowles's stories and the one most representative of her work, is a rending sample of controlled compassion: a comic tale of doom that has at its heart, and *as* its heart, the subtlest comprehension of eccentricity and human apartness. This story alone would require that we accord Jane Bowles high esteem."

Jane Bowles's own remarks about her career are as thorny as the wit of her fiction: "I started to write when I was about fifteen and was obliged to do composition in school. I always thought it the most loathsome of all activities and still do. At the same time I felt even then that I had to do it. Like most adolescents I read a great deal, and had very snobbish tastes. I thought Aldous Huxley wrote only pot-boilers. . . ." She died in 1973 after a long illness.

Jane Bowles
(1917—1973)

CAMP CATARACT

Beryl knocked on Harriet's cabin door and was given permission to enter. She found her friend seated near the window, an open letter in her hand.

"Good evening, Beryl," said Harriet. "I was just reading a letter from my sister." Her fragile, spinsterish face wore a canny yet slightly hysterical expression.

Beryl, a stocky blond waitress with stubborn eyes, had developed a dogged attachment to Harriet and sat in her cabin whenever she had a moment to spare. She rarely spoke in Harriet's presence, nor was she an attentive listener.

"I'll read you what she says; have a seat." Harriet indicated a straight chair and Beryl dragged it into a dark corner where she sat down. It creaked dangerously under the weight of her husky body.

"Hope I don't bust the chair," said Beryl, and she blushed furiously, digging her hands deep into the pockets of the checked plus-fours she habitually wore when she was not on duty.

" 'Dear Sister,' " Harriet read. " 'You are still at Camp Cataract visiting the falls and enjoying them. I always want you to have a good time. This is your fifth week away. I suppose you go on standing behind the falls with much enjoyment like you told me all the guests did. I think you said only the people who don't stay overnight have to pay to stand behind the waterfall . . . you stay ten weeks . . . have a nice time, dear. Here everything is exactly the same as when you left. The apartment doesn't change. I have something I want to tell you, but first let me say that if you get nervous, why don't you come home instead of waiting until you are no good for the train trip? Such a thing could happen. I wonder of course how you feel about the apartment once you are by the waterfall. Also, I want to put this to you. Knowing that you have an apartment and a loving family must make Camp

226

Cataract quite a different place than it would be if it were all the home and loving you had. There must be wretches like that up there. If you see them, be sure to give them loving because they are the lost souls of the earth. I fear nomads. I am afraid of them and afraid for them too. I don't know what I would do if any of my dear ones were seized with the wanderlust. We are meant to cherish those who through God's will are given into our hands. First of all come the members of the family, and for this it is better to live as close as possible. Maybe you would say, "Sadie is old-fashioned; she doesn't want people to live on their own." I am not old-fashioned, but I don't want any of us to turn into nomads. You don't grow rich in spirit by widening your circle but by tending your own. When you are gone, I get afraid about you. I think that you might be seized with the wanderlust and that you are not remembering the apartment very much. Particularly this trip . . . but then I know this cannot be true and that only my nerves make me think such things. It's so hot out. This is a record-breaking summer. Remember, the apartment is not just a row of rooms. It is the material proof that our spirits are so wedded that we have but one blessed roof over our heads. There are only three of us in the apartment related by blood, but Bert Hoffer has joined the three through the normal channels of marriage, also sacred. I know that you feel this way too about it and that just nerves makes me think Camp Cataract can change anything. May I remind you also that if this family is a garland, you are the middle flower; for me you are anyway. Maybe Evy's love is now flowing more to Bert Hoffer because he's her husband, which is natural. I wish they didn't think you needed to go to Camp Cataract because of your spells. Haven't I always tended you when you had them? Bert's always taken Evy to the Hoffers and we've stayed together, just the two of us, with the door safely locked so you wouldn't in your excitement run to a neighbor's house at all hours of the morning. Evy liked going to the Hoffers because they always gave her chicken with dumplings or else goose with red cabbage. I hope you haven't got it in your head that just because you are an old maid you have to go somewhere and be by yourself. Remember, I am also an old maid. I must close now, but I am not satisfied with my letter because I have so much more to say. I know you love the apartment and feel the way I feel. You are simply getting a tourist's thrill out of being there in a cabin like all of us do. I count the days until your sweet return. Your loving sister, Sadie.' "

Harriet folded the letter. "Sister Sadie," she said to Beryl, "is a great lover of security."

"She sounds swell," said Beryl, as if Harriet were mentioning her for the first time, which was certainly not the case.

"I have no regard for it whatsoever," Harriet announced in a positive voice. *"None.* In fact, I am a great admirer of the nomad, vagabonds, gypsies, seafaring men. I tip my hat to them; the old prophets roamed the world for that matter too, and most of the visionaries." She folded her hands in her lap with an air of satisfaction. Then, clearing her throat as if for a public address, she continued. "I don't give a tinker's damn about feeling part of a community. I can assure you. . . . That's not why I stay at the apartment . . . not for a minute, but it's a good reason why she does . . . I mean Sadie; she loves a community spirit and she loves us all to be in the apartment because the apartment is in the community. She can get an actual thrill out of knowing that. But of course I can't . . . I never could, never in a thousand years."

She tilted her head back and half-closed her eyes. In the true style of a person given to interminable monologues, she was barely conscious of her audience. "Now," she said, "we can come to whether I, on the other hand, get a thrill out of Camp Cataract." She paused for a moment as if to consider this. "Actually, I don't," she pronounced sententiously, "but if you like, I will clarify my statement by calling Camp Cataract my *tree house.* You remember tree houses from your younger days. . . . You climb into them when you're a child and plan to run away from home once you are safely hidden among the leaves. They're popular with children. Suppose I tell you pointblank that I'm an extremely original woman, but also a very shallow one . . . in a sense, a *very* shallow one. I am afraid of scandal." Harriet assumed a more erect position. "I despise anything that smacks of a bohemian dash for freedom; I know that this has nothing to do with the more serious things in life . . . I'm sure there are hundreds of serious people who kick over their traces and jump into the gutter; but I'm too shallow for anything like that . . . I know it and I enjoy knowing it. Sadie on the other hand cooks and cleans all day long and yet takes her life as seriously as she would a religion . . . myself and the apartment and the Hoffers. By the Hoffers, I mean my sister Evy and her big pig of a husband Bert." She made a wry face. "I'm the only one with taste in the family but I've never even suggested a lamp for the apartment. I wouldn't lower myself by becoming involved. I do however refuse to make an unseemly dash for freedom. I refuse to be known as 'Sadie's wild sister Harriet.' There is something intensively repulsive to me about unmarried women setting out on their own . . . also a very shallow attitude. You may wonder how a woman can be shallow and know it at the same time, but then, this is precisely the tragedy of any person, if he allows himself to be griped." She paused for a moment and looked into the darkness with a fierce light in her eyes. "Now let's get back to Camp Cataract," she said with renewed vigor. "The pine groves, the canoes, the sparkling purity of the brook water and cascade . . . the cabins . . . the marshmallows, the respectable clientele."

"Did you ever think of working in a garage?" Beryl suddenly blurted out, and then she blushed again at the sound of her own voice.

"No," Harriet answered sharply. "Why should I?"

Beryl shifted her position in her chair. "Well," she said, "I think I'd like that kind of work better than waiting on tables. Especially if I could be boss and own my garage. It's hard, though, for a woman."

Harriet stared at her in silence. "Do you think Camp Cataract smacks of the gutter?" she asked a minute later.

"No, sir . . ." Beryl shook her head with a woeful air.

"Well then, there you have it. It is, of course, the farthest point from the gutter that one could reach. Any blockhead can see that. My plan is extremely complicated and from my point of view rather brilliant. First I will come here for several years . . . I don't know yet exactly how many, but long enough to imitate roots . . . I mean to imitate the natural family roots of childhood . . . long enough so that I myself will feel: 'Camp Cataract is *habit*, Camp Cataract is life, Camp Cataract is not escape.' Escape is unladylike, habit isn't. As I remove myself gradually from within my family circle and establish myself more and more solidly into Camp Cataract, then from here at some later date I can start making my sallies into the outside world almost unnoticed. None of it will seem to the onlooker like an ugly impetuous escape. I intend to rent the same cabin every year and to stay a little longer each time. Meanwhile I'm learning a great deal about

trees and flowers and bushes . . . I am interested in nature."
She was quiet for a moment. "It's rather lucky too," she
added, "that the doctor has approved of my separating from
the family for several months out of every year. He's a blockhead and doesn't remotely suspect the extent of my scheme
nor how perfectly he fits into it . . . in fact, he has even
sanctioned my request that no one visit me here at the camp.
I'm afraid if Sadie did, and she's the only one who would
dream of it, I wouldn't be able to avoid a wrangle and then I
might have a fit. The fits are unpleasant; I get much more nervous than I usually am and there's a blank moment or two."
Harriet glanced sideways at Beryl to see how she was reacting
to this last bit of information, but Beryl's face was impassive.

"So you see my plan," she went on, in a relaxed, offhand
manner, "complicated, a bit dotty and completely original
. . . but then, I *am* original . . . not like my sisters . . .
oddly enough I don't even seem to belong socially to the
same class as my sisters do. I am somehow"—she hesitated
for a second—"more fashionable."

Harriet glanced out of the window. Night had fallen during the course of her monologue and she could see a light
burning in the next cabin. "Do you think I'm a coward?" she
asked Beryl.

The waitress was startled out of her torpor. Fortunately
her brain registered Harriet's question as well. "No, sir," she
answered. "If you were, you wouldn't go out paddling canoes
solo, with all the scary shoots you run into up and down
these rivers. . . ."

Harriet twisted her body impatiently. She had a sudden
and uncontrollable desire to be alone. "Good-bye," she said
rudely. "I'm not coming to supper."

Beryl rose from her chair. "I'll save something for you in
case you get hungry after the dining room's closed. I'll be
hanging around the lodge like I always am till bedtime." Harriet nodded and the waitress stepped out of the cabin, shutting the door carefully behind her so that it would not make
any noise.

Harriet's sister Sadie was a dark woman with loose features
and sad eyes. She was turning slightly to fat in her middle
years, and did not in any way resemble Harriet, who was
only a few years her senior. Ever since she had written her
last letter to Harriet about Camp Cataract and the nomads

Sadie had suffered from a feeling of steadily mounting suspense—the suspense itself a curious mingling of apprehension and thrilling anticipation. Her appetite grew smaller each day and it was becoming increasingly difficult for her to accomplish her domestic tasks.

She was standing in the parlor gazing with blank eyes at her new furniture set—two enormous easy chairs with bulging arms and a sofa in the same style—when she said aloud: "I can talk to her better than I can put it in a letter." Her voice had been automatic and when she heard her own words a rush of unbounded joy flooded her heart. Thus she realized that she was going on a little journey to Camp Cataract. She often made important decisions this way, as if some prearranged plot were being suddenly revealed to her, a plot which had immediately to be concealed from the eyes of others, because for Sadie, if there was any problem implicit in making a decision, it lay, not in the difficulty of choosing, but in the concealment of her choice. To her, secrecy was the real absolution from guilt, so automatically she protected all of her deepest feelings and compulsions from the eyes of Evy, Bert Hoffer and the other members of the family, although she had no interest in understanding or examining these herself.

The floor shook; recognizing Bert Hoffer's footsteps, she made a violent effort to control the flux of her blood so that the power of her emotion would not be reflected in her cheeks. A moment later her brother-in-law walked across the room and settled in one of the easy chairs. He sat frowning at her for quite a little while without uttering a word in greeting, but Sadie had long ago grown accustomed to his unfriendly manner; even in the beginning it had not upset her too much because she was such an obsessive that she was not very concerned with outside details.

"God-damned velours," he said finally. "It's the hottest stuff I ever sat on."

"Next summer we'll get covers," Sadie reassured him, "with a flower pattern if you like. What's your favorite flower?" she asked, just to make conversation and to distract him from looking at her face.

Bert Hoffer stared at her as if she'd quite taken leave of her senses. He was a fat man with a red face and wavy hair. Instead of answering this question, which he considered idiotic, he mopped his brow with his handkerchief.

"I'll fix you a canned pineapple salad for supper," she said to him with glowing eyes. "It will taste better than heavy meat on a night like this."

"If you're going to dish up pineapple salad for supper," Bert Hoffer answered with a dark scowl, "you can telephone some other guy to come and eat it. You'll find me over at Martie's Tavern eating meat and potatoes, if there's any messages to deliver."

"I thought because you were hot," said Sadie.

"I was talking about the velvet, wasn't I? I didn't say anything about the meat."

He was a very trying man indeed, particularly in a small apartment, but Sadie never dwelled upon this fact at all. She was delighted to cook and clean for him and for her sister Evelyn so long as they consented to live under the same roof with her and Harriet.

Just then Evelyn walked briskly into the parlor. Like Sadie she was dark, but here the resemblance ceased, for she had a small and wiry build, with a flat chest, and her hair was as straight as an Indian's. She stared at her husband's shirt sleeves and at Sadie's apron with distaste. She was wearing a crisp summer dress with a very low neckline, an unfortunate selection for one as bony and fierce-looking as she.

"You both look ready for the dump heap, not for the dining room," she said to them. "Why do we bother to have a dining room . . . is it just a farce?"

"How was the office today?" Sadie asked her sister.

Evelyn looked at Sadie and narrowed her eyes in closer scrutiny. The muscles in her face tightened. There was a moment of dead silence, and Bert Hoffer, cocking a wary eye in his wife's direction, recognized the dangerous flush on her cheeks. Secretly he was pleased. He loved to look on when Evelyn blew up at Sadie, but he tried to conceal his enjoyment because he did not consider it a very masculine one.

"What's the matter with you?" Evelyn asked finally, drawing closer to Sadie. "There's something wrong besides your dirty apron."

Sadie colored slightly but said nothing.

"You look crazy," Evelyn yelled. "What's the matter with you? You look so crazy I'd be almost afraid to ask you to go to the store for something. Tell me what's happened!" Evelyn was very excitable; nonetheless hers was a strong and sane nature.

"I'm not crazy," Sadie mumbled. "I'll go get the dinner."

She pushed slowly past Evelyn and with her heavy step she left the parlor.

The mahogany dining table was much too wide for the small oblong-shaped room, clearing the walls comfortably only at the two ends. When many guests were present some were seated first on one side of the room and were then obliged to draw the table toward themselves, until its edge pressed painfully into their diaphragms, before the remaining guests could slide into their seats on the opposite side.

Sadie served the food, but only Bert Hoffer ate with any appetite. Evelyn jabbed at her meat once or twice, tasted it, and dropped her fork, which fell with a clatter on to her plate.

Had the food been more savory she might not have pursued her attack on Sadie until later, or very likely she would have forgotten it altogether. Unfortunately, however, Sadie, although she insisted on fulfilling the role of housewife, and never allowed the others to acquit themselves of even the smallest domestic task, was a poor cook and a careless cleaner as well. Her lumpy gravies were tasteless, and she had once or twice boiled a good cut of steak out of indifference. She was lavish, too, in spite of being indifferent, and kept her cupboards so loaded with food that a certain quantity spoiled each week and there was often an unpleasant odor about the house. Harriet, in fact, was totally unaware of Sadie's true nature and had fallen into the trap her sister had instinctively prepared for her, because beyond wearing an apron and simulating the airs of other housewives, Sadie did not possess a community spirit at all, as Harriet had stated to Beryl the waitress. Sadie certainly yearned to live in the grown-up world that her parents had established for them when they were children, but in spite of the fact that she had wanted to live in that world with Harriet, and because of Harriet, she did not understand it properly. It remained mysterious to her even though she did all the housekeeping and managed the apartment entirely alone. She couldn't ever admit to herself that she lived in constant fear that Harriet would go away, but she brooded a great deal on outside dangers, and had she tried, she could not have remembered a time when this fear had not been her strongest emotion.

Sometimes an ecstatic and voracious look would come into her eyes, as if she would devour her very existence because she loved it so much. Such passionate moments of appreciation were perhaps her only reward for living a life which she knew in her heart was one of perpetual narrow escape. Although Sadie was neither sly nor tricky, but on the contrary profoundly sincere and ingenuous, she schemed unconsciously to keep the Hoffers in the apartment with them, because she did not want to reveal the true singleness of her interest either to Harriet or to herself. She sensed as well that Harriet would find it more difficult to break away from all three of them (because as a group they suggested a little society, which impressed her sister) than she would to escape from her alone. In spite of her mortal dread that Harriet might strike out on her own, she had never brooded on the possibility of her sister's marrying. Here, too, her instinct was correct: she knew that she was safe and referred often to the "normal channels of marriage," conscious all the while that such an intimate relationship with a man would be as uninteresting to Harriet as it would to herself.

From a financial point of view this communal living worked out more than satisfactorily. Each sister had inherited some real estate which yielded her a small monthly stipend; these stipends, combined with the extra money that the Hoffers contributed out of their salaries, covered their common living expenses. In return for the extra sum the Hoffers gave toward the household expenses, Sadie contributed her work, thus saving them the money they would have spent hiring a servant, had they lived alone. A fourth sister, whose marriage had proved financially more successful than Evy's, contributed generously toward Harriet's support at Camp Cataract, since Harriet's stipend certainly did not yield enough to cover her share of their living expenses at the apartment and pay for a long vacation as well.

Neither Sadie nor Bert Hoffer had looked up when Evy's fork clattered onto her plate. Sadie was truly absorbed in her own thoughts, whereas Bert Hoffer was merely pretending to be, while secretly he rejoiced at the unmistakable signal that his wife was about to blow up.

"When I find out why Sadie looks like that if she isn't going to be crazy, then I'll eat," Evelyn announced flatly, and she folded her arms across her chest.

"I'm not crazy," Sadie said indistinctly, glancing toward Bert Hoffer, not in order to enlist his sympathies, but to avoid her younger sister's sharp scrutiny.

"There's a big danger of your going crazy because of

Grandma and Harriet," said Evelyn crossly. "That's why I get so nervous the minute you look a little out of the way, like you do tonight. It's not that you get Harriet's expression . . . but then you might be getting a different kind of craziness . . . maybe worse. She's all right if she can go away and there's not too much excitement . . . it's only in spells anyway. But you—you might get a worse kind. Maybe it would be steadier."

"I'm not going to be crazy," Sadie murmured apologetically.

Evelyn glowered in silence and picked up her fork, but then immediately she let it fall again and turned on her sister with renewed exasperation. "Why don't you ask me why *I'm* not going to be crazy?" she demanded. "Harriet's my sister and Grandma's my grandma just as much as she is yours, isn't she?"

Sadie's eyes had a faraway look.

"If you were normal," Evelyn pursued, "you'd give me an intelligent argument instead of not paying any attention. Do you agree, Hoffer?"

"Yes, I do," he answered soberly.

Evelyn stiffened her back. "I'm too much like everybody else to be crazy," she announced with pride. "At a picture show, I feel like the norm."

The technical difficulty of disappearing without announcing her plan to Evelyn suddenly occurred to Sadie, who glanced up quite by accident at her sister. She knew, of course, that Harriet was supposed to avoid contact with her family during these vacation months at the doctor's request and even at Harriet's own; but like some herd animal, who though threatened with the stick continues grazing. Sadie pursued her thoughts imperturbably. She did not really believe in Harriet's craziness nor in the necessity of her visits to Camp Cataract, but she was never in conscious opposition to the opinions of her sisters. Her attitude was rather like that of a child who is bored by the tedium of grown-up problems and listens to them with a vacant ear. As usual she was passionately concerned only with successfully dissimulating what she really felt, and had she been forced to admit openly that there existed such a remarkable split between her own opinions and those of her sisters, she would have suffered unbelievable torment. She was able to live among them, listening to their conferences with her dead outside ear (the more affluent sister was also present at these sessions, and her husband as well), and even to contribute a pittance toward Harriet's support at the camp, without questioning the validity either of their decisions or of her own totally divergent attitude. By a self-imposed taboo, awareness of this split was denied her, and she had never reflected upon it.

Harriet had gone to Camp Cataract for the first time a year ago, after a bad attack of nerves combined with a return of her pleurisy. It had been suggested by the doctor himself that she go with his own wife and child instead of traveling with one of her sisters. Harriet had been delighted with the suggestion and Sadie had accepted it without a murmur. It was never her habit to argue, and in fact she had thought nothing of Harriet's leaving at the time. It was only gradually that she had begun writing the letters to Harriet about Camp Cataract, the nomads and the wanderlust—for she had written others similar to her latest one, but never so eloquent or full of conviction. Previous letters had contained a hint or two here and there, but had been for the main part factual reports about her summer life in the apartment. Since writing this last letter she had not been able to forget her own wonderful and solemn words (for she was rarely eloquent), and even now at the dinner table they rose continually in her throat so that she was thrilled over and over again and could not bother her head about announcing her departure to Evelyn. "It will be easier to write a note," she said to herself. "I'll pack my valise and walk out tomorrow afternoon, while they're at business. They can get their own dinners for a few days. Maybe I'll leave a great big meat loaf." Her eyes were shining like stars.

"Take my plate and put it in the warmer. Hoffer," Evelyn was saying. "I won't eat another mouthful until Sadie tells us what we can expect. If she feels she's going off, she can at least warn us about it. I deserve to know how she feels . . . I tell every single thing I feel to her and Harriet . . . I don't sneak around the house like a thief. In the first place I don't have any time for sneaking, I'm at the office all day! Is this the latest vogue, this sneaking around and hiding everything you can from your sister? Is it?" She stared at Bert Hoffer, widening her eyes in fake astonishment. He shrugged his shoulders.

"I'm no sneak or hypocrite and neither are you, Hoffer,

you're no hypocrite. You're just sore at the world, but you don't pretend you love the world, do you?"

Sadie was lightheaded with embarrassment. She had blanched at Evy's allusion to her going, which she mistook naturally for a reference to her intention of leaving for Camp Cataract.

"Only for a few days . . ." she mumbled in confusion, "and then I'll be right back here at the table."

Evelyn looked at her in consternation. "What do you mean by announcing calmly how many days it's going to be?" she shouted at her sister. "That's really sacrilegious! Did you ever hear of such a crusty sacrilegious remark in your life before?" She turned to Bert Hoffer, with a horror-stricken expression on her face. "How can I go to the office and look neat and clean and happy when this is what I hear at home . . . when my sister sits here and says she'll only go crazy for a few days? How *can* I go to the office after that? How can I look right?"

"I'm not going to be crazy," Sadie assured her again in a sorrowful tone, because although she felt relieved that Evelyn had not, after all, guessed the truth, hers was not a nature to indulge itself in trivial glee at having put someone off her track.

"You just said you were going to be crazy," Evelyn exclaimed heatedly. "Didn't she, Bert?"

"Yes," he answered, "she did say something like that. . . ."

The tendons of Evelyn's neck were stretched tight as she darted her eyes from her sister's face to her husband's. "Now, tell me this much," she demanded, "do I go to the office every day looking neat and clean or do I go looking like a bum?"

"You look O.K.," Bert said.

"Then why do my sisters spit in my eye? Why do they hide everything from me if I'm so decent? I'm wide open, I'm frank, there's nothing on my mind besides what I say. Why can't they be like other sisters all over the world? One of them is so crazy that she must live in a cabin for her nerves at *my* expense, and the other one is planning to go crazy deliberately and behind my back." She commenced to struggle out of her chair, which as usual proved to be a slow and laborious task. Exasperated, she shoved the table vehemently away from her toward the opposite wall. "Why don't we leave the space all on one side when there's no company?"

she screamed at both of them, for she was now annoyed with
Bert Hoffer as well as with Sadie. Fortunately they were
seated at either end of the table and so did not suffer as a
result of her violent gesture, but the table jammed into four
chairs ranged on the opposite side, pinning three of them
backward against the wall and knocking the fourth onto the
floor.

"Leave it there," Evelyn shouted dramatically above the
racket. "Leave it there till doomsday," and she rushed headlong out of the room.

They listened to her gallop down the hall.

"What about the dessert?" Bert Hoffer asked Sadie with a
frown. He was displeased because Evelyn had spoken to him
sharply.

"Leftover bread pudding without raisins." She had just gotten up to fetch the pudding when Evelyn summoned them
from the parlor.

"Come in here, both of you," she hollered. "I have something to say."

They found Evelyn seated on the couch, her head tilted
way back on a cushion, staring fixedly at the ceiling. They
settled into easy chairs opposite her.

"I could be normal and light in any other family," she
said, "I'm normally a gay light girl . . . not a morose one. I
like all the material things."

"What do you want to do tonight?" Bert Hoffner interrupted, speaking with authority. "Do you want to be excited or
do you want to go to the movies?" He was always bored by
these self-appraising monologues which succeeded her explosions.

Evy looked as though she had not heard him, but after a
moment or two of sitting with her eyes shut she got up and
walked briskly out of the room; her husband followed her.

Neither of them had said good-bye to Sadie, who went
over to the window as soon as they'd gone and looked down
on the huge unsightly square below her. It was crisscrossed
by trolley tracks going in every possible direction. Five phar-
macies and seven cigar stores were visible from where she
stood. She knew that modern industrial cities were considered
ugly, but she liked them. "I'm glad Evy and Bert have gone
to a picture show," Sadie remarked to herself after a while.
"Evy gets highstrung from being at the office all day."

A little later she turned her back on the window and went to the dining room.

"Looks like the train went through here," she murmured, gazing quietly at the chairs tilted back against the wall and the table's unsightly angle; but the tumult in her breast had not subsided, even though she knew she was leaving for Camp Cataract. Beyond the first rush of joy she had experienced when her plan had revealed itself to her earlier, in the parlor, the feeling of suspense remained identical, a curious admixture of anxiety and anticipation, difficult to bear. Concerning the mechanics of the trip itself she was neither nervous nor foolishly excited. "I'll call up tomorrow," she said to herself, "and find out when the buses go, or maybe I'll take the train. In the morning I'll buy three different meats for the loaf, if I don't forget. It won't go rotten for a few days, and even if it does they can eat at Martie's or else Evy will make bologna and eggs . . . she knows how, and so does Bert." She was not really concentrating on these latter projects any more than she usually did on domestic details.

The lamp over the table was suspended on a heavy iron chain. She reached for the beaded string to extinguish the light. When she released it the massive lamp swung from side to side in the darkness.

"Would you like it so much by the waterfall if you didn't know the apartment was here?" she whispered into the dark, and she was thrilled again by the beauty of her own words. "How much more I'll be able to say when I'm sitting right next to her," she murmured almost with reverence. ". . . And then we'll come back here," she added simply, not in the least startled to discover that the idea of returning with Harriet had been at the root of her plan all along.

Without bothering to clear the plates from the table, she went into the kitchen and extinguished the light there. She was suddenly overcome with fatigue.

When Sadie arrived at Camp Cataract it was raining hard.

"This shingled building is the main lodge," the hack driver said to her. "The ceiling in there is three times higher than average, if you like that style. Go up on the porch and just walk in. You'll get a kick out of it."

Sadie reached into her pocketbook for some money.

"My wife and I come here to drink beer when we're in the mood," he continued, getting out his change. "If there's nobody much inside, don't get panicky; the whole camp goes to the movies on Thursday nights. The wagon takes them and brings them back. They'll be along soon."

After thanking him she got out of the cab and climbed the wooden steps on to the porch. Without hesitating she opened the door. The driver had not exaggerated; the room was indeed so enormous that it suggested a gymnasium. Wicker chairs and settees were scattered from one end of the floor to the other and numberless sawed-off tree stumps had been set down to serve as little tables.

Sadie glanced around her and then headed automatically for a giant fireplace, difficult to reach because of the accumulation of chairs and settees that surrounded it. She threaded her way between these and stepped across the hearth into the cold vault of the chimney, high enough to shelter a person of average stature. The andirons, which reached to her waist, had been wrought in the shape of witches. She fingered their pointed iron hats. "Novelties," she murmured to herself without enthusiasm. "They must have been especially made." Then, peering out of the fireplace, she noticed for the first time that she was not alone. Some fifty feet away a fat woman sat reading by the light of an electric bulb.

"She doesn't even know I'm in the fireplace," she said to herself. "Because the rain's so loud, she probably didn't hear me come in." She waited patiently for a while and then, suspecting that the woman might remain oblivious to her presence indefinitely, she called over to her. "Do you have anything to do with managing Camp Cataract?" she asked, speaking loudly so that she could be heard above the rain.

The woman ceased reading and switched her big light off at once, since the strong glare prevented her seeing beyond the radius of the bulb.

"No, I don't," she answered in a booming voice. "Why?"

Sadie, finding no answer to this question, remained silent.

"Do you think I look like a manager?" the woman pursued, and since Sadie had obviously no intention of answering, she continued the conversation by herself.

"I suppose you might think I was manager here, because I'm stout, and stout people have that look; also I'm about the right age for it. But I'm not the manager . . . I don't manage anything, anywhere. I have a domineering cranium all right, but I'm more the French type. I'd rather enjoy myself than give orders."

"French . . ." Sadie repeated hesitantly.

"Not French," the woman corrected her. "French *type*, with a little of the actual blood." Her voice was cold and severe.

For a while neither of them spoke, and Sadie hoped the conversation had drawn to a definite close.

"Individuality is my god," the woman announced abruptly, much to Sadie's disappointment. "That's partly why I didn't go to the picture show tonight. I don't like doing what the groups do, and I've seen the film." She dragged her chair forward so as to be heard more clearly. "The steadies here—we call the ones who stay more than a fortnight steadies—are all crazy to get into birds-of-a-feather-flock-together arrangements. If you look around, you can see for yourself how clubby the furniture is fixed. Well, they can go in for it, if they want, but I won't. I keep my chair out in the open here, and when I feel like it I take myself over to one circle or another . . . there's about ten or twelve circles. Don't you object to the confinement of a group?"

"We haven't got a group back home," Sadie answered briefly.

"I don't go in for group worship either," the woman continued, "any more than I do for the heavy social mixing. I don't even go in for individual worship, for that matter. Most likely I was born to such a vigorous happy nature I don't feel the need to worry about what's up there over my head. I get the full flavor out of all my days whether anyone's up there or not. The groups don't allow for that kind of zip . . . never. You know what rotten apples in a barrel can do to the healthy ones."

Sadie, who had never before met an agnostic, was profoundly shocked by the woman's blasphemous attitude. "I'll bet she slept with a lot of men she wasn't married to when she was younger," she said to herself.

"Most of the humanity you bump into is unhealthy and nervous," the woman concluded, looking at Sadie with a cold eye, and then without further remarks she struggled out of her chair and began to walk toward a side door at the other end of the room. Just as she approached it the door was flung open from the other side by Beryl, whom the woman immediately warned of the new arrival. Beryl, without ceasing to spoon some beans out of a can she was holding, walked over to Sadie and offered to be of some assistance. "I can show you rooms," she suggested. "Unless you'd rather wait till the manager comes back from the movies."

When she realized, however, after a short conversation with Sadie, that she was speaking to Harriet's sister, a malevolent scowl darkened her countenance, and she spooned her beans more slowly.

"Harriet didn't tell me you were coming," she said at length; her tone was unmistakably disagreeable.

Sadie's heart commenced to beat very fast as she in turn realized that this woman in plus-fours was the waitress, Beryl, of whom Harriet had often spoken in her letters and at home.

"It's a surprise," Sadie told her. "I meant to come here before. I've been promising Harriet I'd visit her in camp for a long time now, but I couldn't come until I got a neighbor in to cook for Evy and Bert. They're a husband and wife . . . my sister Evy and her husband Bert."

"I know about those two," Beryl remarked sullenly. "Harriet's told me all about them."

"Will you please take me to my sister's cabin?" Sadie asked, picking up her valise and stepping forward.

Beryl continued to stir her beans around without moving.

"I thought you folks had some kind of arrangement," she said. She had recorded in her mind entire passages of Harriet's monologues out of love for her friend, although she felt no curiosity concerning the material she had gathered. "I thought you folks were supposed to stay in the apartment while she was away at camp."

"Bert Hoffer and Evy have never visited Camp Cataract," Sadie answered in a tone that was innocent of any subterfuge.

"You bet they haven't," Beryl pronounced triumphantly. "That's part of the arrangement. They're supposed to stay in the apartment while she's here at camp; the doctor said so."

"They're not coming up," Sadie repeated, and she still wore, not the foxy look that Beryl expected would betray itself at any moment, but the look of a person who is attentive though being addressed in a foreign language. The waitress sensed that all her attempts at starting a scrap had been successfully blocked for the present and she whistled carefully, dragging some chairs into line with a rough hand. "I'll tell you what," she said, ceasing her activities as suddenly as she had begun them. "Instead of taking you down there to the

Pine Cones—that's the name of the grove where her cabin is—I'll go myself and tell her to come up here to the lodge. She's got some nifty rain equipment so she won't get wet coming through the groves like you would . . . lots of pine trees out there."

Sadie nodded in silence and walked over to a fantasy chair, where she sat down.

"They get a lot of fun out of that chair. When they're drunk," said Beryl pointing to its back, made of a giant straw disc. "Well . . . so long. . . ." She strode away. "Dear Valley . . ." Sadie heard her sing as she went out the door.

Sadie lifted the top off the chair's left arm and pulled two books out of its woven hamper. "The larger volume was entitled *The Growth and Development of the Texas Oil Companies,* and the smaller, *Stories from Other Climes.* Hastily she replaced them and closed the lid.

Harriet opened the door for Beryl and quickly shut it again, but even in that instant the wooden flooring of the threshold was thoroughly soaked with rain. She was wearing a lavender kimono with a deep ruffle at the neckline; above it her face shone pale with dismay at Beryl's late and unexpected visit. She feared that perhaps the waitress was drunk. "I'm certainly not hacking out a free place for myself in this world just in order to cope with drunks," she said to herself with bitter verve. Her loose hair was hanging to her shoulders and Beryl looked at it for a moment in mute admiration before making her announcement.

"Your sister Sadie's up at the lodge," she said, recovering herself; then, feeling embarrassed, she shuffled over to her usual seat in the darkest corner of the room.

"What are you saying?" Harriet questioned her sharply.

"Your sister Sadie's up at the lodge," she repeated, not daring to look at her. "Your sister Sadie who wrote you the letter about the apartment."

"But she can't be!" Harriet screeched. "She can't be! It was all arranged that no one was to visit me here."

"That's what I told her," Beryl put in.

Harriet began pacing up and down the floor. Her pupils were dilated and she looked as if she were about to lose all control of herself. Abruptly she flopped down on the edge of the bed and began gulping in great draughts of air. She was actually practicing a system which she believed had often

saved her from complete hysteria, but Beryl, who knew nothing about her method, was horrified and utterly bewildered.
"Take it easy," she implored Harriet. "Take it easy!"

"Dash some water in my face," said Harriet in a strange
voice, but horror and astonishment anchored Beryl securely
to her chair, so that Harriet was forced to stagger over to the
basin and manage by herself. After five minutes of steady
dousing she wiped her face and chest with a towel and
resumed her pacing. At each instant the expression on her
face was more indignant and a trifle less distraught. "It's the
boorishness of it that I find so appalling," she complained, a
suggestion of theatricality in her tone which a moment before
had not been present. "If she's determined to wreck my
schemes, why doesn't she do it with some style, a little slight
bit of cunning? I can't picture anything more boorish than
hauling oneself onto a train and simply chugging straight up
here. She has no sense of scheming, of intrigue in the grand
manner . . . none whatever. Anyone meeting only Sadie
would think the family raised potatoes for a living. Evy
doesn't make a much better impression, I must say. If they
met her they'd decide we were all clerks! But at least she goes
to business. . . . She doesn't sit around thinking about how to
mess my life up all day. She thinks about Bert Hoffer. Ugh!"
She made a wry face.

"When did you and Sadie start fighting?" Beryl asked her.

"I don't fight with Sadie," Harriet answered, lifting her
head proudly. "I wouldn't dream of fighting like a common
fishwife. Everything that goes on between us goes on under-
cover. It's always been that way. I've always hidden everything from her ever since I was a little girl. She's perfectly
aware that I know she's trying to hold me a prisoner in the
apartment out of plain jealousy and she knows too that I'm
afraid of being considered a bum, and that makes matters
simpler for her. She pretends to be worried that I might forget myself if I left the apartment and commit a folly with
some man I wasn't married to, but actually she knows perfectly well that I'm as cold as ice. I haven't the slightest interest in men . . . nor in women either for that matter; still if I
stormed out of the apartment dramatically the way some do,
they might think I was a bum on my way to a man . . . and
I won't give Sadie that satisfaction, ever. As for marriage, of
course I admit I'm peculiar and there's a bit wrong with me,
but even so I shouldn't want to marry: I think the whole sys-

tem of going through life with a partner is replusive in every way." She paused, but only for a second. "Don't you imagine, however," she added severely, looking directly at Beryl, "don't you imagine that just because I'm a bit peculiar and different from the others, that I'm not fussy about my life. I *am* fussy about it, and I *hate* a scandal."

"To hell with sisters!" Beryl exclaimed happily. "Give 'em all a good swift kick in the pants." She had regained her own composure watching the color return to Harriet's cheeks and she was just beginning to think with pleasure that perhaps Sadie's arrival would serve to strengthen the bond of intimacy between herself and Harriet, when this latter buried her head in her lap and burst into tears. Beryl's face fell and she blushed at her own frivolousness.

"I can't any more," Harriet sobbed in anguished tones. "I can't . . . I'm old . . . I'm much too old." Here she collapsed and sobbed so pitifully that Beryl, wringing her hands in grief, sprang to her side, for she was a most tenderhearted person toward those whom she loved. "You are not old . . . you are beautiful," she said, blushing again, and in her heart she was thankful that Providence had granted her the occasion to console her friend in a grief-stricken moment, and to compliment her at the same time.

After a bit, Harriet's sobbing subsided, and jumping up from the bed, she grabbed the waitress. "Beryl," she gasped, "you must run back to the lodge right away." There was a beam of cunning in her tear-filled eyes.

"Sure will," Beryl answered.

"Go back to the lodge and see if there's a room left up there, and if there is, take her grip into it so that there will be no question of her staying in my cabin. I can't have her staying in my cabin. It's the only place I have in the whole wide world." The beam of cunning disappeared again and she looked at Beryl with wide, frightened eyes. ". . . And if there's no room?" she asked.

"Then I'll put her in my place," Beryl reassured her. "I've got a neat little cabin all to myself that she can have and I'll go bunk in with some dopey waitress."

"Well, then," said Harriet, "go, and hurry! Take her grip to a room in the upper lodge annex or to your own cabin before she has a chance to say anything, and then come straight back here for me. I can't get through these pine

groves alone . . . now . . . I know I can't." It did not occur
to her to thank Beryl for the kind offer she had made.

"All right," said the waitress, "I'll be back in a jiffy and
don't worry about a thing." A second later she was lumbering
through the drenched pine groves with shining eyes.

When Beryl came into the lodge and snatched Sadie's grip
up without a word of explanation, Sadie did not protest. Opposite her there was an open staircase which led to a narrow
gallery hanging halfway between the ceiling and the floor.
She watched the waitress climbing the stairs, but once she
had passed the landing Sadie did not trouble to look up and
follow her progress around the wooden balcony overhead.

A deep chill had settled into her bones, and she was like a
person benumbed. Exactly when this present state had
succeeded the earlier one Sadie could not tell, nor did she
think to ask herself such a question, but a feeling of dread
now lay like a stone in her breast where before there had
been stirring such powerful sensations of excitement and suspense. "I'm so low," she said to herself. "I feel like I was sitting at my own funeral." She did not say this in the spirit of
hyperbolic gloom which some people nurture to work themselves out of a bad mood, but in all seriousness and with her
customary attitude of passivity; in fact, she wore the humble
look so often visible on the faces of sufferers who are being
treated in a free clinic. It did not occur to her that a connection might exist between her present dismal state and the
mission she had come to fulfill at Camp Cataract, nor did she
take any notice of the fact that the words which were to en-
chant Harriet and accomplish her return were no longer well-
ing up in her throat as they had done all the past week. She
feared that something dreadful might happen, but whatever it
was, this disaster was as remotely connected with her as a
possible train wreck. "I hope nothing bad happens . . ." she
thought, but she didn't have much hope in her.

Harriet slammed the front door and Sadie looked up. For
the first second or two she did not recognize the woman who
stood on the threshold in her dripping rubber coat and hood.
Beryl was beside her; puddles were forming around the feet
of the two women. Harriet had rouged her cheeks rather more
highly than usual in order to hide all traces of her crying
spell. Her eyes were bright and she wore a smile that was
fixed and hard.

"Not a night fit for man or beast," she shouted across to Sadie, using a voice that she thought sounded hearty and yet fashionable at the same time; she did this, not in order to impress her sister, but to keep her at a safe distance.

Sadie, instead of rushing to the door, stared at her with an air of perplexity. To her Harriet appeared more robust and coarse-featured than she had five weeks ago at the apartment, and yet she knew that such a rapid change of physiognomy was scarcely possible. Recovering, she rose and went to embrace her sister. The embrace failed to reassure her because of Harriet's wet rubber coat, and her feeling of estrangement bcame more defined. She backed away.

Upon hearing her own voice ring out in such hearty and fashionable tones, Harriet had felt crazily confident that she might, by continuing to affect this manner, hold her sister at bay for the duration of her visit. To increase her chances of success she had determined right then not to ask Sadie why she had come, but to treat the visit in the most casual and natural way possible.

"Have you put on fat?" Sadie asked, at a loss for anything else to say.

"I'll never be fat," Harriet replied quickly. "I'm a fruit lover, not a lover of starches."

"Yes, you love fruit," Sadie said nervously. "Do you want some? I have an apple left from my lunch."

Harriet looked aghast. "Now!" she exclaimed. "Beryl can tell you that I never eat at night; in fact I never come up to the lodge at night, *never*. I stay in my cabin. I've written you all about how early I get up . . . I don't know anything about the lodge at night," she added almost angrily, as though her sister had accused her of being festive.

"You don't?" Sadie looked at her stupidly.

"No, I don't. Are you hungry, by the way?"

"If she's hungry," put in Beryl, "we can go into the Grotto Room and I'll bring her the food there. The tables in the main dining room are all set up for tomorrow's breakfast."

"I despise the Grotto," said Harriet with surprising bitterness. Her voice was getting quite an edge to it, and although it still sounded fashionable it was no longer hearty.

"I'm not hungry," Sadie assured them both. "I'm sleepy."

"Well, then," Harriet replied quickly, jumping at the opportunity, "we'll sit here for a few minutes and then you must go to bed."

The three of them settled in wicker chairs close to the cold hearth. Sadie was seated opposite the other two, who both remained in their rubber coats.

"I really do despise the Grotto," Harriet went on. "Actually I don't hang around the lodge at all. This is not the part of Camp Cataract that interests me. I'm interested in the pine groves, my cabin, the rocks, the streams, the bridge, and all the surrounding natural beauty . . . the sky also."

Although the rain still continued its drumming on the roof above them, to Sadie, Harriet's voice sounded intolerably loud, and she could not rid herself of the impression that her sister's face had grown fatter. "Now," she heard Harriet saying in her loud voice, "tell me about the apartment. . . . What's new, how are the dinners coming along, how are Evy and Bert?"

Fortunately, while Sadie was struggling to answer these questions, which unaccountably she found it difficult to do, the stout agnostic reappeared, and Harriet was immediately distracted.

"Rover," she called gaily across the room, "come and sit with us. My sister Sadie's here."

The woman joined them, seating herself beside Beryl, so that Sadie was now facing all three.

"It's a surprise to see you up at the lodge at night, Hermit," she remarked to Harriet without a spark of mischief in her voice.

"You see!" Harriet nodded at Sadie with immense satisfaction. "I was not fibbing, was I? How are Evy and Bert?" she asked again, her face twitching a bit. "Is the apartment hot?"

Sadie nodded.

"I don't know how long you plan to stay," Harriet rattled on, feeling increasingly powerful and therefore reckless, "but I'm going on a canoe trip the day after tomorrow for five days. We're going up the river to Pocahontas Falls. . . . I leave at four in the morning, too, which rather ruins tomorrow as well. I've been looking forward to this trip ever since last spring when I applied for my seat, back at the apartment. The canoes are limited, and the guides. . . . I'm devoted to canoe trips, as you know, and can fancy myself a red-skin all the way to the Falls and back, easily."

Sadie did not answer.

"There's nothing weird about it," Harriet argued. "It's in keeping with my hatred of industrialization. In any case, you can see what a chopped-up day tomorrow's going to be. I have to make my pack in the morning and I must be in bed by eight-thirty at night, the latest, so that I can get up at four. I'll have only one real meal, at two in the afternoon. I suggest we meet at two behind the souvenir booth; you'll notice it tomorrow." Harriet waited expectantly for Sadie to answer in agreement to this suggestion, but her sister remained silent.

"Speaking of the booth," said Rover. "I'm not taking home a single souvenir this year. They're expensive and they don't last."

"You can buy salf-water taffy at Gerald's Store in town," Beryl told her. "I saw some there last week. It's a little stale but very cheap."

"Why could they sell salt-water taffy in the mountains?" Rover asked irritably.

Sadie was half listening to the conversation; as she sat watching them, all three women were suddenly unrecognizable; it was as if she had flung open the door to some dentist's office and seen three strangers seated there. She sprang to her feet in terror.

Harriet was horrified. "What is it?" she yelled at her sister. "Why do you look like that? Are you mad?"

Sadie was pale and beads of sweat were forming under her felt hat, but the women opposite her had already regained their correct relation to herself and the present moment. Her face relaxed, and although her legs were trembling as a result of her brief but shocking experience, she felt immensely relieved that it was all over.

"Why did you jump up?" Harriet screeched at her. "Is it because you are at Camp Cataract and not at the apartment?"

"It must have been the long train trip and no food . . ." Sadie told herself, "only one sandwich."

"Is it because you are at Camp Cataract and not at the apartment?" Harriet insisted. She was really very frightened and wished to establish Sadie's fit as a purposeful one and not as an involuntary seizure similar to one of hers.

"It was a long and dirty train trip," Sadie said in a weary voice. "I had only one sandwich all day long, with no mustard or butter . . . just the processed meat. I didn't even eat my fruit."

"Beryl offered to serve you food in the Grotto!" Harriet

ranted. "Do you want some now or not? For heaven's sake, speak up!"

"No . . . no." Sadie shook her head sorrowfully. "I think I'd best go to bed. Take me to your cabin . . . I've got my slippers and my kimono and my nightgown in my satchel," she added, looking around her vaguely, for the fact that Beryl had carried her grip off had never really impressed itself upon her consciousness.

Harriet glanced at Beryl with an air of complicity and managed to give her a quick pinch. "Beryl's got you fixed up in one of the upper lodge annex rooms," she told Sadie in a false, chatterbox voice. "You'll be much more comfortable up here than you would be down in my cabin. We all use oil lamps in the grove and you know how dependent you are on electricity."

Sadie didn't know whether she was dependent on electricity or not since she had never really lived without it, but she was so tired that she said nothing.

"I get up terribly early and my cabin's drafty, besides," Harriet went on. "You'll be much more comfortable here. You'd hate the Boulder Dam wigwams as well. Anyway, the wigwams are really for boys and they're always full. There's a covered bridge leading from this building to the annex on the upper floor, so that's an advantage."

"O.K., folks," Beryl cut in, judging that she could best help Harriet by spurring them on to action. "Let's get going."

"Yes," Harriet agreed, "if we don't get out of the lodge soon the crowd will come back from the movies and we certainly want to avoid them."

They bade good night to Rover and started up the stairs.

"This balustrade is made of young birch limbs," Harriet told Sadie as they walked along the narrow gallery overhead. "I think it's very much in keeping with the lodge, don't you?"

"Yes, I do," Sadie answered.

Beryl opened the door leading from the balcony onto a covered bridge and stepped through it, motioning to the others. "Here we go onto the bridge," she said, looking over her shoulder. "You've never visited the annex, have you?" she asked Harriet.

"I've never had any reason to," Harriet answered in a huffy tone. "You know how I feel about my cabin."

They walked along the imperfectly fitted boards in the darkness. Gusts of wind blew about their ankles and they

were constantly spattered with rain in spite of the wooden
roofing. They reached the door at the other end very quickly,
however, where they descended two steps leading into a short,
brightly lit hall. Beryl closed the door to the bridge behind
them. The smell of fresh plaster and cement thickened the
damp air.

"This is the annex," said Beryl. "We put old ladies here
mostly, because they can get back and forth to the dining
room without going outdoors . . . and they've got the toilet
right here, too." She flung open the door and showed it to
them. "Then also," she added, "we don't like the old ladies
dealing with oil lamps and here they've got electricity." She
led them into a little room just at their left and switched on
the light. "Pretty smart, isn't it?" she remarked, looking
around her with evident satisfaction, as if she herself had
designed the room; then, sauntering over to a modernistic
wardrobe-bureau combination, she polished a corner of it
with her pocket handkerchief. This piece was made of shiny
brown wood and fitted with a rimless circular mirror. "Strong
and good-looking," Beryl said, rapping on the wood with her
knuckles. "Every room's got one."

Sadie sank down on the edge of the bed without removing
her outer garments. Here, too, the smell of plaster and cement permeated the air, and the wind still blew about their
ankles, this time from under the badly constructed doorsill.

"The cabins are much draftier than this," Harriet assured
Sadie once again. "You'll be more comfortable here in the
annex." She felt confident that establishing her sister in the
annex would facilitate her plan, which was still to prevent her
from saying whatever she had come to say.

Sadie was terribly tired. Her hat, dampened by the rain,
pressed uncomfortably against her temples, but she did not
attempt to remove it. "I think I've got to go to sleep," she
muttered. "I can't stay awake any more."

"All right," said Harriet, "but don't forget tomorrow at
two by the souvenir booth . . . you can't miss it. I don't want
to see anyone in the morning because I can make my canoe
pack better by myself . . . it's frightfully complicated. . . .
But if I hurried I could meet you at one-thirty; would you
prefer that?"

Sadie nodded.

"Then I'll do my best. . . . You see, in the morning I always practice imagination for an hour or two. It does me lots

of good, but tomorrow I'll cut it short." She kissed Sadie lightly on the crown of her felt hat. "Good night," she said. "Is there anything I forgot to ask you about the apartment?"

"No," Sadie assured her. "You asked everything."

"Well, good night," said Harriet once again, and followed by Beryl, she left the room.

When Sadie awakened the next morning a feeling of dread still rested like a leaden weight on her chest. No sooner had she left the room than panic, like a small wing, started to beat under her heart. She was inordinately fearful that if she strayed any distance from the main lodge she would lose her way and so arrive late for her meeting with Harriet. This fear drove her to stand next to the souvenir booth fully an hour ahead of time. Fortunately the booth, situated on a small knoll, commanded an excellent view of the cataract, which spilled down from some high rock ledges above a deep chasm. A fancy bridge spanned this chasm only a few feet below her, so that she was able to watch the people crossing it as they walked back and forth between the camp site and the waterfall. An Indian chief in full war regalia was seated at the bridge entrance on a kitchen chair. His magnificent feather headdress curved gracefully in the breeze as he busied himself collecting the small toll that all the tourists paid on returning from the waterfall; he supplied them with change from a nickel-plated conductor's belt which he wore over his deer-hide jacket, embroidered with minute beads. He was an Irishman employed by the management, which supplied his costume. Lately he had grown careless, and often neglected to stain his freckled hands the deep brick color of his face. He divided his time between the bridge and the souvenir booth, clambering up the knoll whenever he sighted a customer.

A series of wooden arches, Gothic in conception, succeeded each other all the way across the bridge; bright banners fluttered from their rims, each one stamped with the initials of the camp, and some of them edged with a glossy fringe. Only a few feet away lay the dining terrace, a huge flagstone pavilion whose entire length skirted the chasm's edge.

Unfortunately, neither the holiday crowds, nor the festooned bridge, nor even the white waters of the cataract across the way could distract Sadie from her misery. She constantly glanced behind her at the dark pine groves wherein Harriet's cabin was concealed. She dreaded to see Harriet's shape define itself between the trees, but at the same time she feared that if her sister did not arrive shortly some terrible catastrophe would befall them both before she'd had a chance to speak. In truth all desire to convince her sister that she should leave Camp Cataract and return to the apartment had miraculously shriveled away, and with the desire, the words to express it had vanished too. This did not in any way alter her intention of accomplishing her mission: on the contrary, it seemed to her all the more desperately important now that she was almost certain, in her innermost heart, that her trip was already a failure. Her attitude was not an astonishing one, since like many others she conceived of her life as separate from herself; the road was laid out always a little ahead of her by sacred hands, and she walked down it without a question. This road, which was her life, would go on existing after death, even as her death existed now while she still lived.

There were close to a hundred people dining on the terrace, and the water's roar so falsified the clamor of voices that one minute the guests seemed to be speaking from a great distance and the next right at her elbow. Every now and then she thought she heard someone pronounce her name in a dismal tone, and however much she told herself that this was merely the waterfall playing its tricks on her ears she shuddered each time at the sound of her name. Her very position next to the booth began to embarrass her. She tucked her hands into her coat sleeves so that they would not show, and tried to keep her eyes fixed on the foaming waters across the way, but she had noticed a disapproving look in the eyes of the diners nearest her, and she could not resist glancing back at the terrace every few minutes in the hope that she had been mistaken. Each time, however, she was more convinced that she had read their expressions correctly, and that these people believed, not only that she was standing there for no good reason, but that she was a genuine vagrant who could not afford the price of a dinner. She was therefore immensely relieved when she caught sight of Harriet advancing between the tables from the far end of the dining pavilion. As she drew nearer, Sadie noticed that she was wearing her black winter coat trimmed with red fur, and that her marceled hair remained neatly arranged in spite of the strong wind. Much to her relief Harriet had omitted to rouge her cheeks and her face therefore had regained its natural proportions. She saw Harriet wave at the sight of her and quicken her step. Sadie was pleased that the diners were to witness the impending meeting. "When they see us together," she thought, "they'll realize that I'm no vagrant, but a decent woman visiting her sister." She herself started down the knoll to hasten the meeting. "I thought you'd come out of the pine grove," she called out, as soon as they were within a few feet of one another. "I kept looking that way."

"I would have ordinarily," Harriet answered, reaching her side and kissing her lightly on the cheek, "but I went to the other end of the terrace first, to reserve a table for us from the waiter in charge there. That end is quieter, so it will be more suitable for a long talk."

"Good," thought Sadie as they climbed up the knoll together. "Her night's sleep has done her a world of good." She studied Harriet's face anxiously as they paused next to the souvenir booth, and discovered a sweet light reflected in her eyes. All at once she remembered their childhood together and the great tenderness Harriet had often shown towards her then.

"They have Turkish pilaff on the menu," said Harriet, "so I told the waiter to save some for you. It's such a favorite that it usually runs out at the very beginning. I know how much you love it."

Sadie, realizing that Harriet was actually eager for this dinner, the only one they would eat together at Camp Cataract, to be a success, felt the terrible leaden weight lifted from her heart; it disappeared so suddenly that for a moment or two she was like a balloon without its ballast; she could barely refrain from dancing about in delight. Harriet tugged on her arm.

"I think we'd better go now," she urged Sadie, "then after lunch we can come back here if you want to buy some souvenirs for Evy and Bert . . . and maybe for Flo and Carl and Bobby too. . . ."

Sadie bent down to adjust her cotton stockings, which were wrinkling badly at the ankles, and when she straightened up again her eyes lighted on three men dining very near the edge of the terrace; she had not noticed them before. They were all eating corn on the cob and big round hamburger sandwiches in absolute silence. To protect their clothing from spattering kernels, they had converted their napkins into bibs.

"Bert Hoffer's careful on his clothes too," Sadie reflected, and then she turned to her sister. "Don't you think men look different sitting all by themselves without women?" she asked her. She felt an extraordinary urge to chat—an urge which she could not remember ever having experienced before.

"I think," Harriet replied, as though she had not heard Sadie's comment, "that we'd better go to our table before the waiter gives it to someone else."

"I don't like men," Sadie announced without venom, and she was about to follow Harriet when her attention was arrested by the eyes of the man nearest her. Slowly lowering his corn cob to his plate, he stared across at her, his mouth twisted into a bitter smile. She stood as if rooted to the ground, and under his steady gaze all her newborn joy rapidly drained away. With desperation she realized that Harriet, darting in and out between the crowded tables, would soon be out of sight. After making what seemed to her a superhuman effort she tore herself away from the spot where she stood and lunged after Harriet shouting her name.

Harriet was at her side again almost instantly, looking up at her with a startled expression. Together they returned to the souvenir booth, where Sadie stopped and assumed a slightly bent position as if she was suffering from an abdominal pain.

"What's the trouble?" she heard Harriet asking with concern. "Are you feeling ill?"

Instead of answering Sadie laid her hand heavily on her sister's arm and stared at her with a hunted expression in her eyes.

"Please try not to look so much like a gorilla," said Harriet in a kind voice, but Sadie, although she recognized the accuracy of this observation (for she could feel very well that she was looking like a gorilla), was powerless to change her expression, at least for a moment or two. "Come with me," she said finally, grabbing Harriet's hand and pulling her along with almost brutal force. "I've got something to show you."

She headed down a narrow path leading into a thickly planted section of the grove, where she thought they were less likely to be disturbed. Harriet followed with such a quick, light step that Sadie felt no pull behind her at all and her sister's hand, folded in her own thick palm, seemed as delicate as the body of a bird. Finally they entered a small clearing where they stopped. Harriet untied a handkerchief from around her neck and mopped her brow. "Gracious!" she said. "It's frightfully hot in here." She offered the kerchief to Sadie. "I suppose it's because we walked so fast and because the pine trees shut out all the wind. . . . First I'll sit down and then you must tell me what's wrong." She stepped over to a felled tree whose length blocked the clearing. Its torn roots were shockingly exposed, whereas the upper truck and branches lay hidden in the surrounding grove. Harriet sat down; Sadie was about to sit next to her when she noticed a dense swarm of flies near the roots. Automatically she stepped toward them. "Why are they here?" she asked herself—then immediately she spotted the cause, an open can of beans some careless person had deposited inside the small hollow at the base of the trunk. She turned away in disgust and looked at Harriet. Her sister was seated on the fallen tree, her back gracefully erect and her head tilted in a listening attitude. The filtered light imparted to her face an incredibly fragile and youthful look, and Sadie gazed at her with tenderness and wonder. No sound reached them in the clearing, and she realized with a pounding heart that she could no longer postpone telling Harriet why she had come. She could not have wished for a moment more favorable to the accomplishment of her purpose. The stillness in the air, their isolation, the expectant and gentle light in Harriet's eye, all these elements should have combined to give her back her faith—faith in her own powers to persuade Harriet to come home with her and live among them once again, winter and summer alike, as she had always done before. She opened her mouth to speak and doubled over, clutching at her stomach as though an animal were devouring her. Sweat beaded her forehead and she planted her feet wide apart on the ground as if this animal would be born. Though her vision was barred with pain, she saw Harriet's tear-filled eyes, searching hers.

"Let's not go back to the apartment," Sadie said, hearing her own words as if they issued not from her mouth but from a pit in the ground. Let's not go back there . . . let's you and me go out in the world . . . just the two of us." A second before covering her face to hide her shame Sadie glimpsed Harriet's eyes, impossibly close to her own, their pupils pointed with a hatred such as she had never seen before.

It seemed to Sadie that it was taking an eternity for her sister to leave. "Go away . . . go away . . . or I'll suffocate." She was moaning the words over and over again, her face buried deep in her hands. "Go away . . . please go away . . . I'll suffocate. . . ." She could not tell, however, whether she was thinking these words or speaking them aloud.

At last she heard Harriet's footstep on the dry branches, as she started out of the clearing. Sadie listened, but although one step followed another, the cracking sound of the dry branches did not grow any fainter as Harriet penetrated farther into the grove. Sadie knew then that this agony she was suffering was itself the dreaded voyage into the world—the very voyage she had always feared Harriet would make. That she herself was making it instead of Harriet did not affect her certainty that this was it.

Sadie stood at the souvenir booth looking at some birchbark canoes. The wind was blowing colder and stronger than it had a while ago, or perhaps it only seemed this way to her, so recently returned from the airless clearing. She did not recall her trip back through the grove; she was conscious only of her haste to buy some souvenirs and to leave. Some chains of paper tacked to the side of the booth as decoration kept flying into her face. The Indian chief was smiling at her from behind the counter of souvenirs.

"What can I do for you?" he asked.

"I'm leaving," said Sadie, "so I want souvenirs. . . ."

"Take your choice; you've got birchbark canoes with or without mailing cards attached, Mexican sombrero ashtrays, exhilarating therapeutic pine cushions filled with the regional needles . . . and banners for a boy's room."

"There's no boy home," Sadie said, having caught only these last words.

"How about cushions . . . or canoes?"

She nodded.

"Which do you want?"

"Both," she answered quickly.

"How many?"

Sadie closed her eyes. Try as she would she could not count up the members of the family. She could not even reach an approximate figure. "Eleven," she blurted out finally, in desperation.

"Eleven of each?" he asked raising his eyebrows.

"Yes . . . yes," she answered quickly, batting the paper chains out of her face, "eleven of each."

"You sure don't forget the old folks at home, do you?" he said, beginning to collect the canoes. He made an individual package of each souvenir and then wrapped then all together in coarse brown paper which he bound with thick twine.

Sadie had given him a note and he was punching his money belt for the correct change when her eyes fell on his light, freckled hand. Startled, she shifted her glance from his hand punching the nickel belt to his brick-colored face streaked with purple and vermilion paint. For the first time she noticed his Irish blue eyes. Slowly the hot flush of shame crept along the nape of her neck. It was the same unbearable mortification that she had experienced in the clearing; it spread upward from her neck to the roots of her hair, coloring her face a dark red. That she was ashamed for the Indian this time, and not of her own words, failed to lessen the intensity of her suffering; the boundaries of her pride had never been firmly fixed inside herself. She stared intently at his Irish blue eyes, so oddly light in his brick-colored face. What was it? She was tormented by the sight of an incongruity she couldn't name. All at once she remembered the pavilion and the people dining there; her heart started to pound. "They'll see it," she said to herself in a panic. "They'll see it and they'll know that I've seen it too." Somehow this latter possibility was the most perilous of all.

"They must never know I've seen it," she said, grinding her teeth, and she leaned over the counter, crushing some canoes under her chest. "Quickly," she whispered. "Go out your little door and meet me back at the booth. . . ."

A second later she found him there. "Listen!" She clutched his hand. "We musy hurry . . . I didn't mean to see you . . . I'm sorry . . . I've been trying not to look at you for years . . . for years and years and years. . . ." She gaped at him in horror. "Why are you standing there? We've got to hurry. . . . They haven't caught us looking at you yet, but we've got to hurry." She headed for the bridge, leading the Indian behind her. He followed quickly without saying a word.

The water's roar increased in volume as they approached the opposite bank of the chasm, and Sadie found relief in the sound. Once off the bridge she ran as fast as she could along the path leading to the waterfall. The Indian followed close on her heels, his hand resting lightly in her own, as Harriet's had earlier when they'd sped together through the grove. Reaching the waterfall, she edged along the wall of rock until she stood directly behind the water's cascade. With a cry of delight she leaned back in the curve of the wall, insensible to its icy dampness, which penetrated even through the thickness of her woollen coat. She listened to the cataract's deafening roar and her heart almost burst with joy, because she had hidden the Indian safely behind the cascade where he could be neither seen nor heard. She turned around and smiled at him kindly. He too smiled, and she no longer saw in his face any trace of the incongruity that had shocked her so before.

The foaming waters were beautiful to see. Sadie stepped forward, holding her hand out to the Indian.

When Harriet awakened that morning all traces of her earlier victorious mood had vanished. She felt certain that disaster would overtake her before she could start out for Pocahontas Falls. Heavyhearted and with fumbling hands, she set about making her pack. Luncheon with Sadie was an impossible cliff which she did not have the necessary strength to scale. When she came to three round cushions that had to be snapped into their rainproof casings she gave up with a groan and rushed headlong out of her . cabin in search of Beryl.

Fortunately Beryl waited table on the second shift and so she found her reading a magazine, with one leg flung over the arm of her chair.

"I can't make my pack," Harriet said hysterically, bursting into Beryl's cabin without even knocking at the door.

Beryl swung her leg around and got out of her chair, "I'll make your pack," she said in a calm voice, knocking some tobacco out of her pipe. "I would have come around this morning, but you said last night you wanted to make it alone."

"It's Sadie," Harriet complained. "It's that cursed lunch with Sadie. I can't go through with it. I know I can't. I shouldn't have to in the first place. She's not even supposed to be here . . . I'm an ass. . . ."

"To hell with sisters," said Beryl. "Give 'em a good swift kick in the pants."

"She's going to stop me from going on my canoe trip . . . I know she is. . . ." Harriet had adopted the whining tone of a little girl.

"No, she isn't," said Beryl, speaking with authority.

"Why not?" Harriet asked. She looked at Beryl almost wistfully.

"She'd better not try anything . . ." said Beryl. "Ever hear of jujitsu?" She grunted with satisfaction. "Come on, we'll go make your pack." She was so pleased with Harriet's new state of dependency that she was rapidly overcoming her original shyness. An hour later she had completed the pack, and Harriet was dressed and ready.

"Will you go with me to the souvenir booth?" she begged the waitress. "I don't want to meet her alone." She was in a worse state of nerves than ever.

"I'll go with you," said Beryl, "but let's stop at my cabin on the way so I can change into my uniform. I'm on duty soon."

They were nearly twenty minutes late arriving at the booth, and Harriet was therefore rather surprised not to see Sadie standing there. "Perhaps she's been here and gone back to the lodge for a minute," she said to Beryl. "I'll find out." She walked up to the souvenir counter and questioned the Indian, with whom she was slightly familiar. "Was there a woman waiting here a while ago, Timothy?" she asked.

"A dark middle-aged woman?"

"That's right."

"She was here for an hour or more," he said, "never budged from this stall until about fifteen minutes ago."

"She couldn't have been here an hour!" Harriet argued. "Not my sister. . . . I told her one-thirty and it's not yet two."

"Then it wasn't your sister. The woman who was here stayed more than an hour, without moving. I noticed her because it was such a queer-looking thing. I noticed her first from my chair at the bridge and then when I came up here she was still standing by the booth. She must have stood here over an hour."

"Then it was a different middle-aged woman."

"That may be," he agreed, "but anyway, this one left about fifteen minutes ago. After standing all that time she turned around all of a sudden and bought a whole bunch of souvenirs from me . . . then just when I was punching my belt for the change she said something I couldn't understand—it sounded like Polish—and then she lit out for the bridge before I could give her a penny. That woman's got impulses," he added with a broad grin. "If she's your sister, I'll give you

her change, in case she don't stop here on her way back. . . .
But she sounded to me like a Polak."

"Beryl," said Harriet, "run across the bridge and see if Sadie's behind the waterfall. I'm sure this Polish woman wasn't
Sadie, but they might both be back there. . . . If she's not
there, we'll look in the lodge."

When Beryl returned her face was dead white; she stared
at Harriet in silence, and even when Harriet finally grabbed
hold of her shoulders and shook her hard, she would not say
anything.

MURIEL SPARK was born in 1918 in Edinburgh ("the saturine Heart of Midlothian, never mine") of a Jewish father and Presbyterian mother. She spent some of the years of World War II in South Africa (she married, had a child, and was divorced there) and then returned to London to work in the Political Intelligence Department of the British Foreign Office. She also worked as a reviewer and editor. She edited the letters of Cardinal Newman in 1954 and it was his influence that helped persuade her to convert to Roman Catholicism. In an interview she said things seemed to fall into place on her becoming a Catholic. According to some critics, her Roman Catholicism has lent her work a somberness and depth that belie the charge, sometimes leveled at her, that she is a mere miniaturist. "Her apparently glib novels," writes Karl Malkoff, "comprise a serious attempt to probe the dark moral heart of man." Her position through most of her life as an outsider—not Protestant, not Jew, not a born Catholic— has strengthened her sense of the ridiculous. She is a great satirist. In an address to the American Academy of Arts and Letters in 1970 she called for a literature of savage ridicule, "the only honorable weapon we have left," that would galvanize the reader, not cater to his sentiments. John Updike calls her "one of the few writers of the language on either side of the Atlantic with enough resources, daring, and stamina to be altering, as well as feeding, the fiction machine." She is best known, of course, for *The Prime of Miss Jean Brodie*. But some critics think her finest work is in the short stories, especially those having Africa as their background ("The Go-Away Bird," "Bang-bang You're Dead," "The Curtain Blown by the Breeze," "The Pawnbroker's Wife"). The autobiographical piece that follows is a fine example of the "deliberate clarity" and "curt diffidence of style" that Updike so admires.

Muriel Spark
(1918—   )

THE FIRST YEAR OF MY LIFE

I was born on the first day of the second month of the last year of the First World War, a Friday. Testimony abounds that during the first year of my life I never smiled. I was known as the baby whom nothing and no one could make smile. Everyone who knew me then has told me so. They tried very hard, singing and bouncing me up and down, jumping around, pulling faces. Many times I was told this later by my family and their friends; but, anyway, I knew it at the time.

You will shortly be hearing of that new school of psychology, or maybe you have heard of it already, which, after long and far-adventuring research and experiment, has established that all of the young of the human species are born omniscient. Babies, in their waking hours, know everything that is going on everywhere in the world; they can tune in to any conversation they choose, switch on to any scene. We have all experienced this power. It is only after the first year that it was brainwashed out of us; for it is demanded of us by our immediate environment that we grow to be of use to it in a practical way. Gradually, our know-all brain-cells are blacked out, although traces remain in some individuals in the form of E.S.P., and in the adults of some primitive tribes.

It is not a new theory. Poets and philosophers, as usual, have been there first. But scientific proof is now ready and to hand. Perhaps the final touches are being put to the new manifesto in some cell at Harvard University. Any day now it will be given to the world, and the world will be convinced.

Let me therefore get my word in first, because I feel pretty sure, now, about the authenticity of my remembrance of things past. My autobiography, as I very well perceive at the time, started in the very worst year that the world had ever seen so far. Apart from being born bedridden and toothless, unable to raise myself on the pillow or utter anything but farmyard squawks or police-siren wails, my bladder and my bowels totally out of control, I was further depressed by the curious behavior of the two-legged mammals around me. There were those black-dressed people, females of the species to which I appeared to belong, saying they had lost their sons. I slept a great deal. Let them go and find their sons. It was like the special pin for my nappies which my mother or some other hoverer dedicated to my care was always losing. These careless women in black lost their husbands and their brothers. Then they came to visit my mother and clucked and crowed over my cradle. I was not amused.

"Babies never really smile till they're three months old," said my mother. "They're not *supposed* to smile till they're three months old."

My brother, aged six, marched up and down with a toy rifle over his shoulder.

> The grand old Duke of York
> He had ten thousand men;
> He marched them up to the top of the hill
> And he marched them down again.
>
> And when they were up, they were up.
> And when they were down, they were down.
> And when they were neither down nor up
> They were neither up nor down.

"Just listen to him!"
"Look at him with his rifle!"

I was about ten days old when Russia stopped fighting. I tuned in to the Czar, a prisoner, with the rest of his family, since evidently the country had put him off his throne and there had been a revolution not long before I was born. Everyone was talking about it. I tuned in to the Czar. "Nothing would ever induce me to sign the treaty of Brest-Litovsk," he said to his wife. Anyway, nobody had asked him to.

At this point I was sleeping twenty hours a day to get my strength up. And from what I discerned in the other four hours of the day I knew I was going to need it. The Western Front on my frequency was sheer blood, mud, dismembered bodies, blistering crashes, hectic flashes of light in the night skies, explosions, total terror. Since it was plain I had been born into a bad moment in the history of the world, the future bothered me, unable as I was to raise my head from the pillow and as yet only twenty inches long. "I truly wish I were a fox or a bird," D. H. Lawrence was writing to somebody. Dreary old creeping Jesus. I fell asleep.

Red sheets of flame shot across the sky. It was 21 March, the fiftieth day of my life, and the German Spring Offensive had started before my morning feed. Infinite slaughter. I scowled at the scene, and made an effort to kick out. But the attempt was feeble. Furious, and impatient for some strength, I wailed for my feed. After which I stopped wailing but continued to scowl.

> The grand old Duke of York
> He had ten thousand men. . . .

They rocked the cradle. I never heard a sillier song. Over in Berlin and Vienna the people were starving, freezing, striking, rioting and yelling in the streets. In London everyone was bustling to work and muttering that it was time the whole damn business was over.

The big people around me bared their teeth; that meant a smile, it meant they were pleased or amused. They spoke of ration cards for meat and sugar and butter.

"Where will it all end?"

I went to sleep. I woke and tuned in to Bernard Shaw who was telling someone to shut up. I switched over to Joseph Conrad who, strangely enough, was saying precisely the same thing. I still didn't think it worth a smile, although it was expected of me any day now. I got on to Turkey. Women draped in black huddled and chattered in their harems; yak-yak-yak. This was boring, so I came back to home base.

In and out came and went the women in British black. My mother's brother, dressed in his uniform, came coughing. He had been poison-gassed in the trenches. *"Tout le monde à la bataille!"* declaimed Marshal Foch the old swine. He was now Commander-in-Chief of the Allied Forces. My uncle coughed from deep within his lungs, never to recover but destined to return to the Front. His brass buttons gleamed in the firelight. I weighed twelve pounds by now; I stretched and kicked for exercise, seeing that I had a lifetime before me, coping with this crowd. I took six feeds a day and kept most of them down by the time the *Vindictive* was sunk in Ostend harbour, on which day I kicked with special vigour in my bath.

In France the conscripted soldiers leapfrogged over the dead on the advance and littered the fields with limbs and hands, or drowned in the mud. The strongest men on all fronts were dead before I was born. Now the sentries used bodies for barricades and the fighting men were unhealthy from the start. I checked my toes and my fingers, knowing I was going to need them. *The Playboy of the Western World* was playing at the Court Theatre in London, but occasionally I beamed over to the House of Commons which made me drop off gently to sleep. Generally, I preferred the Western Front where one got the true state of affairs. It was essential to know the worst, blood and explosions and all, for one had to be prepared, as the boy scouts said. Virginia Woolf yawned and reached for her diary. Really, I preferred the Western Front.

In the fifth month of my life I could raise my head from my pillow and hold it up. I could grasp the objects that were held out to me. Some of these things rattled and squawked. I gnawed on them to get my teeth started. "She hasn't smiled yet?" said the dreary old aunties. My mother, on the defensive, said I was probably one of those late smilers. On my wavelength Pablo Picasso was getting married and early in that month of July the Silver Wedding of King George V and Queen Mary was celebrated in joyous pomp at St Paul's Cathedral. They drove through the streets of London with their children. Twenty-five years of domestic happiness. A lot of fuss and ceremonial handing over of swords went on at the Guildhall where the King and Queen received a cheque for £53,000 to dispose of for charity as they thought fit. *Tout le monde à la bataille!* Income tax in England had reached six shillings in the pound. Everyone was talking about the Silver Wedding; yak-yak-yak, and ten days later the Czar and his family, now in Siberia, were invited to descend to a little room in the basement. Crack, crack, went the guns; screams and blood all over the place, and that was the end of the Romanoffs. I flexed my muscles. "A fine healthy baby," said the doctor; which gave me much satisfaction.

Tout le monde à la bataille! That included my gassed uncle. My health had improved to the point where I was able to crawl in my playpen. Bertrand Russell was still cheerily in prison for writing something seditious about pacifism. Tuning in as usual to the Front Lines it looked as if the Germans were winning all the battles yet losing the war. And so it was. The upper-income people were upset about the income tax at six shillings to the pound. But all women over thirty got the vote. "It seems a long time to wait," said one of my drab old aunts, aged twenty-two. The speeches in the House of Commons always sent me to sleep which was why I missed, at the actual time, a certain oration by Mr. Asquith following the armistice on 11 November. Mr. Asquith was a greatly esteemed former prime minister later to be an Earl, and had been ousted by Mr. Lloyd George. I clearly heard Asquith, in private, refer to Lloyd George as "that damned Welsh goat."

The armistice was signed and I was awake for that. I pulled myself on to my feet with the aid of the bars of my cot. My teeth were coming through very nicely in my opinion, and well worth all the trouble I was put to in bringing them forth. I weighed twenty pounds. On all the world's fighting fronts the men killed in action or dead of wounds numbered 8,538,315 and the warriors wounded and maimed were 21,219,452. With these figures in my mind I sat up in my high chair and banged my spoon on the table. One of my mother's black-draped friends recited:

I have a rendezvous with Death
At some disputed barricade,
When spring comes back with rustling shade
And apple blossoms fill the air—
I have a rendezvous with Death.

Most of the poets, they said, had been killed. The poetry made them dab their eyes with clean white handkerchiefs.

Next February on my first birthday, there was a birthday-cake with one candle. Lots of children and their elders. The war had been over two months and twenty-one days. "Why doesn't she smile?" My brother was to blow out the candle. The elders were talking about the war and the political situation. Lloyd George and Asquith, Asquith and Lloyd George. I remembered recently having switched on to Mr. Asquith at a private party where he had been drinking a lot. He was playing cards and when he came to cut the cards he tried to cut a large box of matches by mistake. On another occasion I had seen him putting his arm around a lady's shoulder in a Daimler motor car, and generally behaving towards her in a very friendly fashion. Strangely enough she said, "If you don't stop this nonsense immediately I'll order the chauffeur to stop and I'll get out." Mr. Asquith replied, "And pray, what reason will you give?" Well anyway it was my feeding time.

The guests arrived for my birthday. It was so sad, said one of the black widows, so sad about Wilfred Owen who was killed so late in the war, and she quoted from a poem of his:

> What passing-bells for these who die as cattle?
> Only the monstrous anger of the guns.

The children were squealing and toddling around. One was sick and another wet the floor and stood with his legs apart gaping at the puddle. All was mopped up. I banged my spoon on the table of my high chair.

> But I've a rendezvous with Death
> At midnight in some flaming town;
> When spring trips north again this year,
> And I to my pledged word am true,
> I shall not fail that rendezvous.

More parents and children arrived. One stout man who was warming his behind at the fire, said, "I always think those words of Asquith's after the armistice were so apt. . . ."

They brought the cake close to my high chair for me to see, with the candle shining and flickering above the pink icing. "A pity she never smiles."

"She'll smile in time," my mother said, obviously upset.

"What Asquith told the House of Commons just after the war," said that stout gentleman with his backside to the fire, "—so apt, what Asquith said. He said that the war has cleansed and purged the world, by God! I recall his actual words: 'All things have become new. In this great cleansing and purging it has been the privilege of our country to play her part. . . .'"

That did it. I broke into a decided smile and everyone noticed it, convinced that it was provoked by the fact that my brother had blown out the candle on the cake. "She smiled!" my mother exclaimed. And everyone was clucking away about how I was smiling. For good measure I crowed like a demented raven. "My baby's smiling," said my mother.

"It was the candle on her cake," they said.

The cake be damned. Since that time I have grown to smile quite naturally, like any other healthy and house-trained person, but when I really mean a smile, deeply felt from the core, then to all intents and purposes it comes in response to the words uttered in the House of Commons after the First World War by the distinguished, the immaculately dressed and the late Mr. Asquith.

SHIRLEY JACKSON was born in San Francisco in 1919 and spent most of her early life in California. She and the critic Stanley Edgar Hyman were undergraduates together at the University of Syracuse (they co-edited *The Spectre*, a publication much maligned and finally suppressed by the administration). They married immediately after graduation and had four children. They settled finally in Bennington, Vermont, where Hyman taught at Bennington College and Shirley Jackson maintained the rigorous schedule of the mother—housewife—hostess—prolific writer. She wrote at night when the children were small, during the day after they entered school. In the last decade of her life she suffered from attacks of anxiety and depression and, for a time, was under the care of a psychiatrist. She loved the novels of Jane Austen and Samuel Richardson more than those of Kafka, with whom she is often compared.

Lenemaja Friedman, author of the Twayne Series' volume about Shirley Jackson, has illuminated the connections between Jackson's stories and novels and her personality. She writes: "As a writer, Miss Jackson has been little understood; and, because people insist upon associating her with witches and demons, her true literary worth becomes obscured. Part of this misunderstanding is the fault of the publicity that surrounded 'The Lottery' and the subsequent collection of stories of the same title. She has herself been responsible for part of the myth, for she humorously called herself a witch. She believed that there were many mysteries in life that man has not been able to fathom; and her magic lies in these realms—not in the exploration of witchcraft or in secret glimpses into demonic practices."

When Shirley Jackson died suddenly of heart failure in 1965, the obituary in *Newsweek* read in part: "In her art, as in her life, Shirley Jackson who died last week at 45 was an absolute original. She belonged to no literary movement and was a member of 'no school.' She listened to her own voice, kept her own counsel, isolated herself from all fashionable intellectual and literary currents. She was not an urban, or existential, or 'new' or 'anti-novelist.' She was unique."

Shirley Jackson
(1919—1965)

PILLAR OF SALT

For some reason a tune was running through her head when she and her husband got on the train in New Hampshire for their trip to New York; they had not been to New York for nearly a year, but the tune was from further back than that. It was from the days when she was fifteen or sixteen, and had never seen New York except in movies, when the city was made up, to her, of penthouses filled with Noel Coward people; when the height and speed and luxury and gaiety that made up a city like New York were confused inextricably with the dullness of being fifteen, and beauty unreachable and far in the movies.

"What *is* that tune?" she said to her husband, and hummed it. "It's from some old movie, I think."

"I know it," he said, and hummed it himself. "Can't remember the words."

He sat back comfortably. He had hung up their coats, put the suitcases on the rack, and had taken his magazine out. "I'll think of it sooner or later," he said.

She looked out the window first, tasting it almost secretly, savoring the extreme pleasure of being on a moving train with nothing to do for six hours but read and nap and go into the dining-car, going farther and farther every minute from the children, from the kitchen floor, with even the hills being incredibly left behind, changing into fields and trees too far away from home to be daily. "I love trains," she said, and her husband nodded sympathetically into his magazine.

Two weeks ahead, two unbelievable weeks, with all arrangements made, no further planning to do, except perhaps what theatres or what restaurants. A friend with an apartment went on a convenient vacation, there was enough money in the bank to make a trip to New York compatible with new snow suits for the children; there was the smoothness of unopposed arrangements, once the initial obstacles had been overcome, as though when they had really made up their minds, nothing dared stop them. The baby's sore throat cleared up. The plumber came, finished his work in two days, and left. The dresses had been altered in time; the hardware store could be left safely, once they had found the excuse of looking over new city products. New York had not burned down, had not been quarantined, their friend had gone away according to schedule, and Brad had the keys to the apartment in his pocket. Everyone knew where to reach everyone else; there was a list of plays not to miss and a list of items to look out for in the stores—diapers, dress materials, fancy canned goods, tarnish-proof silverware boxes. And, finally, the train was there, performing its function, pacing through the afternoon, carrying them legally and with determination to New York.

Margaret looked curiously at her husband, inactive in the middle of the afternoon on a train, at the other fortunate people traveling, at the sunny country outside, looked again to make sure, and then opened her book. The tune was still in her head, she hummed it and heard her husband take it up softly as he turned a page in his magazine.

In the dining-car she ate roast beef, as she would have done in a restaurant at home, reluctant to change over too quickly to the new, tantalizing food of a vacation. She had ice cream for dessert but became uneasy over her coffee because they were due in New York in an hour and she still had to put on her coat and hat, relishing every gesture, and Brad must take the suitcases down and put away the magazines. They stood at the end of the car for the interminable underground run, picking up their suitcases and putting them down again, moving restlessly inch by inch.

The station was a momentary shelter, moving visitors gradually into a world of people and sound and light to prepare them for the blasting reality of the street outside. She saw it for a minute from the sidewalk before she was in a taxi moving into the middle of it, and then they were bewilderingly caught and carried on uptown and whirled out on to another sidewalk and Brad paid the taxi driver and put his head back to look up at the apartment house. "This is it, all right," he said, as though he had doubted the driver's ability to find a number so simply given. Upstairs in the elevator, and the key fit the door. They had never seen their friend's apartment before, but it was reasonably familiar—a friend moving from

New Hampshire to New York carries private pictures of a home not erasable in a few years, and the apartment had enough of home in it to settle Brad immediately in the right chair and comfort her with instinctive trust of the linen and blankets.

"This is home for two weeks," Brad said, and stretched. After the first few minutes they both went to the windows automatically; New York was below, as arranged, and the houses across the street were apartment houses filled with unknown people.

"It's wonderful," she said. There were cars down there, and people, and the noise was there. "I'm so happy," she said, and kissed her husband.

They went sight-seeing the first day; they had breakfast in an Automat and went to the top of the Empire State Building. "Got it all fixed up now," Brad said, at the top. "Wonder just where that plane hit."

They tried to peer down on all four sides, but were embarrassed about asking. "After all," she said reasonably, giggling in a corner, "if something of mine got broken I wouldn't want people poking around asking to see the pieces."

"If you owned the Empire State Building you wouldn't care," Brad said.

They traveled only in taxis the first few days, and one taxi had a door held on with a piece of string; they pointed to it and laughed silently at each other, and on about the third day, the taxi they were riding in got a flat tire on Broadway and they had to get out and find another.

"We've only got eleven days left," she said one day, and then, seemingly minutes later, "we've already been here six days."

They had got in touch with the friends they had expected to get in touch with, they were going to a Long Island summer home for a week end. "It looks pretty dreadful right now," their hostess said cheerfully over the phone, "and we're leaving in a week ourselves, but I'd never *forgive* you if you didn't see it *once* while you were here." The weather had been fair but cool, with a definite autumn awareness, and the clothes in the store windows were dark and already hinting at furs and velvets. She wore her coat every day, and suits most of the time. The light dresses she had brought were hanging in the closet in the apartment, and she was thinking now of getting a sweater in one of the big stores, something impractical for New Hampshire, but probably good for Long Island.

"I have to do some shopping, at least one day," she said to Brad, and he groaned.

"Don't ask me to carry packages," he said.

"You aren't up to a good day's shopping," she told him, "not after all this walking around you've been doing. Why don't you go to a movie or something?"

"I want to do some shopping myself," he said mysteriously. Perhaps he was talking about her Christmas present; she had thought vaguely of getting such things done in New York; the children would be pleased with novelties from the city, toys not seen in their home stores. At any rate she said, "You'll probably be able to get to your wholesalers at last."

They were on their way to visit another friend, who had found a place to live by a miracle and warned them consequently not to quarrel with the appearance of the building, or the stairs, or the neighborhood. All three were bad, and the stairs were three flights, narrow and dark, but there was a place to live at the top. Their friend had not been in New York long, but he lived by himself in two rooms, and had easily caught the mania for slim tables and low bookcases which made his rooms look too large for the furniture in some places, too cramped and uncomfortable in others.

"What a lovely place," she said when she came in, and then was sorry when her host said, "Some day this damn situation will let up and I'll be able to settle down in a really decent place."

There were other people there; they sat and talked companionably about the same subjects then current in New Hampshire, but they drank more than they would have at home and it left them strangely unaffected; their voices were louder and their words more extravagant; their gestures, on the other hand, were smaller, and they moved a finger where in New Hampshire they would have waved an arm. Margaret said frequently, "We're just staying here for a couple of weeks, on a vacation," and she said, "It's wonderful, so *exciting*," and she said, "We were *terribly* lucky; this friend went out of town just at the right. . . ."

Finally the room was very full and noisy, and she went into a corner near a window to catch her breath. The window had been opened and shut all evening, depending on whether the person standing next to it had both hands free; and now it was shut, with the clear sky outside. Someone came and stood next to her, and she said, "Listen to the noise outside. It's as bad as it is inside."

He said, "In a neighborhood like this someone's always getting killed."

She frowned. "It sounds different than before. I mean, there's a different sound to it."

"Alcoholics," he said. "Drunks in the streets. Fighting going on across the way." He wandered away, carrying his drink.

She opened the window and leaned out, and there were people hanging out the windows across the way shouting, and people standing in the street looking up and shouting, and from across the way she heard clearly, "Lady, lady." They must mean me, she thought, they're all looking this way. She leaned out farther and the voices shouted incoherently but somehow making an audible whole, "Lady, your house is on fire, lady, lady."

She closed the window firmly and turned around to the other people in the room, raising her voice a little. "Listen," she said, "they're saying the house is on fire." She was desperately afraid of their laughing at her, of looking like a fool while Brad across the room looked at her blushing. She said again, "The *house* is on *fire*," and added, "They say," for fear of sounding too vehement. The people nearest to her turned and someone said, "She says the house is on fire."

She wanted to get to Brad and couldn't see him; her host was not in sight either, and the people all around were strangers. They don't listen to me, she thought, I might as well not be here, and she went to the outside door and opened it. There was no smoke, no flame, but she was telling herself, I might as well not be here, so she abandoned Brad in panic and ran without her hat and coat down the stairs, carrying a glass in one hand and a package of matches in the other. The stairs were insanely long, but they were clear and safe, and she opened the street door and ran out. A man caught her arm and said, "Everyone out of the house?" and she said, "No, Brad's still there." The fire engines swept around the corner, with people leaning out of the windows watching them, and the man holding her arm said, "It's down here," and left her. The fire was two houses away; they could see flames behind the top windows, and smoke against the night sky, but in ten minutes it was finished and the fire engines pulled away with an air of martyrdom for hauling out all their equipment to put out a ten-minute fire.

She went back upstairs slowly and with embarrassment, and found Brad and took him home.

"I was so frightened," she said to him when they were safely in bed, "I lost my head completely."

"You should have tried to find someone," he said.

"They wouldn't listen," she insisted. "I kept telling them and they wouldn't listen and then I thought I must have been mistaken. I had some idea of going down to see what was going on."

"Lucky it was no worse," Brad said sleepily.

"I felt trapped," she said. "High up in that old building with a fire; it's like a nightmare. And in a strange city."

"Well, it's all over now," Brad said.

The same faint feeling of insecurity tagged her the next day; she went shopping alone and Brad went off to see hardware, after all. She got on a bus to go downtown and the bus was too full to move when it came time for her to get out. Wedged standing in the aisle she said, "Out, please," and, "Excuse me," and by the time she was loose and near the door the bus had started again and she got off a stop beyond. "No one *listens* to me," she said to herself. "Maybe it's because I'm too polite." In the stores the prices were all too high and the sweaters looked disarmingly like New Hampshire ones. The toys for the children filled her with dismay; they were so obviously for New York children: hideous little parodies of adult life, cash registers, tiny pushcarts with imitation fruit, telephones that really worked (as if there weren't enough phones in New York that really worked), miniature milk bottles in a carrying case. "We get our milk from cows," Margaret told the salesgirl. "My children wouldn't know what these were." She was exaggerating, and felt guilty for a minute, but no one was around to catch her.

She had a picture of small children in the city dressed like their parents, following along with a miniature mechanical civilization, toy cash registers in larger and larger sizes that eased them into the real thing, millions of clattering jerking small imitations that prepared them nicely for taking over the large useless toys their parents lived by. She bought a pair of skis for her son, which she knew would be inadequate for the New Hampshire snow, and a wagon for her daughter inferior to the one Brad could make at home in an hour. Ignoring the toy mailboxes, the small phonographs with special small records, the kiddie cosmetics, she left the store and started home.

She was frankly afraid by now to take a bus; she stood on the corner and waited for a taxi. Glancing down at her feet, she saw a dime on the sidewalk and tried to pick it up, but there were too many people for her to bend down, and she was afraid to shove to make room for fear of being stared at. She put her foot on the dime and then saw a quarter near it, and a nickel. Someone dropped a pocketbook, she thought, and put her other foot on the quarter, stepping quickly to make it look natural; then she saw another dime and another nickel, and a third dime in the gutter. People were passing her, back and forth, all the time, rushing, pushing against her, not looking at her, and she was afraid to get down and start gathering up the money. Other people saw it and went past, and she realized that no one was going to pick it up. They were all embarrassed, or in too much of a hurry, or too crowded. A taxi stopped to let someone off, and she hailed it. She lifted her feet off the dime and the quarter, and left them there when she got into the taxi. This taxi went slowly and bumped as it went; she had begun to notice that the gradual decay was not peculiar to the taxis. The buses were cracking open in unimportant seams, the leather seats broken and stained. The buildings were going, too—in one of the nicest stores there had been a great gaping hole in the tiled foyer, and you walked around it. Corners of the buildings seemed to be crumbling away into fine dust that drifted downward, the granite was eroding unnoticed. Every window she saw on her way uptown seemed to be broken; perhaps every street corner was peppered with small change. The people were moving faster than ever before; a girl in a red hat appeared at the upper side of the taxi window and was gone beyond the lower side before you could see the hat; store windows were so terribly bright because you only caught them for a fraction of a second. The people seemed hurled on in a frantic action that made every hour forty-five minutes long, every day nine hours, every year fourteen days. Food was so elusively fast, eaten in such a hurry, that you were always hungry, always speeding to a new meal with new people. Everything was imperceptibly quicker every minute. She stepped into the taxi on one side and stepped out the other side at her home; she pressed the fifth-floor button on the elevator and was coming down again, bathed and dressed and ready for dinner with Brad. They went out for dinner and were coming in again, hungry and hurrying to bed in order to get to breakfast with lunch beyond. They had been in New York nine days; tomorrow was Saturday and they were going to Long Island, coming home Sunday, and then Wednesday they were going home, really home. By the time she had thought of it they were on the train to Long Island; the train was broken, the seats torn and the floor dirty; one of the doors wouldn't open and the windows wouldn't shut. Passing through the outskirts of the city, she thought, It's as though everything were traveling so fast that the solid stuff couldn't stand it and were going to pieces under the strain, cornices blowing off and windows caving in. She knew she was afraid to say it truly, afraid to face the knowledge that it was a voluntary neck-breaking speed, a deliberate whirling faster and faster to end in destruction.

On Long Island, their hostess led them into a new piece of New York, a house filled with New York furniture as though on rubber bands, pulled this far, stretched taut, and ready to snap back to the city, to an apartment, as soon as the door was opened and the lease, fully paid, had expired. "We've had this place every year for simply ages," their hostess said. "Otherwise we couldn't have gotten it *possibly* this year."

"It's an awfully nice place," Brad said. "I'm surprised you don't live here all year round."

"Got to get back to the city *some* time," their hostess said, and laughed.

"Not much like New Hampshire," Brad said. He was beginning to be a little homesick, Margaret thought; he wants to yell, just once. Since the fire scare she was apprehensive about large groups of people gathering together; when friends began to drop in after dinner she waited for a while, telling herself they were on the ground floor, she could run right outside, all the windows were open; then she excused herself and went to bed. When Brad came to bed much later she woke up and he said irritably, "We've been playing anagrams. Such crazy people." She said sleepily, "Did you win?" and fell asleep before he told her.

The next morning she and Brad went for a walk while their host and hostess read the Sunday papers. "If you turn to the right outside the door," their hostess said encouragingly, "and walk about three blocks down, you'll come to our beach."

"What do they want with our beach?" their host said. "It's too damn cold to do anything down there."

"They can look at the *water*," their hostess said.

They walked down to the beach; at this time of year it was bare and windswept, yet still nodding hideously under traces of its summer plumage, as though it thought itself warmly inviting. There were occupied houses on the way there, for instance, and a lonely lunchstand was open, bravely advertising hot dogs and root beer. The man in the lunchstand watched them go by, his face cold and unsympathetic. They walked far past him, out of sight of houses, on to a stretch of grey pebbled sand that lay between the grey water on one side and the grey pebbled sand dunes on the other.

"Imagine going swimming here," she said with a shiver. The beach pleased her; it was oddly familiar and reassuring and at the same time that she realized this, the little tune came back to her, bringing a double recollection. The beach was the one where she had lived in imagination, writing for herself dreary love-broken stories where the heroine walked beside the wild waves; the little tune was the symbol of the golden world she escaped into to avoid the everyday dreariness that drove her into writing depressing stories about the beach. She laughed out loud and Brad said, "What on earth's so funny about this Godforsaken landscape?"

"I was just thinking how far away from the city it seems," she said falsely.

The sky and the water and the sand were grey enough to make it feel like late afternoon instead of midmorning; she was tired and wanted to go back, but Brad said suddenly, "Look at that," and she turned and saw a girl running down over the dunes, carrying her hat, and her hair flying behind her.

"Only way to get warm on a day like this," Brad remarked, but Margaret said, "She looks frightened."

The girl saw them and came toward them, slowing down as she approached them. She was eager to reach them but when she came within speaking distance the familiar embarrassment, the not wanting to look like a fool, made her hesitate and look from one to the other of them uncomfortably.

"Do you know where I can find a policeman?" she asked finally.

Brad looked up and down the bare rocky beach and said solemnly, "There don't seem to be any around. Is there something we can do?"

"I don't think so," the girl said. "I really need a policeman."

They go to the police for everything, Margaret thought, these people, these New York people, it's as though they had selected a section of the population to act as problem-solvers, and so no matter what they want they look for a policeman.

"Be glad to help you if we can," Brad said.

The girl hesitated again. "Well, if you *must* know," she said crossly, "there's a leg up there."

They waited politely for the girl to explain, but she only said, "Come *on*, then," and waved to them to follow her. She led them over the dunes to a spot near a small inlet, where the dunes gave way abruptly to an intruding head of water. A leg was lying on the sand near the water, and the girl gestured at it and said, "There," as though it were her own property and they had insisted on having a share.

They walked over to it and Brad bent down gingerly. "It's a leg all right," he said. It looked like part of a wax dummy, a death-white wax leg neatly cut off at top-thigh and again just above the ankle, bent comfortably at the knee and resting on the sand. "It's real," Brad said, his voice slightly different. "You're right about that policeman."

They walked together to the lunchstand and the man listened unenthusiastically while Brad called the police. When the police came they all walked out again to where the leg was lying and Brad gave the police their names and addresses, and then said, "Is it all right to go on home?"

"What the hell you want to hang around for?" the policeman inquired with heavy humor. "You waiting for the rest of him?"

They went back to their host and hostess, talking about the leg, and their host apologized, as though he had been guilty of a breach of taste in allowing his guests to come on a human leg; their hostess said with interest, "There was an arm washed up in Bensonhurst, I've been reading about it."

"One of these killings," the host said.

Upstairs Margaret said abruptly, "I suppose it starts to happen first in the suburbs," and when Brad said, "What starts to happen?" she said hysterically, "People starting to come apart."

In order to reassure their host and hostess about their minding the leg, they stayed until the last afternoon train to New York. Back in their apartment again it seemed to Margaret that the marble in the house lobby had begun to age a little; even in two days there were new perceptible cracks. The elevator seemed a little rusty, and there was a fine film of dust over everything in the apartment. They went to bed feeling uncomfortable, and the next morning Margaret said immediately, "I'm going to stay in today."

"You're not upset about yesterday, are you?"

"Not a bit," Margaret said. "I just want to stay in and rest."

After some discussion Brad decided to go off again by himself; he still had people it was important to see and places he must go in the few days they had left. After breakfast in the Automat Margaret came back alone to the apartment, carrying the mystery story she had bought on the way. She hung up her coat and hat and sat down by the window with the noise and the people far below, looking out at the sky where it was grey beyond the houses across the street.

I'm not going to worry about it, she said to herself, no sense thinking all the time about things like that, spoil your vacation and Brad's too. No sense worrying, people get ideas like that and then worry about them.

The nasty little tune was running through her head again, with its burden of suavity and expensive perfume. The houses across the street were silent and perhaps unoccupied at this time of day; she let her eyes move with the rhythm of the tune, from window to window along one floor. By gliding quickly across two windows, she could make one line of the tune fit one floor of windows, and then a quick breath and a drop down to the next floor; it had the same number of windows and the tune had the same number of beats, and then the next floor and the next. She stopped suddenly when it seemed to her that the windowsill she had just passed had soundlessly crumpled and fallen into fine sand; when she looked back it was there as before but then it seemed to be the windowsill above and to the right, and finally a corner of the roof.

No sense worrying, she told herself, forcing her eyes down to the street, stop thinking about things all the time. Looking down at the street for long made her dizzy and she stood up and went into the small bedroom of the apartment. She had made the bed before going out to breakfast, like any good housewife, but now she deliberately took it apart, stripping the blankets and sheets off one by one, and then she made it again, taking a long time over the corners and smoothing out every wrinkle. "*That's* done," she said when she was through, and went back to the window. When she looked across the street the tune started again, window to window, sills dissolving and falling downward. She leaned forward and looked down at her own window, something she had never thought of before, down to the sill. It was partly eaten away; when she touched the stone a few crumbs rolled off and fell.

It was eleven o'clock; Brad was looking at blowtorches by now and would not be back before one, if even then. She thought of writing a letter home, but the impulse left her before she found paper and pen. Then it occurred to her that she might take a nap, a thing she had never done in the morning in her life, and she went in and lay down on the bed. Lying down, she felt the building shaking.

No sense worrying, she told herself again, as though it were a charm against witches, and got up and found her coat and hat and put them on. I'll just get some cigarettes and some letter paper, she thought, just run down to the corner. Panic caught her going down in the elevator; it went too fast, and when she stepped out in the lobby it was only the people standing around who kept her from running. As it was, she went quickly out of the building and into the street. For a minute she hesitated, wanting to go back. The cars were going past so rapidly, the people hurrying as always, but the panic of the elevator drove her on finally. She went to the corner, and, following the people flying along ahead, ran out into the street, to hear a horn almost overhead and a shout from behind her, and the noise of brakes. She ran blindly on and reached the other side where she stopped and looked around. The truck was going on its appointed way around the corner, the people going past on either side of her, parting to go around her where she stood.

No one even noticed me, she thought with reassurance, everyone who saw me has gone by long ago. She went into the drugstore ahead of her and asked the man for cigarettes; the apartment now seemed safer to her than the street—she could walk up the stairs. Coming out of the store and walking to the corner, she kept as close to the buildings as possible, refusing to give way to the rightful traffic coming out of the doorways. On the corner she looked carefully at the light; it was green, but it looked as though it were going to change. Always safer to wait, she thought, don't want to walk into another truck.

People pushed past her and some were caught in the middle of the street when the light changed. One woman, more cowardly than the rest, turned and ran back to the curb, but the others stood in the middle of the street, leaning forward and then backward according to the traffic moving past them on both sides. One got to the farther curb in a brief break in the line of cars, the others were a fraction of a second too late and waited. Then the light changed again and as the cars slowed down Margaret put a foot on the street to go, but a taxi swinging wildly around her corner frightened her back and she stood on the curb again. By the time the taxi had gone the light was due to change again and she thought, I can wait once more, no sense getting caught out in the middle. A man beside her tapped his foot impatiently for the light to change back; two girls came past her and walked out into the street a few steps to wait, moving back a little when cars came too close, talking busily all the time. I ought to stay right with them, Margaret thought, but then they moved back against her and the light changed and the man next to her charged into the street and the two girls in front waited a minute and then moved slowly on, still talking, and Margaret started to follow and then decided to wait. A crowd of people formed around her suddenly; they had come off a bus and were crossing here, and she had a sudden feeling of being jammed in the center and forced out into the street when all of them moved as one with the light changing, and she elbowed her way desperately out of the crowd and went off to lean against a building and wait. It seemed to her that people passing were beginning to look at her. What do they think of me, she wondered, and stood up straight as though she were waiting for someone. She looked at her watch and frowned, and then thought, What a fool I must look like, no one here ever saw me before, they all go by too fast. She went back to the curb again but the green light was just changing to red and she thought, I'll go back to the drugstore and have a Coke, no sense going back to that apartment.

The man looked at her unsurprised in the drugstore and she sat and ordered a Coke but suddenly as she was drinking it the panic caught her again and she thought of the people who had been with her when she first started to cross the street, blocks away by now, having tried and made perhaps a dozen lights while she had hesitated at the first; people by now a mile or so downtown, because they had been going steadily while she had been trying to gather her courage. She paid the man quickly, restrained an impulse to say that there was nothing wrong with the Coke, she just had to get back, that was all, and she hurried down to the corner again.

The minute the light changes, she told herself firmly; there's no sense. The light changed before she was ready and in the minute before she collected herself traffic turning the corner overwhelmed her and she shrank back against the curb. She looked longingly at the cigar store on the opposite corner, with her apartment house beyond; she wondered, How do people ever manage to get there, and knew that by wondering, by admitting a doubt, she was lost. The light changed and she looked at it with hatred, a dumb thing, turning back and forth, back and forth, with no purpose and no meaning. Looking to either side of her slyly, to see if anyone were watching, she stepped quietly backward, one step, two, until she was well away from the curb. Back in the drugstore again she waited for some sign of recognition from the clerk and saw none; he regarded her with the same apathy as he had the first time. He gestured without interest at the telephone; he doesn't care, she thought, it doesn't matter to him who I call.

She had no time to feel like a fool, because they answered the phone immediately and agreeably and found him right away. When he answered the phone, his voice sounding surprised and matter-of-fact, she could only say miserably, "I'm in the drugstore on the corner. Come and get me."

"What's the matter?" He was not anxious to come.

"Please come and get me," she said into the black mouthpiece that might or might not tell him, "please come and get me, Brad. *Please.*"

MAVIS GALLANT was born in Montreal in 1922. After her father died when she was a small child she was shifted from school to school, from province to province, here speaking English, there writing French. In all she attended seventeen schools and, in her own estimation, received no education. She sold her first story to *The New Yorker* in 1951 and since then has been a regular contributor. She worked for a newspaper in Montreal for a few years and then went to live in France. Her desire to be a writer derives, she says, from a source common to the experience of many writers. "I have discovered that writers' lives tend to fall into a pattern, and mine is no different. They are often the product of a solitary childhood, and have known, early, the shocks of violent change. The vocation exists, and so does the gift; but vocation and gift are seldom of equal proportions, and I suppose that the struggle to equate them is the true and secret tension." Such a pattern is clear in the biographies of Jean Rhys, Frank O'Connor, Elizabeth Bowen, Rudyard Kipling, Mary McCarthy. The list could be much longer.

Like many working artists Gallant is impatient with the categories of self-revelation imposed by interviewers. "Nothing is as obnoxious to me as a writer talking about himself and his aims and theories. These things should be evident in the work (I am talking about serious writers). I have noticed that what interests people is irrelevant. Whenever I have been interviewed I have been asked if I write on a typewriter, if I work in the morning or afternoon, how I first sold a story to *The New Yorker*. My answer to the last of these—that I typed a story and sent it in—never seems satisfactory. Yet that is all there was to it. The beginning is easy; what happens next is much harder."

Mavis Gallant
(1922—   )

ACCEPTANCE OF THEIR WAYS

Prodded by a remark from Mrs. Freeport, Lily Littel got up and fetched the plate of cheese. It was in her to say, "Go get it yourself," but a reputation for coolness held her still. Only the paucity of her income, at which *The Sunday Express* horoscope jeered with its smart talk of pleasure and gain, kept her at Mrs. Freeport's, on the Italian side of the frontier. The coarse and grubby gaiety of the French Riviera would have suited her better, and was not far away; unfortunately it came high. At Mrs. Freeport's, which was cheaper, there was a whiff of infirm nicety to be breathed, a suggestion of regularly aired decay; weakly, because it was respectable, Lily craved that, too. "We seem to have finished with the pudding," said Mrs. Freeport once again, as though she hadn't noticed that Lily was on her feet.

Lily was not Mrs. Freeport's servant, she was her paying guest, but it was a distinction her hostess rarely observed. In imagination, Lily became a punishing statue and raised a heavy marble arm; but then she remembered that this was the New Year. The next day, or the day after that, her dividends would arrive. That meant she could disappear, emerging as a gay holiday Lily up in Nice. Then, Lily thought, turning away from the table, then watch the old tiger! For Mrs. Freeport couldn't live without Lily, not more than a day. She could not stand Italy without the sound of an English voice in the house. In the hush of the dead season, Mrs. Freeport preferred Lily's ironed-out Bayswater to no English at all.

In the time it took her to pick up the cheese and face the table again, Lily had added to her expression a permanent-looking smile. Her eyes, which were a washy blue, were tolerably kind when she was plotting mischief. The week in Nice, desired, became a necessity; Mrs. Freeport needed a scare. She would fear, and then believe, that her most docile boarder, her most pliant errand girl, had gone forever.

287

Stealing into Lily's darkened room, she would count the dresses with trembling hands. She would touch Lily's red with the white dots, her white with the poppies, her green wool with the scarf of mink tails. Mrs. Freeport would also discover—if she carried her snooping that far—the tooled-leather box with Lily's daisy-shaped earrings, and the brooch in which a mother-of-pearl pigeon sat on a nest made of Lily's own hair. But Mrs. Freeport would not find the diary, in which Lily had recorded her opinion of so many interesting things, nor would she come upon a single empty bottle. Lily kept her drinking to Nice, where, anonymous in a large hotel, friendly and lavish in a bar, she let herself drown. "Your visits to your sister seem to do you so much good," was Mrs. Freeport's unvarying comment when Lily returned from these excursions, which always followed the arrival of her income. "But you spend far too much money on your sister. You are much too kind." But Lily had no regrets. Illiberal by circumstance, grudging only because she imitated the behavior of other women, she became, drunk, an old forgotten Lily-girl, tender and warm, able to shed a happy tear and open a closed fist. She had been cold sober since September.

"Well, there you are," she said, and slapped down the plate of cheese. There was another person at the table, a Mrs. Garnett, who was returning to England the next day. Lily's manner toward the two women combined bullying with servility. Mrs. Freeport, large, in brown chiffon, wearing a hat with a water lily upon it to cover her thinning hair, liked to feel served. Lily had been a paid companion once; she had never seen a paradox in the joining of those two words. She simply looked on Mrs. Freeport and Mrs. Garnett as more of that race of ailing, peevish elderly children whose fancies and delusions must be humored by the sane.

Mrs. Freeport pursed her lips in acknowledgement of the cheese. Mrs. Garnett, who was reading a book, did nothing at all. Mrs. Garnett had been with them four months. Her blued curls, her laugh, her moist baby's mouth, had the effect on Lily of a stone in the shoe. Mrs. Garnett's husband, dead but often mentioned, had evidently liked them saucy and dim in the brain. Now that William Henry was no longer there to protect his wife, she was the victim of the effects of her worrying beauty—a torment to shoe clerks and bus conductors. Italians were dreadful; Mrs. Garnett hardly dared put her wee nose outside the house. "You are a little monkey,

Edith!" Mrs. Freeport would sometimes say, bringing her head upward with a jerk, waking out of a sweet dream in time to applaud. Mrs. Garnett would go on telling how she had been jostled on the pavement or offended on a bus. And Lily Littel, who knew—but truly knew—about being followed and hounded and pleaded with, brought down her thick eyelids and smiled. Talk leads to overconfidence and errors. Lily had guided her life to this quiet shore by knowing when to open her mouth and when to keep it closed.

Mrs. Freeport was not deluded but simply poor. Thirteen years of pension keeping on a tawdry stretch of Mediterranean coast had done nothing to improve her fortunes and had probably diminished them. Sentiment kept her near Bordighera, where someone precious to her had been buried in the Protestant part of the cemetery. In Lily's opinion, Mrs. Freeport ought to have cleared out long ago, cutting her losses, leaving the servants out of pocket and the grocer unpaid. Lily looked soft; she was round and pink and yellow-haired. The imitation pearls screwed on to her doughy little ears seemed to devour the flesh. But Lily could have bitten a real pearl in two and enjoyed the pieces. Her nature was generous, but an admiration for superior women had led her to cherish herself. An excellent cook, she had dreamed of being a poisoner, but decided to leave that for the loonies; it was no real way to get on. She had a moral program of a sort—thought it wicked to set a poor table, until she learned that the sort of woman she yearned to become was often picky. After that she tried to put it out of her mind. At Mrs. Freeport's she was enrolled in a useful school, for the creed of the house was this: It is pointless to think about anything so temporary as food; coffee grounds can be used many times, and moldy bread, revived in the oven, mashed with raisins and milk, makes a delicious pudding. If Lily had settled for this bleached existence, it was explained by a sentence scrawled over a page of her locked diary: "I live with gentlewomen now." And there was a finality about the statement that implied acceptance of their ways.

Lily removed the fly netting from the cheese. There was her bit left over from luncheon. It was the end of a portion of Dutch so dry it had split. Mrs. Freeport would have the cream cheese, possibly still highly pleasing under its coat of pale fur, while Mrs. Garnett, who was a yoghurt fancier, would require none at all.

"Cheese, Edith," said Mrs. Freeport loudly; and little Mrs. Garnett blinked her doll eyes and smiled: "No, thank you." Let others thicken their figures and damage their souls.

The cheese was pushed along to Mrs. Freeport, then back to Lily, passing twice under Mrs. Garnett's nose. She did not look up again. She was moving her lips over a particularly absorbing passage in her book. For the last four months, she had been reading the same volume, which was called *Optimism Unlimited*. So as not to stain the pretty dust jacket, she had covered it with brown paper, but now even that was becoming soiled. When Mrs. Freeport asked what the book was about, Mrs. Garnett smiled a timid apology and said, "I'm *afraid* it is philosophy." It was, indeed, a new philosophy, counseling restraint in all things, but recommending smiles. Four months of smiles and restraint had left Mrs. Garnett hungry, and to mark her last evening at Mrs. Freeport's, she had asked for an Italian meal. Mrs. Freeport thought it extravagant—after all, they were still digesting an English Christmas. But little Edith was so sweet when she begged, putting her head to one side, wrinkling her face, that Mrs. Freeport, muttering about monkeys, had given in. The dinner was prepared and served, and Mrs. Garnett, suddenly remembering about restraint, brought her book to the table and decided not to eat a thing.

It seemed that the late William Henry had found this capriciousness adorable, but Mrs. Freeport's eyes were stones. Lily supposed this was how murders came about—not the hasty, soon-regretted sort but the plan that is sown from an insult, a slight, and comes to flower at temperate speed. Mrs. Garnett deserved a reprimand. Lily saw her, without any emotion, doubled in two and shoved in a sack. But did Mrs. Freeport like her friend enough to bother teaching her lessons? Castigation, to Lily, suggested love. Mrs. Garnett and Mrs. Freeport were old friends, and vaguely related. Mrs. Garnett had been coming to Mrs. Freeport's every winter for years, but she left unfinished letters lying about, from which Lily—a great reader—could learn that dear Vanessa was becoming meaner and queerer by the minute. Thinking of Mrs. Freeport as "dear Vanessa" took flexibility, but Lily had that. She was not "Miss" and not "Littel"; she was, or rather had been, a Mrs. Cliff Littel, who had taken advantage of the disorders of war to get rid of Cliff. He vanished, and his memory grew smaller and faded from the sky. In the bright new day strolled Miss Lily Littel, ready for anything. Then a lonely, fretful widow had taken a fancy to her and, as soon as travel was possible, had taken Lily abroad. There followed eight glorious years of trains and bars and discreet afternoon gambling, of eating éclairs in English-style tearooms, and discovering cafés where bacon and eggs were fried. Oh, the discovery of that sign in Monte Carlo: *Every Friday Sausages and Mashed!* That was the joy of being in foreign lands. One hot afternoon, Lily's employer, hooked by Lily into her stays not an hour before, dropped dead in a cinema lobby in Rome. Her will revealed she had provided for "Miss Littel," for a fox terrier, and for an invalid niece. The provision for the niece prevented the family from coming down on Lily's head; all the same, Lily kept out of England. She had not inspired the death of her employer, but she had nightmares for some time after, as though she had taken the wish for the deed. Her letters were so ambiguous that there was talk in England of an inquest. Lily accompanied the coffin as far as the frontier, for a letter of instructions specified cremation, which Lily understood could take place only in France. The coffin was held up rather a long time at customs, documents went back and forth, and in the end the relatives were glad to hear the last of it. Shortly after that, the fox terrier died, and Lily appropriated his share, feeling that she deserved it. Her employer had been living on overdrafts; there was next to nothing for the dog, companion, or niece. Lily stopped having nightmares. She continued to live abroad.

With delicate nibbles, eyes down, Lily ate her cheese. Glancing sideways, she noticed that Mrs. Garnett had closed the book. She wanted to annoy; she had planned the whole business of the Italian meal, had thought it out beforehand. Their manners were still strange to Lily, although she was a quick pupil. Why not clear the air, have it out? Once again she wondered what the two friends meant to each other. "Like" and "hate" were possibilities she had nearly forgotten when she stopped being Mrs. Cliff and became this curious, two-faced Lily Littel.

Mrs. Freeport's pebbly stare was focused on her friend's jar of yoghurt. "Sugar?" she cried, giving the cracked basin a shove along the table. Mrs. Garnett pulled it toward her defiantly. She spoke in a soft martyred voice, as though Lily weren't there. She said that it was her last evening and it no longer mattered. Mrs. Freeport had made a charge for extra sugar—yes, she had seen it on her bill. Mrs. Garnett asked only to pay and go. She was never coming again.

"I look upon you as essentially greedy." Mrs. Freeport leaned forward, enunciating with care. "You pretend to eat nothing, but I cannot look at a dish after you have served yourself. The *wreck* of the lettuce. The *destruction* of the pudding."

A bottle of wine, adrift and forgotten, stood by Lily's plate. She had not seen it until now. Mrs. Garnett, who was fearless, covered her yoghurt thickly with sugar.

"Like most people who pretend to eat like birds, you manage to keep your strength up," Mrs. Freeport said. "That sugar is the equivalent of a banquet, and you also eat between meals. Your drawers are stuffed with biscuits, and cheese, and chocolate, and heaven knows what."

"Dear Vanessa," Mrs. Garnett said.

"People who make a pretense of eating nothing always stuff furtively," said Mrs. Freeport smoothly. "Secret eating is exactly the same as secret drinking."

Lily's years abroad had immunized her to the conversation of gentlewomen, their absorption with money, their deliberate over- or underfeeding, their sudden animal quarrels. She wondered if there remained a great deal more to learn before she could wear their castoff manners as her own. At the reference to secret drinking she looked calm and melancholy. Mrs. Garnett said, "That is most unkind." The yoghurt remained uneaten. Lily sighed, and wondered what would happen if she picked her teeth.

"My change man stopped by today," said Mrs. Garnett, all at once smiling and widening her eyes. How Lily admired that shift of territory—that carrying of banners to another field. She had not learned everything yet. "I *wish* you could have seen his face when he heard I was leaving! There was really no need for his coming, because I'd been in to his office only the week before, and changed all the money I need, and we'd had a lovely chat."

"The odious little merchant in the bright-yellow automobile?" asked Mrs. Freeport.

Mrs. Garnett, who often took up farfetched and untenable arguments, said, "William Henry wanted me to be happy."

"Edith!"

Lily hooked her middle finger around the bottle of wine and pulled it gently toward her. The day after tomorrow was years away. But she did not take her eyes from Mrs. Freeport, whose blazing eyes perfectly matched the small sapphires hanging from her ears. Lily could have matched the expression if she had cared to, but she hadn't arrived at the sapphires yet. Addressing herself, Lily said, "Thanks," softly, and upended the bottle.

"I meant it in a general way," said Mrs. Garnett. "William Henry wanted me to be happy. It was nearly the last thing he said."

"At the time of William Henry's death, he was unable to say anything," said Mrs. Freeport. "William Henry was my first cousin. Don't use him as a platform for your escapades."

Lily took a sip from her glass. Shock! It hadn't been watered—probably in honor of Mrs. Garnett's last meal. But it was sour, thick, and full of silt. "I have always thought a little sugar would improve it," said Lily chattily, but nobody heard.

Mrs. Freeport suddenly conceded that William Henry might have wanted his future widow to be happy. "It was because he spoiled you," she said. "You were vain and silly when he married you, and he made conceited and foolish. I don't wonder poor William Henry went off his head."

"Off his head?" Mrs. Garnett looked at Lily; calm, courteous Miss Littel was giving herself wine. "We might have general conversation," said Mrs. Garnett, with a significant twitch of face. "Miss Littel has hardly said a word."

"Why?" shouted Mrs. Freeport, throwing her table napkin down. "The meal is over. You refused it. There is no need for conversation of any kind."

She was marvelous, blazing, with that water lily on her head. Ah, Lily thought, but you should have seen me, in the old days. How I could let fly . . . poor old Cliff.

They moved in single file down the passage and into the sitting room, where, for reasons of economy, the hanging luster contained one bulb. Lily and Mrs. Freeport settled down directly under it, on a sofa; each had her own newspaper to read, tucked down the side of the cushions. Mrs. Garnett walked about the room. "To think that I shall never see this room again," she said.

"I should hope not," said Mrs. Freeport. She held the paper before her face, but as far as Lily could tell she was not reading it.

"The trouble is"—for Mrs. Garnett could never help giving herself away—"I don't know where to *go* in the autumn."

"Ask your change man."

"Egypt," said Mrs. Garnett, still walking about. "I had friends who went to Egypt every winter for years and years, and now they have nowhere to go, either."

"Let them stay home," said Mrs. Freeport. "I am trying to read."

"If Egypt continues to carry on, I'm sure I don't know where we shall all be," said Lily. Neither lady took the slightest notice.

"They were perfectly charming people," said Mrs. Garnett, in a complaining way.

"Why don't you do the *Times* crossword, Edith?" Mrs. Freeport asked.

From behind them Mrs. Garnett said, "You know that I can't, and you said that only to make me feel small. But William Henry did it until the very end, which proves, I think, that he was not o.h.h. By o.h.h. I mean *off his head.*"

The break in her voice was scarcely more than a quaver, but to the two women on the sofa it was a signal, and they got to their feet. By the time they reached her, Mrs. Garnett was sitting on the floor in hysterics. They helped her up, as they had often done before. She tried to scratch their faces and said they would be sorry when she died.

Between them, they got her to bed. "Where is her hotwater bottle?" said Mrs. Freeport. "No, not that one. She must have her own—the bottle with the bunny head."

"My yoghurt," said Mrs. Garnett, sobbing. Without her makeup she looked shrunken, as though padding had been removed from her skin.

"Fetch the yoghurt," Mrs. Freeport commanded. She stood over the old friend while she ate the yoghurt, one tiny spoonful at a time. "Now go to sleep," she said.

In the morning, Mrs. Garnett was taken by taxi to the early train. She seemed entirely composed and carried her book. Mrs. Freeport hoped that her journey would be comfortable. She and Lily watched the taxi until it was out of sight on the road, and then, in the bare wintry gardens, Mrs. Freeport wept into her hands.

"I've said good-bye to her," she said at last, blowing her nose. "It is the last good-bye. I shall never see her again. I was so horrid to her. And she is so tiny and frail. She might die. I'm convinced of it. She won't survive the summer."

"She has survived every other," said Lily reasonably.

"Next year she must have the large room with the balcony. I don't know what I was thinking, not to have given it to her. We must begin planning now for next year. She will want a good reading light. Her eyes are so bad. And, you know, we should have chopped her vegetables. She doesn't chew. I'm sure that's at the bottom of the yoghurt affair."

"I'm off to Nice tomorrow," said Lily, the stray. "My sister is expecting me."

"You are so devoted," said Mrs. Freeport, looking wildly for her handkerchief, which had fallen on the gravel path. Her hat was askew. The house was empty. "So devoted . . . I suppose that one day you will want to live in Nice, to be near her. I suppose that day will come."

Instead of answering, Lily set Mrs. Freeport's water lily straight, which was familiar of her; but they were both in such a state, for different reasons, that neither of them thought it strange.

NADINE GORDIMER, the daughter of an English mother and a Jewish father who emigrated to Africa from a Baltic town, was born in 1923 at Springs, near Johannesburg in South Africa. At convent school she was a good student with a "bossy vitality" that made her popular, restless, and a frequent truant. At the University of Witwatersrand in Johannesburg she read D. H. Lawrence, who influenced her way of looking at the natural world, Henry James, from whom she acquired a sense of form, and Hemingway, who gave her an ear for the essential in dialogue. After her first stories were published in *The New Yorker* and *Harper's*, reviewers, praising her verbal dexterity and her "mercilessly accurate" sensory responses, announced the arrival of a "potentially major writer."

Honor Tracy has said, there is "no living writer of short stories more interesting, varied and fertile than Miss Gordimer at her best." She knows why she writes. "I think that a writer's purpose is to make sense of life. Even the most esoteric of linguistic innovations, the wildest experiments with form, are an expression of this purpose. The only dictum I always remember is André Gide's—'Salvation, for the writer, lies in being sincere even against one's better judgement.' The ideal way to write is as if oneself and one's readers were already dead." Married and the mother of two children, she has been adjunct professor of writing at Columbia University since 1971.

Nadine Gordimer
(1923—   )

THE TRAIN FROM RHODESIA

The train came out of the red horizon and bore down toward them over the single straight track.

The stationmaster came out of his little brick station with its pointed chalet roof, feeling the creases in his serge uniform in his legs as well. A stir of preparedness rippled through the squatting native vendors waiting in the dust; the face of a carved wooden animal, eternally surprised, stuck out of a sack. The stationmaster's barefoot children wandered over. From the gray mud huts with the untidy heads that stood within a decorated mud wall, chickens, and dogs with their skin stretched like parchment over their bones, followed the piccanins down to the track. The flushed and perspiring west cast a reflection, faint, without heat, upon the station, upon the tin shed marked "Goods," upon the walled kraal, upon the gray tin house of the stationmaster and upon the sand, that lapped all around, from sky to sky, cast little rhythmical cups of shadow, so that the sand became the sea, and closed over the children's black feet softly and without imprint.

The stationmaster's wife sat behind the mesh of her verandah. Above her head the hunk of a sheep's carcass moved slightly, dangling in a current of air.

They waited.

The train called out, along the sky; but there was no answer; and the cry hung on: I'm coming . . . I'm coming . . .

The engine flared out now, big, whisking a dwindling body behind it; the track flared out to let it in.

Creaking, jerking, jostling, gasping, the train filled the station.

Here, let me see that one—the young woman curved her body further out of the corridor window. Missus? smiled the old boy, looking at the creatures he held in his hand. From a piece of string on his gray finger hung a tiny woven basket; he lifted it, questioning. No, no, she urged, leaning down toward him, across the height of the train, toward the man in the piece of old rug; that one, that one, her hand commanded. It was a lion, carved out of soft dry wood that looked like spongecake; heraldic, black and white, with impressionistic detail burnt in. The old man held it up to her still smiling, not from the heart, but at the customer. Between its Vandyke teeth, in the mouth opened in an endless roar too terrible to be heard, it had a black tongue. Look, said the young husband, if you don't mind! And round the neck of the thing, a piece of fur (rat? rabbit? meerkat?); a real mane, majestic, telling you somehow that the artist had delight in the lion.

All up and down the length of the train in the dust the artist sprang, walking bent, like performing animals, the better to exhibit the fantasy held toward the faces on the train. Buck, startled and stiff, staring with round black and white eyes. More lions, standing erect, grappling with strange, thin, elongated warriors who clutched spears and showed no fear in their slits of eyes. How much, they asked from the train, how much?

Give me penny, said the little ones with nothing to sell. The dogs went and sat, quite still, under the dining car, where the train breathed out the smell of meat cooking with onion.

A man passed beneath the arch of reaching arms meeting gray-black and white in the exchange of money for the staring wooden eyes, the stiff wooden legs sticking up in the air; went along under the voices and the bargaining, interrogating the wheels. Past the dogs; glancing up at the dining car where he could stare at the faces, behind glass, drinking beer, two by two, on either side of a uniform railway vase with its pale dead flower. Right to the end, to the guard's van, where the stationmaster's children had just collected their mother's two loaves of bread; to the engine itself, where the stationmaster and the driver stood talking against the steaming complaint of the resting beast.

The man called out to them, something loud and joking. They turned to laugh, in a twirl of steam. The two children careered over the sand, clutching the bread, and burst through the iron gate and up the path through the garden in which nothing grew.

Passengers drew themselves in at the corridor windows and turned into compartments to fetch money, to call someone to look. Those sitting inside looked up: suddenly different, caged faces, boxed in, cut off, after the contact of outside. There was an orange a piccanin would like. . . . What about that chocolate? It wasn't very nice. . . .

A young girl had collected a handful of the hard kind, that no one liked, out of the chocolate box, and was throwing them to the dogs, over at the dining car. But the hens darted in, and swallowed the chocolates, incredibly quick and accurate, before they had even dropped in the dust, and the dogs, a little bewildered, looked up with their brown eyes, not expecting anything.

—No, leave it, said the girl, don't take it. . . .

Too expensive, too much, she shook her head and raised her voice to the old boy, giving up the lion. He held it up where she had handed it to him. No, she said, shaking her head. Three-and-six? insisted her husband, loudly. Yes baas! laughed the boy. *Three-and-six?*—the young man was incredulous. Oh leave it—she said. The young man stopped. Don't you want it? he said, keeping his face closed to the boy. No, never mind, she said, leave it. The old native kept his head on one side, looking at them sideways, holding the lion. Three-and-six, he murmured, as old people repeat things to themselves.

The young woman drew her head in. She went into the coupé and sat down. Out of the window, on the other side, there was nothing; sand and bush; a thorn tree. Back through the open doorway, past the figure of her husband in the corridor, there was the station, the voices, wooden animals waving, running feet. Her eye followed the funny little valance of scrolled wood that outlined the chalet roof of the station; she thought of the lion and smiled. That bit of fur round the neck. But the wooden buck, the hippos, the elephants, the baskets that already bulked out of their brown paper under the seat and on the luggage rack! How will they look at home? Where will you put them? What will they mean away from the places you found them? Away from the unreality of the last few weeks? The man outside. But he is not part of the unreality; he is for good now. Odd . . . somewhere there

was an idea that he, that living with him, was part of the
holiday, the strange places.

Outside, a bell rang. The stationmaster was leaning against
the end of the train, green flag rolled in readiness. A few men
who had got down to stretch their legs sprang on to the train,
clinging to the observation platforms, or perhaps merely
standing on the iron step, holding the rail; but on the train,
safe from the one dusty platform, the one tin house, the
empty sand.

There was a grunt. The train jerked. Through the glass the
beer drinkers looked out, as if they could not see beyond it.
Behind the fly-screen, the stationmaster's wife sat facing back
at them beneath the darkening hunk of meat.

There was a shout. The flag drooped out. Joints not yet
coordinated, the segmented body of the train heaved and
bumped back against itself. It began to move; slowly the
scrolled chalet moved past it, the yells of the natives, running
alongside, jetted up into the air, fell back at different levels.
Staring wooden faces waved drunkenly, there, then gone,
questioning for the last time at the windows. Here, one-and-
six baas!—As one automatically opens a hand to catch a
thrown ball, a man fumbled wildly down his pocket, brought
up the shilling and sixpence and threw them out; the old native, gasping, his skinny toes splaying the sand, flung the lion.

The piccanins were waving, the dogs stood, tails uncertain,
watching the train go: past the mud huts, where a woman
turned to look, up from the smoke of the fire, her hand
pausing on her hip.

The stationmaster went slowly in under the chalet.

The old native stood, breath blowing out the skin between
his ribs, feet tense, balanced in the sand, smiling and shaking
his head. In his opened palm, held in the attitude of receiving, was the retrieved shilling and sixpence.

The blind end of the train was being pulled helplessly out
of the station.

The young man swung in from the corridor, breathless. He
was shaking his head with laughter and triumph. Here! he
said. And waggled the lion at her. One-and-six!

What? she said.

He laughed. I was arguing with him for fun, bargaining—
when the train had pulled out already, he came tearing
after.... One-and-six baas! So there's your lion.

She was holding it away from her, the head with the open jaws, the pointed teeth, the black tongue, the wonderful ruff of fur facing her. She was looking at it with an expression of not seeing, of seeing something different. Her face was drawn up, wryly, like the face of a discomforted child. Her mouth lifted nervously at the corner. Very slowly, cautious, she lifted her finger and touched the mane, where it was joined to the wood.

But how could you, she said. He was shocked by the dismay of her face.

Good Lord, he said, what's the matter?

If you wanted the thing, she said, her voice rising and breaking with the shrill impotence of anger, why didn't you buy it in the first place? If you wanted it, why didn't you pay for it? Why didn't you take it decently, when he offered it? Why did you have to wait for him to run after the train with it, and give him one-and-six? One-and-six!

She was pushing it at him, trying to force him to take it. He stood astonished, his hands hanging at his sides.

But you wanted it! You liked it so much!

—It's a beautiful piece of work, she said fiercely, as if to protect it from him.

You liked it so much! You said yourself it was too expensive—

Oh *you*—she said, hopeless and furious. *You.* . . . She threw the lion on to the seat.

He stood looking at her.

She sat down again in the corner and, her face slumped in her hand, stared out of the window. Everything was turning round inside her. One-and-six. One-and-six. One-and-six for the wood and the carving and the sinews of the legs and the switch of the tail. The mouth open like that and the teeth. The black tongue, rolling, like a wave. The mane round the neck. To give one-and-six for that. The heat of shame mounted through her legs and body and sounded in her ears like the sound of sand pouring. Pouring, pouring. She sat there, sick. A weariness, a tastelessness, the discovery of a void made her hands slacken their grip, atrophy emptily, as if the hour was not worth their grasp. She was feeling like this again. She had thought it was something to do with singleness, with being alone and belonging too much to oneself.

She sat there not wanting to move or speak, or to look at anything, even; so that the mood should be associated with

nothing, no object, word or sight that might recur and so recall the feeling again. . . . Smuts blew in grittily, settled on
her hands. Her back remained at exactly the same angle,
turned against the young man sitting with his hands drooping
between his sprawled legs, and the lion, fallen on its side in
the corner.

The train had cast the station like a skin. It called out to
the sky, I'm coming, I'm coming; and again, there was no answer.

MARGARET LAURENCE was born in Manitoba in 1926. Educated at the University of Manitoba, Winnipeg, she has lived in Canada, Somaliland, Ghana, and England. Her early stories are set in Africa. She is perhaps best known for her novel *A Jest of God* which was made into the film *Rachel, Rachel*. This story of an introspective thirty-four-year-old spinster who suddenly falls in love has a theme implicit in the story reprinted here: the need to escape from the stifling world of convention and habit into a new and free world. The critic A. Norman Jeffares has described her gifts in words that apply to the fine story that follows: "Mrs. Laurence has a capacity for conveying the intensity of emotion which racks her characters; she chooses detail illuminatingly and economically; and she develops her human sympathies steadily from book to book. The reader is left with a comforting sense of architectonic control at work, however uncontrolled the actions of the characters may seem at some crucial point of story or novel."

Margaret Laurence
(1926—   )

A BIRD IN THE HOUSE

The parade would be almost over by now, and I had not
gone. My mother had said in a resigned voice, "All right,
Vanessa, if that's the way you feel," making me suffer twice
as many jabs of guilt as I would have done if she had lost her
temper. She and Grandmother MacLeod had gone off, my
mother pulling the low boxsleigh with Roddie all dolled up in
his new red snowsuit, just the sort of little kid anyone would
want people to see. I sat on the lowest branch of the birch
tree in our yard, not minding the snowy wind, even welcoming its punishment. I went over my reasons for not going, trying to believe they were good and sufficient, but in my heart I
felt I was betraying my father. This was the first time I had
stayed away from the Remembrance Day parade. I wondered
if he would notice that I was not there, standing on the sidewalk at the corner of River and Main while the parade
passed, and then following to the Court House grounds where
the service was held.

I could see the whole thing in my mind. It was the same
every year. The Manawaka Civic Band always led the way.
They had never been able to afford full uniforms, but they
had peaked navy-blue caps and sky-blue chest ribbons. They
were joined on Remembrance Day by the Salvation Army
band, whose uniforms seemed too ordinary for a parade, for
they were the same ones the bandsmen wore every Saturday
night when they played "Nearer My God to Thee" at the
foot of River Street. The two bands never managed to prac-
tise quite enough together, so they did not keep in time too
well. The Salvation Army band invariably played faster, and
afterwards my father would say irritably, "They play those
marches just like they do hymns, blast them, as though they
wouldn't get to heaven if they didn't hustle up." And my
mother, who had great respect for the Salvation Army because of the good work they did, would respond chidingly,

"Now, now, Ewen—" I vowed I would never say "Now, now" to my husband or children, not that I ever intended having the latter, for I had been put off by my brother Roderick, who was now two years old with wavy hair, and everyone said what a beautiful child. I was twelve, and no one in their right mind would have said what a beautiful child, for I was big-boned like my Grandfather Connor and had straight lanky black hair like a Blackfoot or Cree.

After the bands would come the veterans. Even thinking of them at this distance, in the white and withdrawn quiet of the birch tree, gave me a sense of painful embarrassment. I might not have minded so much if my father had not been among them. How could he go? How could he not see how they all looked? It must have been a long time since they were soldiers, for they had forgotten how to march in step. They were old—that was the thing. My father was bad enough, being almost forty, but he wasn't a patch on Howard Tully from the drugstore, who was completely grey-haired and also fat, or Stewart MacMurchie, who was bald at the back of his head. They looked to me like imposters, plump or spindly caricatures of past warriors. I almost hated them for walking in that limping column down Main. At the Court House, everyone would sing *Lord God of Hosts, be with us yet, lest we forget, lest we forget.* Will Masterson would pick up his old Army bugle and blow the last Post. Then it would be over and everyone could start gabbling once more and go home.

I jumped down from the birch bough and ran to the house, yelling, making as much noise as I could.

> *I'm a poor lonesome cowboy*
> *An' a long way from home—*

I stepped inside the front hall and kicked off my snow boots. I slammed the door behind me, making the dark ruby and emerald glass shake in the small leaded panes. I slid purposely on the hall rug, causing it to bunch and crinkle on the slippery polished oak of the floor. I seized the newel post, round as a head, and spun myself to and fro on the bottom stair.

> *I ain't got no father*
> *To buy the clothes I wear.*
> *I'm a poor lonesome—*

At this moment my shoulders were firmly seized and shaken by a pair of hands, white and delicate and old, but strong as talons.

"Just what do you think you're doing, young lady?" Grandmother MacLeod enquired, in a voice like frost on a windowpane, infinitely cold and clearly etched.

I went limp and in a moment she took her hands away. If you struggled, she would always hold on longer.

"Gee, I never knew you were home yet."

"I would have thought that on a day like this you might have shown a little respect and consideration," Grandmother MacLeod said, "even if you couldn't make the effort to get cleaned up enough to go to the parade."

I realised with surprise that she imagined this to be my reason for not going. I did not try to correct her impression. My real reason would have been even less acceptable.

"I'm sorry," I said quickly.

In some families, *please* is described as the magic word. In our house, however, it was *sorry*.

"This isn't an easy day for any of us," she said.

Her younger son, my Uncle Roderick, had been killed in the Great War. When my father marched, and when the hymn was sung, and when that unbearably lonely tune was sounded by the one bugle and everyone forced themselves to keep absolutely still, it would be that boy of whom she was thinking. I felt the enormity of my own offence.

"Grandmother—I'm sorry."

"So you said."

I could not tell her I had not really said it before at all. I went into the den and found my father there. He was sitting in the leather-cushioned armchair beside the fireplace. He was not doing anything, just sitting and smoking. I stood beside him, wanting to touch the light-brown hairs on his forearm, but thinking he might laugh at me or pull his arm away if I did.

"I'm sorry," I said, meaning it.

"What for, honey?"

"For not going."

"Oh—that. What was the matter?"

I did not want him to know, and yet I had to tell him, make him see.

"They look silly," I blurted. "Marching like that."

For a minute I thought he was going to be angry. It would

have been a relief to me if he had been. Instead, he drew his eyes away from mine and fixed them above the mantelpiece where the sword hung, the handsome and evil-looking crescent in its carved bronze sheath that some ancestor had once brought from the Northern Frontier of India.

"Is that the way it looks to you?" he said.

I felt in his voice some hurt, something that was my fault. I wanted to make everything all right between us, to convince him that I understood, even if I did not. I prayed that Grandmother MacLeod would stay put in her room, and that my mother would take a long time in the kitchen, giving Roddie his lunch. I wanted my father to myself, so I could prove to him that I cared more about him than any of the others did. I wanted to speak in some way that would be more poignant and comprehending than anything of which my mother could possibly be capable. But I did not know how.

"You were right there when Uncle Roderick got killed, weren't you?" I began uncertainly.

"Yes."

"How old was he, Dad?"

"Eighteen," my father said.

Unexpectedly, that day came into intense being for me. He had had to watch his own brother die, not in the antiseptic calm of some hospital, but out in the open, the stretches of mud I had seen in his snapshots. He would not have known what to do. He would just have had to stand there and look at it, whatever that might mean. I looked at my father with a kind of horrified awe, and then I began to cry. I had forgotten about impressing him with my perception. Now I needed him to console me for this unwanted glimpse of the pain he had once known.

"Hey, cut it out, honey," he said, embarrassed. "It was bad, but it wasn't all as bad as that part. There were a few other things."

"Like what?" I said, not believing him.

"Oh—I don't know," he replied evasively. "Most of us were pretty young, you know, I and the boys I joined up with. None of us had ever been away from Manawaka before. Those of us who came back mostly came back here, or else went no further away from town than Winnipeg. So when we were overseas—that was the only time most of us were ever a long way from home."

"Did you want to be?" I asked, shocked.

"Oh well—" my father said uncomfortably. "It was kind of interesting to see a few other places for a change, that's all."

Grandmother MacLeod was standing in the doorway.

"Beth's called you twice for lunch, Ewen. Are you deaf, you and Vanessa?"

"Sorry," my father and I said simultaneously.

Then we went upstairs to wash our hands.

That winter my mother returned to her old job as nurse in my father's medical practice. She was able to do this only because of Noreen.

"Grandmother MacLeod says we're getting a maid," I said to my father, accusingly, one morning. "We're not, are we?"

"Believe you me, on what I'm going to be paying her," my father growled, "she couldn't be called anything as classy as a maid. Hired girl would be more like it."

"Now, now, Ewen," my mother put in, "it's not as if we were cheating her or anything. You know she wants to live in town, and I can certainly see why, stuck out there on the farm, and her father hardly ever letting her come in. What kind of life is that for a girl?"

"I don't like the idea of your going back to work, Beth," my father said. "I know you're fine now, but you're not exactly the robust type."

"You can't afford to hire a nurse any longer. It's all very well to say the Depression won't last forever—probably it won't, but what else can we do for now?"

"I'm damned if I know," my father admitted. "Beth—"

"Yes?"

They both seemed to have forgotten about me. It was at breakfast, which we always ate in the kitchen, and I sat rigidly on my chair, pretending to ignore and thus snub their withdrawal from me. I glared at the window, but it was so thickly plumed and scrolled with frost that I could not see out. I glanced back to my parents. My father had not replied, and my mother was looking at him in that anxious and half-frowning way she had recently developed.

"What is it, Ewen?" Her voice had the same nervous sharpness it bore sometimes when she would say to me, "For mercy's sake, Vanessa, what is it *now*?" as though whatever was the matter, it was bound to be the last straw.

My father spun his sterling silver serviette ring, engraved with his initials, slowly around on the table.

"I never thought things would turn out like this, did you?"

"Please—" my mother said in a low strained voice, "please, Ewen, let's not start all this again. I can't take it."

"All right," my father said. "Only—"

"The MacLeods used to have money and now they don't," my mother cried. "Well, they're not alone. Do you think all that matters to me, Ewen? What I can't bear is to see you forever reproaching yourself. As if it were your fault."

"I don't think it's the comedown," my father said. "If I were somewhere else, I don't suppose it would matter to me, either, except where you're concerned. But I suppose you'd work too hard wherever you were—it's bred into you. If you haven't got anything to slave away at, you'll sure as hell invent something."

"What do you think I should do, let the house go to wrack and ruin? That would go over well with your mother, wouldn't it?"

"That's just it," my father said. "It's the damned house all the time. I haven't only taken on my father's house, I've taken on everything that goes with it, apparently. Sometimes I really wonder—"

"Well, it's a good thing I've inherited some practicality even if you haven't," my mother said. "I'll say that for the Connors—they aren't given to brooding, thank the Lord. Do you want your egg poached or scrambled?"

"Scrambled," my father said. "All I hope is that this Noreen doesn't get married straightaway, that's all."

"She won't," my mother said. "Who's she going to meet who could afford to marry?"

"I marvel at you, Beth," my father said. "You look as though a puff of wind would blow you away. But underneath, by God, you're all hardwood."

"Don't talk stupidly," my mother said. "All I hope is that she won't object to taking your mother's breakfast upon a tray."

"That's right," my father said angrily. "Rub it in."

"Oh Ewen, I'm sorry!" my mother cried, her face suddenly stricken. "I don't know why I say these things. I don't mean to."

"I know," my father said. "Here, cut it out, honey. Just for God's sake please don't cry."

"I'm sorry," my mother repeated, blowing her nose.

"We're both sorry," my father said. "Not that that changes anything."

After my father had gone, I got down from my chair and went to my mother.

"I don't want you to go back to the office. I don't want a hired girl here. I'll hate her."

My mother sighed, making me feel that I was placing an intolerable burden on her, and yet making me resent having to feel this weight. She looked tired, as she often did these days. Her tiredness bored me, made me want to attack her for it.

"Catch me getting along with a dumb old hired girl," I threatened.

"Do what you like," my mother said abruptly. "What can I do about it?"

And then, of course, I felt bereft, not knowing which way to turn.

My father need not have worried about Noreen getting married. She was, as it turned out, interested not in boys but in God. My mother was relieved about the boys but alarmed about God.

"It isn't natural," she said, "for a girl of seventeen. Do you think she's all right mentally, Ewen?"

When my parents, along with Grandmother MacLeod, went to the United Church every Sunday, I was made to go to Sunday school in the church basement, where there were small red chairs which humiliatingly resembled kindergarten furniture, and pictures of Jesus wearing a white sheet and surrounded by a whole lot of well-dressed kids whose mothers obviously had not suffered them to come unto Him until every face and ear was properly scrubbed. Our religious observances also included grace at meals, when my father would mumble "For what we are about to receive the Lord make us truly thankful Amen," running the words together as though they were one long word. My mother approved of these rituals, which seemed decent and moderate to her. Noreen's religion, however, was a different matter. Noreen belonged to the Tabernacle of the Risen and Reborn, and she had got up to testify no less than seven times in the past two years, she told us. My mother, who could not imagine anyone's voluntarily making a public spectacle of themselves, was profoundly shocked by this revelation.

"Don't worry," my father soothed her. "She's all right. She's just had kind of a dull life, that's all."

My mother shrugged and went on worrying and trying to help Noreen without hurting her feelings, by tactful remarks about the advisability of modulating one's voice when singing hymns, and the fact that there was plenty of hot water so Noreen really didn't need to hesitate about taking a bath. She even bought a razor and a packet of blades and whispered to Noreen that any girl who wore transparent blouses so much would probably like to shave under her arms. None of these suggestions had the slightest effect on Noreen. She did not cease belting out hymns at the top of her voice, she bathed once a fortnight, and the sorrel-coloured hair continued to bloom like a thicket of Indian paintbrush in her armpits.

Grandmother MacLeod refused to speak to Noreen. This caused Noreen a certain amount of bewilderment until she finally hit on an answer.

"Your poor grandma," she said. "She is deaf as a post. These things are sent to try us here on earth, Vanessa. But if she makes it into Heaven, I'll bet you anything she will hear clear as a bell."

Noreen and I talked about Heaven quite a lot, and also Hell. Noreen had an intimate and detailed knowledge of both places. She not only knew what they looked like—she even knew how big they were. Heaven was seventy-seven thousand miles square and it had four gates, each one made out of a different kind of precious jewel. The Pearl Gate, the Topaz Gate, the Amethyst Gate, the Ruby Gate—Noreen would reel them off, all the gates of Heaven. I told Noreen they sounded like poetry, but she was puzzled by my reaction and said I shouldn't talk that way. If you said poetry, it sounded like it was just made up and not really so, Noreen said.

Hell was larger than Heaven, and when I asked why, thinking of it as something of a comedown for God, Noreen said naturally it had to be bigger because there were a darn sight more people there than in Heaven. Hell was one hundred and ninety million miles deep and was in perpetual darkness, like a cave or under the sea. Even the flames (this was the awful thing) *did not give off any light.*

I did not actually believe in Noreen's doctrines, but the images which they conjured up began to inhabit my imagination. Noreen's fund of exotic knowledge was not limited to religion, although in a way it all seemed related. She could do many things which had a spooky tinge to them. Once when she was making a cake, she found we had run out of eggs. She went outside and gathered a bowl of fresh snow and used it instead. The cake rose like a charm, and I stared at Noreen as though she were a sorceress. In fact, I began to think of her as a sorceress, someone not quite of this earth. There was nothing unearthly about her broad shoulders and hips and her forest of dark red hair, but even these features took on a slightly sinister significance to me. I no longer saw her through the eyes or the expressed opinions of my mother and father, as a girl who had quit school at grade eight and whose life on the farm had been endlessly drab. I knew the truth—Noreen's life had not been drab at all, for she dwelt in a world of violent splendours, a world filled with angels whose wings of delicate light bore real feathers, and saints shining like the dawn, and prophets who spoke in ancient tongues, and the ecstatic souls of the saved, as well as denizens of the lower regions—mean-eyed imps and crooked cloven-hoofed monsters and beasts with the bodies of swine and the human heads of murderers, and lovely depraved jezebels torn by dogs through all eternity. The middle layer of Creation, our earth, was equally full of grotesque presences, for Noreen believed strongly in the visitation of ghosts and the communication with spirits. She could prove this with her Ouija board. We would both place our fingers lightly on the indicator, and it would skim across the board and spell out answers to our questions. I did not believe wholeheartedly in the Ouija board, either, but I was cautious about the kind of question I asked, in case the answer would turn out unfavourable and I would be unable to forget it.

One day Noreen told me she could also make a table talk. We used the small table in my bedroom, and sure enough, it lifted very slightly under our fingertips and tapped once for *Yes*, twice for *No*. Noreen asked if her Aunt Ruthie would get better from the kidney operation, and the table replied *No*. I withdrew my hands.

"I don't want to do it any more."

"Gee, what's the matter, Vanessa?" Noreen's plain placid face creased in a frown. "We only just begun."

"I have to do my homework."

My heart lurched as I said this. I was certain Noreen would know I was lying, and that she would know not by any ordinary perception, either. But her attention had been caught by something else, and I was thankful, at least until I saw what it was.

My bedroom window was not opened in the coldest weather. The storm window, which was fitted outside as an extra wall against the winter, had three small circular holes in its frame so that some fresh air could seep into the house. The sparrow must have been floundering in the new snow on the roof, for it had crawled in through one of these holes and was now caught between the two layers of glass. I could not bear the panic of the trapped bird, and before I realised what I was doing, I had thrown open the bedroom window. I was not releasing the sparrow into any better a situation, I soon saw, for instead of remaining quiet and allowing us to catch it in order to free it, it began flying blindly around the room, hitting the lampshade, brushing against the walls, its wings seeming to spin faster and faster.

I was petrified. I thought I would pass out if those palpitating wings touched me. There was something in the bird's senseless movements that revolted me. I also thought it was going to damage itself, break one of those thin wing-bones, perhaps, and then it would be lying on the floor, dying, like the pimpled and horribly featherless baby birds we saw sometimes on the sidewalks in the spring when they had fallen out of their nests. I was not any longer worried about the sparrow. I wanted only to avoid the sight of it lying broken on the floor. Viciously, I thought that if Noreen said, *God sees the little sparrow fall,* I would kick her in the shins. She did not, however, say this.

"A bird in the house means a death in the house," Noreen remarked.

Shaken, I pulled my glance away from the whirling wings and looked at Noreen.

"What?"

"That's what I've heard said, anyhow."

The sparrow had exhausted itself. It lay on the floor, spent and trembling. I could not bring myself to touch it. Noreen bent and picked it up. She cradled it with great gentleness between her cupped hands. Then we took it downstairs, and when I had opened the back door, Noreen set the bird free.

"Poor little scrap," she said, and I felt struck to the heart, knowing she had been concerned all along about the sparrow, while I, perfidiously, in the chaos of the moment, had been concerned only about myself.

"Wanna do some with the ouija board, Vanessa?" Noreen asked.

I shivered a little, perhaps only because of the blast of cold air which had come into the kitchen when the door was opened.

"No thanks, Noreen. Like I said, I got my homework to do. But thanks all the same."

"That's okay," Noreen said in her guileless voice. "Any time."

But whenever she mentioned the Ouija board or the talking table, after that, I always found some excuse not to consult these oracles.

"Do you want to come to church with me this evening, Vanessa?" my father asked.

"How come you're going to the evening service?" I enquired.

"Well, we didn't go this morning. We went snowshoeing instead, remember? I think your grandmother was a little bit put out about it. She went alone this morning. I guess it wouldn't hurt you and me, to go now."

We walked through the dark, along the white streets, the snow squeaking dryly under our feet. The streetlights were placed at long intervals along the sidewalks, and around each pole the circle of flimsy light created glistening points of blue and crystal on the crusted snow. I would have liked to take my father's hand, as I used to do, but I was too old for that now. I walked beside him, taking long steps so he would not have to walk more slowly on my account.

The sermon bored me, and I began leafing through the Hymnary for entertainment. I must have drowsed, for the next thing I knew, my father was prodding me and we were on our feet for the closing hymn.

> *Near the Cross, near the Cross,*
> *Be my glory ever,*
> *Till my ransomed soul shall find*
> *Rest beyond the river.*

I knew the tune well, so I sang loudly for the first verse. But the music to that hymn is sombre, and all at once the words themselves seemed too dreadful to be sung. I stopped singing, my throat knotted. I thought I was going to cry, but I did not know why, except that the song recalled to me my

Grandmother Connor, who had been dead only a year now. I wondered why her soul needed to be ransomed. If God did not think she was good enough just as she was, then I did not have much use for His opinion. *Rest beyond the river*—was that what had happened to her? She had believed in Heaven, but I did not think that rest beyond the river was quite what she had in mind. To think of her in Noreen's flashy Heaven, though—that was even worse. Someplace where nobody ever got annoyed or had to be smoothed down and placated, someplace where there were never any family scenes—that would have suited my Grandmother Connor. Maybe she wouldn't have minded a certain amount of rest beyond the river, at that.

When we had the silent prayer, I looked at my father. He sat with his head bowed and his eyes closed. He was frowning deeply, and I could see the pulse in his temple. I wondered then what he believed. I did not have any real idea what it might be. When he raised his head, he did not look uplifted or anything like that. He merely looked tired. Then Reverend McKee pronounced the benediction, and we could go home.

"What do you think about all that stuff, Dad?" I asked hesitantly, as we walked.

"What stuff, honey?"

"Oh, Heaven and Hell, and like that."

My father laughed. "Have you been listening to Noreen too much? Well, I don't know. I don't think they're actual places. Maybe they stand for something that happens all the time here, or else doesn't happen. It's kind of hard to explain. I guess I'm not so good at explanations."

Nothing seemed to have been made any clearer to me. I reached out and took his hand, not caring that he might think this a babyish gesture.

"I hate that hymn!"

"Good Lord," my father said in astonishment. "Why, Vanessa?"

But I did not know and so could not tell him.

Many people in Manawaka had flu that winter, so my father and Dr. Cates were kept extremely busy. I had flu myself, and spent a week in bed, vomiting only the first day and after that enjoying poor health, as my mother put it, with Noreen bringing me ginger ale and orange juice, and each evening my father putting a wooden tongue-depressor into my mouth and peering down my throat, then smiling and saying he thought I might live after all.

Then my father got sick himself, and had to stay at home and go to bed. This was such an unusual occurrence that it amused me.

"Doctors shouldn't get sick," I told him.

"You're right," he said. "That was pretty bad management."

"Run along now, dear," my mother said.

That night I woke and heard voices in the upstairs hall. When I went out, I found my mother and Grandmother MacLeod, both in their dressing-gowns. With them was Dr. Cates. I did not go immediately to my mother, as I would have done only a year before. I stood in the doorway of my room, squinting against the sudden light.

"Mother—what is it?"

She turned, and momentarily I saw the look on her face before she erased it and put on a contrived calm.

"It's all right," she said. "Dr. Cates has just come to have a look at Daddy. You go on back to sleep."

The wind was high that night, and I lay and listened to it rattling the storm windows and making the dry and winter-stiffened vines of the Virginia creeper scratch like small persistent claws against the red brick. In the morning, my mother told me that my father had developed pneumonia.

Dr. Cates did not think it would be safe to move my father to the hospital. My mother began sleeping in the spare bedroom, and after she had been there for a few nights, I asked if I could sleep in there too. I thought she would be bound to ask me why, and I did not know what I would say, but she did not ask. She nodded, and in some way her easy agreement upset me.

That night Dr. Cates came again, bringing with him one of the nurses from the hospital. My mother stayed upstairs with them. I sat with Grandmother MacLeod in the living room. That was the last place in the world I wanted to be, but I thought she would be offended if I went off. She sat as straight and rigid as a totem pole, and embroidered away at the needlepoint cushion cover she was doing. I perched on the edge of the chesterfield and kept my eyes fixed on *The White Company* by Conan Doyle, and from time to time I turned a page. I had already read it three times before, but luckily Grandmother MacLeod did not know that. At nine o'clock she looked at her gold brooch watch, which she always wore pinned to her dress, and told me to go to bed, so I did that.

I wakened in darkness. At first, it seemed to me that I was in my own bed, and everything was as usual, with my parents in their room, and Roddie curled up in the crib in his room, and Grandmother MacLeod sleeping with her mouth open in her enormous spool bed, surrounded by half a dozen framed photos of Uncle Roderick and only one of my father, and Noreen snoring fitfully in the room next to mine, with the dark flames of her hair spreading out across the pillow, and the pink and silver motto cards from the Tabernacle stuck with adhesive tape onto the wall beside her bed—*Lean on Him, Emmanuel Is My Refuge, Rock of Ages Cleft for Me.*

Then in the total night around me, I heard a sound. It was my mother, and she was crying, not loudly at all, but from somewhere very deep inside her. I sat up in bed. Everything seemed to have stopped, not only time but my own heart and blood as well. Then my mother noticed that I was awake.

I did not ask her, and she did not tell me anything. There was no need. She held me in her arms, or I held her, I am not certain which. And after a while the first mourning stopped, too, as everything does sooner or later, for when the limits of endurance have been reached, then people must sleep.

In the days following my father's death, I stayed close beside my mother, and this was only partly for my own consoling. I also had the feeling that she needed my protection. I did not know from what, nor what I could possibly do, but something held me there. Reverend McKee called, and I sat with my grandmother and my mother in the living room. My mother told me I did not need to stay unless I wanted to, but I refused to go. What I thought chiefly was that he would speak of the healing power of prayer, and all that, and it would be bound to make my mother cry again. And in fact, it happened in just that way, but when it actually came, I could not protect her from this assault. I could only sit there and pray my own prayer, which was that he would go away quickly.

My mother tried not to cry unless she was alone or with me. I also tried, but neither of us was entirely successful.

Grandmother MacLeod, on the other hand, was never seen crying, not even the day of my father's funeral. But that day, when we had returned to the house and she had taken off her black velvet overshoes and her heavy sealskin coat with its black fur that was the softest thing I had ever touched, she stood in the hallway and for the first time she looked unsteady. When I reached out instinctively towards her, she sighed.

"That's right," she said. "You might just take my arm while I go upstairs, Vanessa."

That was the most my Grandmother MacLeod ever gave in, to anyone's sight. I left her in her bedroom, sitting on the straight chair beside her bed and looking at the picture of my father that had been taken when he graduated from medical college. Maybe she was sorry now that she had only the one photograph of him, but whatever she felt, she did not say.

I went down into the kitchen. I had scarcely spoken to Noreen since my father's death. This had not been done on purpose. I simply had not seen her. I had not really seen anyone except my mother. Looking at Noreen now, I suddenly recalled the sparrow. I felt physically sick, remembering the fearful darting and plunging of those wings, and the fact that it was I who had opened the window and let it in. Then an inexplicable fury took hold of me, some terrifying need to hurt, burn, destroy. Absolutely without warning, either to her or to myself, I hit Noreen as hard as I could. When she swung around, appalled, I hit out at her once more, my arms and legs flailing. Her hands snatched at my wrists, and she held me, but still I continued to struggle, fighting blindly, my eyes tightly closed, as though she were a prison all around me and I was battling to get out. Finally, too shocked at myself to go on, I went limp in her grasp and she let me drop to the floor.

"Vanessa! I never done one single solitary thing to you, and here you go hitting and scratching me like that! What in the world has got into you?"

I began to say I was sorry, which was certainly true, but I did not say it. I could not say anything.

"You're not yourself, what with your dad and everything," she excused me. "I been praying every night that your dad is with God, Vanessa. I know he wasn't actually saved in the regular way, but still and all—"

"Shut up," I said.

Something in my voice made her stop talking. I rose from the floor and stood in the kitchen doorway.

"He didn't need to be saved," I went on coldly, distinctly. "And he is not in Heaven, because there is no Heaven. And it doesn't matter, see? *It doesn't matter!*"

Noreen's face looked peculiarly vulnerable now, her high wide cheekbones and puzzled childish eyes, and the thick russet tangle of her hair. I had not hurt her much before, when I hit her. But I had hurt her now, hurt her in some inexcusable way. Yet I sensed, too, that already she was gaining some satisfaction out of feeling sorrowful about my disbelief.

I went upstairs to my room. Momentarily I felt a sense of calm, almost of acceptance. *Rest beyond the river.* I knew now what that meant. It meant Nothing. It meant only silence, forever.

Then I lay down on my bed and spent the last of my tears, or what seemed then to be the last. Because, despite what I had said to Noreen, it did matter. It mattered, but there was no help for it.

Everything changed after my father's death. The MacLeod house could not be kept up any longer. My mother sold it to a local merchant who subsequently covered the deep red of the brick over with yellow stucco. Something about the house had always made me uneasy—that tower room where Grandmother MacLeod's potted plants drooped in a lethargic and lime-green confusion, those long stairways and hidden places, the attic which I had always imagined to be dwelt in by the spirits of the family dead, that gigantic portrait of the Duke of Wellington at the top of the stairs. It was never an endearing house. And yet when it was no longer ours, and when the Virginia creeper had been torn down and the dark walls turned to a light marigold, I went out of my way to avoid walking past, for it seemed to me that the house had lost the stern dignity that was its very heart.

Noreen went back to the farm. My mother and brother and myself moved into Grandfather Connor's house. Grandmother MacLeod went to live with Aunt Morag in Winnipeg. It was harder for her than for anyone, because so much of her life was bound up with the MacLeod house. She was fond of Aunt Morag, but that hardly counted. Her men were gone, her husband and her sons, and a family whose men are gone is no family at all. The day she left, my mother and I did not know what to say. Grandmother MacLeod looked even smaller than usual in her fur coat and her black velvet toque. She became extremely agitated about trivialities, and fussed about the possibility of the taxi not arriving on time. She had forbidden us to accompany her to the station. About my father, or the house, or anything important, she did not say a word. Then, when the taxi had finally arrived, she turned to my mother.

"Roddie will have Ewen's seal ring, of course, with the MacLeod crest on it," she said. "But there is another seal as well, don't forget, the larger one with the crest and motto. It's meant to be worn on a watch chain. I keep it in my jewel-box. It was Roderick's. Roddie's to have that, too, when I die. Don't let Morag talk you out of it."

During the Second World War, when I was seventeen and in love with an airman who did not love me, and desperately anxious to get away from Manawaka and from my grandfa-ther's house, I happened one day to be going through the old mahogany desk that had belonged to my father. It had a number of small drawers inside, and I accidentally pulled one of these all the way out. Behind it there was another drawer, one I had not known about. Curiously, I opened it. Inside there was a letter written on almost transparent paper in a cramped angular handwriting. It began—*Cher Monsieur Ewen*—That was all I could make out, for the writing was nearly impossible to read and my French was not good. It was dated 1919. With it, there was a picture of a girl, looking absurdly old-fashioned to my eyes, like the faces on long-dis-carded calendars or chocolate boxes. But beneath the dated quality of the photograph, she seemed neither expensive nor cheap. She looked like what she probably had been—an ordi-nary middle-class girl, but in another country. She wore her hair in long ringlets, and her mouth was shaped into a sweetly sad posed smile like Mary Pickford's. That was all. There was nothing else in the drawer.

I looked for a long time at the girl, and hoped she had meant some momentary and unexpected freedom. I remem-bered what he had said to me, after I hadn't gone to the Remembrance Day parade.

"What are you doing, Vanessa?" my mother called from the kitchen.

"Nothing," I replied.

I took the letter and picture outside and burned them. That

was all I could do for him. Now that we might have talked together, it was many years too late. Perhaps it would not have been possible anyway. I did not know.

As I watched the smile of the girl turn into scorched paper, I grieved for my father as though he had just died now.

RUTH PRAWER JHABVALA was born in 1927 in Cologne, Germany, of Jewish parents who emigrated to England in 1939. She was educated in Coventry and London, and married an Indian architect in 1951. She has lived in Delhi ever since and is the mother of three daughters.

She talks about her writing with the same straightforwardness that gives her fiction its unforgettable voice: "I started writing as soon as I had learned the alphabet, at six. My infant writings were all religious and Jewish. When we migrated to England, . . . I began writing stories in English . . . all about the English lower middle classes. Similarly, the moment I set foot in India I began writing about Indians. . . . Lately I have changed. I find I still want to write about India and Indians, but now from a European viewpoint. That change of subject may reflect a change in myself. I used to feel very much at home in India, but as the years go by I feel more and more an exile and a stranger. Writing is the only thing I can do, and so I think it has become a substitute for many things. For instance, for my inability to cook, or play games, or get interested in politics, or take much pleasure in other people's company. Or it may be an apologia for living in a country full of poverty and sickness and misery and sitting by without once lifting a finger for anyone. Or again, it may be a substitute for that religious experience which India continually seems to promise but which I have not yet even remotely approached. The act of writing gets increasingly difficult but also increasingly pleasurable. I want to say rather more complicated things, but usually find I am not up to them. So I start again, and again. I am dissatisfied with everything I have ever written and regard it all only as a preparation for that one work which probably I don't have it in me to write but which I hope I can go on trying for."

Reviewers and critics agree that she is "one of India's best novelists writing in English at the present time." In her quiet humor and deft obliquity they have heard the influence of Jane Austen. Her moral consciousness, however, is original, shaped by times that Austen never dreamed of.

Ruth Prawer Jhabvala
(1927–   )

THE ENGLISHWOMAN

The Englishwoman—her name is Sadie—was fifty-two years old when she decided to leave India. She could hardly believe it. She felt young and free. At fifty-two! Her bag is packed and she is running away. She is eloping, leaving everything behind her—husband, children, grandchildren, thirty years of married life. Her heart is light and so is her luggage. It is surprising how few things she has to take with her. Most of her clothes are not worth taking. These last years she has been mostly wearing dowdy cotton frocks sewn by a little turbaned tailor. She still has a few saris but she is not taking them with her. She doesn't ever intend to wear those again.

The person who is crying the most at her impending departure is Annapurna, her husband's mistress. Annapurna has a very emotional nature. She looks into the packed bag; like Sadie, she is surprised by its meager contents. "Is that all you are taking with you?" she asks. Sadie answers, "It's all I've got." Annapurna breaks into a new storm of tears.

"But that's good," Sadie urges. "Not to accumulate things, to travel light—what could be better?"

"Oh, you're so spiritual," Annapurna tells her, wiping her eyes on the other's sleeve. "Really you are far more Indian than I am."

"Nonsense," Sadie says, and she means it. What nonsense.

But it is true that if Indian means "spiritual"—as so many people like to believe—then Annapurna is an exception. She is a very, very physical sort of person. She is stout, with a tight glowing skin, and shining eyes and teeth, and hair glossy with black dye. She loves clothes and jewelry and rich food. Although she is about the same age as the Englishwoman, she is far more vigorous, and when she moves, her sari rustles and her bracelets jingle.

"But are you really going?"

Annapurna keeps asking this question. And Sadie keeps

asking it of herself too. But they ask it in two very different ways. Annapurna is shocked and grieved (yes, grieved—she loves the Englishwoman). But Sadie is incredulous with happiness. Can it really be true? she keeps asking herself. I'm going? I'm leaving India? Her heart skips with joy and she has difficulty in repressing her smiles. She doesn't want anyone to suspect her feelings. She is ashamed of her own callousness—and yet she goes on smiling, more and more, and happiness wells up in her like a spring.

Last week she went to say goodbye to the children. They are both settled in Bombay now with their families. Dev, her son, has been married for two years and has a baby girl; Monica, the daughter, has three boys. Dev has a fine job with an advertising company; and Monica is working too, for she has too much drive to be content with just staying at home. She calls herself a go-go girl and that is what she is, charging around town interviewing people for the articles she writes for a women's magazine, talking in the latest slang current in Bombay, throwing parties of which she herself is the life and soul. Monica looks quite Indian—her eyes are black, her skin glows; she is really more like Annapurna than like the Englishwoman, who is gaunt and pale.

Although so gay, Monica also likes to have serious discussions. She attempted to have such a discussion with her mother. She said, "But, Mummy, *why* are you going?" and she looked at her with the special serious face she has for serious moments.

Sadie didn't know what to answer. What could she say? But she had to say something, or Monica would be hurt. So she too became solemn, and she explained to her daughter that when people get older they begin to get very homesick for the place in which they were born and grew up and that this homesickness becomes worse and worse till in the end life becomes almost unbearable. Monica understood what she said and sympathised with it. She made plans how they would all come and visit her in England. She promised that when the boys became bigger, she would send them to her for long holidays. She was now in full agreement with her mother's departure, so Sadie was glad she told her what she did. She was prepared to tell Dev the same thing if he asked her, but he didn't ask. He and his wife were rather worried in those days because there was an outbreak of chicken pox in their apartment building and they were afraid Baby might catch it. But they too promised frequent visits to her in England.

Only Annapurna is still crying. She looks at Sadie's little suitcase and cries, and then she looks at Sadie and cries. She keeps asking, "But why, *why?*" Sadie tries to tell her what she told Monica, but Annapurna waves her aside; for her it is not a good enough reason and she is right, Sadie herself knows it isn't. She asks wouldn't Sadie miss all of them and their love for her, and wouldn't she miss the life she has lived and the place in which she has lived it, her whole past, everything she has been and done for thirty years? Thirty years! she cries, again and again, appalled—and Sadie too is appalled, it is such a long time. Annapurna says that an Indian wife also yearns for her father's house, and at the beginning of her marriage she is always waiting to go off there to visit; but as the years progress and she becomes deeper and deeper embedded in her husband's home, these early memories fade till they are nothing more than a sweet sensation enshrined in the heart. Sadie knows that what Annapurna is saying is true, but also that it does not in the least apply in her own case because her feelings are not ones of gentle nostalgia.

The Englishwoman doesn't like to remember the early years when she first came to live here. It is as if she wished to disown her happiness then. How she loved everything! She never gave a backward glance to home or England. Her husband's family enjoyed and abetted her attempts to become Indian. A whole lot of them—mother-in-law, sister-in-law, aunts, cousins and friends—would cram into the family car (with blue silk curtains discreetly drawn to shield them from view) and drive to the bazaar to buy saris for Sadie. She was never much consulted about their choice, and when they got home, she was tugged this way and that while they argued with each other about the best way to drape it round her. When they had finished, they stood back to admire, only instead of admiring they often could not help smiling at her appearance. She didn't care. Yes, she knew she was too tall for the sari, and too thin, and too English, but she loved wearing it and to feel herself Indian. She also made attempts to learn Hindi, and this too amused everyone and they never tired of making her repeat certain words, going into peals of laughter at her pronunciation. Everyone, all the ladies of the household, had a lot of fun. They were healthy, rich and gay. They were by no means a tradition-bound family, and although their life in the house did have something of the enclosed, languorous quality of purdah living, the minds flowering within it were full of energy and curiosity. The mother-in-law herself, at that time well over sixty, spent a lot of her time reading vernacular novels, and she also attempted to write some biographical sketches of her own, describing life in a high-caste household of the 1880s. She took to smoking cigarettes quite late in life and liked them so much that she ended up as a chain-smoker. When Sadie thinks of her, she sees her reclining on an embroidered mat spread on the floor, one elbow supported on a bolster, some cushions at her back, reading a brown tattered little volume through her glasses and enveloping herself in clouds of scented cigarette smoke.

Annapurna often speaks about those days. Annapurna was a relative, some sort of cousin. She had run away from her husband (who drank and, it was whispered, went in for unnatural practices) and had come to live with them in the house. When Annapurna speaks about those distant times, she does so as if everyone were still alive and all of them as young and gay as they were then. Often she says, "If only Srilata [or Radhika—or Raksha—or Chandralekha] were here now, how she would laugh!" But Srilata died of typhoid twenty years ago; Raksha married a Nepalese general and has gone to live in Kathmandu; Chandralekha poisoned herself over an unhappy love affair. To Annapurna, however, it is as if everyone is still there and she recalls and brings to life every detail of a distant event so that to Sadie too it begins to appear that she can hear the voices of those days. Till Annapurna returns to the present and with an outstretched hand, her plump palm turned up to heaven, she acknowledges that they are all gone and many of them are dead; and she turns and looks at the Englishwoman and says, "And now you are going too," and her eyes are full of reproach.

It may seem strange that the mistress should reproach the wife, but Annapurna is within her rights to do so. For so many years now it is she who has taken over from the Englishwoman all the duties of a wife. There has never been any bitterness or jealousy between them. On the contrary, Sadie has always been grateful to her. She knows that before her husband became intimate with Annapurna, he used to go to other women. He *had* to go; he was such a healthy man and needed women as strong and healthy as he was. These were often young prostitutes. But for a long time now he has been content with Annapurna. He has put on an enormous amount of weight in these last years. It is Annapurna's fault; she feeds him too well and panders to his passion for good food. His meals are frequent and so heavy that in between them, he is not capable of moving. He lies on a couch arranged for him on a verandah and breathes heavily. Sometimes he puffs at a hookah which stands within easy reach. He lies there for hours while Annapurna sits on the other end of the couch and entertains him with lively gossip. He enjoys that, but doesn't mind at all if she has no time for him. When he feels like talking, he summons one of the servants to come and squat on the carpet near his couch.

When Sadie first knew him, as a student at Oxford, he was a slim boy with burning eyes and a lock of hair on his forehead. He was always smiling and always on the go. He loved being a student, and though he never managed to graduate, got a lot out of it. He gave breakfast parties and had his own wine merchant and a red car in which he drove up to London several times a week; he was always discovering new pleasures, like hampers from Fortnum and Mason's and champagne parties on the river. Sadie had grown up in rather an austere atmosphere. Her family were comfortably off but had high principles of self-restraint and preferred lofty thought to lavish living. Sadie herself—a serious girl, a spare, stringent, high-bred English beauty—thought she had the same principles, but the young Indian made her see another side to her nature. When he went back to India, it was impossible to stay behind. She followed him, married him, and loved him even more than she had in England. He belonged here so completely. Sometimes Sadie didn't see him for days on end—when he went on shooting parties and other expeditions with his friends—but she didn't mind. She stayed at home with the other women and enjoyed life as much as he did. There were summer nights when they all sat out in the garden by the fountain, and Chandralekha, who had a very sweet voice, sang sad songs from the hills while Radhika accompanied her on a lutelike instrument; and the moon shone, and Annapurna cut up mangoes for all of them, and the smell of these mangoes mingled with that exuding from the flowering bushes in a mixture so pungent, so heady, that when the Englishwoman recalls those nights now, it is always by their scent that they become physical and present to her.

Annapurna and Sadie's husband play cards every evening. They play for money and Annapurna usually loses and then she gets cross; she always refuses to pay up, and the next evening they conveniently forget her debt and start again from scratch. But if he loses, then she insists on immediate payment: she laughs in triumph, and holding out her hand, opens and shuts it greedily and shouts, "Come on, pay up!" She also calls to Sadie and the servants to witness his discomfiture; those evenings are always merry. But sooner or later, and often in the middle of a game, she falls asleep. Once Annapurna is asleep, everything is very quiet. The servants turn off the lights and go to their quarters; the husband sits on his couch and looks out into the garden and takes a few puffs at his hookah; Sadie is upstairs in her bedroom. Nothing stirs, there isn't a sound, until the husband gives a loud sigh as he heaves himself up. He wakes Annapurna and they support each other up the stairs to their bedroom, where they sink onto their large, soft bed and are asleep immediately and totally until it is morning. It is a long time before Sadie can get to sleep. She walks up and down the room. She argues with herself to and fro, and her mind heaves in turmoil like a sea in storm. The fact that everything else is calm and sleeping exacerbates her restlessness. She longs for some response, for something or someone other than herself to be affected by what is going on within her. But there is only silence and sleep. She steps out of her room and onto the verandah. The garden is in imperfect darkness, dimly and fitfully lit by the moon. Occasionally—very, very occasionally—a bird wakes up and rustles in a tree.

It was during these hours of solitude that she came to her decision to leave. To others—and at the actual moment of making it, even to herself—it seemed like a sudden decision, but in fact, looking back, she realizes that she has been preparing for it for twenty years. She can even mark the exact day, twenty years ago, when first she knew that she did not want to go on living here. It was when her son was sick with one of those sudden mysterious illnesses that so often attack children in India. He lay burning in the middle of a great bed, with his eyes full of fever; he was very quiet except for an occasional groan. All the women in the house had gathered round his bedside and all were giving advice and different remedies. Some sat on chairs, some on the floor; the mother-in-law squatted crosslegged on the end of his bed, her

spectacles on her nose, smoking cigarettes and turning the
pages of a novel; from time to time she made soothing noises
at Dev and squeezed his ankles. Annapurna sat by his side
and rubbed ice on his head. Every time Dev groaned they all
said, "Oh, poor Baba, poor Baba." The servants moved in and
out; they too said, "Oh, poor Baba," and looked at him
pityingly. The Englishwoman remembered the sickbeds of her
own childhood, how she lay for hours comfortable and bored
with nothing to do except watch the tree outside the window
and the fat wet raindrops squashing against and sliding down
the window-pane. The only person who ever came in was her
mother, when it was time for her medicine. But Dev wouldn't
have liked that. He wanted everyone with him, and if one of
the aunts was out of the room for too long a time, he would
ask for her in a weak voice and someone would have to go
and fetch her.

Sadie went out onto the verandah. But it was no better
there. The day was one of those murky yellow ones when the
sun is stifled in vapours of dust. She felt full of fears, for Dev
and for herself, as if they were both being sucked down
by—what was it? the heat? the loving women inside? the air
thick as a swamp in which fevers breed? She longed to be
alone with her sick child in some cool place. But she knew
this was not possible and that they belonged here in this
house crammed full with relatives and choking under a yellow sky. She could never forget the despair of that moment,
though in the succeeding years there were many like it. But
that was the first.

As she stood there on the verandah, she saw her husband
arrive home. He was a very bright spot in that murky day.
He was dressed in a starched white kurta with little jewels for
buttons, and his face was raised towards her as she stood up
on the verandah, and he was smiling. He was no longer the
slim boy she had first known but neither was he as fat as he
is today: no, he was in the prime of life then, and what a
prime! He came bounding up the outside staircase towards
her and said, "How is he?"

"How can he be," she answered, "with all of them in
there?"

Surprised at her tone, he stopped smiling and looked at her
anxiously. Her anger mounted, and there were other things
mixed in with it now: not only the heat and the overcrowded
room but also that he was so sleek and smiling and young

while she—oh, she felt worn out, wrung out, and knew she looked it. She thought of the prostitutes he went to. It seemed to her that she could see and smell their plump, brown, wriggling young bodies greasy with scented oil.

In a shaking voice she said, "They're stifling that poor boy—they won't let him breathe. No one seems to have the least idea of hygiene."

He knew it was more than she was saying and continued to look at her anxiously. "Are you ill?" he asked and put out his hand to feel her forehead. When she drew back, he asked, "What is it?" full of sympathy.

They had been speaking in low voices, but all the same from inside the crowded room Annapurna had sensed that something was wrong. She left the bedside and came out to join them. She looked enquiringly at Sadie's husband. They were not yet lovers at the time, but there was that instinctive understanding between them there was between all the members of that household.

"She is not well," he said.

"I *am* well! I'm perfectly well!" Sadie burst into tears. She had no control over this. Furiously she wiped the foolish tears from her cheeks.

Both of them melted with tenderness. Annapurna folded her in an embrace; the husband stroked her back. When she struggled to get free, they thought it was a new outbreak of anguish and redoubled their attentions. At last she cried, "It's so *hot!*" and indeed she could hardly breathe and perspiration ran down her in runnels from her being squashed against fat Annapurna. Then Annapurna let her go. They both stood and looked at her, full of anxiety for her; and these two round healthy shining faces looking at her with love, *pitying* her, were so unbearable to her that, to prevent herself from bursting into the tears that she despised but that they, she knew, not only awaited but even expected, she turned and, hurrying along the verandah that ran like a gallery all round the house, she hid herself in her bedroom and locked the door. They followed and knocked urgently and begged to be allowed to enter. She refused to open. She could hear them discussing her outside the door: they were full of understanding; they realized that people did get upset like this and that then it was the duty of others to soothe and help them.

She was always being soothed and helped. She is still being

soothed and helped. Annapurna has taken everything out of her suitcase and is repacking it in what she considers is a better way. She has had special shoe bags sewn. As a matter of fact, she would like to have a completely new outfit of clothes made for her. She says how will it look if Sadie arrives with nothing better than those few shabby rags in that little suitcase? Sadie thinks silently to herself: Look to whom? She knows almost no one there. A few distant relatives, one old school friend; she hasn't been there for thirty years, she has no contacts, no correspondence—and yet she is going home! Home! And again happiness rushes over her in waves, and she takes a deep breath to be able to bear it.

"And not a single piece of jewelry," Annapurna grumbles.

Sadie laughs. She has given it all away long ago to Monica and to Dev's wife: and very glad she was to get rid of all those heavy costly gold ornaments. They were her share of the family jewels, but she never knew what to do with them. Certainly she couldn't wear them—she was always too thin and pale to be able to carry off those pieces fit for a barbarian queen; so she had left them lying around for years in a cupboard till Annapurna had taken them away from her to lock up in a safe.

"At least *one* piece you could have let me keep for you," Annapurna now says. "Then you would have had something to show them. What will they think of us?"

"What will *who* think?" Sadie asks, and the idea of the distant relatives and her poor school friend (Clare, still unmarried and still teaching) having any thoughts on the subject of what properties she has brought back with her from India makes her laugh again. And there is a lightheartedness in her laughter that hasn't been there for a long time, and Annapurna hears it and is hurt by it.

They are both hurt by her attitude. It has been years since Sadie saw her husband so upset; but then it has been years since anything really upset him. He has led a very calm life lately. Not that his life was not always calm and comfortable, but there were times in his younger days when he, like everyone else in the house, had his outbursts. She particularly remembers one he had with his sister Chandralekha. Actually, at that time, the whole house was in upheaval. Chandralekha had formed an unfortunate attachment to a man nobody approved of. They were not a rigid family that way—there had been several love matches—but it seemed Chandralekha's choice was entirely unsuitable. Sadie had met the man, who struck her as intelligent and of a strong character. In fact, she thought Chandralekha had shown excellent taste. But when she told her husband so, he waved her aside and said she didn't understand. And it was true, she didn't; everything that went on in the house during those days was a mystery to her. Oh, she understood vaguely what it was all about—the man was of *low birth*, and all his virtues of character and self-made position could not wipe that stain away—but the passions that were aroused, the issues that were thought to be at stake, were beyond her comprehension. Yet she could see that all of them were suffering deeply, and Chandralekha was in a torment of inner conflict (indeed, she later committed suicide).

One day Chandralekha came in carrying a dish of sweet rice which she had made herself. She said, "Just wait till you taste this," and she lovingly ladled a spoonfull onto her brother's plate. He began to eat with relish, but quite suddenly he pushed the plate away and began to cry out loud. Everyone at once knew why, of course. The only person who was surprised was Sadie—both at the suddenness of the outburst and at the lengths to which he went. He banged his head against the wall, flung himself on the ground at Chandralekha's feet, and at one point he snatched up a knife and held it at his own throat and had to have it wrested away from him by all the women there surrounding him. "The children, the children!" he kept crying, and at first Sadie thought he meant their own children, Monica and Dev, and she couldn't understand what was threatening them; but everyone else knew he meant Chandralekha's children who were yet unborn but who would be born, and if she married this man, born with polluted blood. Sadie didn't know how that scene ended; she went away and locked herself up in her bedroom. She covered her ears with her hands to shut out the noise and cries that echoed through the house.

When he learned of her decision to leave, Sadie's husband begged and pleaded with her in the same way he had done with Chandralekha all those years ago. The Englishwoman felt embarrassed and ashamed for him. He looked so ridiculous, being so heavy and fat, with his great bulk heaving, and emitting cries like those of a hysterical woman. No one else found him ridiculous—on the contrary, the servants and Annapurna were deeply affected by his strong emotions and tried to comfort him. But he wouldn't be comforted till in the end his passion spent itself. Then he became resigned and even quite practical and sent for his lawyer to make a settlement. He was very generous toward his wife, and indeed keeps pressing her to accept more and is distressed because she doesn't need it. So now she feels ashamed not of him but of herself and her own lack of feeling.

It is her last night in India. As usual, her husband and Annapurna are playing cards together. When she joins them, they look at her affectionately and treat her like a guest. Annapurna offers tea, sherbet, lime water, and is distressed when she declines all these suggestions. She is always distressed by the fact that Sadie needs less food than she does. She says, "How can you live like that?" After a moment's thought, she adds, "How will you live *there?* Who will look after you and see that you don't starve yourself to death?" When Sadie looks at her, it is as she feared: tears are again flowing down Annapurna's cheeks. A sob also breaks from out of her bosom. It is echoed by another sob: Sadie looks up and sees that tears are also trickling down her husband's face. Neither of them speaks, and in fact they go on playing cards. The Englishwoman lowers her eyes away from them; she sits there, silent, prim, showing no emotion. She hopes they think she *has* no emotion; she does her best to hide it—the happiness that will not be suppressed, even at the sight of their tears.

Annapurna has had enough of playing. She flings down the cards (she has been losing). She wipes her tears away with her forearm like a child, yawns, sighs, says, "Well, time to go to bed," in resignation. He says, "Yes, it's time," with the same sigh and the same resignation. They have accepted the Englishwoman's departure; it grieves them, but they submit to it, as human beings have to submit to everything, such as old age and disease and loss of every kind. They walk upstairs slowly, leaning on each other.

When Sadie goes up to her own room, she is almost running in her excitement. She looks in the mirror and is surprised at the drained face that looks back at her. She doesn't feel like that at all—no, she feels the way she used to do, so that now she expects her bright eyes back again and her pink cheeks. She turns away from the mirror, laughing at her own foolishness; and she can hear her own laughter and it is just the way it used to be. She knows she won't sleep tonight. She doesn't want to sleep. She loves this feeling of excitement and youth and to pace the room with her heart beating and wild thoughts storming in her head. The servants have turned out the lights downstairs and gone to bed. The lights are out in her husband and Annapurna's room too; they must be fast asleep, side by side on their bed.

The Englishwoman can't see the moon, but the garden is lit up by some sort of faint silver light. She can make out the fountain with the stone statue, and the lime trees, and the great flowering bush of Queen of the Night; there is the bench where they used to sit in the evenings when Chandralekha sang in her sweet voice. But as she goes on looking, the moonlit scene brightens until it is no longer that silver garden but English downs spreading as far as the eye can see, yellow on one side, green on another. The green side is being rained upon by mild soft rain coming down like a curtain, and the yellow side is being shone upon by a sun as mild and soft as that rain. On a raised knoll in the foreground there is an oak tree with leaves and acorns, and she is standing by this tree; and as she stands there, on that eminence overlooking the downs, strong winds blow right through her. They are as cold and fresh as the waters of a mountain torrent. They threaten to sweep her off her feet so that she has to plant herself down very firmly and put out her hand to support herself against the trunk of the tree (she can feel the rough texture of its bark). She raises her face, and her hair—not *her* hair but the shining hair of her youth—flies wild and free in that strong wind.

DORIS BETTS was born in Statesville, North Carolina, in 1932. She attended the University of North Carolina at Greensboro and Chapel Hill and is now Associate Professor of English at Chapel Hill. She has also lectured in creative writing at Duke University, Indiana University Summer Writers Conference, and Squaw Valley Writers Conference. Her fiction has won a number of literary prizes including a Guggenheim fellowship. She was a National Book Award finalist in 1974 for *Beasts of the Southern Wild*, from which the following story is taken. Her short stories have been published in *Redbook, Mademoiselle, Cosmopolitan, Ms.*, and anthologized in *Best American Short Stories, North Carolina in the Short Story, A New Southern Reader, Young Writers at Work, Red Clay Anthology, Archetypes in the Short Story*, and other collections. She is married and has three children.

Doris Betts
(1932—   )

STILL LIFE WITH FRUIT

Although Gwen said three times she felt fine, the sister made her sit in a wheelchair and be rolled to the elevator like some invalid. Looking over her shoulder for Richard, she let one hand drop onto the rubber tire, which scraped heat into her fingertips. Immediately Gwen repeated on the other side, for her fingers felt clammy and disconnected from the rest of her.

"Your husband can't come up for a while, dear," said the sister, parking her neatly in one corner and pressing the Number 4 button. Sister was broad in the hip and wore a white skirt starched stiff as poster paper. "Are the pains bad?" "No." Gwen sat rigid and cold, all the blood gone to her fingers. There was so much baby jammed toward her lungs that lifting her chest would have been ridiculous. Surely the sister knew enough to say "contraction," and never "pain." For some women—not Gwen, of course—that could be a serious psychological mistake.

Besides, they weren't bad. Maybe not bad enough. Gwen had no fear of childbirth since she understood its stages perfectly, but to make a fool of herself with false labor? She'd never bear the embarrassment. To so misread the body's deepest messages—that would be like wetting one's pants onstage.

She said uneasily, "I hope they're not slowing down."

The sister's face grew briefly alert, perhaps suspicious. "When's your due date?"

Gwen told her ten days ago, and the sister said, "That's all right, then." Maybe if Gwen were Catholic, the sister's face would seem kinder, even blessed. That led to the idea—quickly pushed aside—that, had she been Catholic, bearing the first in a long row of unimpeded babies, the sister would like her better. On Ward Four she was rolled to a special room, told to put on the hospital gown and get into bed.

"And drink water. Drink lots of water," the sister said, took her blood pressure, and left her with a thermometer cocked at an angle in her mouth.

Gwen couldn't recall anything in the doctor's pamphlets about drinking water. Maybe in this hospital it was sanctified? She jerked both hands to her abdomen, relieved when it tightened and hardened the way Dr. Somers had been promising for months. She hoped this new pang was on schedule; Richard's watch was still on Richard's arm, downstairs. She felt no pain, since she was a well-adjusted modern who accepted her womanhood. Two months ago, however, she'd decided not to try natural childbirth, mainly because the doctor who advocated it was male. She was drifting, then, away from everything male. Lately she had withdrawn from everything, period. (The baby has eaten me, she sometimes thought.)

She climbed into the high bed, suddenly angry and alone, and discovered on the wall facing her a bronze statuette of Jesus wrenched on His cross, each shoulder drawn in its joint, His neck roped from pain, His face turned out with agony. It struck Gwen that Catholics might be downright insensitive. The Virgin Mary was one thing, but in this room on this day, this prince . . . this chaste bachelor on his way to God's bosom? To Gwen it seemed . . . well . . . tasteless.

Another sister recorded her 98.6 temperature and drew an assortment of blood samples on glass slides and in phials. She sucked these up through a flexible brown tube and Gwen wondered if she ever sipped too hard and got a mouthful. The sister also wrote down that Mrs. Gower had eaten and how recently and made her urinate into a steel bowl. "You take a nap, till the barber comes," she said. And giggled.

But Gwen, crackling with energy, doubled her pillow behind her and sat nearly upright, wide eyes fixed on the racked form of Jesus in a loincloth. They must have already cast lots for His seamless robe (down on the cool, gray hospital tile), but at this stage in the crucifixion no one had yet buried a spear point in His side. He was skinnier than Gwen had always pictured Him.

Ah, to be skinny herself! To sleep on her flat stomach, walk lightly again on the balls of her feet. To own a navel that would be a hole and not a hill! Gwen made herself bear down once, as if on the toilet. No effect at all. Too early.

The Labor Room, pale green, was furnished in buffed

aluminum. Its single chair was dull metal, straight, uncomfortable. Her clothes had been hung in a green wall locker next to Jesus, including the linen dress with the twenty-four-inch-waist she hoped to wear home next week. On her bedside table was a pitcher of water and crushed ice, and a glass with a clear tube in it. She drank water as the sister had ordered. Maybe it went down the sliding ramp where Junior, like some battleship, would be launched to the open sea. He felt to her like a battleship, plated turrets and stacks and projections, each pricking her own organs until they withdrew and gave him room. She sometimes felt as if her lungs had slipped slightly into each arm and her entrails been driven down her thighs.

The next nurse wore black religious garb, its hem nearly to the floor. With a black arm she set her covered tray on Gwen's mattress, said it was time for the first shave in Mrs. Gower's life, and flicked off the sheet. Gwen pressed into the pillow. She had never felt so naked—even after months of probes with gloved fingers and cold entries of the doctor's periscope. It must be a sign of her failing brain that one minute she saw her baby as a battleship; now there were periscopes thrust up his launching ramp. She had not thought clearly since that first sperm hit the egg and blew fuses all the way upstairs. Even her paintings showed it. Haphazard smears on canvas, with no design at all. Richard pretended, still, to admire them. He pretended the thought never crossed his mind that she might slice off one ear. She might have, too, if she could remember where the thing was growing.

It was the stare of a woman which embarrassed her. A religious. The young sister gazed with interest between Gwen's thighs as she made ready to repeat (here Gwen giggled) what Delilah did to Samson. She thought of asking the nun whether work in a maternity ward lent new appeal to chastity.

The nun said brightly, "Here we are."

"Here *we* are?" Gwen laughed again. I'm getting giddy. There must be dope in that water pitcher.

"You're very hairy." The sister couldn't be over twenty years old. Perhaps she was still apprenticed, a novice. Sleeping single in her narrow bed, spending her days with women who slept double and who now brought her the ripe fruits of God. Her face looked pale as if she were preparing to cross herself in some holy place. So it was a shock when she said, "All beautiful women are hairy. We had a movie star here once, miscarried on a promotion tour, and you could have combed her into ringlets."

Gwen could not match that so she lay, eyes closed, while the dull razor yanked out her pubic essence by the roots. She could no longer remember how she would look there, bald. She could recall sprouting her first scattered hairs as a girl, each lying flat and separate. Sparse, very soft in texture. Now would she grow back prickly? Now, when she most needed to recapture Richard, would she scrape him like a cheese grater? Five o'clock shadow in the midnight place? When Gwen opened her eyes it seemed to her Jesus had been nailed at just the right height to get a good view from His cross.

At last the sister's pan was black with sheep shearings. Black Sheep, have you any wool? One for the unborn boy, who lives up the lane? Gwen drank more water while the sister took out the razor blade and wiped the last hairs on a cloth.

"When can my husband come?" asked Gwen. She felt her face pucker. "I don't have anything to read."

The sister smiled. "Maybe after the enema." She carried out her wooly pan. Maybe she stuffed sofa cushions. And the bloodletting nun reclined on these and sipped Type O cocktails through her soft rubber tube. Maybe a "hair shirt" really meant . . .

Why, I'm just furious! Gwen thought, surprised. I'm almost homicidal!

The nurse with the enema must have been poised outside the door. Gwen barely had time to test her shaved skin with shocked fingers. Plucked chicken butt. She ought to keep her fingers away—germs—had she not just lately picked her own nose? Maybe she bore some deep, subconscious hostility against her baby!

She jerked her hand away and lifted her hips as told onto the rubber sheet. She refused to hear the cheery conversation floating between her knees. Inside her the liquid burned. When she belched she feared the enema had risen all the way. She might sneeze and twin spurts jet out her ears. She gasped, "I can't, can't hold it in."

Quickly she was helped across the room to the toilet cubicle. God, she would never make it. She carried herself, a brimming bowl, with the least possible movement. Then she could let go and spew full every sewer pipe in the whole hospital. Through the plastic curtain the nun said happily, "You doing just fine, Mrs. Gower?" Now *there* was psychology!

"O.K.," she managed to say. "Can my husband come now?"

"You just sit there awhile," said the nun, and carried her equipment to the plucked chicken down the hall.

Disgusting how clean the bathroom was. Gwen was a bad housekeeper—as Richard's parents kept hinting—twenty projects under way at once; yet, while she emptied the wastebasket, soap crud caked in the soap dish and flecks of toothpaste flew from nowhere onto the mirror. Nor could she keep pace with Richard's bladder. The disinfectant was hardly dry before he peed again and splattered everything. Yet, enemas and all, this place was as clean as a monk's/nun's cell.

Gwen flushed the toilet but did not stand. In case. She had never felt so alone. Ever since she crossed two states to live in a house clotted with Gowers, she had been shrinking. The baby ate her. Now the baby's container was huge but Gwen, invisible, had no body to live in. Today she had been carried to the hospital like a package. This end up. Open with care.

"Ready for bed?"

She cleaned herself one more time and tottered out. The new nurse was in plain uniform, perhaps even agnostic. She set a cheap clock by the water pitcher. "How far apart are your pains now?"

Gwen had forgotten them. "I don't know." She was sleepy.

"Have you had any show?"

Gwen couldn't remember what "show" was. Some plug? Mucus. She didn't know. Was she expected to know everything? Couldn't the fool nurse look on the sheets and tell? She was probably Catholic, too, and her suit was in the cleaners.

"Your husband can visit a minute, now. And your doctor's on the floor."

Gwen fell back on the skimpy pillow. She drowsed, one hand dropped like a fig leaf over her cool pubis.

"How's it going?" Richard said. His voice was very loud.

"Going!" Gwen flew awake. "It's gone!" she said bitterly. "Gone down the toilet! I don't even have any phlegm left in my throat. All of it. Whoosh." Suddenly he looked a good five years younger than she, tanned, handsome. Joe College. He looked well fed, padded with meat and vegetables and plump with his own cozy waste from meat and vegetables. "Where in hell have you been?"

"In the waiting room." He yanked his smile into a straight line. "You having a bad time?"

She stared at the ceiling. "They shaved me."

"Oh." He gave a laugh nearly dry enough for a sympathetic cluck. Give the little chicken a great big cluck. Ever since they'd moved in with his parents Gwen had been the Outsider and Richard the Hypocrite. If she talked liberal and Mr. Gower conservative, Richard said nervously they shared the same goals. When he left mornings for work, he kissed her goodbye in the bedroom and his mother in the kitchen. If Gwen fixed congealed salad and Mother Gower made tossed fruit, Richard ate heartily of both and gave equal praise. Lately Gwen had been drawing his caricature, in long black strokes, and he thought it was Janus.

He said, "I never thought about shaving, but it must be necessary. The doctor can probably see things better."

Things? Gwen turned her face away. Cruelly she said, "It's probably easier to clean off the blood."

"Hey, Gwen," he said, and bent to kiss as much cheek as he could reach. She grabbed him. So hard it must have pinched his neck. Poor little man with a pinch on his neck! She stuck her tongue deep in his mouth and then bit his lower lip.

Uneasy, he sat in the metal chair and held her hand. "Whatever they're giving you, let's take some home," he said.

And go through this again? At first, in their rented room, she and Richard had lain in bed all day on Sundays. Sleeping and screwing, and screwing and sleeping. My come got lost in the baby's coming. I don't even remember how it feels.

But Dr. Somers, when he came in, looked to Gwen for the first time virile and attractive. A little odd, but he'd never be clumsy. For medical reasons alone, he'd never roll sleepily away and leave her crammed against the wall with a pillow still under her ass, swollen and hot. With Richard's parents on the other side of that wall, breathing lightly and listening.

She gave Dr. Somers a whore's smile to show him her hand lay in Richard's with no more feeling than paper in an envelope.

"You look just fine, Gwendolyn," he said. He nodded to Richard as if he could hardly believe a young squirt with no obvious merits could have put her in such a predicament.

"We'll take a look now and see how far along things are. Mr. Gower?"

Richard went into the hall. She watched Dr. Somers put ooze on his rubber gloves. Talking with him down the valley of uplifted knees seemed now more normal than over the supper table to Richard. She lost her embarrassment with him. Besides, Dr. Somers liked art. He continued to talk to her as if the baby had not yet eaten her painting hand, her eye for line and color. As if there would still be something of Gwen left when this was over.

While he fumbled around in her dampness, he often asked what she was painting now, or raved about Kandinsky. When she first went to his office with two missed menstrual periods, she mentioned the prints hung in his waiting room. "Black lines" was Dr. Somers' favorite—he had seen the original at the Guggenheim on a convention in New York.

Gwen had not told him when, in her sixth month, her own admiration settled instead on Ivan Albright. Her taste shifted to Albright's warty, funereal textures, even while her disconnected hand continued to play with a palette knife and lampblack dribble. The few times her brain could get hold of the proper circuits, it made that hand pour together blobs of Elmer's glue, lighter fluid, and India ink. *Violà!* Mitosis extended! She had done also a few charcoal sketches of herself nude and pregnant, with no face at all under the wild black hair, or with a face rounded to a single, staring eye.

Oh, she was sore where he slid his finger! Politely he nodded uphill toward her head. "Glaswell has a sculpture in the lobby, did you see it?"

"We came in the other door."

"I was on the purchasing committee. It's metal and fiberglass, everything straining upward. That answered the board's request for a modern work consistent with the Christian view of man." He frowned. "You're hardly dilated at all. When did you feel the last one?"

"I stopped feeling anything right after that enema."

He thrust deeper. "False alarm, I'm afraid. But your departure date—when is it? I want you well rested before a long trip."

"In two weeks." Richard was being drafted. Once he left for the Army, Gwen would take the baby home to her parents. The Gowers expected her to stay here, of course, but she would not. Last week she had given Dr. Somers all her good reasons, one by one. When the baby came, she planned to give them to Richard. And, if he dared balk, she intended to go into a post-partum depression which would be a medical classic.

He laughed. "The baby's not following your schedule." His round head shook, and behind his thick glasses his eyes floated like ripe olives. "It's a false alarm, all right."

"But it happened just the way you said. An ache in the back. That cramp feeling. And it settled down right by the clock." To her humiliation, Gwen started to cry. "I'm overdue, goddamnit. He must weigh fifty pounds up there. What in hell is he waiting for?"

Dr. Somers withdrew and stripped off the glove. He looked at Jesus thoughtfully. He scrubbed his hands in a steel pan. "Tell you what, Gwendolyn. Stop crying now. It's suppertime anyway; let's keep you overnight. A little castor oil at bedtime. If nothing happens by morning, I'll induce labor."

"You can skip the castor oil," Gwen said, sniffing hard. "It'll go through me like . . . like a marble down a drainpipe." She did not know how he might induce labor. Some powerful uterine drug? She pictured herself convulsing, held down by a crowd of orderlies and priests. "Induce it how?"

"Puncture the membranes," he said cheerfully. He looked so merry she got an ugly superimposed picture: boy, straight pin, balloons. "I'll just have a word with your husband."

An hour later they demoted Gwen from the Labor Room and down the hall to a plain one, where she lay alongside a woman who was pleased to announce she had just had her tubes tied. "And these old Roman biddies hate it. Anybody that screws ought to get caught at it—that's their motto."

The Roman biddy who happened to be helping Gwen into bed did not even turn, although her face blotched an uneven red. Her cheeks ripened their anger as disconnected from her soul as Gwen's painting hand was adrift from her brain. Among the red patches her mouth said, perfectly controlled, "I wouldn't talk too much, Mrs. Gower. I'd get my rest."

The woman in the next bed was Ramona Plumpton, and she had had four babies already. With this last one she'd nearly bled to death. "This is the best hospital in town, though, and I'm a Baptist. The food's good and it's the cleanest. No staph infections." Behind one hand she added, "I hear, though, they'll save the baby first, no matter what. That puts it down to a 50-50 chance in my book. Is this your first, honey?"

"Yes. They're going to induce labor so I can travel soon. My husband's joining the Army." She hoped Richard would not mention false labor, not in front of this veteran.

"You're smart to follow him from camp to camp." Perhaps to counteract her hemorrhage, Mrs. Plumpton had painted rosy apples on each cheek. "The women that hang around after soldiers! You wouldn't believe it!"

Gwen thought about that. There she'd be, home with her beard growing out, while Richard entered some curly practiced woman. Huge breasts with nipples lined like a pair of prunes. Like Titian, she arranged the woman, adjusted the light. She made the woman cock one heavy arm so she could stipple reddish fur underneath.

"Bringing it on like that, you'll birth fast," said Mrs. Plumpton. "A dry birth, but fast. I was in labor a day and a half with my first and I've got stretch marks you wouldn't believe. Calvin says I look like the tattooed lady."

Gwen assigned Mrs. Plumpton's broad, blushing face to the prostitute in Fort Bragg and tied off her tubes with a scarlet ribbon.

Richard came by but said he wasn't allowed to stay. He'd driven all the way uptown to bring Gwen some books—one of Klee prints and a *Playboy* magazine and three paperbacks about British murders. Gwen usually enjoyed multiple murders behind the vicarage, after tea, discovered by spinsters and solved by Scotland Yard.

He kissed her very tenderly and she stared into one of his eyes. The large woman was imprinted there already, peach-colored, her heart-of-gold glowing through her naked skin.

"It's very common and you're not to feel bad about it."

She touched Richard's mouth with her fingers. Did a dry birth have anything in common with dry sex? It sounded harder. She reached beyond him and drank a whole glass of water.

". . . Dr. Somers says there's nothing to it. I'll be here tomorrow long before anything happens."

"Now, don't you worry," Gwen said, just to remind him what his duty was. She got down a little more water.

Richard said his parents, downstairs, were not allowed to visit. "They send you their love. Mom's getting everything ready."

Sweeping lint from under our marriage bed. Straightening my skirts on their hangers. She can't come near my cosmetics without tightening every lid and bottle cap.

"Mom's a little worried about induced labor. Says it doesn't seem natural." He patted her through the sheet. "They've both come to love you like a daughter."

When he had gone Ramona Plumpton said, "Well, he's good *looking*." It wasn't much, she meant, but it was something. "Between you and him that ought to be a pretty baby. You want a boy or a girl?"

"Girl." They had mainly discussed a son, to bear both grandfather's names. William Everest Gower. Suddenly she did want a daughter. And she'd tell her from the first that school dances, fraternity pins, parked cars—it all led down to this. This shaved bloat in a bed with a reamed-out gut.

She read until the nurse brought castor oil, viscous between two layers of orange juice. It made her gag, but she got it down.

For a long time she could not sleep. Too many carts of metal implements were rolled down the hall; ploughshares rattled in buckets, and once a whole harvesting machine clashed out of the elevator.

When she finally drifted off she dreamed she found her baby hanging on a wall. Its brain had grown through the skull like fungus; and suspended from its wafer head was a neckless wet sack with no limbs at all. Gwen started to cry and a priest came in carrying a delicate silver pitchfork. He told her to hush, he hadn't opened the membranes yet. When he pricked the soft bag it fell open and spilled out three perfect male babies, each of them no bigger than her hand, and each with a rosebud penis tipped with one very tiny thorn. The priest began to circumcise them in the name of the Father, Son, and Holy Ghost; and when a crowd gathered Gwen was pushed to the rear where she couldn't see anything but a long row or pictures—abstracts—down a long snaky hall.

She woke when somebody put a thermometer in her mouth, straight out of the refrigerator. It was no-time, not dark or light, not late, not early. She could not even remember if the year bent toward Easter or Halloween.

Pressure bloomed suddenly in her gut. She barely made it to the toilet, still munching the glass rod. She filled the bowl with stained oil and walked carefully back to bed, rubbing her swollen abdomen for tremors. She had not wakened in the night when the baby thumped, not once felt the long leg cramps which meant he had leaned on her femoral arteries. It came to Gwen suddenly that the baby must be dead, had smothered inside her overnight. By her bed Gwen stood first on one foot, then the other, shaking herself in case he might rattle in her like a peanut. She laid the thermometer on the table, knowing it measured her cold terror. She thumped herself. Nothing thumped back.

"Time to eat!" said Ramona Plumpton, peeling a banana from her tray.

She got into bed, pressing her belly with both palms.

A tall black man brought her breakfast tray. He said it was six-thirty. She had nothing but juice and black coffee, which she must not drink until a nurse checked her temperature and said it was fine. "No labor pains?"

"No. And he isn't moving!"

"He's waiting for *you* to move him," she said with a smile, and marked a failing grade on Gwen's chart. Later a resident pulled the curtain around her bed and thrust a number of fingers into her, all the wrong size. He said they'd induce at nine o'clock. She played with that awhile: induce, seduce, reduce, produce. She folded out *Playboy*'s nude Girl-of-the-Month, also hairless, with tinted foam rubber skin. There was an article which claimed Miss April read Nietzsche and collected Guatemalan postage stamps, preferred the Ruy Lopez in chess, and had once composed an oratorio. Miss April owned two glistening nipples which someone—the photographer?—had just sucked to points before the shutter clicked.

At nine, strangers rolled Gwen into what looked like a restaurant kitchen, Grade A, and strapped her feet wide into steel stirrups on each side of a hard table. The small of her back hurt. Gwen wanted to brace it with the flat of one hand, but somebody tied it alongside her hip.

"Don't do that!" Gwen said, flapping her left out of reach. A nurse plucked it from the air like a tame partridge. "Regular procedure," said the nurse, and tied it in place.

Through a side door came Dr. Somers, dressed in crisp lettuce-colored clothes. He talked briefly about the weather and Vietnam while he drove both hands into powdered rubber gloves.

Gwen broke in, "Is my baby dead?"

Above the gauze mask his eyes flared and shrank. "Certainly not." He sounded muffled and insincere.

Gwen let down her lids. Spider patterns of light and dark. Caught in the web, tiny sunspots and eclipses.

Someone spread her legs wider. She felt strange, cold things sliding in, one of them shaped like a mailed fist on a hard bronze forearm. The witches did that for Black Mass. Used a metal dildo. Gwen was not frightened, only shocked as a witch to find the devil's part icy, incapable of being warmed even there, at her deepest. She cracked her lids and saw the rapist bend, half bald, beyond the white sheet which swaddled her knees.

Fine, said the gauze, *just fine*. He called over a mummified henchman and he too admired the scene. Gwen felt herself the reverse of some tiny pocket peepshow, some key charm through which men look at spread technicolor thighs, magnified and welcoming. Now she enclosed the peephole, and through their cold tube they gloated over her dimpled cervix, which throbbed in rhythm like a winking pear.

Helpless and angry she thought: Everything's filthy.

"Looks just fine," the henchman said, fidgeting in his green robe. Gwen wondered what the sister thought as she rolled an enamel table across the room like the vicar's tea cart. Full of grace? Fruit of *whose* womb?

Dr. Somers said, "There'll be one quick pain, Gwendolyn. Don't jump."

Until then she had given up jumping, spread and tied down as she was. Now she knew at his lightest touch she would leap, shrieking, and his scalpel would pierce her through like a spear. The sweat on her upper lip ran hot into her mouth. Sour.

"Lie very still now," said the sister.

The pain, when it came, was not great. If fluid spilled, Gwen could not tell since the sharp prick spilled her all over with exhalations, small grunts, muscles she did not even own falling loose. "Nothing to it," Dr. Somers said.

She shivered when the devil took himself out of her.

"Now we just wait awhile." He gave a mysterious message to the sister, who injected something high in Gwen's arm. They freed her trembly hands and feet and rolled her back to the room she remembered well from yesterday.

Everything, magically, had been shifted here—Klee, clock, her magazines and mysteries. Mrs. Plumpton had even sent a choice collection from her candy box, mostly chocolate-covered cherries, which the sister said Gwen couldn't eat yet. Overnight Jesus had moved very slightly on His cross and dropped His chin onto one shoulder. Yet His exhaustion looked faked. Forewarned, He awaited the shaking and dark. He was listening for that swift zipper rent in the veil of the tabernacle, ceiling to floor. Three days from now (count them: three) and the great stone would roll.

Gwen stared at the sister who helped her into bed. Was this the one who shifted the figurines? Did she carry under her habit, even now, the next distraught bronze, who, when cued, would cry out about being forsaken?

Politely, Gwen asked, "You like your work here?"

"Of course. All my patients are happy. You should sleep now, Mrs. Gower, and catnap from now on. Things will happen by themselves."

Trusting no one, Gwen opened her eyes as wide as they would go. Her face was one huge wakeful eye, like a headlamp. "Is my husband outside?"

"Not yet," said the sister, smiling. "Can I get you anything before I go? No? And drink water."

The baby might have died from drowning. Unbaptized, but drowned. Gwen was certain she did not sleep, yet Dr. Somers was suddenly there in a business suit, patting her arm. "You've started nicely," he said.

She felt dizzy from the hypodermic. She announced she would not give birth after all, having changed her mind. Her body felt drawn and she sat up to see if her feet had been locked into traction. Dr. Somers said Mr. Gower had come by and been sent on to work—there was plenty of time. He faded, sharpened again to say Gwendolyn was to ask the nurse when she needed it.

The next thing she noticed was a line of figures who climbed in her window, rattling aside the venetian blinds and straddling a radiator, then crossing her room and marching out into the hall. It was very peculiar, since her room was on the hospital's fourth floor. Most of the people did not speak or even notice her. A few nodded, slightly embarrassed to find her lying by their path, then drew away toward the wall and passed by like Levites on the other side.

One was a frightened young Jewish girl, hardly fourteen, whose weary face showed what a hard climb it had been up the sheer brick side of the hospital. Behind her came an aging athlete in lederhosen, drunk; he wore one wing like a swan's and was yodeling *Leda-leda-Ledal-lay*. He gave Gwen a sharp look, half lecherous, as he went by her bed, flapping his snowy wing as if it were a nuisance he could not dislodge. A workman in coveralls climbed in next; he thrust head and shoulders back out the window and called to someone, "I tell you it's already open wide enough!" After much coaxing, the penguin followed him in and rode through the room on his shoulder, so heavy the workman tottered under the glossy weight. Several of the parade kept their rude backs to her. Angry, Gwen called them by name but they would not turn, and two of the women whispered about her when they went by.

It was noon when Gwen next looked at the clock. Richard had not come back. Instantly awake and furious, Gwen swung out of the high bed. She nearly fell. She grabbed for the metal chair—Good God!—something thudded in her middle like a pile driver. She felt curiously numb and in pain at the same time. She clumped to the doorway and hung on to the frame. There was a nun at a small desk to her right, filling out charts in a lovely, complex script.

"Going to telephone my husband," Gwen said. Her voice box had fallen and each word had to be grunted up from a long distance.

A chair was slid under her. ". . . shouldn't be out of bed . . . Quickly." The nurse balanced the telephone on Gwen's knees.

She dialed and Mrs. Gower said, "Hello?" Her voice was high and sweet as if she had just broken off some soprano melody. Gwen said nothing. "Hello? Hello? Is anybody there?"

With great effort, short of breath, she said, "May I speak to Richard Gower? Please?"

"He's eating lunch."

Gwen looked at the far wall. A niche, some figurines, a lighted candle. She took a deep breath. When she screamed full blast, no doubt, the candle would blow out twelve feet away and across town the old lady's eardrum would spatter all over the telephone. But before she got half enough air sucked in she heard, "Gwen? That's not you? Gwen, good heavens, you're not out of bed? Richard! Richard, come quick!"

Gwen could hear the chair toppling at the table, Richard's

heavy shoes running down the hall and then, "Gwen? Gwen, you're all right?"

Wet and nasal, the breath blew out of her. "You just better get yourself over here, Richard Gower. That's all," she wailed. "You just quit eating and come this very minute. How can you eat at a time like this?"

Richard swore the doctor said they had hours yet. He was on his way right now and he hadn't even been *able* to eat, thinking of her.

She told him to hurry and slammed down the phone. The nun was looking at her, shaking her headdress. She half pushed Gwen into bed. "Now you've scared him," she said gently.

Gwen shook free of her wide black sleeve. The next pain hit her and this one was pain—not a "contraction" at all. One more lie in a long line of lies. "Long-line-of-lies," she recited to herself, and got through the pain by keeping rhythm.

> One more lie
> In a
> Long line
> Of lies.

On the next pain she remembered to breathe deep and count. She needed fourteen long breaths to get through it, and only the six gasps in the middle were really bad.

By the time Richard trotted in she was up to twenty-two breaths, and most of them were hard ones in the center without much taper on either end. He stopped dead, his mouth crooked, and Gwen knew she must look pale. Perhaps even ugly. She could no longer remember why she had wanted him there.

"Good," said Dr. Somers. "We were just taking her in."

Richard kissed her. Gwen would not say anything. He rubbed her forehead with his fingers. New wrinkles had broken there, perhaps, like Ramona's stretch marks. As they rolled her into the Delivery Room, Gwen saw that Jesus had perked up a lot, gotten His second wind. She closed her eyes, counting mentally her pains in tune: One and two and three-three-three. Four-four-four. Five-five-five. Words caught up slowly with the music in her head: Mary had a little lamb. Little lamb. Little . . .

When they made her sit upright on the table so an anes-

thetic could be shot into her spine, Gwen hurt too much from
the bending even to feel the puncture. They had trouble getting her spread and tied into this morning's position; she had
begun to thrash around and moan. She could not help the
thrashing, yet she enjoyed it, too. If they'd let go of me once,
I'd flop all over this damn sterile floor like a whale on the
beach. I'd bellow like a elephant.

That reminded her of something Dr. Somers had said—
that in the delivery room most Negro women prayed. *Jesus,
oh, Lord, Sweet Jesus!* And most white women, including the
high-born, cursed. Oh, you damn fool, Gwen groaned (aloud,
probably). It's *all* swearing!

Oh Jesus!
Oh Hell!

They scratched at her thighs with pins and then combs and
then Kleenex and Dr. Somers said that proved the anesthetic
was working. Gwen fell rather quickly from agony to half
death and floated loose, broken in two at the waist.

"Move your right foot," said the doctor, and somebody's
right foot moved. He explained she would be able to bear
down, by will, even though she would notice only the intent
to do so, and not feel herself pushing. So when they said bear
down, Gwen thought about that, and somebody else bore
down somewhere to suit them.

"High forceps." Two hands molded something below her
navel, outside, and pressed it.

"Now," said the mummified henchman.

The huge overhead light had the blueness of a gas flame.
She might paint it, staring, on a round canvas. She might call
the painting "Madonna's Eye." She might even rise up into it
and float loose in the salty eye of the Blessed Damozel like a
dust mote.

Suddenly the doctor was very busy and, like a magician,
tugged out of nowhere a long and slimy blue-gray thing, one
gut spilling from its tail. No, that was cord, umbilical cord.
He dropped the mass wetly on the sheet near Gwen's waist,
groped into an opening at one end. Then that blunt end of it
rolled, became a face, bas relief, carved shallow on one side.
The mouth gave a sickly mew and, before her eyes, the whole
length began to bleach and to pinken. Gwen could hardly
breathe from watching while it lay loosely on her middle and

somehow finished being born of its own accord, by will, finally shaped itself and assumed a new color. Ribs tiny as a bird's sprang outward—she could see their whiteness through the skin. The baby screamed and shook a fist wildly at the great surgical light.

Like electricity, that scream jolted Gwen's every cell. She vibrated all over. "That's natural," said Dr. Somers, "that little nervous chill." He finished with the cord, handed the baby to a man in a grocer's apron and began to probe atop her abdomen. "We'll let the placenta come and it's all done. He's a beautiful boy, Gwendolyn."

The pediatrician she and Richard had chosen was already busy at another table. Cleaning him, binding him, piling him into a scale for weight. Dr. Somers explained that Gwen must lie perfectly flat in bed, no pillow, so the spinal block would not give her headaches. If she'd drunk enough water, as ordered, her bladder would soon recover from the drug. Otherwise they'd use a catheter—no problem.

The sister, her face as round as the operating light, bent over her. "Have you picked out a name?"

"No," Gwen lied. *She* needed the new name. *She* was the one who would never be the same.

". . . a small incision so you wouldn't be torn by the birth. An episiotomy. I'll take the stitches now." Dr. Somers winked between her knees. "Some women ask me to take an extra stitch to tighten them for their husbands."

Stitch up the whole damn thing, Gwen thought. They were scraping her numb thighs with combs again.

". . . may feel like hemorrhoids for a few days . . ."

She went to sleep. When she woke there was a small glass pram alongside, and they were ready to roll her back to her room. Gwen tried to sit up but a nun leaned on her shoulder. "Flat on your back, Mrs. Gower."

"I want to see."

"Shh." The sister bent over the small transparent box and lifted the bundle and flew it face down at her, so Gwen could see the baby as if he floated prone in the air. His head was tomato red, now, and the nun's starched wide sleeves flew out beyond his flaming ears. A flat, broad nose. Gwen would never be able to get the tip of her own breast into that tiny mouth. There was peach fuzz dusted on his skull except on the top, where a hank of coarse black hair grew forward.

Gwen touched her own throat to make sure no other hand had grabbed it. Something crawled under her skin, like the spider which webbed her eyelids, tightening all lines. In both her eyes the spider spilled her hot, wet eggs—those on the right for bitterness, and those on the left for joy.

ELIZABETH CULLINAN was born in 1933 in New York City. After graduating from Marymount Manhattan College, she went to work at *The New Yorker* for fiction editor William Maxwell. She received the New Writers Award given by the Great Lakes Colleges Association for 1970, and in the same year her first novel, *House of Gold,* was awarded a Houghton Mifflin Literary Fellowship.

In his review in *The New York Times* novelist Richard Elman praised the novel's Joycean rendering of the textures of ordinary lives. Maeve Brennan has defined Cullinan's gift most exactly—she calls it a contemplative prose. *Yellow Roses,* her most recent collection of short stories, has been well received. She performs small miracles, said one review, having "an uncanny ability to take a small commonplace event, or thought, and from it ferret out deep meanings that move from the particular to the universal. As she does she illuminates, moves, bestows a particular grace on the human condition." John Leonard wrote in *The New York Times*: ". . . this book makes me feel better about the world. It hedges, as though to hide behind that hedge while careless thugs on black horses gallop by, but it seems essentially to endorse the uses of intelligence and the stamina of love . . . When you can say in eight pages what most novelists have never been able to say at all . . . you are a first-rate writer. Elizabeth Cullinan . . . is a first-rate writer."

In a way that Conrad would approve, she has made her readers see and hear and feel the experience of being a daughter. And no other writer has caught better than she the uneasy, jittery tempos of Irish Catholics.

Elizabeth Cullinan
(1933—   )

IDIOMS

Now that my parents are old, I dread the prospect of their dying the way I dreaded it as a child, when the loss of one or the other always seemed to me to be imminent. My mother used to have weak spells that left her moaning and weeping, and afterward she had to be put to bed. I suppose it was a question of being both tired and discouraged, but in the world where she grew up tiredness and discouragement were inadmissible, and so she developed these alarming symptoms, which she called a heart condition.

My worries about my father centered on the Second World War. I was afraid he'd be drafted and sent to Europe and killed there or listed as missing in action, but as it turned out he was never called up. Instead, a front of another sort opened at home. My father, too, had begun to be sick and tired of the limitations of his life, and his struggle against them took the form of betting on horse races. He lost all interest in our family, and my fears for his life changed to the fear that he'd leave us. Eventually he did, but after six months he returned, though he and my mother never resolved their quarrel with each other. It entered permanently into our lives, like matters of taste or domestic routine.

Rosemary, my middle sister, was the hardest hit. She became unstable, going from school to school, job to job, friend to friend, boyfriend to boyfriend. Grace, who's the oldest, left home and got married when she was twenty-two. As for me, I looked around and saw that there were people who didn't dwell under any such cloud as we did and I became preoccupied with these people and the way they lived, down to the smallest detail. The pictures on their walls, the slipcovers on their furniture, the dishes on their tables—all of it mattered to me and mattered a lot in the long run, for at some point my envy turned to ambition; or at least that's how I explain to myself why I became a decorator. It was a way of making an impression on a world where my parents, by virtue of their failure to get along, had no entrée. I was ready to leave them and their troubles behind but I wasn't taking into account the magnetism of family feeling, whatever its quality, and in fact I've never got beyond the pull of my parents' love and unhappiness. It's they who'll leave me behind one of these days, in the ordinary way that used to terrify me and now gives me a different cause for anxiety.

"Is everything all right?" my sisters and I ask each other after one of us has just been home. There are two or three things that can start trouble, the same two or three small things that have always started it. My mother might have been talking to one or another of her brothers and sisters, who are conceited, clannish people and make her discontented. Or my father could have paid a visit to his favorite sister, Adele, whose company makes the rest of us like strangers to him. Or he could have been drowning his sorrows. Or my mother could have been housecleaning, exhausting herself and driving my father mad with the smell of furniture polish and the sound of the vacuum cleaner. Why should my sisters and I take these things so to heart? Other people seem to build up a resistance to their family situation, but Grace and Rosemary and I can still be laid low when the old quarrel erupts, as if even now our lives depended on coming from a good family, having a happy home.

Yesterday when I visited my parents everything was all right except for a few sharp words just after I arrived. My father was sitting at one end of the sofa with the newspaper; at the other end was my mother, reading her prayer book, wearing a lavender wool shirtwaist dress. She was also wearing sneakers that belonged to my father, who was once persuaded to buy them for the beach, though he never put them on. It was quite a sight—my mother in sneakers. I can't remember ever seeing her so much as throw a ball, let alone take part in a sport; it's years since she even walked to the supermarket. I had to laugh, and then to pretend the laugh was meant not to criticize but to encourage: "You look nice and comfortable in your sneakers."

My mother wasn't fooled. "Someone might as well get some use out of them," she said both defensively and offensively.

My father was wearing gray flannel trousers and a red

plaid shirt and he looked at least ten years younger than his age, which is seventy-six. After a minute he raised his eyes from the paper and said, "I came across a phrase the other day—'*Reader's Digest* mentality.' Is that a common expression?"

I said, "I don't know." My mother's sister Marie gets the *Reader's Digest,* and my father can't stand Aunt Marie.

He said, "But there must be such a thing, don't you think, as the '*Reader's Digest* mentality'?"

There is, of course, and my aunt is a perfect example, but I said, "Don't ask me." I resented his trying to line me up on his side and I wondered, as I have before, about the nature of his affections. He seems never to have investigated them, never to have noticed the various inflections of his own heart, and when he's called on to say how he feels he uses ready-made expressions. It's not as if he had no way with words. He's a witty man but when it comes to his feelings he resorts to clichés. "My children mean everything to me," he'll say, or "My family comes first." Recently he told me, "I'll never be able to thank you for what you've done." This was a few weeks ago, after we'd had a glimpse—or, as Rosemary called it, a dress rehearsal—of the scene we'll play in earnest one of these days.

At one o'clock on a Tuesday afternoon my mother telephoned and said in the measured voice that's so reassuring and so misleading, "I don't like to disturb you, Connie, but I thought I'd better tell you that Daddy's just been taken to the hospital."

The week before, he'd slipped on the ice and cracked a rib, having gone out for the paper very early in the morning in his bedroom slippers. On account of his carelessness he got no more than the required sympathy, and I felt guilty about this now that it appeared there were complications. "Has the rib got worse?" I asked my mother.

She said, "Apparently it's not the rib at all."

In my experience, catastrophe—the real thing—is always heralded by just some such unexpected twist. I braced myself. "Not the rib?" I said.

"It doesn't look like it. When he sat down to lunch he was white as a sheet. He said, 'I don't feel so well,' and he went in and lay down on the bed. The next thing I knew he was calling me from the bathroom. The bowl was full of blood, and when I helped him back to bed he said, 'I don't want to

worry you, but I think this is it.' I called an ambulance and
got him to the hospital, and Dr. Bowen put him right into Intensive Care." Her voice came to rest on those last two
words. My mother loves authority and its citadels. The bank,
the hospital, the supermarket, department stores, school,
church—she feels equally safe in all these places and, feeling
safe, she also feels confident. For me, confidence is a matter
of confronting the worst.

I said, "It sounds like at least an ulcer."

Mother said, "I've called Rosemary. She'll be here any
minute."

Rosemary lives near my parents. I said, "What about
Grace?" Grace lives in Baltimore.

Mother said, "I thought I'd hold off till there's something
definite."

"When will that be?"

"I'm to call the hospital at two o'clock."

"I'll be up as soon as I can." I caught the one-fifty-five
train. Riding past the slums and on into the soothing vistas of
Westchester County, I thought of my childhood fear of being
orphaned. I'd believed that without a father or mother I'd
have no future, that I'd be emotionally stunted and, for all
practical purposes, prevented from moving on into real life,
but the fact of the matter is, any wholly or partly parentless
people I've known have displayed a far greater aptitude for
reality than I, who seem to lack the basic technique or perhaps the right approach. But I work at it, and here was the
proof, here I was—a daughter on a speeding train, moving
toward a bedside. What could be more true to life?

When I got to my parents' apartment, Rosemary and my
mother were sitting in the living room with their coats on.
From this I jumped to the conclusion that my father had died,
but there were no red-rimmed eyes, no one was at a loss for
words, and so I had to backtrack. "What's happening?" I asked.

Rosemary said, "I called the hospital half an hour ago.
They told me he was resting."

"Whatever that means." I began unbuttoning my coat. I
felt a little let down. Tragedy isn't preferable to mere trouble,
but there's something to be said for having to rise to an occasion as well as deal with it.

"I imagine they've given him a sedative," Rosemary said.
She's a literal person. Her green eyes are distractingly clear.
Her short, reddish-brown hair curls naturally around her

face. She has a ready smile and she cries easily, and when we're together she's usually mistaken for the younger. I strike people, by comparison, as distant and I also have an air of responsibility that's especially noticeable when I'm around Rosemary. Even when we were growing up I was the dependable one, the child who always put away her toys, the little girl who learned to iron and to cook before her older sister, the young woman who knew what she wanted to do and did it. But the balance has a way of shifting in families, and usually in the interest of the truth. When she was thirty Rosemary decided to go to law school, and her life took a turn for the better. Now she's married and lives in Mamaroneck and is in practice there with her husband. And it's my turn to be worried over. I'm the one who in fact inherited my father's streak of perversity. I'm choosy about the jobs I'll take on and I prefer to work at my own pace, so the living I make is precarious.

My mother said, "Did you have your lunch, Connie?"

I said, "Not really." I'd bought a bar of chocolate in Grand Central Station.

"Let me make you a sandwich," she said.

"How are we fixed for time?" I glanced over at Rosemary in a way that said *We've got to talk*. From the time we were children, my sisters and I have been exchanging these distress signals.

Rosemary said, "Actually, we're running late."

I said, "Let's get going then."

Hospitals have a mortal dullness along with their deadly glamour. The sick are pitiable in their boredom as well as in their pain—or so I thought until I visited my father in Intensive Care. It was a big room with a row of beds along one wall; opposite the open beds there were a number of glassed-in booths full of electronic equipment, and my father lay in one of these. There was a wonderful stillness about him, which the machine monitoring his heart and the tubes attached to his arm seemed to feed rather than intrude on. His fine, straight hair was spread out and thin-looking against the pillowcase. His eyes were closed; his lips were parted, and his mouth a little caved in. On his left wrist was a plastic identification bracelet that struck me as the right touch, for he bore no resemblance to his real, chipper self. He'd become an old man—any old man. After a minute or two he sensed our presence and opened his eyes and looked at us with such terror and sweetness that my heart went out to him. He's someone who asks for very little in the way of attention, and what comes to him even in the normal course of events he doesn't know what to make of. We moved over to the bed and kissed him, one by one, like communicants. "How do you feel, Frank?" my mother asked.

"I'm awfully tired." He smiled apologetically. "I suppose it's all the tests," he said.

"Are there any results yet?" Mother asked.

"Not that I know of." His eyes closed and then opened again. "I guess I lost a lot of blood," he said.

"You've had four transfusions," said my mother.

"Holy smoke! That's a lot of blood." He smiled again. "For a little guy like me." He has no great opinion of himself, maybe even no particular thoughts on his own relative merits, which could be why he was never successful. Success, after all, requires a certain amount of self-importance, and he's too reasonable to have any illusions along that line.

Mother said, "Do you need anything?"

He said, "I wish I had my glasses."

She said, "Aren't they in your shaving kit?"

"Are they?" He looked confused; he began fingering the bedclothes.

"I thought I stuck them in there." Beside the bed was a low metal cabinet where my father's belongings had been put. Mother got down on her knees and began going through his things. When in doubt, in need, in sorrow, in anger, in frustration my mother will act. To be helpless is the closest she can come to despair, and when she got to her feet empty-handed she was wild-eyed. "You don't really need your glasses, do you?" she asked my father.

"I might get hold of a newspaper," he said.

"I'll drop them off," said Rosemary.

A pretty young nurse came into the booth and looked at us suspiciously. "How long have you been here?" she asked.

I said, "Just a few minutes."

"He's very weak." The nurse felt for my father's pulse. "I think you'd better leave."

My mother leaned over the bed. "Shall I call Adele?" she asked my father.

For a minute he looked irritated and a little less sick, a little more himself. "No, don't do that," he said. Adele, companion of his youth, partner in a hundred private jokes, would have been out of place in that cramped and businesslike cubicle. We who'd shared his bad times were the ones who belonged there, and the consciousness of this weighed on us and made us sharp with each other on the way back to the apartment.

My mother said, "If anything happens, Adele would want to be there."

I said, "Who knows?"

Rosemary said, "What have you got in the house in the way of food?"

"Will you be staying for supper?" Mother asked.

"I ought to go and see how Jake's fixed," said Rosemary.

"Why couldn't Jake come and eat with us?" My mother knows why or at least she should know—my sister's husband is Jewish; he observes the dietary laws to the letter, and though Mother makes an effort at keeping special pots and dishes, she gets thing mixed up, and Jake is nervous at my parents' table.

Rosemary said, "I think I'd better check in with him and then come back."

"What about you, Connie?"

"I'm staying." It occurred to me that over the next few days I might be having quite a few suppers with my mother.

"Would you rather have fried chicken or lamb chops?"

I said, "I don't care."

That was how it went as we drove through the hard sunlight of that freezing winter afternoon. When we reached the apartment, Rosemary said, "You run in with Mother and get the glasses, Connie. I'll wait in the car."

I said, "O.K., I'll only be a minute." But I was several minutes. The glasses weren't where my father usually leaves them, on the end table in the living room. Mother headed for the kitchen. I went into the bedroom and looked through his pockets, then through his chest of drawers, but I had no luck. I tried the desk and as I was shuffling through the mess of papers I accidentally overturned a small cardboard box. There was the sound of a multitude of small objects falling in all directions; I bent over and began picking things up. There were two shoehorns, a folded yardstick, two hard candies wrapped in colored cellophane, four pencils worn down to stubs, a tarnished souvenir tie clasp, a pocket magnifying glass, a brass drawer handle in the shape of a daisy, a moldy gum eraser, an American-flag lapel pin (the most mystifying item in the collection; my father's patriotic but not rabid, and not in the least ostentatious), half a dozen rubber bands, masses of paper clips, a penknife, and a strip of photographs of himself taken in a coin-operated machine. The photos were slightly overexposed, and the bleached look on his face reminded me of the look he had now in the hospital. It was the look of someone facing a gun or a ghost. I picked everything up and dumped it back in the box. My mother came into the bedroom with the glasses. "They were on top of the refrigerator," she announced, as if to say "Where else?"

"I'll drive back with Rosemary and bring them up to him. It'll save time," I told her, but this was the chance my sister and I were waiting for, and we took a few minutes to sit in the car reviewing the situation. Usually when we talk things over we dwell on the past, rehashing the events of our parents' lives that have led to this or that crisis, but my father's condition forced us into the future. Things will be changed by his death—or by my mother's. The survivor will probably go and live with Rosemary. I worry about this, but she was philosophical that afternoon. "There isn't any other way, really, and it'll be all right," she said. "Jake is so wonderful. The problem will be to keep him from being too indulgent. He has very tribal ideas about old people."

"Tribal?" I said, but I knew what she was getting at. Jake is an idealistic man, full of kindness and noble principles.

"He thinks they're sort of sacred," Rosemary said sheepishly.

I groaned. We both couldn't help laughing. "All the same, it doesn't seem fair," I said.

But we were premature with our speculation. When I went up to my father with his glasses, the doctor was there and he said, "I was just telling your dad he seems to be O.K." Dr. Bowen has a cast in his left eye which gives the effect of a twinkle, and it made me think he was making light of things for my father's benefit, but no, he was perfectly serious. "Nothing showed up on the X-rays," he went on.

"What caused all the bleeding?" I asked.

"He said he took a lot of aspirin for the cracked rib. That, combined with the painkiller we gave him, probably brought on acute gastritis."

"Gastritis?" It struck me as too trivial a term to apply to my father's dire symptoms, to the shocking change in his ap-

pearance, and, by extension, to the emotional workout my
mother and my sister and I had been given.

"That's an inflammation of the stomach lining," the doctor
explained.

I turned to my father. He looked relieved and embarrassed.
I said, "How do you like that?"

He was a good patient but a high-handed one and he complained very amusingly about everything, especially the food.
The first two days he was given nothing but antacid solution;
then it was soup and jello. By that time he was ravenous, but
when he was finally offered a menu and allowed to choose
from it the lamb cutlet turned out to be ground lamb served
in a paper cup, the peas were puréed, there was no salt and
pepper, no gravy. He took to making up his own order and
scrawling it across the card: "I'll have a ham sandwich with
mustard on rye bread." Or "Give me a T-bone steak and
some French-fried potatoes." I'd have thought this behavior
would antagonize the nurses, but when I visited him I was
impressed by the way he was treated. No one talked down to
him or patronized him; instead they acted as if he were a
well man, and an unusual one, and the day we took him
home they asked that he come back and visit them. "Not on
your life," he said. "From now on I go out of my way to
avoid this place."

There was no holding him. The next day he was out and
about, but I stayed home for nearly a week. It wasn't a bad
time, all things considered. My mother has had to learn, over
the years, to curb the generous impulses that come most
naturally to her, but with a convalescent she lets herself go,
and though my father hates fuss he'd had a good scare and it
made him tolerant; he accepted the eggnogs and the cups of
beef broth and the chicken sandwiches with fairly good grace.
Still, I was glad when I could get back to New York. I left
after dinner on a Thursday. My father drove me to the train
and, as we drew up to the station, he said, "I'll never be able
to thank you for what you've done, Con." I shrugged it off as
I usually do when he comes out with these things, but then I
turned to say goodbye and I was struck by the look on his
face. It showed an appreciation of his position and of mine
which was surely beyond words and it made me question my
own attitude. Is there any great virtue, I asked myself, in try-

ing to put things well? For whose sake am I continually doing that—isn't it a matter of pleasing myself? And why should my father be required to strain after words of his own if the ready-made sentiments satisfy him? They lack originality, but the personal element is there, as it was there however obscurely in the objects I found when I overturned the box on his desk. I leaned over and kissed him and said, "Take care of yourself."

I was five minutes early for my train. It was cold out, but I stayed on the platform rather than in the waiting room, where it was stuffy. It was a beautiful evening—clear and still, with a sky full of stars—and I had a sense of returning to the world, that world I'd been so anxious to flee to when I was younger. It occurred to me that when my parents die my life will truly be stunted, for my thrilling flight will then be broken—I'll have no one to flee except myself, nothing to escape from except the confines of my own body. But for the present I'd been given a reprieve and as I waited for my train I had the old vague awareness of possibilities to be explored and time at my disposal. I was aware, too, of an affinity among the three or four other people on the platform and myself. That we were travelling in the middle of the week and at an off-hour showed that we all meant business of one kind or another—the woman with the overnight case who was nervously smoking a cigarette, the middle-aged man holding on to a musical-instrument case that was as tall as he was, the sailor who came out of the waiting room with a duffelbag on his back. Not a joyride among us, I thought.

In the middle of the platform there was a bench with an empty place that I decided to take advantage of. The girl I sat down next to was reading a book, a French grammar open to a lesson on idioms which began with a paragraph of explanation. An idiom, it said, can be an expression that's peculiar in itself by virtue of its grammatical construction, such as "You had better go." Or an expression may be idiomatic in that it has a meaning that can't be derived as a whole from the combined meaning of its elements. There were three examples, three separate sentences with their translations. The French vocabulary was easy enough, but indeed I couldn't derive the meaning from the combined meaning of its elements and so I took a look at the English. I found that the three sentences added up to something, a set of ideas that fell somewhere between syllogism and non sequitur—on the one hand methodical, on the other hand inspired:

> *There will be moonlight tonight.*
> *It will be necessary to leave early.*
> *There will always be problems.*

A Selected Bibliography

DORIS BETTS (1932–   )

The Gentle Insurrection (1954); *Tall Houses in Winter* (1957); *The Scarlet Thread* (1964); *The Astronomer and Other Stories* (1966); *The River to Pickle Beach* (1972); *Beasts of the Southern Wild and Other Stories* (1973).

MARIA-LUISA BOMBAL (1910–   )

Her two novels have not been translated into English.

ELIZABETH BOWEN (1899–1973)

Encounters (1926); *Ann Lee's and Other Stories* (1926); *The Hotel* (1928); *Joining Charles and Other Stories* (1929); *The Last September* (1929); *Friends and Relations* (1931); *To the North* (1933); *The Cat Jumps and Other Stories* (1934); *The House in Paris* (1936); *The Death of the Heart* (1939); *Look at All Those Roses* (1941); *Seven Winters* (1942); *Ivy Gripped the Steps* (1946); *Selected Stories* (1946); *The Heat of the Day* (1949); *A World of Love* (1955); *Stories* (1959); *The Little Girls* (1964); *A Day in the Dark and Other Stories* (1965); *Eva Trout* (1969).

JANE BOWLES (1917–1973)

Two Serious Ladies (1943); *In the Summer House* (1954); *Plain Pleasures* (1966); *The Collected Works of Jane Bowles* (1966); *My Sister's Hand in Mine: An Expanded Edition of the Collected Works* (1977).

ELIZABETH CULLINAN (1933–   )

House of Gold (1970); *A Time of Adam* (1971); *Yellow Roses* (1977).

ISAK DINESEN (1885–1962)

Seven Gothic Tales (1934); *Out of Africa* (1937); *Winter's Tales* (1942); *The Angelic Avengers* (1947); *Farah* (1950); *Last Tales* (1957); *Anecdotes of Destiny* (1958); *Shadows on the Grass* (1960); *On Mottoes of My Life* (1962); *Osceola* (1962); *Essays* (1965); *Carnival: Entertainments and Posthumous Tales* (1977).

DOROTHY CANFIELD FISHER (1879–1958)

Gunhild (1907); *The Squirrel Cage* (1912); *Hillsboro People* (1915); *The Bent Twig* (1915); *The Real Motive* (1916); *Home Fires in France* (1918); *Day of Glory* (1919); *The Brimming Cup* (1921); *Rough-Hewn* (1922); *Raw Material* (1923); *The Home-Maker* (1924); *Made-to-Order Stories* (1925); *Her Son's Wife* (1926); *The Deepening Stream* (1930); *Basque People* (1936); *Seasoned Timber* (1939).

GERTRUD FUSSENEGGER (1912–)

Her works have not been translated into English.

MAVIS GALLANT (1922–)

The Other Paris (1956); *Green Water, Green Sky* (1959); *My Heart Is Broken* (1964); *A Fairly Good Time* (1970); (with Raymond Jean) *The Affair of Gabrielle Russier* (1971).

NATALIA GINZBURG (1916–)

The Road to the City (published with *The Dry Heart*) (1949); *A Light for Fools* (1956); *Voices in the Evening* (1963); *Family Sayings* (1967); *Never Must You Ask Me* (1973); *No Way* (1974).

NADINE GORDIMER (1923–)

Face to Face (1949); *The Soft Voice of the Serpent* (1952); *The Lying Days* (1953); *A World of Strangers* (1958); *Friday's Footprint* (1960); *Occasion for Loving* (1963); *Not for Publication* (1965); *The Late Bourgeois World* (1966); *A Guest of Honour* (1970); *Livingstone's Companions* (1971); *The Conservationist* (1975); *Selected Stories* (1976); *Burger's Daughter* (1979).

CAROLINE GORDON (1895–)

Penhally (1931); *Aleck Maury, Sportsman* (1934); *None Shall Look Back* (1937); *The Garden of Adonis* (1937); *Green Centuries* (1941); *The Women on the Porch* (1944); *The Forest of the South* (1945); *The Strange Children* (1951); *The Malefactors* (1956); *Old Red and Other Stories* (1963); *The Glory of Hera* (1972).

ZORA NEALE HURSTON (1903–1960)

Jonah's Gourd Vine (1934); *Mules and Men* (1935); *Their Eyes Were Watching God* (1937); *Tell My Horse* (1938); *Moses: Man of the Mountain* (1939); *Dust Tracks on a Road: An Autobiography* (1942).

SHIRLEY JACKSON (1919–1965)

The Road Through the Wall (1948); *The Lottery; or the Adventures of James Harris* (short stories) (1949); *Hangsaman* (1951); *Life Among the Savages* (1953); *The Bird's Nest* (1954); *The Haunting of Hill House* (1959); *We Have Always Lived in the Castle* (1962).

SARAH ORNE JEWETT (1849–1909)

Deephaven (1877); *Old Friends and New* (1899); *Country By-Ways* (1881); *The Mate of the Daylight and Friends Ashore* (1883); *A Country Doctor* (1884); *A Marsh Island* (1885); *A White Heron and Other Stories* (1886); *The King of Folly Island and Other People* (1888); *Strangers and Wayfarers* (1890); *A Native of Winby and Other Tales* (1893); *The Country of the Pointed Firs* (1896); *The Queen's Twin and Other Stories* (1899); *The Tory Lover* (1901).

RUTH PRAWER JHABVALA (1927–   )

To Whom She Will (1955); *The Nature of Passion* (1956); *Esmond in India* (1958); *The Householder* (1960); *Get Ready for Battle* (1962); *Like Birds, Like Fishes* (1963); *A Backward Place* (1965); *A Stronger Climate* (1968); *An Experience of India* (1971); *A New Dominion* (1973); *Heat and Dust* (1976); *How I Became a Holy Mother and Other Stories* (1976).

SELMA LAGERLÖF (1858–1940)

Invisible Links (1899); *The Miracles of Antichrist* (1899); *The Girl from the Marsh Croft* (1910); *The Emperor of Portugallia* (1916); *The Queens of Kungahalla* (1917); *The Outcast* (1920); *The Tale of a Manor* (1922); *Herr Arne's Hoard* (1923); *The Ring of the Lowenskolds* (1931); *Harvest* (1935); *Collected Works*, 12 volumes (1933).

MARGARET LAURENCE (1926–   )

This Side Jordan (1960); *The Stone Angel* (1964); *The Tomorrow-Tamer* (1964); *A Jest of God* (1966); *The Fire-Dwellers* (1969); *A Bird in the House* (1970).

OLIVIA MANNING (1914–   )

The Wind Changes (1938); *Growing Up: A Collection of Short Stories* (1948); *Artist Among the Missing* (1949); *School for Love* (1951); *A Different Face* (1957); *Doves of Venus* (1958); *The Balkan Trilogy: The Great Fortune* (1961); *The Spoilt City* (1963); *Friends and Heroes* (1966); *A Romantic Hero and Other Stories* (1967); *Penguin Modern Stories 12*, with others (1972); *The Danger Tree* (1977).

KATHARINE PRICHARD (1883–1969)

The Pioneers (1915); *Windlestraws* (1916); *Black Opal* (1921); *The Grey Horse* (short stories) (1924); *Working Bullocks* (1926); *Coonardoo* (1929); *Haxby's Circus* (1930); *Kiss on the Lips* (1932); *Intimate Strangers* (1937); *Moon of Desire* (1941); *Potch and Colour* (1944); *The Roaring Nineties* (1946); *Golden Miles* (1948); *Winged Seeds* (1950); *N'Goola* (1959); *On Strenuous Wings* (1965); *Subtle Flame* (1968).

JEAN RHYS (1894–   )

The Left Bank and Other Stories (1927); *Postures* (1929) published in U.S. as *Quartet* (1929); *After Leaving Mr. Mackenzie* (1931); *Voyage in the Dark* (1935); *Good Morning Midnight* (1939); *Wide Sargasso Sea* (1966); *Tigers Are Better Looking* (1968); *Penguin Modern Stories, I* (1969); *Quartet* (1971); *Sleep It Off, Lady* (1976).

DOROTHY RICHARDSON (1873–1957)

Pilgrimage (collected in 4 vols., 1938; expanded ed., 1967): *Pointed Roofs* (1915); *Backwater* (1916); *Honeycomb* (1917); *The Tunnel* (1919); *Interim* (1919); *Deadlock* (1921); *Revolving Lights* (1923); *The Trap* (1925); *Oberland* (1927); *Dawn's Left Hand* (1931); *Clear Horizon* (1935); *Dimple Hill* (1938); *March Moonlight* (1967).

MURIEL SPARK (1918–   )

The Comforters (1957); *Robinson* (1958); *The Go-Away Bird and Other Stories* (1958); *Memento Mori* (1959); *The Ballad of Peckham Rye* (1960); *The Bachelors* (1960); *The Prime of Miss Jean Brodie* (1961); *Voices at Play* (1961); *The Girls of Slender Means* (1963); *Doctors of Philosophy* (1963); *The Mandelbaum Gate* (1965); *Collected Stories*, vol. 1 (1967); *The Public Image* (1968); *The Driver's Seat* (1970); *Not to Disturb* (1971); *The Hothouse by the East River* (1973); *The Takeover* (1976).

SIGRID UNDSET (1882–1949)

Selected works. Dates refer to the year in which the English translation became available.
Gunnar's Daughter (1936); *Kristin Lavransdatter* (3 vols., 1930); *Olav Audunssen* (4 vols., 1925-1927); *The Master of Hestviken* (1934); *Stages on the Road* (1934); *The Wild Orchid* (1931); *The Burning Bush* (1932); *Ida Elisabeth* (1932); *The Longest Years* (1935); *The Faithful Wife* (1937).

MARGUERITE YOUNG (1909–   )

Prismatic Ground (1937); *Moderate Fable* (1944); *Miss MacIntosh, My Darling* (1965).